T0041033

Los Voraces 2019

Also by Andy Soltis
and from McFarland

Chess Lists (2d ed., 2002)

The 100 Best Chess Games of the 20th Century, Ranked (2000)

Soviet Chess 1917–1991 (2000)

Frank Marshall, United States Chess Champion: A Biography with 220 Games (1993)

With Gene H. McCormick

The United States Chess Championship, 1845–1996 (2d ed., 1997)

Los Voraces 2019

— *A Chess Novel* —

ANDY SOLTIS

Drawings by Linda Campbell Franklin

McFarland & Company, Inc., Publishers
Jefferson, North Carolina, and London

Library of Congress Cataloguing-in-Publication Data

Soltis, Andy, 1947–
Los Voraces 2019 : a chess novel / Andy Soltis.
p. cm.

ISBN 0-7864-1637-8 (softcover : 50# alkaline paper)

1. Chess—Fiction. 2. New Mexico—Fiction. 3. Chess players—Fiction. 4. Chess—Tournaments—Fiction. I. Title.
PS3619.O438L67 2004
813'.6—dc22 2003022661

British Library cataloguing data are available

©2004 Andy Soltis. All rights reserved

No part of this book may be reproduced or transmitted in any form or by any means, electronic or mechanical, including photocopying or recording, or by any information storage and retrieval system, without permission in writing from the publisher.

Cover illustration ©2003 PhotoSpin

Manufactured in the United States of America

McFarland & Company, Inc., Publishers
Box 611, Jefferson, North Carolina 28640
www.mcfarlandpub.com

Author's Note

THIS STORY FIRST APPEARED, in somewhat different form, as a serial of monthly installments on the Chess Cafe website (www.chesscafe.com), beginning in September 2001. I've tried to remain faithful to chess tournament traditions. The pairings follow the standard sequence for a 14-player round robin tournament. The FIDE laws mentioned are real (with the exception of the "anti-hair pulling rule"). And, yes, there is a poison called Compound 1080.

Some readers have wondered about the games. Most of them are real, some of them were played by me. A few are elaborations of long-forgotten games. The eight queens game from the *Friday, August 23* chapter was composed by Dr. Julio César Infantozzi of Montevideo, Uruguay.

Tuesday, August 20, 2019

EVERY TIME I'D COME TO Los Voraces I learned something about grandmasters. I learned more about grandmasters, in fact, than about chess. Or, for that matter, about Los Voraces. This time, I thought, might be different.

This time was supposed to be "The Greatest Tournament in Chess History." There'd been hype like that for a lot of big-deal events, beginning with Wijk aan Zees and Linareses back in the '90s. But for the Sheldrake Memorial Tournament—a.k.a. Los Voraces 2019—it was supposed to be true.

What I knew was true was that the world's 14 highest rated players had signed contracts to compete in the first-ever $20 million chess tournament. There'd be more genius, anxiety and attitude packed into the town's twelve square blocks than in Silicon Valley, Hollywood and the Harvard Yard combined.

And my job, at least for two and a half weeks, was to play referee and nursemaid to more than a dozen of the world's most easily bruised egos. I was the arbiter.

As I drove south along the Interstate, down from Albuquerque and towards Elephant Butte and Las Cruces, memories of past Sheldrake tournaments came flooding back to me.

Old man Sheldrake had made his first $200 million selling short in the dot.com depression of '01–'04 and his last $650 million strip mining what was left of North Dakota. But in 2009 he retired to the one-time mud village of Los Voraces, New Mexico. There in a remote, hilly area just east of town he built a neo-adobe estate that cost upwards of eight figures.

And he discovered chess. Maybe it was because he knew he was slowly dying and wanted to buy a page of history on the cheap. Or maybe he really fell in love with the game. Who really knew what Sheldrake was thinking?

Whatever the reason, in 2011 he sponsored a tournament, the Sheldrake International-Ultra, the first-ever Category XXIV event. That translates to an average rating of 2825-plus, a figure once unheard of. Only "world-class" players—whatever that meant—were invited. The playing site was the auditorium of the Los Voraces High School, in the only four-story building in the county, and it was built entirely with Sheldrake's money. Not much of a site, really. But he knew it was the players, not the venue, that make a tournament. Throw enough money their way and you could get grandmasters to compete in igloos.

There were seven more International-Ultras in the next seven Augusts, each with a bigger prize fund and a higher category, as Sheldrake managed to lure more and more of the super–Elo crowd to southern New Mexico. After he died in 2018, he left an obscene amount of money for another tournament. This tournament, his Memorial.

And if it weren't for the money I wouldn't be here either. After 32 years in big-league chess, first as a grandmaster and the last 12 years as an International Arbiter, I'd seen a lot of chess and very little money. It was time to cash in. If running tournaments for Sheldrake was selling out, I was glad to name my price. And besides, I was getting paid to watch some pretty good chess.

As I reminisced, I turned off the Interstate onto a state highway for 20 or so miles, then onto a one-lane black-top, and finally onto the barely paved former Navajo trail that runs straight through Las Voraces and serves as the town's main drag.

Outside the Casa Yucca Grande Hotel ("The Friendliest Spot Between Here and Taos"), I stopped and spotted a few familiar faces: The unlikely trio of International Grandmasters Gabor, Vilković and Qi. I was barely out of my car when it started.

"What have you done to us this time?" Gabor said. "This is an insult to chess!"

Everything that happened to Attila Gabor seemed to be an insult to chess—and there had been a lot of insults in his 67 years. The heavy-set Hungarian was notoriously hard to please. But even I had to admit he was worth the invitation. He was clearly the strongest player his age since Smyslov qualified for the Candidates Finals back in '84.

"An insult to chess!" Gabor repeated.

"What seems to be the problem this time, Attila?"

It didn't really matter. Gabor needed to be angry about something. It was essential to his playing well. He managed to put 110 percent of himself into every game, mainly by working up a maniacal hatred for his opponent. Or for the playing site. Or the playing conditions. Or me.

"It's an insult to hold us captive and alone in this oven. It's 50 degrees and 500 kilometers from civilization."

At least he had the distance about right. We were a six-hour drive east of Phoenix, and more than four hours north of Chihuahua. Between here and the Mexican border there were fewer than 20,000 people—but about 100,000 scorpions. As for the temperature, well, it was barely 40 Celsius today.

"Look, Attila, Los Voraces is hardly new to you. You've played here before. And you didn't have to call the weather bureau to know it gets hot here in August."

"Furthermore, international grandmasters cannot be expected to perform in solitary confinement," he added.

"You also knew the rules were going to be different this time," I said. "Just the players will be here—no seconds, no agents, no computers, no entourages, no phone calls, no pagers, no power palms, no hand-held anythings. In short, no outsiders or outside contact."

"And that's why I'm going to have to confiscate that," I said as I relieved him of the lapel phone he kept above his jacket breast pocket.

Actually I also thought the new rules were stupid. They were Sheldrake's legacy, his idea of maintaining a news blackout for his Memorial. The outcome was supposed to remain a secret until the last round was over. It seemed like a cross between a private training match and those old reality TV shows—a kind of "Chess Survivor."

"I still say chess cannot be played in a furnace," Gabor said, adjusting his tinted glasses. Gabor's high-prescription lenses were a necessity. Without them he was literally playing blindfold chess.

He turned to his right for support from Qi Yuanzhi. Qi smiled diplomatically—and said nothing. The pencil-thin grandmaster from Shanghai would never let himself become part of one of Gabor's rants. But Predrag Vilković certainly would.

"Precisely!" he said in his high-pitched voice.

Vilković was the world's oldest prodigy. He'd won the first under-8 world championship when it was introduced in 2005, became the youngest-ever GM at 9 years, nine months, 13 days, and then the world's first professional 10-year-old in 2007.

But he was now pushing 23 and hadn't won anything stronger than an Advanced Chess open in the last three years. The Serb was living off a bubble reputation. Yet another "next Bobby Fischer." As Gabor would put it—and he often did, privately—Vilković has a great future behind him.

"Look," I said, "You all played here before when it was hotter than this and spectators were rarer than rain puddles. And may I remind you that you are professionals. International Grandmaster Gabor is rated No. 9 in the world. International Grandmaster Vilković is rated—"

"Except," Qi interrupted, "in the People's Republic of China, Hong Kong and the Administrative District of Macau." He was always the first to remind listeners that the latest tinkering with FIDE ratings wasn't accepted in certain quarters.

"All right, Grandmaster Gabor is rated No. 9 in the world except in China, Hong Kong and Macau," I said. "My point is that you men are highly regarded players who have been invited to the most prestigious tournament in history."

"Speaking of prestige in the oblivion of Los Voraces is an oxymoron," Gabor said.

"Precisely!"

Vilković had acquired a lot of annoying habits since dropping out of the third grade in Novy Belgrade. But the worst was to suddenly blurt out "Precisely!" whenever he was within earshot of a conversation. It usually meant he didn't have anything to say yet felt obligated to participate anyway.

But I wasn't up to dealing with this. Not yet. The first round wasn't for two days, and Gabor and Vilković were in mid-tournament form.

"Let me remind all of you why you are here," I said, with a bit of an edge.

"You mean to put on a spectacle that will glorify the odious memory of a rich, dead American," Gabor said.

"No, I mean because you are each guaranteed at least $1 million."

Vilković caught my wording and looked up at Gabor and Qi.

He had to look up: he was 4 foot 8. Being a prodigy must have stunted his physical growth as well as the emotional.

"*At least* one million?"

Poor Predrag. He believed me when I sent him his contract and lied about each invitee getting the same $1 million he was.

We all knew the economics of big league chess had changed long ago. The real money is up front nowadays and highly confidential. Even 20 years ago or so, a big tournament, say a Wijk aan Zee, would have an announced prize fund of $20,000. But for every $1 in prizes there was at least $10 in discreet appearance fees. And even back then there was quite a different fee for a Kramnik than there was for ... well, for a Predrag Vilković.

Anyway, I could see Vilković's embarrassment was my opportunity.

"You gentleman may want to compare notes about financial matters, so I won't detain you."

I turned away and headed up Main Street. Out of the corner of my eye I could see Gabor and Qi quickly step away, in opposite directions, leaving Vilković alone to wonder if he was going to be the poorest millionaire in Los Voraces for the next 17 days.

Halfway to the high school, I ran into two of the locals, Aloisius Zachariah Gibbs and Josiah Phelps, M.D.

Sheriff Gibbs was what passed for law enforcement in Los Voraces and Phelps, a sixty-ish G.P. with a perpetually worried look, was his crony. Like most everyone else in town, they didn't know a thing about chess. And during my eight years as Sheldrake's tournament arbiter I'd always found them to be amiable, harmless and totally clueless.

"I see you people are back again this year," Gibbs said.

"Must be something in the air that attracts us," I said.

"Actually the sulfur dioxide index is up throughout the Valley this summer," Phelps said. "Also the particulates..."

"You don't sound happy to see us," I said to Gibbs.

"Town doesn't really like the chessplayers," he said with a grin and a shake of the head.

I suspected he'd smile the same way if he had to tell next-of-kin their relative had been eaten by iguanas.

"Nope, town doesn't like the chessplayers," Gibbs said. "Never did. Never will."

That I could understand. I remembered how back in the '70s the grandmasters would descend on Lone Pine, California, for the first of the big-bucks internationals conducted on a Swiss System basis. They arrived each April like off-season locusts. They'd hog the diners, litter the streets and let the locals know how grateful they should be to have grandmasters in their midsts. One year, the owner of an all-night restaurant put up a sign—"No chessplayers allowed." He was upset because a GM occupied one of the handful of booths for 19 hours straight, analyzing his most recent loss with anyone who would listen, while nursing a single cup of coffee. The sign stayed up until Louis Statham, the Sheldrake of Lone Pine, threatened to buy the place.

In Los Voraces I knew that part of my job was to keep the residents quiet, contented and off my back.

"The town only has to put up with us once a year, Sheriff. By September 6th, we're history until next year."

Gibbs and Phelps looked blankly at one another and then at me.

"But I thought this was going to be the last one, seeing as how Mr. Sheldrake had passed on," the doctor said.

"I'm afraid not. We only said it'd be the last one in order to hype it. But I happen to know Sheldrake's pockets were deep enough to run Memorials for another 20 years," I said.

And the estate had better run them. I was already counting on the arbiter fees through 2028 at least.

"Is that so?" Gibbs said with a bit less grin.

There was another exchange of glances and what seemed like a strained pause. I wondered how I was going to get out of *this* pointless conversation.

"We'll have to discuss this at the town meeting," Gibbs said. Phelps acknowledged with a jerky bob of the head.

I took that as my cue to escape. After an exchange of obligatory "See ya's," I headed back towards the high school.

And I was thinking: Two and a half weeks and I'll be back in the real world.

I knew all about the town meetings that Los Voraces prided itself on. "Prairie democracy," they called it. From time to time all 183 adult residents of town would pile into the Valley of the Polecat Eternal Life and Redemption Church for a meeting. They'd discuss pressing town issues, such as when to schedule the Green Chile Cheeseburger Eating Contest.

As I headed on up Main Street, Los Voraces High School stood out in front of me. Three blocks away, it looked like a Hollywood space ship. The school was the only marble, steel-and-glass, 21st century building in a town of brick and stucco. And for two and a half weeks each year it was all mine. I got exclusive use of it for the Sheldrake tournament, provided we were done in time for the fall semester.

I walked up the front steps and through the main double-door entrance, hoping I wouldn't run into any more of the players. They'd be coming soon enough, arriving from Phoenix or Santa Fe by air-conditioned limos that were costing the Sheldrake estate an amount roughly equivalent to the GNP of Honduras.

The school lobby was unlit and empty. I headed through the central auditorium door and up the main aisle to the stage, the tournament's traditional playing area. Everything seemed in order. The clocks I'd ordered were new, the players' chairs were still in good shape and the videotaping system was state-of-the-art. The only telephone backstage had the standard silent lights to signal incoming calls. The post-mortem room, down the backstage hall, was immaculate. My office was again set up in an anteroom several yards away, where I could conduct business without being heard or, hopefully, bothered.

All the miniature flags of the players' countries were accounted for except Dareh Bohigian's. I made a mental note to rush-order a red-blue-orange Armenian flag. And just to make sure, I measured the squares of the new boards: they were exactly 2¼ inches, just right. Most important of all, the air conditioning worked.

In the dim light I suddenly realized I wasn't alone.

"Darling, I was wondering when you were going to get around to telling me she was invited," Zhenya Bastrikova said.

The Russians had landed.

"Nothing in my contract mentioned *she* would be here," Bastrikova purred in her St. Petersburg accent.

She was Kersti Karlson of Helsinki, winner of four women's world championship tournaments—compared with Bastrikova's three. They had been archenemies since they were 12-year-olds competing at their first Kasparov chess camp more than 20 years ago, and had been in fights, verbal and otherwise, ever since.

Bastrikova, tall, high-cheekboned and raven-haired, and Karlson, a 5 foot 2 strawberry blond, fought at invitationals, Olympiads, candidates matches, even a charity simul. They were, in fact, the sole reason for Article 17.1 of FIDE's Laws of Chess, "the anti–hair-pull rule."

In short, the Gulf of Finland wasn't big enough for the two of them.

"Nothing in your contract said that she wouldn't be here," I said. "Besides, you knew we wanted the Elo top 14 this time and that money was no object."

"This is not about money. This is about her."

"Look, Zhenya, she's probably not happy about seeing you here either. In fact, you can bank on that. But you're both going to have to get over it."

"I demand protection, darling," she said. "I will not be assaulted again by that woman."

"You won't be," I said, and patted the top of a mahogany table. "At least when you're playing here."

It was the table I'd specially prepared just to avoid trouble in the inevitable Karlson vs. Bastrikova pairing. Their clock would be bolted in place: no more dragging it closer to one player's side after each move. Also, since both women followed the ritual of writing down a move before playing it, I had a pair of small crevices dug into the table deep enough to shield each scoresheet from opposing eyes. Finally, an oakwood slat extended from under the table, directly below the fourth and fifth ranks, to the floor. There would be no repeat of the shin-kicking war that turned the fourth round at Barcelona 2017 into a scandal.

Bastrikova was not impressed.

"I prefer to be in a separate room from her."

"I prefer to be in Vegas at the $100-minimum table," I replied. "But we're both going to have to live with being disappointed, at least for 13 rounds here."

And with that I left. I knew that whenever Bastrikova and Karlson played there might be a problem. There always had been. But with their talent they were well worth the trouble.

I headed back down Main Street and checked into my room at the Casa Yucca Grande. The Casa was not four stars by any stretch of an over-zealous travel writer's imagination. But at least the plumbing worked, the bed was firm and vermin didn't bite. Much.

After unpacking, a wave of fatigue came over me, and I realized I'd been exhausted by a 6:30 A.M. wakeup, a six-hour drive and by two short encounters with grandmasters.

When I struggled awake, it was already dusk. A glance outside my second-story window told me all the stores on the block seemed to be closed. Must be "prairie democracy" time.

After a long, hot bath and a change of clothes, I felt like a new man and went downstairs. In the Casa's lobby, I could see Phelps and a few of the locals in easy chairs, burping back dinner. Several of the players were seated around the hotel's big faux-turquoise table where Gabor was holding court. At heart, every master is a bit of a showoff and Gabor was in ringmaster mode as he set up a position on a board.

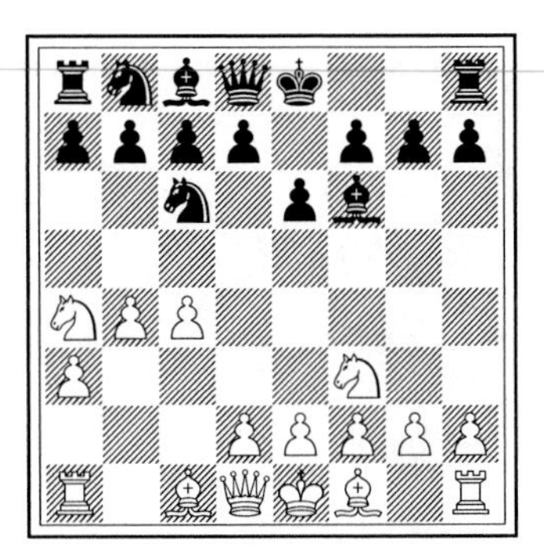

After Black's 6th move

"You'll enjoy this one. It's from one of my earliest games," Gabor told his audience, which included three of the newest arrivals, Zdravko Popov of Bulgaria, Johnny Eichler of Germany, and the Dutchman Van Siclen.

"I was White. Now I ask you: How is it possible that this position could come about after six full moves?"

"If it was one of your games, Attila, I'm surprised White isn't already totally busted," Gert Van Siclen said.

Gabor ignored him.

"All the moves made perfectly logical sense. Perfectly logical," he said. "I will give you one hint. My first move was c4."

After a moment, Bastrikova spoke up.

"Then Black must have played 1. ... e6. Nothing else works."

Another pause.

"Oh, it's easy," Vilković piped up. "I count five more moves by White, three by knights and two by pawns."

"I didn't realize you could count that high, little man," Van Siclen said. "Maybe then you'd also like to explain Black's next five moves—because he seems to have only made four."

"May I remind you, I said this position shows six full moves," Gabor said. "Six by White and six by Black. And all perfectly logical."

"We heard you the first time," Bastrikova said.

This time there was a longer pause. No one seemed to notice me standing behind Gabor. Qi broke the silence.

"Black can only make two knight moves, knight to e7 then to c6. Therefore by logic there must be three bishop moves."

"Chinese logic is like a Chinese firecracker," Popov said. "It looks brilliant and powerful but ends up with just a lot of smoke."

But Bastrikova had grabbed a Black bishop.

"No, for once he is right," she said. "Black plays out to some square like c5, like so. Then back to e7—and then to f6."

Eichler jumped in: "Okay, so it is 1. c4 e6. Then, maybe 2. Nc3 for White and 2. ... Bb4 for Black. Followed by 3. Nf3 and 3. ... Ne7."

"White's fourth move is Na4, threatening a3," Qi added. "Black does something like N from e7 to c6."

"So with your 'perfectly logical sense,' Attila, you played 5. a3 and he made ... Be7," Popov said. "That leaves 6. b4 and 6. ... Bf6. Q.E.D."

"And it only took six of the world's strongest grandmasters several minutes to solve a problem any 12-year-old Hungarian could do in his head," Gabor said, pleased with himself.

"Maybe what this tournament needs is fourteen Hungarian 12-year-olds," I said. "Rather than high-priced grandmasters."

I immediately realized I'd blundered. All eyes turned to me.

"What this tournament does not need is felonious opponents," Bastrikova said. "The kind that starts fights."

"It does need better lighting," Eichler said. "In that auditorium you couldn't see f2 if your nose was stuck on e1."

Van Siclen was next: "What it really needs is dressing rooms for each player. Preferably with separate toilets and showers."

"And the players must be given computers," Popov said. "You can't even post-mortem without them."

"Also you must do something about unequal fees!" Vilković said.

"Most of all we need decent playing conditions!" Gabor said, shouting to be heard. "Not another level of Dante's inferno."

"You cannot expect us to create art," he roared, "in the middle of the great American desert!"

Suddenly Gabor gasped. He grabbed his left arm with his right, then seized his chest with both hands in classic heart-attack pose. Then all 260 pounds of him crumpled to the cinnamon-colored carpet floor.

For the first time since I arrived in Los Voraces, the players were speechless.

Phelps moved surprisingly quickly. In what seemed like a femtosecond he was on the ground, examining Gabor's still body. After a small eternity, he sighed, shook his head and covered Gabor's face with his jacket.

"Which one was he?" Phelps asked, as he stood up.

"The world's ninth highest rated chess player," I said.

As if in shock, Qi added softly: "Except in the People's Republic of China, Hong Kong and the Administrative District of Macau."

"Precisely!"

Wednesday, August 21, 2019

I WOKE UP WRESTLING with pangs of guilt, anxiety and hangover. Of course, I knew I wasn't really responsible for Gabor's death. Heart attacks kill 30,000-plus Americans each year, so it's hardly breaking news when they claim the life of an overweight, 67-year-old, Type-A Hungarian.

Besides, Gabor wasn't the first GM to die at a tournament. Several strong players had gone to the Great Skittles Room in the Sky right after playing games. There were a few who died during games—and Capablanca was fatally stricken just watching a game. Wasn't it Korchnoi who called heart attacks "the occupational disease of chess masters"?

Yet as the arbiter of this $20 million exercise in misplaced philanthropy, I still felt badly. "The Greatest Tournament in Chess History" wasn't supposed to start this way.

Outside the Casa, the air was already 92 degrees at 9:10 A.M. and the sidewalk was a griddle. It was the kind of heat I knew from past Sheldrakes. After a few minutes outside you lose your ability to concentrate on anything but how to reach the next air-conditioner. I resolved to stay indoors as much as possible before the players' meeting.

After breakfast, I checked the Casa's registry. Besides the seven GMs I had seen last night—Bastrikova, Qi, Vilković, Popov, Van Siclen, Eichler, and, of course, Gabor—I knew another six had arrived at some point in the last 12 hours.

Kersti Karlson of Finland was here, along with Klushkov "the Spaceman" and former world champion Bohigian. Also somewhere in the vicinity were Eustace Royce-Smith of the U.K., the Romanian Octav Boriescu and U.S. Champion Todd Krimsditch. Only one player was missing: Grushevky, of course. World champions are like that.

In any event, I posted an updated schedule on the hotel's bulletin board and slipped laser copies under the door of each player's room. The GMs had virtually taken over the Casa's top floors, the second and third. That made the Casa's longtime manager, Brendan Menendez, happy because it was off-season anyway and there were no paying guests to be scared off. It also made it easier for him to enforce my rule about no outgoing or incoming phone calls, faxes, and so on for the players.

I had no trouble getting Menendez to give me a key to Gabor's room so I could take care of the late grandmaster's things.

"Anything else, just holler," he said.

Gabor had been assigned the Arroyo Suite, on the third floor. Some suite. It had the usual antiseptic look of any small-town hotel room, except for a bigger mini-bar, a larger bed—California King size, and a tackier framed still-life on the far wall. And, I guessed, an extra mint when the maid turned the bed down.

I must confess I felt a bit uneasy as I packed up what clothing of Gabor's I found in the closet. I left it on the bed, with his valise and a few books. The bathroom cabinet held the usual items—disposable razor, toothbrush, comb, a few medicine bottles. I left them to be collected later.

In the nightstand I found his passport, address book, the horn-rimmed glasses Gabor used only at the board as well as his dark glasses for bright sunlight, another medicine bottle—the kind of things we call "personal effects." I figured they might have to be mailed separately, so I stuffed them into a large manila envelope I'd brought and dropped it off in my room on the way downstairs.

It was 11:25. There was still nearly an hour before the drawing of lots, so I paid a call on Phelps. He worked out of an office attached to his ranch-style home, a three-minute walk from the hotel. His nurse-secretary-bookkeeper, Mona Barnes, recognized me when I walked in. She waved me on to Phelps, at his desk in the back room.

"How's the chess?" he said, without looking up.

"Just fine, Doc."

I felt slightly ridiculous calling anyone "Doc." But in this one-horse, two-dog town, everyone else addressed Phelps that way.

"I'm going to need some particulars on Gabor."

"Particulars?" He looked up.

"The medical details. I have to contact the Hungarian consulate in Los Angeles to arrange for the return of the body. I'm the one stuck with this because there's nobody else to do it. And I need some basic information, including exact time and cause of death."

Phelps blinked. "Well, you already know the time, because you were there. And the cause was an event of myocardial infarction."

"An event?"

"That's a heart attack in laymen's terms. And I see no reason for an autopsy," he said.

"Maybe so. Anyway, I'm sure the Hungarians will want to do their own once you release the body."

Phelps' eyes told me he was turning something over in his mind.

"Well, you know I could do a preliminary post-mortem here. Strictly routine, of course, but it might help you with the Hungarians."

"Thanks."

After a few minor errands, I was in the auditorium at Los Voraces High School and a little surprised at what I found on. Many grandmasters operate on "GM time," that is, ten-plus minutes late, even when their clock is running. But on this morning several had already shown up to check out this year's improvements to the site. They checked them out in their own way.

Bohigian, the courtly veteran, was trying out each chair in the playing area on the auditorium stage, to see which best accommodated his 6 foot 6 frame. Van Siclen, bearded, chubby and looking older than his 32 years, was carefully evaluating the selection of single-barrel Anejo Tequilas in the makeshift hospitality suite. Tall and tweedy Royce-Smith was anxiously scrutinizing the building's entrances and exits. Security conscious? Or simply paranoid? The jury was still out.

And Qi and Karlson were testing the clocks in a series of four-minute games. They were seated at what would normally be Board One, one of the two tables nearest the edge of the stage and closest to the audience. Boards Three and Four were set a few feet back of

One and Two, and Five and Six were nearest the stage wall. This year, without Gabor, there would be no Board Seven.

There was nothing else to do until the meeting so I grabbed a folding metal chair to watch. I sat down on the side of the board nearest the clock, so I faced the players and had a good view of the auditorium seats behind them. Their first game, with Qi playing White, went:

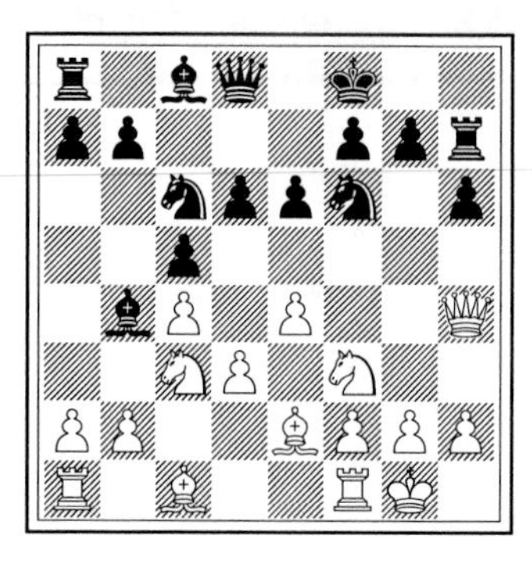

After 9. ... Rh7

1. c4 e6 2. Nc3 Bb4 3. e4 c5 4. Qg4 Kf8!

It's funny: I saw that 4. ... Qf6? 5. Nb5 was bad for Black but I don't think anyone realized at the time that White was getting into trouble.

5. Nf3? Nf6 6. Qh4 d6 7. Be2 Nc6 8. 0–0 h6! 9. d3 Rh7!!

Karlson, the "Karelian Karpov," was known for moves like this. Of course, Qi saw ...g5! coming. Meeting it was another story.

10. Ne1 g5 11. Qg3 Nd4 12. Bd1 e5

As I wondered how Qi was going to untangle his pieces, I heard Vilković trying to bum a smoke from Van Siclen. The Serb had the usual addiction of East European GMs—to other people's cigarettes.

13. h4 Ne6 14. h×g5 h×g5

If Black got in ...Nf4 her game looked to be positionally winning. So:

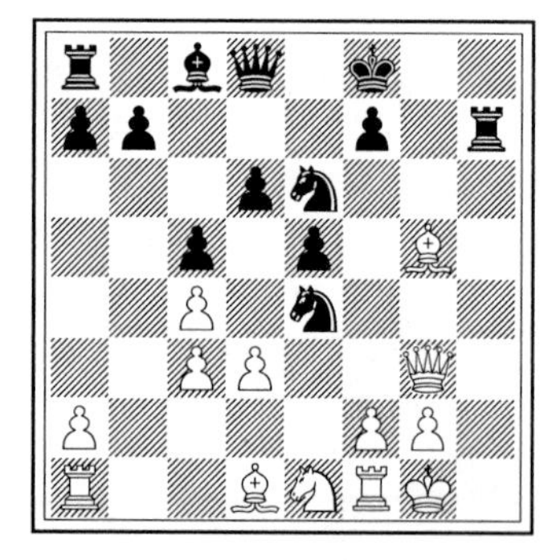

After 16. ... N×e4

15. B×g5? B×c3 16. b×c3 N×e4!

"Cool!" the terminally perky Karlson said as she ripped off the e-pawn. Qi shook his head at his position. While he thought, Popov slipped into a metal chair next to me.

"I am trying to understand what you are doing," he whispered conspiratorially. "You want to make it more unique, yes?"

"I haven't the vaguest idea what you're talking about," I said without turning from the game. I wasn't about to supply Popov with gossip he could swap on the grandmaster grapevine.

Already bald at 28 and dressed in his usual jet black turtleneck and slacks, he looked like a cross between a 19th century anarchist and a low-rent pro wrestler. He also had a reputation for being someone you could never trust.

"The rules," he said. "Forty in two and a half and all that 1960s nonsense."

"Don't blame me," I said. "I didn't make this stuff up. Sheldrake did. Complain to him."

"I will let Gabor do that. He will be seeing him first," Popov replied drily.

Qi was two pawns down in a lost rook endgame. I continued to pretend I cared.

"But okay," Popov said "It's not real chess. It's a lottery. And if you are willing to pay us to play snail chess, so be it."

He stood up to go and added:

"But I'm curious about how you are going to sell this to the Spaceman."

Just as Popov said that I looked out on the auditorium and noticed Klushkov. He was standing at the center door, some 20 yards away from the stage.

Even among the eccentrics that make up the grandmaster elite, Nikolai Pavlovich Klushkov stood out. The gaunt and gangly native of Yaroslavl had been rated in the top three in the world for most of the last decade. But it was his playing style, and his behavior of course, that made him truly distinctive.

When his rivals would be bent over the board, calculating like Deep Blue IX on hyperdrive, Klushkov would let his clock run. He'd stare at the ceiling in a glacial calm, reciting Lermontov to himself. Then he would play a move no one had remotely considered.

At first the others called him "Cosmonaut Klushkov." Then "the Grandmaster from Pluto." And, finally, "The Spaceman," which stuck.

Qi had resigned, and was starting another game with Karlson while I watched Klushkov. As if in a daze, he stood at the auditorium's main entrance without entering. Maybe he had forgotten where he had to be. Or where he was. Or who he was.

Fortunately for him, Eichler and Boriescu arrived together a few seconds later from the Casa, and a flash of recognition came over Klushkov's face:

This was a chess tournament and he was a player.

That settled, Klushkov followed the others inside.

Karlson had White in the rematch with Qi, and seemed determined to bring out her inner Tal.

1. d4 Nf6 2. c4 e6 3. Nf3 c5 4. d5 e×d5 5. c×d5 d6 6. Nc3 g6 7. Bf4 Bg7 8. Qa4+ Bd7 9. Qb3 b5 10. B×d6 Qb6 11. N×b5?!

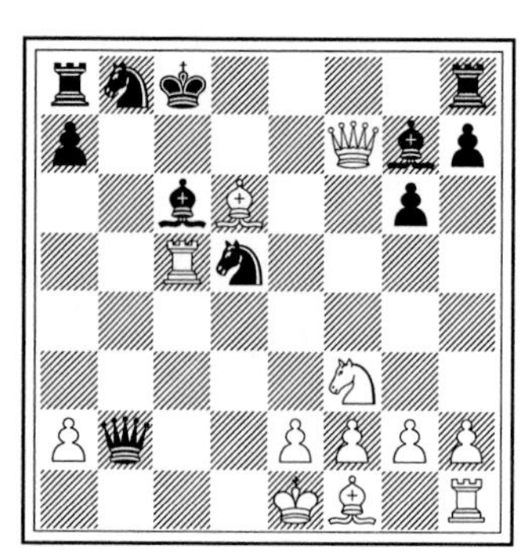

After 16. ... Bc6

She hit the clock and looked at me with an expression that said "Everything's sound at four minutes, right?"

11. ... Q×b5 12. Qe3+ Kd8 13. Qe7+ Kc8 14. Rc1 N×d5!

Wrong.

15. Q×f7 Q×b2 16. R×c5+ Bc6

Only a few tricks were left (17. R×d5 is mated by 17. ... Qc1+).

17. Ne5 B×e5 18. Qe6+ Kb7 19. Q×e5 Qb1+ 20. Kd2 Nd7!

While Karlson searched for the saving cheapo that didn't exist, I took a quick headcount. With Grushevsky unaccounted for and Gabor in an air-conditioned vault at the Los Voraces morgue, I was enjoying the company of 10 world class players. But that meant I was missing two warm bodies.

I called the Casa and left urgent messages for Bastrikova and Krimsditch, telling them to get their 2850-rated tails over to the high school because I was going to start the players' meeting in five minutes.

Eight minutes later, with Zhenya present but still minus the representative of the U. S. of A., I began.

"Gentlemen and ladies: By now you all know of the untimely passing of Grandmaster Gabor. I think I can speak for all of us when I say this was a loss that will be felt wherever the game is played. Chess has suffered greatly."

From the corner of my eye I could see Vilković and Popov smirking at one another from their seats on the stage. They'd hated Gabor with a passion, and his death was all a big joke to them.

A few seats away Bohigian had his 49-year-old eyes closed. Was he asleep? Karlson and Bastrikova accidentally caught sight of one another, so each was adjusting her chair to get the other woman out of her field of vision. Klushkov was carefully counting the stitches in his shaggy gray cardigan. And *talking* to them. Eichler was playing with some silly wrist video game. Only Qi seemed to be listening.

"I've given some thought to the matter and decided it would be too inconvenient to arrange for a replacement," I continued. "Besides, I doubt if any of you would want me to try to bring in the next highest rated player as a last-minute substitute. That would be Grandmaster Krilinsky."

A few nods of agreement. Bohigian woke up at the sound of "Krilinsky," his blood-rival since some long-forgotten Spartak vs. Dinamo junior match during the Brezhnev years. I went on:

"And so, with the authority invested in me by Mr. Sheldrake and the Sheldrake Trust, I've decided to proceed with business as usual. The only difference is that each player will now have a bye. The Sheldrake Memorial will go ahead as scheduled. Attila would have wanted it that way."

I could see Vilković and Popov were on the verge of bursting out laughing at that, so I quickly added:

"You should already be aware of the rules and regulations for this tournament. At least you would if you'd read beyond the dollar signs on your contracts. Most of the rules will remain as they were in past Sheldrakes. The principle difference is the time limit—40 moves in two and a half hours. Followed by adjournment."

I waited for the groans.

"I haven't adjourned since 1993," Bohigian said.

"I've never even seen it done," Popov said.

"*Hangepartie? Incroyable!*" Boriescu said.

In his own way, Boriescu was unique. Almost every other player his strength since the 1970s had been fluent in English. Boriescu understood a bit of the language all right. But when he spoke, he relied on a kind of personal Esperanto, using odd and ends of other languages. As if anyone could ever figure out what he meant. Few bothered to try.

"The rules may be a bit strange for some of you," I added, "but I'm sure you'll be able to adhere easily enough to Mr. Sheldrake's wishes. Now without further ado, I'd like to address the matter that brought us here this morning."

"It is already fifteen minutes to one," Bastrikova said.

"Thank you, Zhenya. I stand corrected. The matter that brought us here this afternoon: the drawing of lots and determination of pairings."

"Excuse me, but aren't you leaving out something more important than pairings?"

The other players all turned to Vilković. *More important than pairings?*

You could see he was embarrassed at the instant attention.

"There were 14 of us and now there will be only 13."

"And your point is…?" Van Siclen asked, boldfacing the last two words.

"My point is—Gabor's fee. We were going to be paid only if we finished all of our games. What happens to his share now?"

There was a brief pause and a few nods.

"Good catch," Eichler said.

"Quite," Royce-Smith said from a seat at the other side of the stage.

"Precisely!" Van Siclen said, mocking Vilković.

"I think we should divide Gabor's share proportionately, according to rating," Eichler said.

"You would," said Popov, who trailed him by 70 Elo points on the July 1 list.

"You know, with Gabor's money we could have one hell of a party," Van Siclen mused. With Gert there was always a 50 percent chance he was serious.

"*Nyet*," said Boriescu. "*Es muy mucho dinero*."

"This is unbecoming of grandmasters," Bohigian said. "We didn't act like this in my day."

"In your day," Vilković giggled, "the first prizes were bottles of vodka and tins of Baltic herring."

"We should vote on an issue of this significance," Qi said.

"I vote we give equal shares of Gabor's fee to everyone," Karlson announced.

"I vote for anything but that," Bastrikova said, several feet away.

I had to regain the floor before this got out of hand.

"Excuse me but you're not voting for anything. A chess tournament is not a democracy."

Several players started to object, but there was no way I'd allow them. I spoke quickly.

"When it comes to rules a chess tournament is a monarchy—and an arbiter is the most absolute monarch this side of a ship's captain. As for the issue Grandmaster Vilković has raised, Mr. Sheldrake had foreseen just such a possibility. I don't mean of a death, of course. But of a player dropping out. Consistent with his wishes, Grandmaster Gabor's appearance fee will be added to the prizes, on a sliding scale. You will all receive a new prize schedule later at the hotel, but I'm at liberty to tell you now that this will mean that first place alone will be worth an additional $200,000."

I let the number sink in a moment before proceeding.

Qi shot me an inquisitive glance and turned to look about the stage. Then Royce-Smith did the same. One by one the GMs began to look uneasily at one another.

For the first time, the players of Los Voraces 2019 realized there would be real money in the prizes, not just in the contracted fees. Everyone was mentally calculating how much that meant for their likely finish:

Assuming Grushevsky took clear first place—no sure thing these days—Klushkov, Bohigian and Royce-Smith would likely be contending for second, third and fourth. That would mean perhaps $300,000 between them.

Eichler would probably get his usual even score—maybe 12 draws this time. But it would still be worth about $75,000 extra for him. The women would figure on finishing somewhere in the middle. And Popov would probably be fighting Vilković to avoid last. But even that was worth $25,000 more than he was expecting to leave town with.

After a long-enough pause, I added: "Not bad for scheduling a game you don't have to play."

"They're the best kind," Van Siclen said.

As it turned out, the pairings went fairly smoothly. Sheldrake had stipulated there would be a "Los Voraces–style drawing," leaving me to read his mind. So in the next order of business I directed the players' attention to a large table at my left. There I had placed some

13

pseudo–Pueblo pottery I'd picked up at a shlock souvenir shop in Albuquerque yesterday before driving down Interstate 25.

Inside each "authentic semi-glazed pitcher" or "handmade Zia ceremonial vessel" I'd put a different number, one to 13, attached to a gift. I instructed the players to come forward—in alphabetical order, starting with Bastrikova—and pick an item. The present inside would determine how they'd stand in the pairing chart.

Bastrikova selected a vase which contained a bracelet of Apatite chips and a paper tag that read "3." Karlson eventually ended up with the "6." That meant she and Bastrikova would meet in Round Eight. I could hardly wait.

The rest of the draw was routine. I designated Gabor as "14" so whenever anyone was due to play that number he or she would have the bye. That gave Vilković a day off in tomorrow's first round because he found the "1" attached to a necklace of Heishi beads hidden inside the clay water-dish he picked.

And since in their infinite wisdom they'd declined to attend, I drew for Grushevsky—he got the "9"—and for Krimsditch, who ended up with the "8."

Krimsditch, the sandy-haired Californian, announced his presence by tripping over a folding chair as he entered from the rear of the auditorium just when we were finishing up. "Sorry," he said, not meaning it in the slightest.

"This all but concludes the business of the Sheldrake Memorial players' meeting," I said. "Before we adjourn—pardon, I meant, recess—I'd like to inform you of something not listed in the prize schedules of your contracts. There is a brilliancy prize this year. And a particularly generous amount has been assigned to it."

"How much?" Popov asked.

"Of course, you can't put an exact price tag on genius..."

"How much?" Bastrikova asked.

"...but in this case Mr. Sheldrake did just that—a half million dollars."

It was an insane amount. No tournament had ever given more than a few thousand for a beauty prize. The top brilliancy at New York 1924 was worth 50 bucks. At Nottingham '36, it was ten pounds sterling. For San Antonio 1972, the first super-tournament after World War II, it was $150. And Kasparov pocketed all of 500 guilders, about $250, for his game with Topalov at Wijk aan Zee 1999.

Adjusted for inflation, the value of genius had been steadily going down. But the brilliancy prize of Los Voraces 2019 would be worth something on the order of $10,000—per move. The GMs seemed suitably impressed, all but Bohigian who shook his head.

"Finally," I said, "there is the matter of the composition of an appeals committee in case there is a protest of one of my decisions. I need three names."

"I nominate Qi Yuanzhi," said Karlson, whose infatuation with Qi was obvious to everyone except him.

"May I decline?" he said.

"Can I nominate myself?" Bastrikova said.

"Is there any money in this?" Krimsditch said.

"The answers to your questions are no, yes and no," I replied. "That gives us two nominees, Grandmasters Qi and Bastrikova. I nominate former world champion Bohigian as the third member. Do I hear any objections?"

Before anyone could open their mouth I concluded:

"Hearing none, I also nominate Grandmasters Royce-Smith and Eichler as alternates, to serve only in case of a dispute involving any of the three committee members. And so, ladies and gentleman, we are done. Barring any further crises I'll see you all here at 2 tomorrow for the first round."

"*Nema problema*," Boriescu mumbled to himself as the crowd dispersed. "*N'importe*."

Two hours later, I'd laserprinted the pairings and new prize schedules and slipped them under the door of each of the players' rooms. I also typed up my notes from the meeting.

I had to keep an exact record. In his desire to bring back the glory days of international chess, Sheldrake wanted a tournament book written about his memorial. An old-fashioned print-on-page book, with glossy photos, round-by-round commentary and post-mortem quotes from the players. And I was deputized to compile it.

By 4:45 I was finished. I found several messages waiting for me at the Casa's main desk. Or rather, several special requests. Each of the players had made a list of things they couldn't live without during the tournament and figured it was my duty to provide them.

Eichler wanted a soccer ball for exercise. Qi urgently sought a source for silken tofu. Popov said he needed a hotel room with a quieter air conditioner. Karlson simply couldn't play chess without her eucalyptus tea. Van Siclen had to have a special TV hookup so he could catch Sparta Rotterdam games.

And so on. I felt like I was back in the old days, scrambling to keep Kasparov supplied with Toblerones during rounds.

But they were still my players. *My* players. I felt strangely responsible for them, almost paternal, despite everything. I made a shopping list of what I could get in town, which wasn't much, and started working the phone to order the rest.

Finally it was dusk. After a so-so dinner at the Rancho Voraces—smoked rabbit tamales with blue corn spoon bread, washed down with a couple of Dos Equis—I got back to my hotel room. Where I noticed the manila envelope I'd left on the bed.

I'd never gotten around to mailing off Gabor's personal effects to Hungary, what with the visit to Phelps, the late start at the high school, the silly argument over fee money and my head start on fulfilling the GM wishlists.

I emptied the contents on the bed, and looked at it: So this is what sums up the life of International Grandmaster Attila Gabor.

Only then did I focus on the orange-colored, white-topped vial. It was labeled "Drogistal," the heart medicine, with the usual fine-print mumbo-jumbo on the back.

But this wasn't Drogistal.

Even before opening the vial I realized something was wrong. I knew Drogistal. It had been the world's most prescribed heart medication for a decade. I'd taken it myself a few years before for a slight arrhythmia.

The small reddish pills I was looking at were something else. Gabor, with his atrocious eyesight, couldn't tell the difference. But I could.

Had he mixed up his medicine in some way, some fatal way? I didn't know. And there was no one around to tell me.

I quickly resealed the manila envelope, opened the closet safe, put in the envelope and locked it up. I left my room, found the service staircase at the end of the hall and walked up a flight of stairs to the third floor.

The hallway was empty. But when I got to Gabor's room I noticed the door was slightly ajar. That alarmed me. If someone was inside, it would almost certainly be a player.

Slowly I opened the door and found: Nothing. No valise. No clothes. Nothing in the bathroom cabinet. Someone had taken everything I'd seen hours before. And as I closed the cabinet and looked at myself in the mirror, it occurred to me.

There was a real possibility that Gabor had been murdered. And that one of *my* players was the murderer.

Thursday, August 22, 2019

THE PHONE ON MY NIGHTSTAND rang at the ungodly hour of 7:22 A.M.

"World Champion Grushevsky must have his own dressing room at playing site," the basso profundo voice said.

"And a very good morning to you, too, Igor," I replied.

"With his own cot, reclining chair, private toilet and shower, dressing table and mirror, food preparing area, refrigerator and live monitor of his board and clock," he continued.

"I'm afraid we can't do that, Igor. If we did that for you, we'd have to provide rooms for the 12 other players."

"They are not World Champion Grushevsky. My contract states you must provide proper facilities for the strongest player of the galaxy."

"Look, Igor, your contract states no such thing. I know because I wrote it. Besides, if we needed the strongest player of the galaxy we would have lured Garry Kimovich out of retirement."

I knew that would get him. Grushevsky liked to claim he was the strongest player in history—and "of the galaxy." He had that wording added to the title page of each of his books, even to his business cards. Eventually, the other players began referring to him as the "Spog," the strongest player of galaxy. As in, "Who gets the Spog today?" "Not me, I got Spogged yesterday."

True, Grushevsky was the highest-rated player in history. But that was because he broke Kasparov's peak with the help of point inflation. I suspect a 2700 player from Garry Kimovich's era could give draw odds to a 2850 player nowadays. But this wasn't worth arguing about. Not at 7:22 A.M.

"There is not enough money in the world to make World Champion Grushevsky happy about this," he said.

"Then one of us is going to be unhappy on this fine New Mexico morning."

And with that I hung up and went back to sleep. It was too good a morning to waste on the problems of grandmasters.

Three hours later, my alarm went off. Normally, I'm not a night person but during tournaments I try to keep the same hours as the GMs. If the rounds were going to begin at 2 P.M., as they always were at a Sheldrake, none of the players would be asleep by midnight. ("I go to bed at 4 A.M.," as Kramnik famously said. "Almost all chessplayers do.")

And none of the GMs would plan on rising before 11 or so. But I didn't have the luxury. Today I needed to get moving early. After I wolfed down a "Sombrero Special" breakfast at the Casa ("Ancho Chile Huevos Rancheros with Red Salsa and Refried Beans—Guacamole $1 extra"), I began my last-minute chores.

First, I checked at the front desk on the status of the supplies I'd ordered.

"How's the chess?" Menendez asked. In eight years of coming to Los Voraces I'd never found a good answer to that greeting.

"The chess is just fine. Anything come in for me?"

"I'll check."

There were a few overnight deliveries, of things I needed for the tournament's needs and to meet the players' "special requests." But still no sign of a miniature flag of the Republic of Armenia. Bohigian would have to be unpatriotic today.

I stopped in at Phelps' office twice before 12:30, but there was no sign of the good doctor.

"Just can't keep track of such a busy man," said Nurse Barnes. "He's on a house call out in the Valley. Try again tomorrow?"

I decided against telling Sheriff Gibbs what I'd found—and not found—in Gabor's room. I needed to know more before I was willing to share information. After all, there could be an innocent explanation for the pills or for the items that disappeared from the Arroyo Suite. And even though I knew Gabor had feuds and enemies—more than even the usual GM's share—his death couldn't be due to foul play. Could it?

After all, who hated him enough to kill him? Vilković? Popov? Not really. Krimsditch? One of the women? It didn't make sense.

Finally it was 1:20. I walked over to the high school to inspect the playing site once more. It was part of my pre-tournament ritual, performing tasks little known outside the brotherhood of International Arbiters. Even veteran grandmasters haven't a clue about all the technical nonsense required of a really dedicated IA these days. For example, it took me nearly 20 minutes just to measure the lighting at all six boards. I know it wasn't necessary but I wanted to make sure it met the world championship standards FIDE had set, at Fischer's insistence, more than 40 years ago.

That 1972 rule read: "Illumination on the chess table shall be variable between 120 and 180 foot-candles with dimmer control, from fluorescent lamps in the 3000K range, shielded by milk-white acrylic Plexiglas or equal no closer than 5 meters to the floor."

Really.

By 1:46, the players began to drift in, joining me and Mrs. Nagle on the stage.

Nancy Nettlesen Nagle was just about the only citizen of Los Voraces who seemed pleased that the town was hosting the world's greatest annual chess tournament.

"I love to watch them think, don't you?" she said as we set up the clocks, one per board. "It's so ... inspirational."

"Yeah, real battle of wits. Maybe this year nobody'll hang their queen in a winning position."

"Exciting!" she said.

At 53, Mrs. Nagle was an early widow who wore her silvering brown hair in a bun. Everyone knew her: she was the town's librarian, voting registrar, and recording secretary of the town council. But for two-plus weeks each August she also served as my semi-official assistant arbiter. And there were times when she was the only spectator.

Unfortunately, she wasn't alone today. Eichler, the *Wunderkind* of German chess, walked in arm in arm with a new arrival to town.

"Good morning, honorable arbiter. Do you know Daphne? I must introduce you."

"Charmed," I fibbed. "But we've already met."

I'd seen Daphne Nardlinger at about half the tournaments I'd run in the last nine years. She was hard to miss. Too blond to be real, with a tad too much makeup and too little skirt for someone of her 35-plus years, she'd become the *Übergoupie* of big-league chess.

But I had to be a bit impressed by Daphne. She always managed to show up with someone new, someone just a little bit stronger than her last GM. I knew she was trading up. But I didn't realize she'd broken 2900.

"I can't say I'm happy to see you here, Miss Nardlinger. The invitees to the Memorial were specifically requested not to bring companions of any kind."

"I'm not a groupie," Daphne said. "I'm a self-actualized person who helps players take control of the super-grandmaster experience."

"And you do that by…?"

"I do it through nurturing, spiritual cherishing and the enhancement of their personal growth."

I stared at her until Eichler made up an excuse.

"Sorry, I must spend quality time with my scoresheet," he said and headed to his board.

Of course, I wasn't really surprised that Sheldrake's dream—sealing off the tournament from the outside world until the last move of the last game—wasn't going to succeed one hundred percent. What troubled me was that Daphne was a potential troublemaker, the kind that congregates around major players at major tournaments, trying to fit in.

Hangers-on are often more of a problem than the players, as a number of past incidents could attest. There was the time at Manila 2012 when fans of Grushevsky's got out of hand at his hotel and trashed one of the public rooms. It was rock-star quality damage, and the hotel refused to host any more tournaments after that. Chess, they said, is too violent.

And that was hardly unique. Something similar occurred during the 1987 U.S. Championship in Colorado, and again at a Hilton in Russia in 2006. I didn't need that type of grief at Los Voraces 2019. Not if I wanted there to be a Los Voraces 2020.

"I'm glad we had this time to share," Daphne said as she bounced off to take a seat in the auditorium's first row.

Ten minutes before the round began, the players were all in their places, all except Vilković, who I guessed was off smoking somewhere.

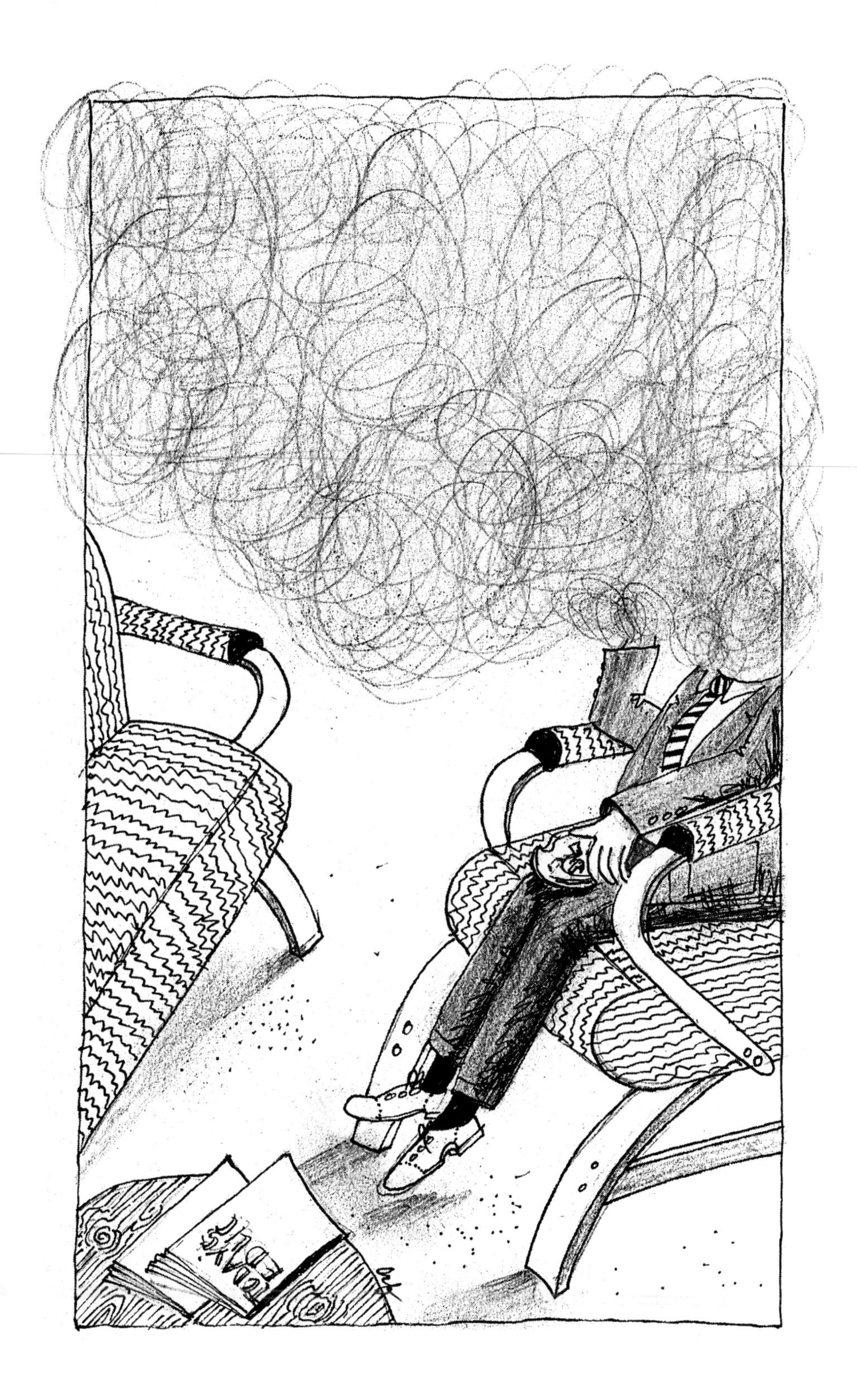

A glance at the boards found everyone going through their pre-round idiosyncrasies:

Bastrikova was using a red pen this year. Her lucky blue pen must have run out of luck. Klushkov had placed a glass and two bottles of distilled Siberian glacier water on his side of the table, facing Bohigian. Qi was bending his head back and forth in isometric exercises. Karlson closed her eyes to meditate. Popov had folded his scoresheet lengthwise, once then twice. His opponent, Van Siclen, was preparing for time pressure by numbering the spaces on his scoresheet next to the final moves of the control. He wrote a "10" next to move 30, a "9" next to 31, on so on, so he would know how many moves he had left to make.

Krimsditch, wearing a University of New Mexico sweatshirt and jeans, methodically twisted his white gold Rolex around so that the clock was on the inside of his wrist.

"Anybody got gum?" he called out, to no one in particular.

"I have!" Daphne exclaimed from the "audience." She began rummaging through her oversized, fake leather handbag in search of a stick of Juicy Fruit.

At his table, Royce-Smith had crossed off the number 13 on his scoresheet.

"Are you really superstitious?" I asked.

"No" he said. "Being superstitious brings bad luck." He didn't smile.

There was some light banter at other boards. But no mention of the man who wasn't there. How quickly Gabor had been forgotten. And then it was time to make history.

"Ladies and gentlemen, let me officially welcome you once again to Los Voraces, New Mexico, this time for the first annual Sheldrake Memorial International Tournament," I said.

"I believe I covered most of the technical matters yesterday. Just a few reminders. I need your signatures on both scoresheets when the game is over. The post-mortem room is where it was last year. And you can find the rest rooms through the doors to the lobby. So let me just add, may the best player win."

Then I began my walk across the stage, starting White's clock on all boards in the time-honored tradition of tournament directors. It felt good.

As usual, nothing much happened in the first hour, while the players settled into their rhythms of thought, trying to adjust to a time control that hadn't been used since *Chess Informant 40*. Qi's game, on Board Four, was the first to make an impression.

Qi–Boriescu
King's Indian Defense E62

1. d4 Nf6 2. c4 g6 3. g3 Bg7 4. Bg2 0–0 5. Nf3 d6 6. Nc3 c6 7. 0–0 Qa5 8. h3 Qa6 9. b3 b5 10. cxb5 cxb5

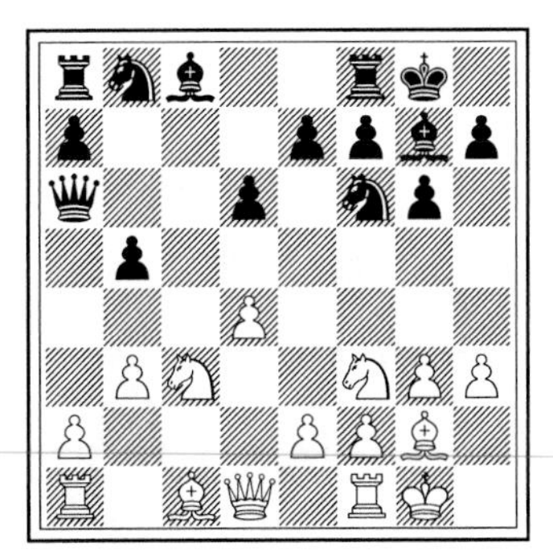

After 10. ... cxb5

A book position so old that, I suspected, no one beside the two players remembered the theory. I seemed to recall that White usually played something positional like 11. b4. Or something complicated like 11. Qd3 b4 12. Ne5!?. Or something.

11. a4 b4 12. Nb5 Qb6 13. Ne5!

Boriescu made a strange sight. His body, all 5 foot 5, 220 pounds of him, arched forward, with toes pointed into the parquet stage floor and hands gripping his bald spot, as he agonized over the position.

He had good reason to agonize: Black was in trouble. He couldn't play 13. ... Bb7?? because 14. Nc4 wins outright. And 13. ... d5 is met by 14. Qc2 followed by invasion at c7 or c6. For example, 14. Qc2 Na6 15. Qc6 Bb7 16. Q×b6 a×b6 17. Nc4!.

After 27 minutes, Boriescu decided to accept the sacrifice, probably because there was nothing better than taking his chances with 13. ... d×e5 14. B×a8 B×h3!?.

13. ... dxe5 14. dxe5!

But he began to turn a shade of dark green after this. On 14. ... Bb7 15. Be3 Black is lost, and 14. ... Nc6 15. Be3 Qb7 16. Rc1 Bd7 17. N×a7 was decidedly unpleasant.

14. ... Rd8 15. Be3!!

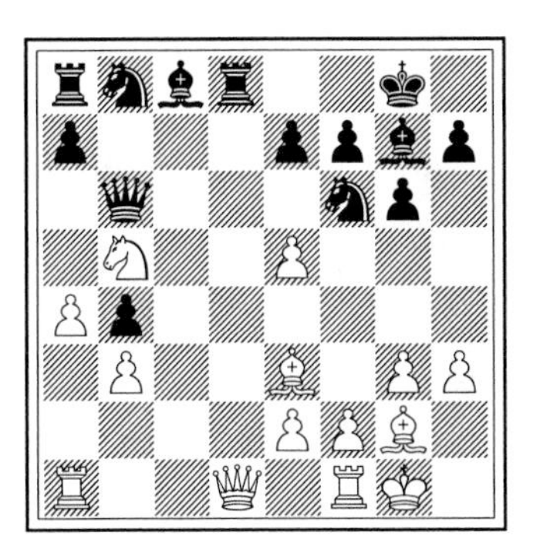

After 15. Be3

Make that chartreuse.

Within a minute or two, Qi's board had attracted a small, silent crowd. Royce-Smith nodded to himself as he calculated Qi's queen sack. Eichler shook his head. Karlson just smiled. Only Van Siclen seemed unimpressed. On his way off the stage, towards the right-hand aisle that led to the men's room, he paused, looked at me and shrugged.

And I wondered if past generations of arbiters appreciated moments like this. Did they know when Fischer or Alekhine was creating a masterpiece in front of them? Or was it just part of their business to get the scoresheets signed, make sure the moves were recorded legibly and get ready for the next round?

In those days you didn't have to be a master to run a master tournament. An arbiter could even be a rook-odds player. But today no IA can be below 2400 strength. Just to enforce rules like FIDE's 10.2—a.k.a. the "making no effort to win by normal means" rule—you have to understand pretty well what's happening on the board.

In any event, the crowd broke up just as there was a result on Board Three. The game, what there was of it, had one highlight, which occurred after seven moves.

It could have been a composition, one of Gabor's how-did-this-come-about-games. In fact, there was a kind of logic to all the moves in this one, too. When I saw the scoresheets I understood that:

Krimsditch–Eichler
Queen's Indian Defense E15

1. d4 Nf6 2. c4 e6 3. Nf3 b6 4. g3 Ba6 5. Qa4 Ne4 6. Bg2 Nd6

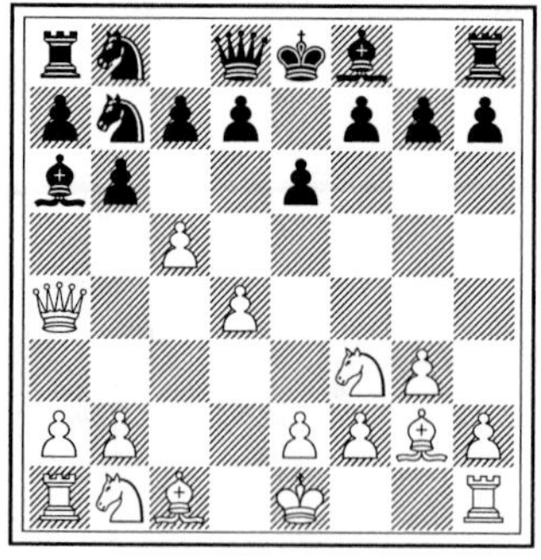

After 7. ... Nb7

Quite a conception: On 7. Nbd2 Black has 7. ... N×c4! 8. N×c4 b5 and he is at least equal.

7. c5! Nb7!

Eichler took a while before he found this move but it was the only good one. White's initiative would be much too strong after 7. ... b×c5 8. d×c5 Nb7 9. c6! d×c6 10. Ne5.

8. b4 c6 9. Nc3 Be7 10. Bf4 b×c5!

On 10. ... d6 11. b5! Black is positionally squashed—

11. B×b8 Bb5 12. N×b5 c×b5 13. Qa6! R×b8 14. b×c5?

—just as he would be after 13. d×c5. Eichler's sense of danger was highly developed for a player of his age, and he extricated himself from the bind by giving Krimsditch a reason to believe he had losing as well as winning chances.

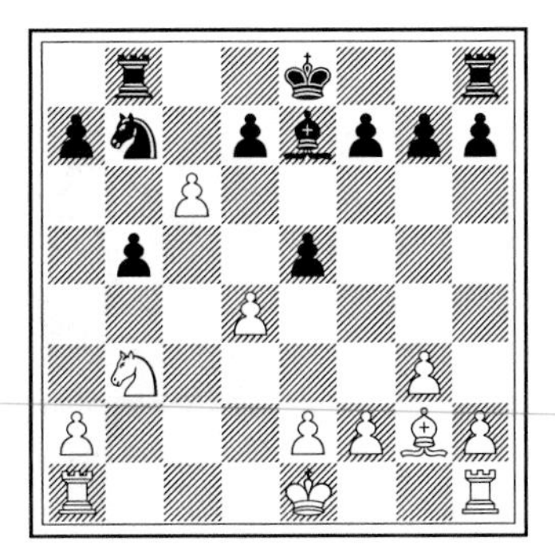

After 18. c6

14. ... Qa5+ 15. Q×a5 N×a5 16. Nd2 e5!

Not 16. ... d6 17. Nb3! with a miserable endgame for Black.

17. Nb3 Nb7 18. c6

18. ... Bb4+ 19. Kd1 d×c6 20. B×c6+ Ke7 Draw

As so often happens, the player who was in trouble a few moves before—Black—didn't appreciate how well off he was when he offered a draw. Eichler would have been winning after 21. d×e5? Rhd8+ 22. Kc2 Rbc8 and would be at least equal after 21. B×b5 e×d4 22. N×d4 Rhd8 23. e3 Bc3.

After I collected the scoresheets and flags I asked the players to follow me to my office. It was time to begin work on another chore: I needed all the participants to sign a special oak "Los Voraces 2019" board—one GM's autograph per square—that the Trust was going to showcase someday in a Sheldrake Chess Museum.

But when I got Krimsditch and Eichler to the office, back of the stage, we discovered their ball-points wouldn't write on wood. We needed a felt-tipped pen.

"I have!" said the ever-helpful Miss Nardlinger, who had tagged along.

Daphne searched through her handbag again until, inevitably, she found one. I wondered what other essentials she might have stored in the bag. First aid kit? Alkaline batteries? Parachute?

"Chess will be eternally indebted to you," I told her.

"Tell me about it," she said.

It looked like Krimsditch and Eichler weren't the only ones starting the tournament with a rest day. Popov was soon on the verge of peace talks with Van Siclen and the negotiations were concluded amicably by the third hour of play. But you couldn't have guessed that outcome by the way they started the afternoon:

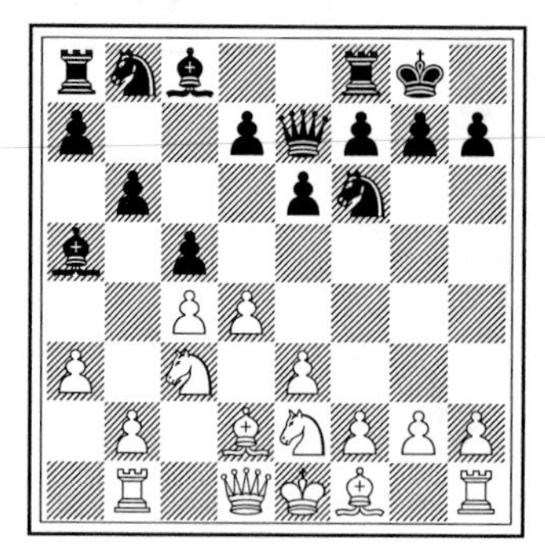

After 8. ... 0–0

Van Siclen–Popov
Nimzo-Indian Defense E42

1. c4 e6 2. Nc3 Nf6 3. d4 Bb4 4. e3 c5 5. Ne2 b6 6. a3 Ba5 7. Rb1 Qe7 8. Bd2 0–0

9. b4?! c×b4 10. a×b4 B×b4 11. R×b4! Q×b4 12. Nd5

The queen wasn't quite trapped (12. ... Qb2 13. Bc3 Qa2). But White had ample compensation for the sacrificed pawn and exchange even if he passed up Nc7. After 17 minutes, Popov wrote something on his scoresheet and covered it with a pen placed horizontally.

But after another minute or so he wrinkled his nose, looked doubtfully at his opponent and crossed out the concealed move.

12. ... N×d5?

He was probably right the first time. After 12. ... Q×c4 13. Nec3 Q×d5 Black had winning chances.

13. B×b4 N×b4 14. Nf4 N8c6 15. d5 Ne5 16. Be2 Na6 17. Qa1 f6!

With this move Black manages to liquidate the dangers and keep enough compensation for the queen to ensure at least a draw.

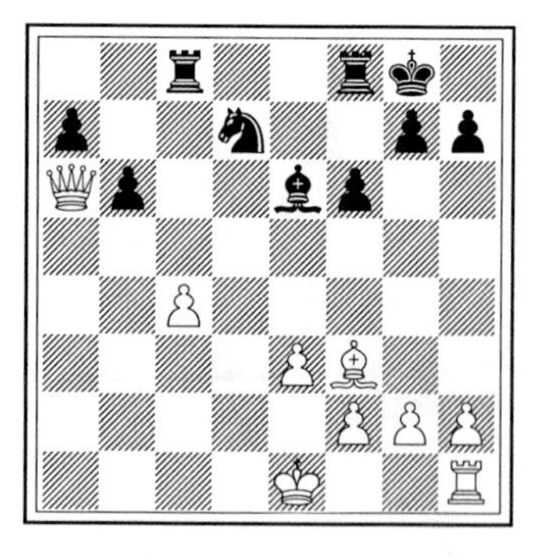

After 21. ... Rac8 Draw

18. d×e6 d×e6 19. N×e6 B×e6 20. Q×a6 Nd7 21. Bf3 Rac8 Draw

Just when it got interesting. As Karpov used to say after a first-round draw, the players were just "testing the equipment."

Not so on Board Five, where Karlson was already in trouble against the world champion.

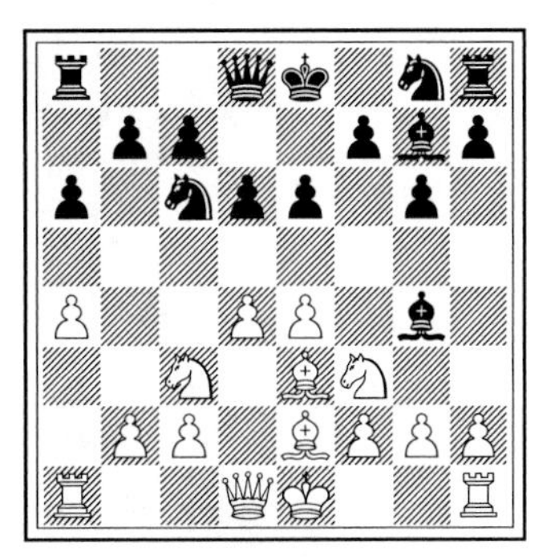

After 7. ... e6

Karlson–Grushevsky
Modern Defense B06

1. e4 g6 2. d4 Bg7 3. Nc3 d6 4. Nf3 a6 5. a4 Bg4 6. Be3 Nc6 7. Be2 e6!

It was another example of Grushevsky's pet system. In the old days Black used to play 7. ... e5 "on principle." But the trouble with having principles in chess is that they don't always agree with what's happening on the board.

This line had come into a bit of vogue because Black had to struggle for equality too often after 7. ... e5 8. dxe5.

8. 0–0 Nge7 9. h3 Bxf3 10. Bxf3 0–0 11. Re1 Re8

Grushevsky's basic idea was to wait in the center. He avoids 11. ... d5 because of 12. e5—as well as 11. ... e5 12. dxe5 dxe5 13. Nd5, with advantage to White in either case.

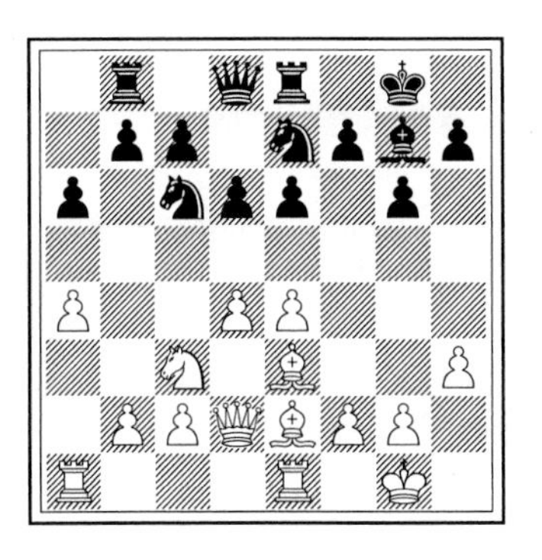

After 13. Be2

But White should also wait. She's in no position to play 12. e5, and 12. d5 exd5 13. exd5 Ne5 only eases Black's position. That means neither side profits from a change in the pawn structure—and it explains why this line was known, informally at least, as the "You First Variation."

12. Qd2 Rb8 13. Be2

It was an excellent choice of opening for Karlson. She liked to have clear-cut middlegame plans that arose naturally out of the positions. Here she had run out of ideas as soon as she completed her development. After this she began to swim. Or, rather, sink.

13. ... d5! 14. Rad1 Qd6 15. Bf4 Qb4

Suddenly the d4- and b2-pawns were falling (16. B×c7 Rbc8 17. Bg3 N×d4 favors Black).

16. e×d5 e×d5 17. Be3 Q×b2 18. Bf3 Nf5 19. Rb1 Qa3

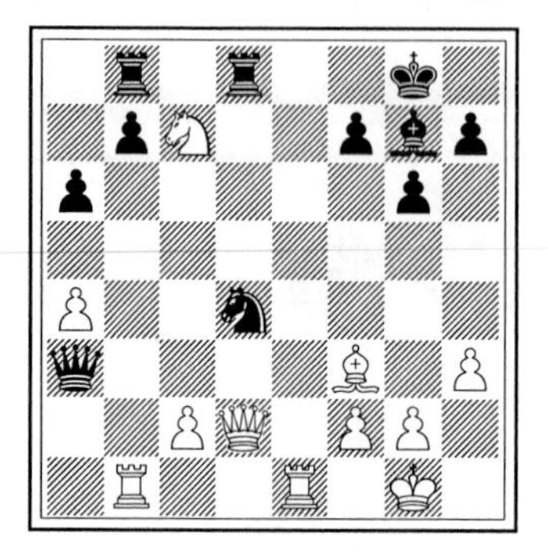

After 22. ... N×d4

If Kersti had realized how badly she stood she probably would have tried 20. B×d5 and prayed.

20. N×d5 Nc×d4 21. N×c7 Red8 22. B×d4 N×d4

Facing 22. ... Qc5, 22. ... N×f3+ or the loss of both queenside pawns, White could have resigned without disgracing the family name. For example, 23. Qf4 Q×a4 24. Nd5 Q×c2.

But she insisted on playing on until she knew the D-players would be able to understand her position was hopeless.

23. B×b7?!

Now 23. ... Nf3+ 24. B×f3 R×d2 grants White a fighting chance with 25. R×b8+ Bf8 26. Ree8.

23. ... R×b7! 24. R×b7 Nf3+ White resigns

As I watched the final moves, Grushevsky looked up at me and quickly shifted his gaze away. Still annoyed about the dressing room, no doubt.

After a few minutes, Krimsditch slithered over to where I stood. I must admit I never liked him. Maybe it was the forearm tattoo that read "World's Sexiest Chess Player." Or the surfer wardrobe. But mostly it was the attitude.

"You tried to screw me royally yesterday. The pairings, I mean."

"They're normal round-robin pairings, the fairest system in chess," I said. "And if you'd been on time, you'd have seen the drawing of lots."

"Don't give me that 'fairest' crap," he said. "We both know there's a lot of luck in a round robin. A different kind of luck than in a Swiss or a knockout. But it's still luck. I nearly got screwed three times yesterday."

"How do you figure that?"

I was torn between mild curiosity and an unwillingness to feed his delusions of persecution. Krimsditch was eager to vent.

"First, you drew me a number in the bottom half of the pairings. If Gabor hadn't stroked out, I'd have ended up with seven blacks and only six whites. Also, you drew 8 for me. I coulda had Black in the first two games, the worst draw you can get."

Having played in round robins since he was 7, Krimsditch had learned the calculus of the draw for pairings before he'd mastered the multiplication tables.

"But as it stands now," I said, "you're scheduled to play Gabor tomorrow. That means you get the bye."

He ignored that and continued: "The third thing you did was to put me in between Eichler and the Spog."

I knew what he meant. Almost all players in a round robin will face opponents in the same sequence. They will play the number 3 opponent in the round after they've faced the number 2, and the day before number 4, and so on. In our tournament, Eichler was number 7 and Grushevsky was 9. So the other GMs would be well-rested and ready to go all out when they played Krimsditch, the 8.

The reason was that Eichler was notorious for offering quick draws—and talented enough to live up to his rating and play punishing chess if his offer was refused. So, after splitting a point with him, each GM would be ready to go for blood against Krimsditch—especially since they saw Grushevsky on their schedule the round after that.

"I feel your pain," I told Krimsditch.

"And?"

"And I suggest you take control of the experience. Perhaps through personal growth, nurturing and spiritual cherishing. And I'm glad we had this time to share."

The most entertaining game of the round—until its abrupt end—was Klushkov's, of course. Truly "Spaceman chess."

Klushkov–Bohigian
Réti Opening A09

1. Nf3 d5 2. c4 d4 3. e3 Nc6 4. b4!?

I confess I only managed to guess about a third of the moves that followed. Most of them looked like "sixth-hour moves"—the kind that made sense only in a quick post-mortem analysis, after a five-hour playing session.

4. ... N×b4 5. e×d4 e5!

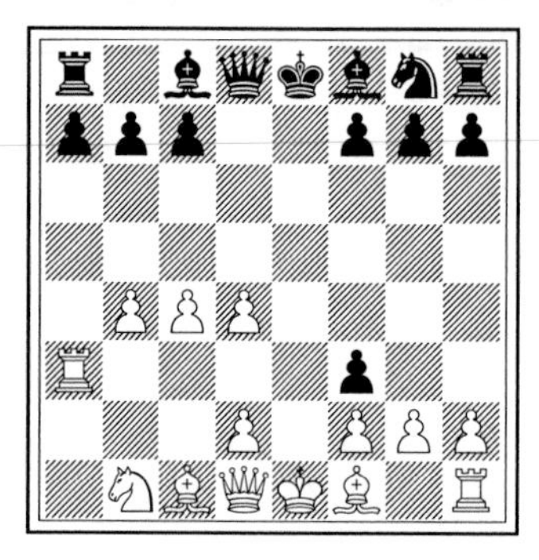

After 8. Ra3

Based on 6. N×e5 Q×d4 or 6. d×e5 Bf5!.

6. a3 e4 7. a×b4 e×f3 8. Ra3!

Bizarre—but White had to meet ...Qe7+ somehow. And it wasn't going to be much fun playing 8. Q×f3 Q×d4 9. Nc3 B×b4 or 9. Qe3+ Q×e3+.

8. ... Q×d4 9. Rd3 f×g2 10. Qe2+ Be6 11. B×g2 Q×c4 12. 0–0 c6 13. f4

Black's last move, my database later revealed, was the first new move (!) of the game. This position looked dangerous for him. For example, 13. ... g6 is met by 14. Bb2, and 13. ... Rd8 14. R×d8+ was risky after 15. Qe5.

But as so often happens in tournaments of this level, the excitement was all over in a few moves, even though it took the players another hour to find them.

13. ... Ne7 14. f5 Bd5 15. Nc3 0–0–0!?

This looked right at the time he played it. But there was something to be said for the queen sack, 15. ... B×g2 16. Rd8+ R×d8 17. Q×c4 B×f1. Maybe it was just too early in the tournament for Bohigian to take risks—or to think about the brilliancy prize.

16. Ba3

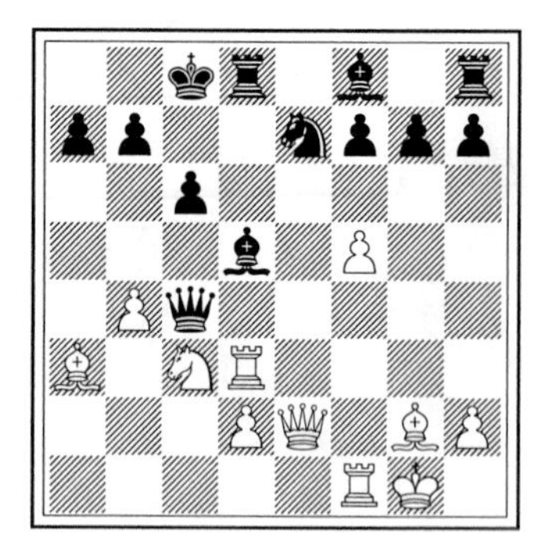

After 16. Ba3

As he pressed the clock, Klushkov muttered something. Not to his opponent, it seemed. Or to me. Maybe to the *clock*.

But it turned out to be a draw offer.

Bohigian, behind on time and facing the dangers of 17. Rc1 or 17. b5, readily accepted. Playing at the disadvantage of half an hour—and of 22 years—it made sense to avoid, say, 16. … Qa6 17. b5!? Q×a3 18. N×d5 Qc5+ 19. Kh1 N×d5 20. b×c6.

Or did it? After I'd made sure the players had signed their scoresheets, Klushkov walked off without a word. I decided to compliment Bohigian.

"People don't often grab material from the Spaceman and live these days. But today might have been the day to test him."

He shook his head.

"As my Russian grandmother used to say, 'Better a dove on the plate than a woodgrouse in the mating place.'"

Right. Another of his proverbs.

"In English we say, 'A bird in hand…'—but I'll defer to the wisdom of your grandmother," I said.

Bohigian quickly gathered up his pen and glasses and left. Some professionals, like him, never spent a second more at the playing site than they needed to. Other GMs couldn't be kept away, even when they weren't playing.

Vilković, for example, had scoped out the openings of the round, then spent most of the next three hours chain-smoking non-filters in the hospitality suite I'd set up in a teachers' lounge. He made occasional visits to the auditorium stage to gauge the day's progress. He was there when I made my 6 P.M. check on the status of the remaining games—just as Qi was ending Boriescu's misery.

Qi–Boriescu

15. … R×d1 16. Rf×d1 Qa5 17. e×f6 B×f6

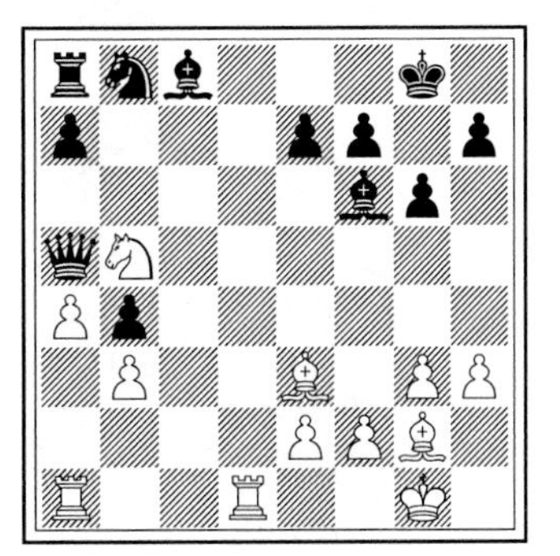

Qi–Boriescu
After 17. … B×f6

18. Rac1!

White had to emerge materially ahead now since virtually all of Black's army is en prise. But frankly I expected the game to last at least until move 25.

18. … Bd7

More hopeful, but also lost was 18. … B×h3 19. B×a8 a6 20. Nd4. By eliminating the knight this way, Black allows White's rooks to take over the board.

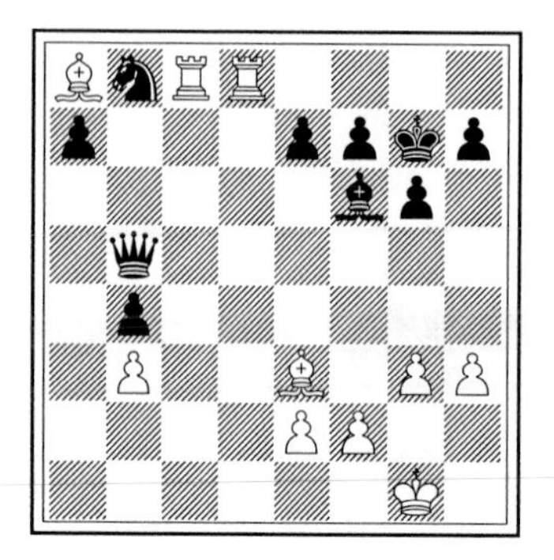

Final position

19. B×a8 B×b5 20. Rc8+ Kg7 21. a×b5 Q×b5 22. Rdd8

"*No mas*," Boriescu said as he stopped the clock. "*Kaput*."

Qi just nodded as he wrote "1–0" on his scoresheet.

Van Siclen, who evidently had nothing better to do, sidled up to me.

"Nothing new," he said. "It was played in Guangzhou last month. Every move."

The final game of the day, Bastrikova versus Royce-Smith, was an afterthought. The St. Petersburg grandmistress blundered on the 29th move of a Kramnik Sicilian and resigned three moves later.

Despite the groans about 40 in 2½, the round was over in just 4 hours, 17 minutes—early enough for everyone to make the fajita buffet at the Rancho Voraces before they ran out of pico de gallo.

Before leaving the high school I posted the standings:

> ***SHELDRAKE MEMORIAL***
> AFTER ROUND ONE
> Grushevsky, Qi, Royce-Smith, 1 point
> Bohigian, Eichler, Klushkov, Krimsditch, Popov, Van Siclen, ½
> Bastrikova, Boriescu, Karlson, Vilković (with bye), 0

"Such a pleasant group," Mrs. Nagle said. "They play so nice together."

One could only hope.

After dinner, I prepared the round's bulletins and headed to the library in search of information about little reddish pills. The *Physicians' Desk Reference* confirmed they weren't Drogistal. But nothing in the PDR or any of the likely Internet sources shed light on the contents of the vial I'd stashed in my room safe.

After Mrs. Nagle had to lock up the library for the night, I took a stroll through the outskirts of town. Okay, stroll is not the word. It was more like a short hike: Past the ranger station, across the Sequoia

Gully Campground, through the Blue Wolf Picnic Area, and along the Locoweed Trail. The air was surprisingly crisp now that the sun was down. There was a night chill, since the temperature had made the usual 25-degree drop in the four hours since sunset, and the stars seemed exceptionally bright.

It really was a beautiful night and it reminded me there were other reasons why I kept coming back year after year. It wasn't just the chess. Or even the money.

When I got back to my hotel room it was nearly midnight, and there were several messages on the voice mail:

"*Beep*. World Champion Grushevsky wishes to remind you he is still without dressing room at playing site."

"*Beep*. Royce-Smith here. Need to talk to you urgently. Someone is following me. I can feel it. Over to you."

"*Beep. Hola*, Boriescu speaking. *Adjournment pas possible. God Natt.*"

"*Beep*. This is Sheriff Gibbs. I've just arrested some of your people. A Mr. Eichler and a Miss Nardlinger. They broke into the municipal swimming pool. If you're willing to assume responsibility for their behavior, I'll release them to you. Otherwise, they'll be spending the night in my lockup."

I called downstairs and told the Casa's front desk not to allow any more calls to my room. And I went to sleep.

It was too good a night to waste on the problems of grandmasters.

Friday, August 23, 2019

THE NEXT MORNING EICHLER WAS blushing. When I got him bailed out of jail, he could have been upset. Or annoyed. Or irritated. But the world's No. 5 rated player only seemed embarrassed over his late night arrest.

Daphne, however, was outraged.

By the time I escorted them back to the Casa she was composing a petition out loud, demanding an apology from the town, county and state. And threatening to sue for false arrest, illegal imprisonment, municipal malfeasance, official misprision and violations of five Amendments of the U.S. Constitution.

"Grandmasters can't be treated like this," she said sullenly.

"You're not a grandmaster, Miss Nardlinger," I reminded her. "You're a spectator."

"I'm a professional spectator."

When we reached the Casa lobby, she searched through her handbag for a leather-covered notebook and began setting down a petition, starting with "To whom it may concern…" and ending with "We the undersigned so demand." Then she proceeded to button-hole every player who passed through the lobby, looking for signers. She should have known better.

"I am sorry, no politics," Qi said as he edged away from her.

"I can't be first on a list," Vilković, her next target, said.

"What's in it for me?" Krimsditch asked. You could never tell with Krimsditch how much was attitude and how much was real.

Daphne had better luck with Karlson.

"Cool! I'll do it," she said. "As soon as you get six of the others."

Grushevsky's excuse was no less evasive: "The World Champion never signs anything without advice of his legal affairs committee."

And so it went. While Nardlinger was making her pitch to Klushkov, he stared blankly at her forehead, then her chest. He waited for her to finish and then walked off without a word.

Next up was Boriescu. He didn't break his stride or make eye-contact.

"*Je pense que non*," he said as he rushed by. "*Verstehen*?"

Then came Van Siclen and Popov, both former boyfriends of Daphne's at previous tournaments. They just glided past her as soon as they saw her pen and paper in hand. It was quite a sight: The world's greatest players fleeing from the sight of a slightly manic superfan.

"I'm not going to forget this," Daphne warned as the last of the GMs escaped through the Casa's glass front door. "And there are other things I'm going to remember!"

I was still wondering what she meant as I posted the day's pairings in the hotel lobby. It shaped up like a good round.

SHELDRAKE MEMORIAL
ROUND TWO PAIRINGS
Grushevsky vs. Eichler
Vilković vs. Qi
Boriescu vs. Bastrikova
Royce-Smith vs. Klushkov
Bohigian vs. Popov
Van Siclen vs. Karlson
Krimsditch–bye

After leaving the Casa, I made another try at finding Phelps at his office. The doctor was out again, Nurse Barnes informed me.

"It's that darn pertussis outbreak," she said.

"Pertussis?"

"Whooping cough. We get it every year about this time. Doc's on call to help out anywhere in the Valley when he's needed."

When I reached the high school all was in order except the temperature. For the moment it was cool enough. But it probably wouldn't be after 20 or so moves had been played. From years of experience as an arbiter I knew that in a typical invitational, with 14 to 16 players, the collective body heat would raise the temperature one degree every 45 minutes in an average room.

Even in an auditorium that can add up in a five-hour session—and Los Voraces's was tiny by high school standards. It was a rectangular room with two seating sections facing the stage, 20 seats in each, with a central aisle between them, and aisles on the left and right side.

After a bit of a hunt I located the school custodian, Cel Sims, in the basement.

The parents who gave him the name Celerity had no powers of foresight: Cel Sims was the slowest human being I had ever seen. His metabolic rate was undetectable. And at 340 pounds, he was one of the biggest I'd ever seen. After a bit of persuasion I got him to lower the thermostat.

"Shurrrre 'nuffff," said Cel.

By then it was drawing near to 2 P.M., and all the players arrived at their boards early, perhaps just to get away from Daphne. It was evident early on what the strangest game was going to be: Board Four. That's where Royce-Smith had challenged the Spaceman to a pawn race. Or was it a memory contest?

Royce-Smith–Klushkov
Semi-Slav Defense D47

1. d4 d5 2. c4 c6 3. Nf3 Nf6 4. e3 e6 5. Nc3 Nbd7 6. Bd3 dxc4 7. Bxc4 b5 8. Be2!? a6 9. e4 b4

Even Daphne could have seen how committed White was now. Either Royce-Smith had to go for a second queen or play the middlegame a pawn down (10. Na4 Nxe4 or 10. e5 bxc3 11. exf6 cxb2 12. Bxb2 Nxf6).

10. e5 bxc3 11. exf6 cxb2 12. fxg7 bxa1(Q)

This used to get a question mark—in place of 12. ... Bxg7—eons ago. What improvement had Klushkov come up with?

13. gxh8(Q) Qxa2! 14. Qxh7 a5! 15. h4!

Both players were finally out of their prep. And both had apparently concluded that the board was too unsafe for normal moves—like merely developing pieces. So...

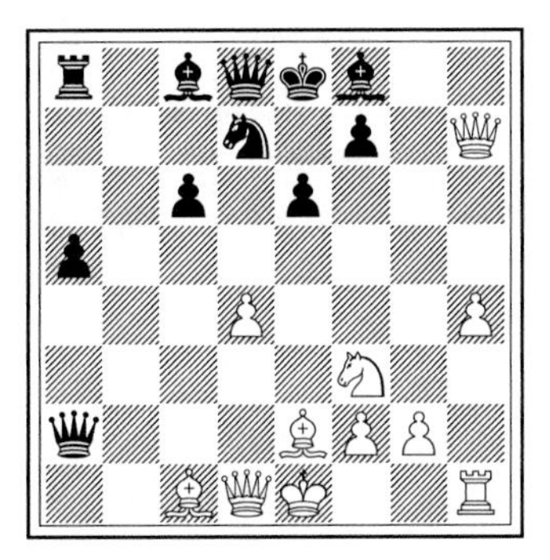

After 15. h4

15. ... a4 16. h5 a3 17. Qg8 Qb1 18. h6 a2 19. h7 a1(Q) 20. 0–0!

I had to break open a new set of pieces to get a second pair of queens. But to find the third I just borrowed from Board One, because by that time the world champion's game was already in an ending.

Grushevsky–Eichler
Ruy Lopez C61

1. e4 e5 2. Nf3 Nc6 3. Bb5 Nd4 4. N×d4 e×d4 5. 0–0 c6 6. Bc4 d5 7. e×d5 c×d5 8. Bb5+ Bd7 9. Re1+ Ne7 10. B×d7+ Q×d7 11. Qh5

Grushevsky screwed the queen onto h5, rose quickly and strode away from the board. He was an intimidating figure. Maybe not in Kasparov's league in terms of stage presence and certainly not in Fischer's. But his mannerisms had an almost palpable effect on most opponents. Grushevsky simply seemed larger than life. Or at least larger than his Armani threads: a 38 medium build bursting out of a 36 short.

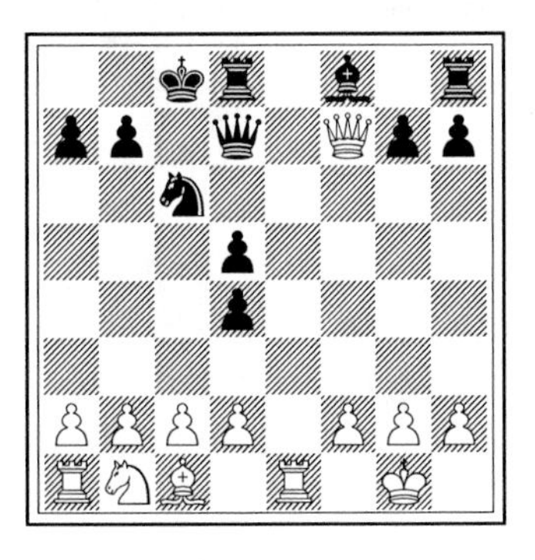

After 12. ... Nc6

But it didn't seem to faze Eichler, not in this position. The standard reply, I learned later, was 11. ... Rc8. But then 12. d3! and Nd2–f3 is supposed to be strong for White.

11. ... 0–0–0!?

Eichler rarely relied on standard moves.

12. Q×f7 Nc6

Now 13. Qf3 or 13. Qh5 are met

nicely by 13. ... d3! followed by ...Bc5/...Nd4 with excellent play for Black's minor pieces.

Grushevsky wasn't used to being surprised in the opening, and he spent a (relatively) long time on the next few (relatively forced) moves.

13. Q×d7+ K×d7

Eichler seemed almost cherubic at the board, too innocent-looking—despite the pencil moustache—to be taken seriously. But here he clearly held the initiative, not a minor accomplishment with the Black pieces against the world champion. And all it cost him was a pawn.

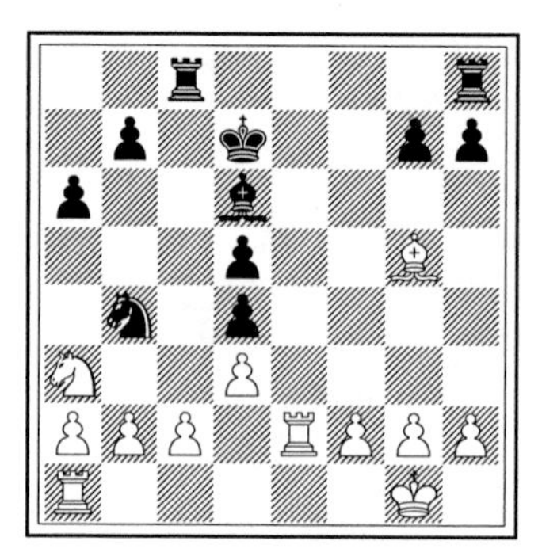

Final position

14. d3 Nb4 15. Na3 Rc8 16. Re2

White has nothing after 16. Bf4 N×c2 17. N×c2 R×c2. But committing his rooks to the defense of a2 and c2 was no way to complete development. Black made his next two moves quickly.

16. ... Bd6 17. Bg5 a6

And Black offered a draw.

After 35 minutes Grushevsky accepted. He just didn't have a clear plan that allowed him to keep his extra pawn. And he wasn't about to risk getting the worst of it in an equal-material ending after, say, 18. Kf1 Rhe8 19. R×e8 K×e8. Not when Eichler had made a quick half point available by offering a draw.

Immediately after the handshake Grushevsky paid a rare visit to my office. He was still fuming when he arrived.

"I am not permitted to play like them," he said, waving his right hand behind him. "They can sacrifice a piece after ten minutes and think nothing of it. Because no one cares if *they* lose. But if I lose, it is historic event."

I wasn't the only one who smiled at this: The world champion felt he had to explain—to me, of all people—why he'd allowed a draw with the White pieces against an 18-year-old.

Eichler trailed him into the office, with Daphne in tow, to hand in his own scoresheet and to sign Grushevsky's. When Grushevsky took notice of him, he rolled his eyes and walked out.

"Tough game?" I asked the German.

"It was quite simple, actually," Eichler said.

I nodded.

"Johnny was just explaining how chess really began in 2012," Daphne said. "Isn't that fascinating?"

"Chess began in 2012?"

"21st century chess. The modern game," Eichler said. "The old guys just don't understand 21st century chess."

"Old guys like Grushevsky," I said.

"Of course, he's nearly 35."

I paused to remember what it was like to be 35. But Eichler and Daphne were already headed for the door.

"Tell me again how you figured it out," she said. "The 21st century chess, I mean."

"Actually, it all began seven years ago, when I was just a 1900 player. Then one weekend I decided to learn the Benko Gambit and all of a sudden—," Eichler said before they disappeared down the hall.

While this was going on, Vilković's game had reached an early crisis. It began with him playing a rare opening with rarer abandon.

Vilković–Qi
English Opening A27

1. c4 e5 2. Nc3 Nc6 3. Nf3 g6 4. d4 e×d4 5. Nd5! Bg7 6. Bg5 Nce7! 7. N×d4 h6 8. Bh4 g5

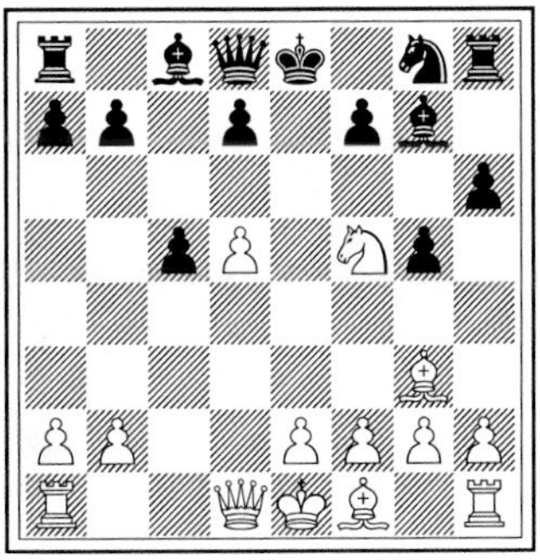

Of course, 8. ... c6 was safer, but Qi probably didn't like White's center pressure after 9. Nc3 and 10. Qd2.

After 11. Nf5

9. Bg3 N×d5 10. c×d5 c5 11. Nf5

The gnome-like Vilković could barely conceal his glee. On 11. ... Bf6 12. Qd2 Qb6 13. 0–0–0! or 12. Nd6+ and e2–e4–e5 White has a terrific initiative.

11. ... B×b2 12. Nd6+ Kf8

Suddenly Vilković's demeanor changed. It wasn't ...B×a1 that bothered him. He must have counted on sacking the exchange when he made his 11th move.

But now he had to find an escape square to answer ... Bc3+!. And after 13. Rc1 Qa5+ 14. Qd2 Qxd2+ 15. Kxd2 Bxc1+ he would be just down material with zero to show for it.

13. f3

On 13. ... Bxa1 14. Qxa1 he would have some compensation (14. ... f6 15. h4! gxh4 16. Rxh4). Maybe not great compensation but still...

13. ... h5! 14. h4

Quite lost was 14. Rb1 Bc3+ 15. Kf2 h4.

14. ... Nh6 15. Kf2?

But here 15. hxg5 Qxg5 16. Ne4! (not 16. Bh4? Qe5!) keeps White in the game.

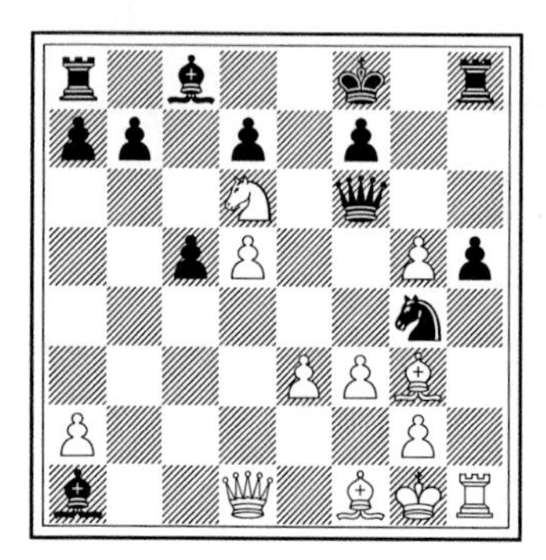

After 18. Kg1

15. ... Qf6!

Now it was obvious that something had gone horribly wrong. The threats of 15. ... Ng4+ and 15. ... Bxa1 were lethal. Vilković took half an hour before replying but there were no good moves any more.

16. e3 Bxa1 17. hxg5 Ng4+ 18. Kg1

18. ... Nxe3!

White resigned after another ten thoroughly irrelevant moves. The two grandmasters moved on to the post-mortem room.

The P-M room: It was really a spacious assistant principal's office I had commandeered some years ago and equipped with a half dozen sets and more comfortable chairs. You got there fastest by walking to the back of the stage, through the door behind the right curtain and then down a short hallway past my office. And as usual, the loser was the first to get to the room. He always has the most to prove.

"I was winning," Vilković was saying when I dropped in.

I made it a practice of trying to attend at least a part of every post-mortem. It was a good way to break away from the tedium of the stage and the dull drone of the ticking clocks. And since the GMs still had some respect for my playing ability—based on games I'd won 30 years ago which lived on in their databases—they didn't mind me listening in on their joint analysis. It was often revealing despite the usual lapses in objectivity.

"Absolutely winning," Vilković said.

"This could be true," Qi said. "But how do you win?"

Vilković was notorious for his optimism in the P-M room. He'd never lost a game there. In fact, if you listened to him, he was winning at some point in every game he ever played at Los Voraces.

"Aha!" Vilković said as he grabbed the White queen and moved it up one square at move 12.

He was right: With 12. Qd2!, White threatens the bishop as well as Qe3+ and turns the evaluation of the position upside down. If Black tries 12. ... Qf6, then 13. Nd6+ Kf8 14. Ne4! and White should not be worse.

Qi readily agreed. It didn't cost him anything to concede he'd been fortunate. But that was no consolation to his opponent.

"This happens to me at least once every tournament," Vilković said, turning to me.

"You must have been unlucky."

"Yes, it is better to be lucky than good. But how do I learn to be lucky?"

"Precisely," I replied. But he was too distraught to get it.

Actually, most super-grandmasters, I'd found, were good losers. Much better losers, in fact, than most 1600 players. That's one of the things I admired about them.

In some cases they took losses well because they were objective and self-critical, in the old Soviet School way, and recognized that losing was part of the game. In other cases, the grandmasters thought the way a sports fan does when he bets on the outcome of a football or baseball game:

If he wins, it's because of superior interpretation and analysis of the often complex and intricate information available to them.

If he loses, it's just bad luck. And you can't do anything about luck.

When I returned to the playing area I saw Karlson was winning back the point she'd lost—due to bad luck, of course—the day before. Her game today lasted nearly four hours but was decided in the first 55 minutes:

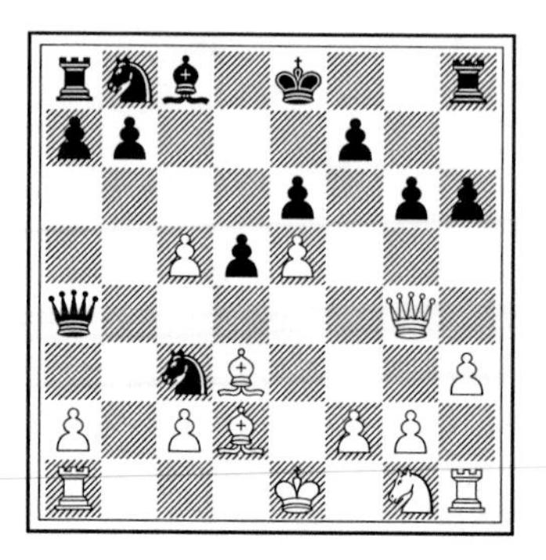

After 13. h3

Van Siclen–Karlson
French Defense C12

1. e4 e6 2. d4 d5 3. Nc3 Nf6 4. Bg5 Bb4 5. e5 h6 6. Bd2 B×c3 7. b×c3 Ne4 8. Qg4 g6 9. Bc1

This bishop move was back in fashion again—perhaps only because there were no secrets left to explore in 9. Bd3.

9. ... c5 10. Bd3 N×c3 11. d×c5 Qa5 12. Bd2 Qa4 13. h3

Van Siclen was regarded in some quarters as Mr. Theory. But he paid a price for it: Everyone had something specially prepared when they faced him. Here Karlson had trotted out one of her old lines. The theory on it showed that White was much better after 13. ... Q×g4? 14. h×g4 Na4 15. R×h6 but Black was supposed to have no trouble after 13. ... h5.

What Van Siclen had in mind was ... something we'll never know. Maybe he had a new wrinkle in the 13. ... h5 14. Q×a4+ endgame. Or a TN after 14. Qf3 Ne4. In any event, he seemed totally undone when it was his opponent who came up with the first original move.

13. ... Ne4!? 14. B×e4?

Played much too quickly. Black was threatening not only 14. ... N×c5 but also 14. ... Qd4.

Yet 14. Ne2 N×c5 15. Qf3 had to be better than this capture.

14. ... Qd4! 15. Rb1?

And this throws almost all of his remaining compensation away. White should have tried 15. Rd1 Q×e5 because he has the terrific shot 16. B×h6!. The idea is that 16. ... R×h6 would be met by 17. R×d5!.

Black can retain an edge after 16. B×h6 with 16. ... d×e4 but following 17. Be3 Karlson would still have a game to play.

15. ... Q×e5 16. Ne2

There was still some hope left after 16. Qf3 because of 16. ... d×e4 17. Qe3 and 18. Bc3 with play for White on the dark squares. But 16. ... Q×e4+ 17. Q×e4 d×e4 should do the trick.

16. ... Q×e4

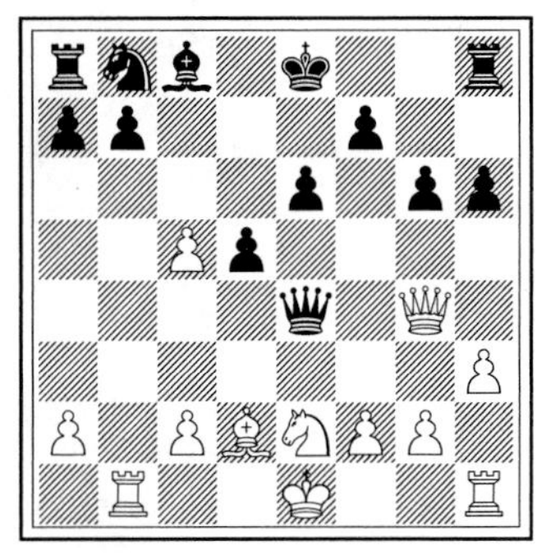

After 16. ... Q×e4

And the outcome was never in doubt after that.

Not much happened in the next half hour. I was on caffeine break in my office close to 5 P.M. when I heard a commotion coming my way.

"But you had it last year," Royce-Smith was telling Popov as they invaded my space.

"That's exactly why I need it again. I was equal fourth last year," Popov said.

"But I had it in '15, '16 and '17."

This grief I didn't need.

"You're arguing about a hotel room?" I guessed.

"The Hacienda Suite," Royce-Smith said. "The one near the end of the hall with the big bay window. My traditional room."

"Tradition has nothing to do with it," Popov said. "Besides, it's my lucky room."

That was a new one for me. I knew about grandmasters and their lucky pens, the lucky jackets they wore until they lost, even the lucky meals they ordered early on the day of a game. But never a lucky room.

"Who has the room now?"

"I do," Popov said. "Possession is nine-tenths of the law."

"You have it only because you arrived in Los Voraces first, by a matter of two hours," Royce-Smith said. "Tradition is on my side."

"This tradition of yours started four years ago," Popov said. "Possession is on my side."

"But I specifically requested the Hacienda in advance. I can show you the laser-mail."

"Don't bother," I said.

I wanted to ask how resolving matters like this had become the responsibility of an International Arbiter. But I knew the answer: There was no one else to complain to. I was the designated lightning rod.

"It seems to me that both of you have valid claims. Therefore, there are two equitable solutions."

"Yes?" Popov said.

"One option is to divide the time. You can have it the first eight days," I said to Popov. "That would include yesterday and today."

"And you can have it for the remaining eight days," I told Royce-Smith.

"You said there was a second solution," he said.

"Correct. The alternative is for me to switch rooms with Popov for the duration of the tournament."

"But..." Popov began.

"That way neither of you will be disappointed about the other having it."

"But..." Royce-Smith said.

"And I suggest you mutually accept the first solution and return to your boards. My guess is you've both lost several minutes by now."

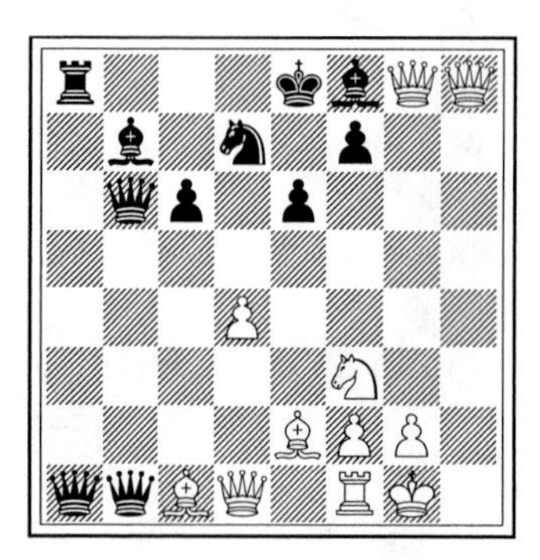

Royce-Smith–Klushkov After 21. ... Qdb6

It wasn't much of a guess, of course. Both their clocks had been running a while by the time they got back to the stage. Klushkov had played **20. ... Bb7!** on Royce-Smith's board and the game continued:

Royce-Smith–Klushkov
21. h8(Q) Qdb6

22. g4

At first this looked ridiculous. But then I realized the idea: four White queens would beat three Black ones.

22. ... 0–0–0 23. Q×f7 c5! 24. Bd3 Qba2 25. Re1 c4 26. Be4 B×e4 27. R×e4 c3! 28. g5!

There was little choice now for either player. But that didn't stop Klushkov from being Klushkov: He closed his eyes. He leaned back in his chair. And he hummed a Russian nursery song for 27 of his remaining 37 minutes.

Then he woke up and played the obvious move as if nothing had happened. The game continued at blitz speed.

28. ... c2 29. Qe1 Kb8 30. g6 Ka7! 31. Kg2 Qd5 32. Ng5 Rc8 33. f3!

Despite the rapid changes on the board it was astonishing how both players managed to set up defensive positions that made the presence of extra queens almost meaningless. In relative terms, there was at least twice as much firepower on the board as in a typical middlegame. Yet neither king was in danger. And the firepower soon grew:

33. ... Rc7 34. Qf4 Ba3 35. B×a3 Q×a3 36. g7 c1(Q) 37. g8(Q)

This was one of three games that threatened to become the tournament's first adjournment. The others were Boriescu–Bastrikova and Bohigian–Popov. In the latter, Bohigian had gotten the edge in a convoluted English Opening hybrid, and soon the Bulgarian's queenside was hemorrhaging badly.

But at 49 Bohigian no longer trusted his calculation powers the way he did 10 or 12 years ago. Too many oversights in checking over variations had cost him too many half-points, and he had begun to rely more and more on intuition. At the cost of accuracy, of course.

After a few second-best moves Bohigain's advantage had evaporated. His draw offer came as soon as Popov made the time control.

"Tough game," I said to Bohigian as he prepared to leave the playing hall.

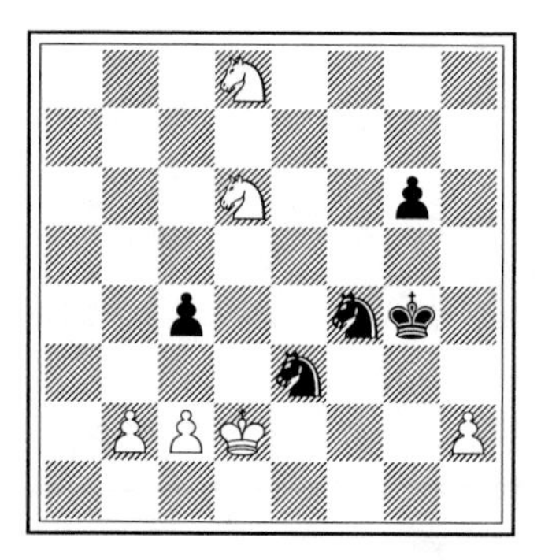

Boriescu–Bastrikova
After 44. Kd2

"Good fortune and bad fortune ride in the same sleigh," he sighed.

Bastrikova, meanwhile, looked like she would be sharing last place with Vilković.

Boriescu–Bastrikova

Black saw that 44. ... Nf1+ 45. Kc3 N×h2 46. K×c4 was not even close. And 44. ... Nfd5 45. Ne6 Kh3 46. Nf4+! wasn't much better. So she went desperate:

44. ... N×c2!? 45. K×c2 Nd3 46. N×c4 N×b2!

This was a consequence of White's 44th move. Black can eliminate the last White pawn by force now.

47. K×b2 Kh3 48. Nf7 g5!

It was the infamous king-and-two-knights versus king-and-pawn ending. Only Troitsky, Rauzer—and God—knew the book theory. And it was extraordinarily hard to handle at the board. After all, didn't Karpov blow a book draw in this ending some 20 years ago?

But one thing was certain: The further advanced the Black pawn was, the better the drawing chances. For example, 48. ... K×h2?? 49. Ng5! was lost. Play continued:

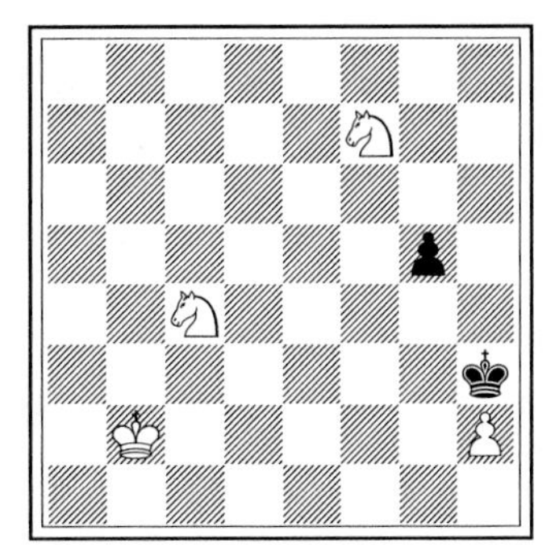

Boriescu–Bastrikova
After 48. ... g5

49. Ne3 K×h2

Not 49. ... g4?? 50. Nf1 Kg2 51. Ne5! and White wins.

50. Ng4+ Kg3 51. Nfe5

Since they were well past the time control at move 40, either player could have sacrificed clock minutes in order to adjourn. But a strange thing happened here:

Bastrikova started playing *faster.* She was convinced that Boriescu would discover the position was a book win as soon as he sealed and found the right book. Or rather, she feared he would find out how to win it.

And Boriescu matched her speed. Maybe he knew that in this kind of ending the player with the pawn blunders more often than the player with the knights. (Okay, I had to look that up. But it turns out that even Smyslov made a double question mark move when he was the defender in a game from the 1941 Absolute Soviet Championship.)

Whatever the case, the players blitzed past the second time control at move 56 and had reached move 65 by 6:30. Black's king had been chased around the edges of the board but was still far from being mated.

That was the story on Board Three. Next door, on Board Four, Royce-Smith and Klushkov were headed for a crescendo. Their position got very crowded and then very empty:

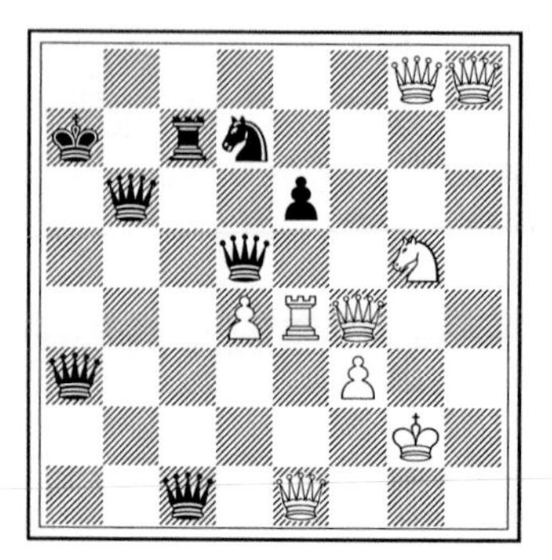

Royce-Smith–Klushkov
After 37. g8(Q)

Royce-Smith–Klushkov

37. ... Qcb2+ 38. Re2 Rc2 39. Rxc2 Qxc2+ 40. Qf2 Q6b2! 41. Qh4 Qaa2 42. Qfg3 Qdxd4! 43. Ne4

White's position just barely holds together. The game ended after the mother of all liquidations:

43. ... Qdxf2+ 44. Qxf2+ Qxf2+ 45. Qxf2+ Qxf2+ 46. Nxf2 Draw

It was a new record—in three moves six queens had left the board. In fact, there were five straight moves that, in a now-dead language, read "queen takes queen check."

Klushkov accepted Royce-Smith's draw offer by writing ½—four inches tall—so that it covered his scoresheet. He left the table without a word.

A bit embarrassed, Royce-Smith shrugged and then loped out of the auditorium, towards his favorite dinner table at the Rancho Voraces. His lucky table.

Moments later I was collecting their scoresheets when my wristwatch alarm went off. It was 7 P.M., the end of the five-hour session. But it was the beginning of a curious ceremony that hadn't been seen at this level in international chess in decades: The adjournment.

I gave Boriescu the sealed-move envelope to fill out. Since it was Bastrikova's turn to move, it was his responsibility to record the names, date, round, position of the pieces and how much time he had spent, on the front of the envelope. He did this quickly, hoping to make the most of the two-hour break.

While Bastrikova fell into deep concentration, I wondered about this antique system of writing down moves. It wasn't just the adjournment that bothered me. Or the fact that Bastrikova could be forfeited for writing an illegal 69th move in this position—yet wouldn't be punished if she made the same illegal move on the board.

No, it went beyond that. There were other problems. Because of the convention that says a player has to keep his own record of the game, you could forfeit on time because you filled in the wrong blank and put down your 39th move as your 40th. Or you could be penalized with the loss of critical minutes because you made a faulty claim of three-time repetition, based on a screwed-up scoresheet.

Only chess—and golf—still required players to chronicle their results on paper. They were the only sports that punished you for making a slip of a pen. So much for 21st century chess.

It turned out Bastrikova took 38 minutes to select her "secret move," as the Russians call it, and then took another five to recheck it. Then she licked the envelope, signed the back and stopped her clock.

That left me with less than an hour to grab a chiliburger at the Rancho. I made sure I was back at the high school by 8:50 P.M. to see that the adjourned position had not been disturbed and the clock settings were right. I found Zhenya still on the stage, studying the position on another board. Boriescu was nowhere in sight.

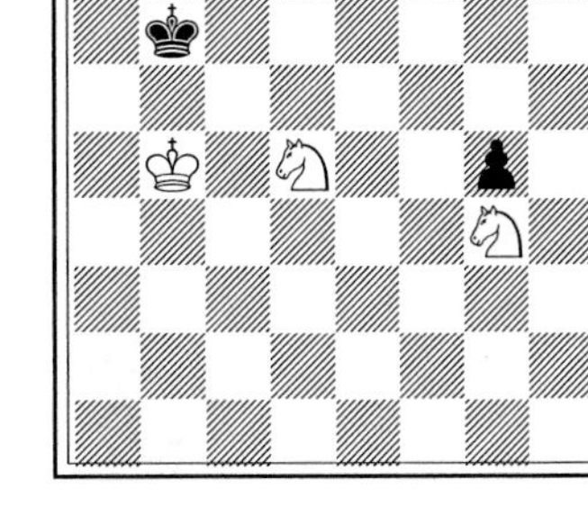

Boriescu–Bastrikova
Black to move

Under normal circumstances he would be relaxing while his second—or, rather, seconds—did most of the analysis of the position during the break. But with no outsiders allowed this year, Boriescu had to perform the analytical chores himself. So would every other invitee this year, another incentive, I hoped, for them not to adjourn. I didn't want to spend my evenings here either.

The envelope remained sealed, as per the rules, when I started White's clock at exactly 9 P.M. Boriescu trundled in three minutes later, sat down without taking off his dark green jacket—and smiled when I opened the envelope and showed him:

Boriescu–Bastrikova
69. ... Ka7

The two players exchanged glances but with decidedly different expressions.

Bastrikova was clearly unhappy. She knew now that she'd sealed a lemon. With 69. ... Kc8! she would have had good chances of reaching move 99, when she could have invoked the 50-move rule and claimed a draw. Boriescu quickly played:

70. Nc7

And Bastrikova replied:

70. ... Kb7

The Rumanian GM reached for the knight again, but pulled his hand back from the board. Then he gripped the back of his head with both hands and began to recheck his analysis.

As his clock ran, I realized we were getting an audience. Eichler and Daphne arrived together, then Karlson and Qi. The GM spectators climbed onto the stage. Karlson and Qi stood over Boriescu's right shoulder and Eichler took up position behind Bastrikova. But I shooed Daphne back to the first row of the auditorium. Mrs. Nagle also showed up, explaining that she'd been delayed by a town meeting.

"We take our civic responsibility very serious," she said.

"Did you happen to see Phelps?"

"You mean at the meeting? Of course, dear, he never misses one," she said. "It's prairie democracy!"

By the time Boriescu broke out of his long think, I saw Van Siclen walking up the right aisle of the auditorium towards the stage. He had an open bottle of Heineken in each hand and the unmistakably unsteady gait of someone feeling no pain. Van Siclen was truly a two-fisted drinker.

And that was a pity. Because he was also one of the handful of players who emerge every generation with the talent to go all the way but don't seem to think it worth the effort. It was easy enough for Gert to remain one of the world's best for ten to fifteen years, and that was good enough for him.

It was a comfortable life. One invitation follows another. Nice hotels. Lavish amenities. Adoring fans. Minimal hours. Gifts and meal stipends, plus plenty of food during the rounds. A chance to see the world.

And little incentive to narrow the considerable distance between being very talented and being world champion. As he was fond of saying, the world can only afford one Grushevsky at a time.

I motioned him to the doorway leading backstage. We were far enough away from the board to talk.

"Shouldn't you be preparing instead of mourning?"

"No need. I know exactly what I will do in the next three—no, make that four rounds."

"Exactly?"

"Exactly," he said. "One of the great beauties of the round robin is that you can script most of the tournament."

I'd heard this before. Van Siclen loved to take about his "tournament plans." So did other grandmasters. Even Fischer, in his first Interzonal, had a plan: Bobby needed a plus-five score to qualify for the Candidates, he explained. So Fischer identified the "five fish" he could beat, and all he needed to do to qualify was draw with everyone else.

When someone suggested that the 15-year-old GM might—perish the thought—lose a game, Bobby replied: "That's okay. Then I'll just find a sixth fish."

Botvinnik went further, writing out scenarios in hand for his Soviet championships once he knew the pairings. Weeks before the tournament began he would detail how, say, he would play for an endgame with White against Kotov in the first round and save his TN in the Slav for Bondarevsky in the fourth and be willing to draw against Keres in the fifth, and so forth.

But Van Siclen wasn't a Fischer or a Botvinnik. Despite his 2869 rating.

"Something didn't go according to the script today," I said. "What makes you so sure it will tomorrow?"

"Tomorrow is easy. I have Black with Eichler. I predict a draw in … oh … 17 moves."

That was hardly crystal-ball work. Eichler's lack of ambition was well known. He was content to exert himself in only three or four games per tournament.

"Then comes Round Four. White against Krimsditch," Van Siclen said. "Well, you know my games with Todd. He hasn't been able to play me since he hung his king at Wijk aan Zee three years ago. If I want it, it will be a draw in 20 moves. And I will probably want it."

"And then?"

"Then is Round Five. Black against Grushevsky. For anyone else, this would be a difficult game. But not for me."

There was a reason for his self-assurance. It was an open secret that Van Siclen had a long-term arrangement with the world champion:

He had agreed to give Grushevsky a draw at Munich 2017 in a position where the Ukrainian was dead lost—but desperate to keep his non-losing streak alive. In return Van Siclen exacted a promise of quick draws in their next four games. The price had evidently gone up since, according to GM legend, Mikhail Tal made a similar deal for three future draws with a lesser opponent.

"Did it occur to you that you shouldn't be telling the arbiter about agreeing to draws in advance?"

"It did occur to me," he grinned. "But I'm sure you wouldn't want to mar the Greatest Tournament in Chess History with a double forfeit." He had a point.

"And then there is Round Six—against the unfortunate Attila Gabor. That's my bye. So, you see, I really don't have to think about chess until I play Bohigian next week."

As he said this, I looked out at the lone board and noticed Eichler, standing next to it and frowning. I went to take a look.

Boriescu had played:

Boriescu–Bastrikova
After 75. Ne4

71. Na6

And Bastrikova's king made a run for safety:

71. ... Kc8 72. Kc6 Kd8 73. Kd6 Ke8! 74. Nc5 Kf7 75. Ne4

Here was a big decision. Where does the king go? To g6 or e8? One was probably losing, the other....?

Bastrikova, who had been moving fairly quickly, took 22 minutes before selecting:

75. ... Ke8!

Nobody knew it at the time but this saved the game.

We later found a forced mate in about 15 moves after 75. ... Kg6??, e.g. 76. Ng3 Kf7 77. Kd7 Kf8 78. Ne5!! g4 79. Kd8 Kg7 80. Ke7 Kg8 81. Nc6!! Kg7 82. Nd8 Kg6 83. Ne6 Kh7 84. Kf7 and so on.

Play continued on for another 25 minutes as more of the players drifted in to check out the position. Royce-Smith and Grushevsky stayed for a few minutes or so, to confirm in their own minds that

Boriescu wasn't winning. Bohigian and Popov took seats in the audience and scanned the first-round bulletin, with an occasional glance at the demonstration wall board. I even spotted Klushkov sitting in the back row of the auditorium, with his eyes closed. I guess there wasn't much else to do on a Friday night in Los Voraces, New Mexico.

After a long think Boriescu made a final try to seal off the king's escape. But it was obvious he wasn't making progress after:

76. Nef6+ Kd8 77. Nd5 Ke8 78. Nb6 Kf7

Twenty-one moves later, Bastrikova invoked the 50-move rule, and I readily acknowledged her claim was valid. As Eichler, Qi, Karlson, Popov and even Van Siclen swooped in for the post-mortem, I updated the standings on the wallchart:

SHELDRAKE MEMORIAL
AFTER TWO ROUNDS
Qi, 2 points
Grushevsky, Royce-Smith, 1½
Bohigian, Eichler, Karlson, Klushkov, Popov, 1
Bastrikova, Boriescu, Krimsditch (with bye) *Van Siclen*, ½
Vilković (with bye) 0

"You blundered on the second move," Eichler was saying at the board.

He retraced the moves and shifted the knight towards the center. With 71. Ne6!, just after the sealed move, White corners the Black king, he explained.

For example, 71. ... Kc8 72. Kc6 Kb8 73. Nc5 Kc8 74. Nb7! Kb8 75. Nd6 with mate on the horizon.

It didn't take much to convince Boriescu he had thrown away a win.

"*Abgabezug*. Blunder," he muttered, as he left the board. "*Fruktansvart. Patzer*!"

Bastrikova wasn't sure who the patzer was. She was just happy to sign her scoresheet and get the game over with. But at that moment, her new lucky pen went dry.

"Out of ink and it's only the second round," I said.

"You need a pen? I have!" Daphne called out from the audience.

No one present could forget what happened next.

Daphne Nardlinger reached once more into her handbag, and pulled something out. It was thin, black and yellow. But at 15 inches long, definitely not a pen. And then she screamed. And collapsed.

Did you know the coral snake is native to New Mexico? And that its venom is twice as deadly as a rattler's?

Saturday, August 24, 2019

A. Z. GIBBS WAS IN HIS MAIN STREET office, reading the weekly *Voice of Voraces*, when I arrived. He was a sandy-haired 47-year-old with a penchant for cowboy boots that bore the town's "LV" insignia and would have seemed more at home in a Western novel than in this speed bump of a town. But for the first time in my eight years of coming to Los Voraces I needed to take him seriously as a professional.

"Knock, knock," I said, sticking my head in the open doorway. He waved me in, and I took one of his gray folding chairs, next to the rusty water cooler.

"Says here the county zoning commission may approve a new campsite," Gibbs said. "If the ranger station approves, 'course."

"Do tell," I replied. I knew how to speak like the locals when I needed to.

"Yep, it's only taken them six years to get around to it," he said from behind a pair of yellow-tinted sunglasses. "Things don't take so long in other counties, like over in Socorro or Colfax or even—"

"Look, Sheriff, let me get to the point. I'm troubled by the events of the last four days."

"You should be. I am, too," he agreed. "Pity about that Mr. Gabor. And Miss Nardlinger. How is her friend taking it?"

"Eichler is pretty upset. He'd really only known her a few days. But still..."

"Must be very smart folks, those grandmasters."

"Daphne wasn't a grandmaster. She was a fan. In fact, a groupie."

"Uh-huh."

"In fact, she was just about our only spectator. The good people of Los Voraces don't seem to show much love for the tournament."

"Well, as I told you," Gibbs replied with a pursed-lip smile. "Town doesn't like the chessplayers. Never did, never will. I remember two years ago when Mr. Gabor flooded his bathroom at the Casa. You know, we take water to be very precious around here."

"I'm sure you do, Sheriff. But what I have in mind is a lot more serious than letting a tub overflow."

"Serious how?"

"Serious as a coral snake bite."

Gibbs raised his eyebrows, then shrugged. "Well I can understand how someone from back East like Miss Nardlinger could make that mistake. Snakes and skinks and other varmints end up in all sorts of places in town. They get into drain pipes and garages. Some walk right in through the front door of homes. Just a week ago, Cel Sims found a leopard frog in a first-floor classroom over at the high school."

"Sheriff—"

"But around these parts, everyone knows to watch out for a coral snake. You can tell him by the color. He has yellow and white rings with black and red bands. We say, 'Black on yellow, kill a fellow.'"

I'd had enough of the wildlife lecture.

"Look, Sheriff, I don't think Daphne picked up the wrong snake by mistake. I don't think she'd knowingly pick up any snake."

"You're saying her death wasn't just a tragic and most unfortunate accident?"

"Sheriff, let's review the bidding: On Tuesday, Gabor dies from a heart attack, a cardiac event, as Dr. Phelps put it. Three days later, Daphne dies from an accident. An event and an accident."

"And you're suggesting there's a pattern."

It was more of a statement than a question.

"I'm suggesting two of our chess people who were very much alive on Tuesday aren't today."

His look told me that for the first time I had his full attention.

"I have no idea how that snake got into Daphne's bag, but I don't think it arrived by accident," I added. "And I'm beginning to wonder about Gabor. Have you considered the possibility that someone is responsible for both of these deaths?"

"Both?"

"Both."

"Who would do it?"

"I don't know. Anyone. A player? One of the townspeople?"

"And what would be the motive?" he asked.

"You've got me there, too. Envy. Jealousy. Settling old scores. Who knows?"

"You mean there are actually reasons why your players would want to harm one another?"

"Harm, maybe," I said. "Everybody loathed playing Gabor. He invited it. Absolutely reveled in it. But kill? No, at least I don't think so."

"And the young woman?" Gibbs asked.

"Daphne was more of nuisance than anything else. Nobody had enough reason to harm her."

"You're sure about that?"

"Sheriff, I'm not sure about anything," I admitted. "There are all sorts of relationships here that I can only guess at. Big money tournaments are like a traveling road show in which every month a dozen-plus egos crash into one another at a new playing site. The players form temporary alliances, share gossip, spread disinformation, do just about anything to get an edge they can use now, or save for the next tournament. I have enough trouble just dealing with them from one day to another."

"Is that so," Gibbs said, again more comment that question. "Well, okay. I'll make some inquiries if you're concerned. But I'm curious about something else."

"Shoot."

"If these chessplayers are such a handful—if they pose so many problems for you—why do you put up with it year after year?"

"Well, Sheriff, we have a saying: 'The arbiter always finishes fourth.'"

"Which means?"

"Which means at major tournaments the arbiter's fee is exceeded only by the first three prizes."

"And?"

"And that means I'm guaranteed to be paid well. That makes up for a lot of grief."

"Is that *so*."

There were never Saturday rounds at Lone Pine. That day was the only rest day in the nine-round schedule of those legendary tournaments back in the late ’70s and early ’80s. The official explanation was that the schedule was arranged so observant Jews like Sammy Reshevsky could play. But there was always the hope that this might be just the format that would lure Robert James Fischer out of retirement.

At Los Voraces, however, hardly anyone noticed the calendar. The players thought only in terms of opponents.

“What’s tomorrow?” I’d heard Popov ask Vilković last night.

“Tomorrow is Bastrikova” was the reply. “Black against Bastrikova.”

Not, I noticed, “Tomorrow is Saturday.”

While the calendar was forgotten, Vilković’s Board One pairing shaped up as one of the more interesting of the day when I posted the schedule:

SHELDRAKE MEMORIAL
ROUND THREE PAIRINGS
Bastrikova vs. Vilković
Klushkov vs. Boriescu
Popov vs. Royce-Smith
Karlson vs. Bohigian
Eichler vs. Van Siclen
Krimsditch vs. Grushevsky
Qi–bye

There was enough of an imbalance in strength on every board to expect at least two, and maybe as many as four, decisive results. That would please Sheldrake, who was never happy with quick draws. He didn’t go as far as Señor Rentero back in the old days of the Linares tournaments—showing envelopes filled with pesetas to reluctant grandmasters in an effort to inspire them to fight. But Sheldrake somehow managed to communicate his pleasure about seeing a good game. And he would have enjoyed the early scrimmaging today, at least on Board Three:

Popov–Royce-Smith
Sicilian Defense B45

1. e4 c5 2. Nf3 Nc6 3. d4 c×d4 4. N×d4 Nf6 5. Nc3 e6 6. Ndb5 Bb4

Back when I was a player, nobody used this fossil of a defense. But in the last few years, it'd come back into fashion when the GMs began to sour on the Sveshnikov Variation, that is, after 6. ... d6 7. Bf4 e5.

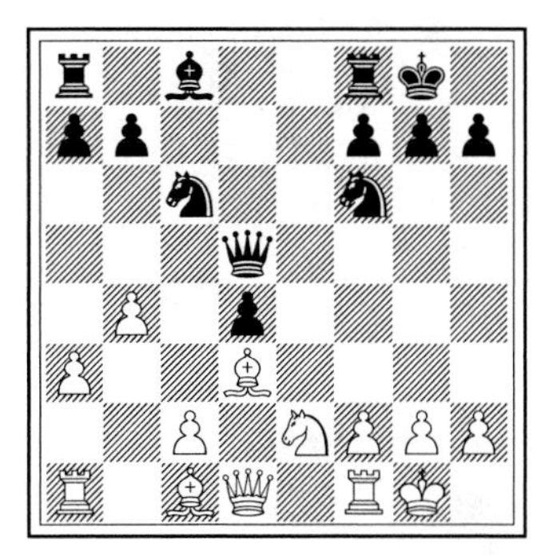

After 13. b4

7. a3 B×c3+ 8. N×c3 d5 9. e×d5 e×d5 10. Bd3 0–0 11. 0–0 d4 12. Ne2 Qd5 13. b4!?

All these positions used to be rated as plus-over-equals for White—for reasons nobody could remember now. Probably the old evaluations were just based on general principles, the most misleading guide there is in chess.

But Popov's move seemed right at the time: if White has an edge, why not put a death sentence on the d-pawn with Bb2 and/or b4–b5? For example, 13. ... a6 14. Bb2 Be6? 15. N×d4!.

13. ... Ne5 14. N×d4

Same idea: 14. ... Q×d4?? 15. B×h7+. But Popov was the one who had missed something tactical.

14. ... Bh3! 15. g×h3 Q×d4

The point: Now 16. B×h7+ K×h7 17. Q×d4 Nf3+ costs White a piece.

While waiting for Popov's reply I caught Mrs. Nagle's eye. She was wearing gold-rimmed glasses that made her look even more grandmotherly today than usual.

"I need to talk to someone confidentially, to get some, uh ... guidance."

She nodded.

"Well, most everybody in the Valley is comfortable about talking out their troubles with Pastor McKittrick. He's good people."

"No, not spiritual guidance. I need to find a kind of specialist. A chemist, or a pharmacist. Someone to analyze something. Someone I can trust."

Now she smiled.

"Don't tell me you're one of those folks who found a shiny rock.

They all want to know if it's pyrites or the real thing. You know we used to have a saying, 'All that glitters—'"

"I'm not talking about ore. I have some medicine that I'd like to check on. You know, to verify that it's what I should be taking."

She narrowed her eyes as she thought for a second.

"Well, there's a medical supplies man over in Endoline that Doc Phelps used to work with on prescriptions. He had some chemistry training. I can find his e-mail."

"Thanks, but do you have a phone number?"

"My, yes," she said.

"Also, do you happen to know which state trooper station covers Los Voraces?"

She wrinkled her nose before replying. "Well, of course. The one in Dolores. Now let me find you that medical man's number."

I made a few mental notes as she ambled off. By the time I looked again at the boards, a lot had transpired, beginning with the action on Board Three.

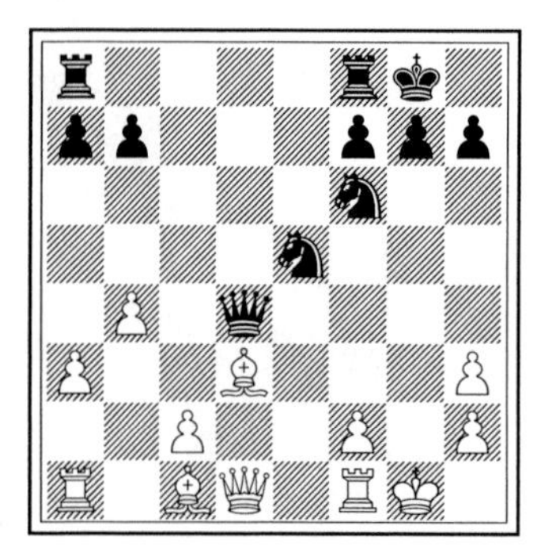

Popov–Royce-Smith
After 15. ... Q×d4

Popov–Royce-Smith

16. Bg5 Rfd8 17. B×f6 g×f6 18. Re1 Kh8! 19. Be4!

Now 19. ... Q×d1 20. Ra×d1 R×d1 favors White's bishop in the ending and 19. ... Rg8+ 20. Kh1! Q×f2 21. Qh5! is a nice middlegame as long as White takes minimal steps to safeguard his king (21. ... Rg7 22. B×b7 Rd8 23. Re2 Qd4 24. Rf1 etc.).

19. ... Rg8+ 20. Bg2? Qf4! 21. Kh1

After Popov moved his king into the corner, he stood up and nodded in approval. (Not 21. Qd5 Nf3+ or 21. Re3 Rad8 22. Qe2 Rd2! 23. Q×d2? Nf3+.)

Then he headed off stage and down the right aisle toward the men's room. Royce-Smith waited until his opponent had closed the auditorium door before he delivered the coup.

21. ... R×g2!

"Ouch!" Karlson, standing to Royce-Smith's right, said—loudly enough to let everyone on stage hear.

Karlson had her own rating scale for surprise moves—"ouch," "super-ouch" and "mega-ouch." An "ouch" meant a nasty oversight. A "mega-ouch" usually meant you just left your queen en prise, and "super-ouch" was something in between.

In this case a mere "ouch" was enough to bring several players to Popov's board to see what happened. Even Grushevsky, who was on move at his board, got up and let his clock run as he took a look. After they saw how much 22. K×g2 Rg8+ 23. Kh1 Nf3 or 23. Kf1 Q×h2 favors Black, the spectators magically turned back into grandmasters and returned to their middlegames.

Moments later Popov opened the auditorium door and headed up the aisle. When he arrived at his board I noticed several heads turning, to watch his reaction to the rook sack. Then they averted their eyes—like drivers who wanted to see the car wreck that caused the traffic tie-up ahead of them but didn't want to know the graphic details of what happened to the accident victim.

22. K×g2 Rg8+ 23. Kf1 Q×h2 24. Qd5 Q×h3+ 25. Ke2 Qh5+ 26. Kf1 Rg5!

The threats (of ...Nf3, etc.) are too numerous.

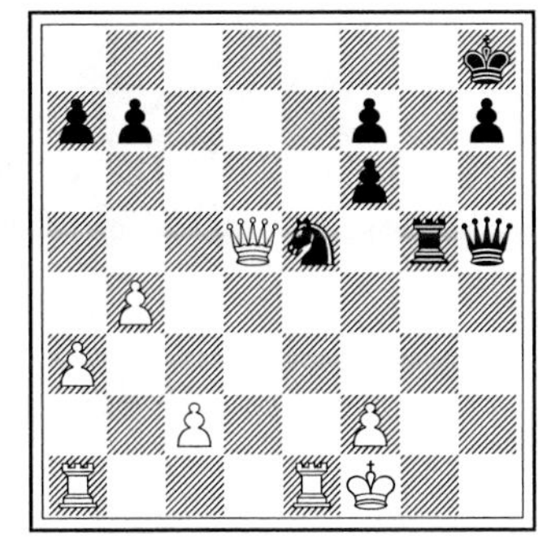

After 26. ... Rg5

27. Re3 Ng4 28. Re8+ Kg7 29. Qd8 Nh2+!

Not 29. ... Qh1+ 30. Ke2 Q×a1 31. Rg8+ Kh6 32. Qf8+.

30. Ke1 Re5+ White resigns

Because of 31. R×e5 Q×e5+ and ...Q×a1, or 31. Kd2 Rd5+.

On the board next door, it turned out that Van Siclen had been wrong about his game with Eichler. It wasn't drawn in 17 moves, as he'd predicted last night. Not even half that:

Eichler–Van Siclen
English Opening A35

1. c4 c5 2. Nc3 Nc6 3. Nf3 Nd4

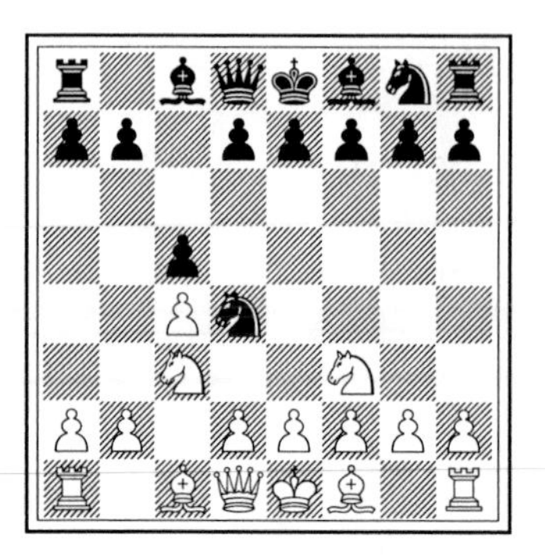

After 3. ... Nd4

Like so many simple moves, this had a fairly short history. It only dated back to the late 1980s. Now 4. g3? N×f3+ or 4. N×d4 c×d4 5. Nb5 e5 and 6. ... a6 were known to favor Black.

4. Ng1

They used to laugh at this, until Kasparov played it some 20-plus years ago. White prepares 5. e3 and 6. d4, to get a kind of d-pawn game. In fact, the first time 4. Ng1 was played, Black replied 4. ... Nf6 5. e3 Nc6 6. d4 d5 and transposed into a Queen's Gambit Declined as if nothing had happened.

4. ... Nc6!

You had to know Van Siclen to understand this move. Or, to be exact, you had to know the way he played Eichler. Gert knew his opponent's repertoire better than his own. He knew Eichler wasn't going to play 5. g3—just as he knew Eichler wouldn't do it when he first had a chance, at move three. Eichler had too much preparation invested in the theory of the English Opening with Nf3 followed by d2–d4.

5. Nf3 Nd4 6. Ne5

What else? White hadn't been doing too well lately with 6. e3 N×f3+ 7. Q×f3 g6.

6. ... Nc6!

Now 7. N×c6 d×c6 8. g3 e5 and ...Bf5 offers White little. And 7. Nd3 d6 just misplaced the knight. So:

7. Nf3 Nd4 8. Ng1

After he retreated the knight, Eichler didn't hit his clock, but just looked up at Van Siclen. His opponent looked up, too. Then Eichler nodded, Van Siclen copied him, and both then circled the word "Draw" at the bottom of the scoresheet. No one said a word.

It reminded me of the incident at the Oympiad seven years ago during the San Salvador–Qatar match. Late in an endgame, the *Sal-*

vadoreño on second board nodded to his opponent instead of making a move. His opponent smiled and nodded in agreement. Then White wrote down "½" on his scoresheet, while Black wrote "0–1."

It took 20 minutes to sort that one out, after heated arguments in Spanish, Arabic, and English. It would have taken longer if the arbiter hadn't threatened to double-forfeit all four games in the match unless the one in dispute was resumed immediately. It was one of my proudest moments.

Meanwhile, Karlson was headed for a long, drawish rook-and-bishop ending with Bohigian. And Klushkov was securing his hold on first place.

Klushkov–Boriescu
Semi-Tarrasch Defense (by transposition) D32

1. c4 Nf6 2. Nc3 e6 3. d4

You never knew which Klushkov was going to show up at the board. Last year at this tournament against the same opponent he played 3. e4 c5 4. e5 Ng8 5. b4!? c×b4 6. Ne4, the Yaroslavl Gambit. He won quickly.

3. ... c5 4. Nf3 c×d4 5. N×d4 d5 6. e3 Nc6 7. c×d5 e×d5 8. Be2

Today it was the positional Klushkov. Despite his predilection for arcane lines, particularly with Black, the Spaceman often adopted quiet setups like this with White.

8. ... Bd6 9. 0–0 0–0 10. b3 Re8 11. Bb2 Qe7

Black has made nothing that remotely resembled an error. And yet in the next five moves his position was clearly on the decline.

12. Nf3! Be6 13. Nb5 Bb8 14. Nbd4 Bd7 15. Rc1 Ne4 16. N×c6 b×c6

Sacrifice or blunder? (After 17. Ba6 and Bb7 White wins material.) The next three moves would tell.

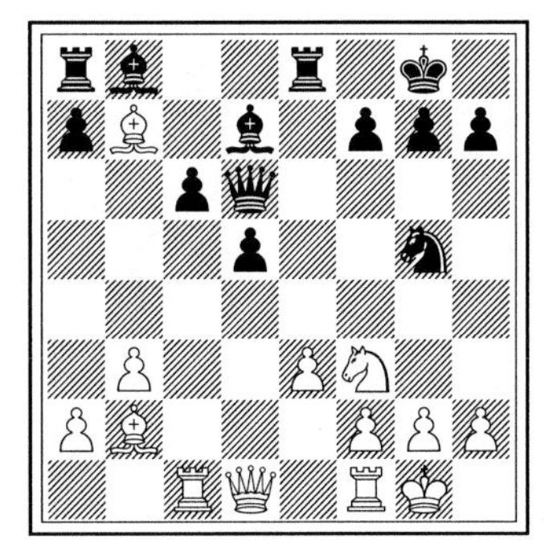

After 18. ... Ng5

17. Ba6! Qd6 18. Bb7 Ng5

This looked dangerous ... for about twenty seconds.

19. Ne5 R×e5 20. f4!

Now 20. ... R×e3 21. Qd4 is even worse.

20. ... Re8 21. B×a8

And White won without further incident (21. ... f6 22. Qc2! Ne4 23. Rfd1 Rc8 24. Bb7 etc.)

The Board Six game got off to a slow start because Krimsditch arrived 35 minutes late for his battle with the world champion. There was a time when players apologized for being only two minutes late. But no more. The nine-time U.S. Champion said nothing as he sat down. Grushevsky just glared at him and refused to shake hands. They soon got down to business.

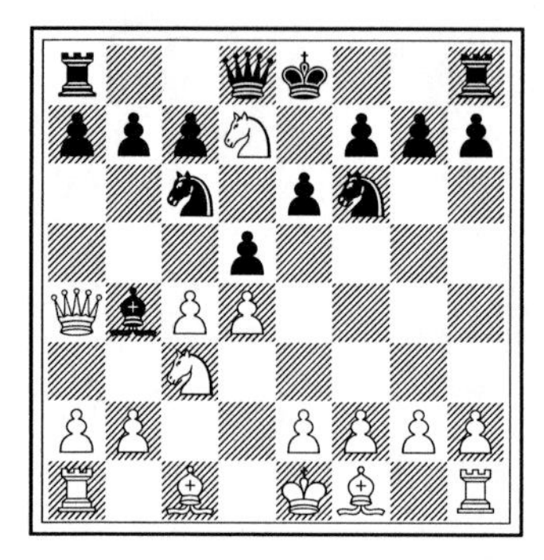

After 7. N×d7

Krimsditch–Grushevsky
Queen's Gambit Declined (by transposition) D38

1. d4 Nf6 2. c4 e6 3. Nc3 Bb4 4. Nf3 d5 5. Qa4+ Nc6 6. Ne5 Bd7 7. N×d7

Here Grushevsky began to recheck his preparation, his ears reddening the way Keres used to at a critical point in a game.

It occurred to me he must be the world's worst poker player. Grushevsky just couldn't conceal his feelings when he was considering a strong move—or when he was upset with a bad position. Which was it here?

7. ... Ne4! 8. Qc2

Grushevsky wouldn't reveal any of his secrets after the game. But it seemed likely that White should have gambled with 8. Ne5, e.g. 8. ... N×c3 9. b×c3 B×c3+ 10. Bd2 B×a1 11. N×c6 b×c6 12. Q×c6+.

8. ... N×d4 9. Qd3 Nc6!

Once again the old saw about retreats being the easiest moves to overlook is proven true. White's knight is trapped behind enemy lines and Krimsditch has to scramble to get his pawn back (not 10. cxd5 exd5 11. Qxd5 Nxc3).

10. f3 Nxc3 11. bxc3 Bd6 12. cxd5 exd5 13. Qxd5 Qxd7 14. e4

White's edge in space was illusory: his weaknesses on dark squares count more.

14. ... Qe7 15. Bg5 f6 16. Be3 0–0–0

The threat is 17. ... Bg3+ and 18. ... Rxd5.

17. Qb5 a6 18. Qa4 Bc5!

This move both defends the queenside and exposes White's own king position.

Krimsditch didn't like the looks of 19. Bd2 f5 so he threw himself on his sword. But adults have been known to resign positions like this instead.

19. Bxa6!? Bxe3 20. Qxc6

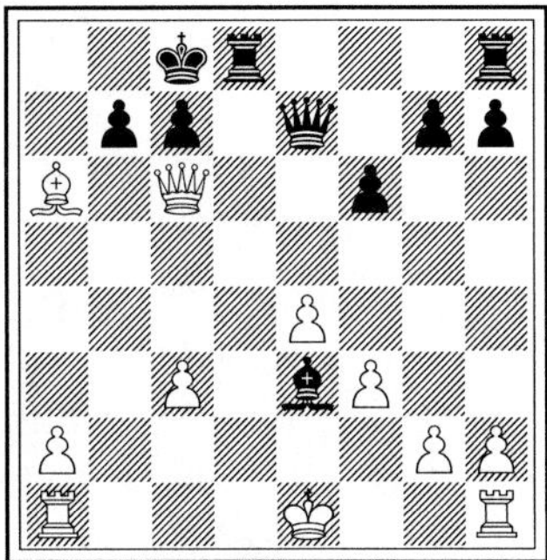

After 20. Qxc6

20. ... bxa6 21. Rb1

Well, some adults. White's sacrifice looked pretty but there were only a few cheap traps left now.

21. ... Bd2+

Not 21. ... Bb6? 22. Rxb6. Black finds a way of coordinating his pieces that is superior to 21. ... Qc5 22. Qe6+ Rd7 23. Rd1.

22. Ke2 Qd6 23. Qc4 Rhe8!

By stopping the possibility of Qe6+, Black frees the queen. His move also ensures that Black can beat off the attack with ...Re5–c5 before White can add his rooks to the mix with Rhd1 and Rb2.

24. Rhd1 Re5 25. Kf1

In some positions the only choice is between bad looking moves—and worse moves.

For example, on 25. Rb2 Black gets out of the pin and wins with 25. ... Rc5 26. Qb3 Qd3+ 27. Kf2 Qe3+ 28. Kf1 Rb5!.

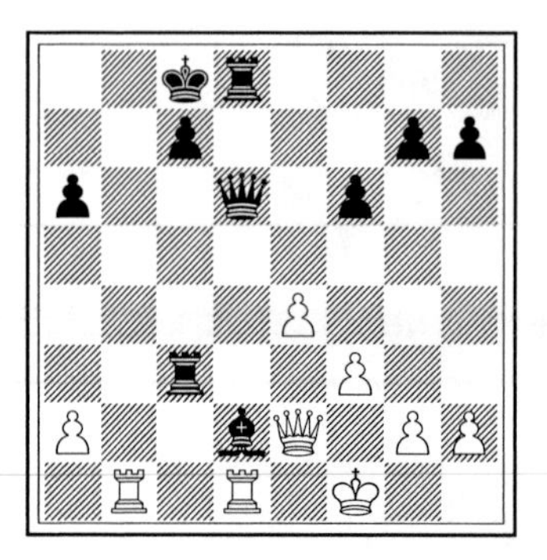

After 26. ... R×c3

25. ... Rc5 26. Qe2 R×c3

Krimsditch played on another 10 moves before conceding. While I watched the game wind down, Royce-Smith pulled me aside. He had finished his own post-mortem with Popov and motioned for me to follow him into the hallway behind the stage.

"The walls have ears," he said.

Royce-Smith was a strange case. Unquestionably the finest mind in the tournament, the pipe-smoking GM from Manchester was a genuine intellectual, a rarity at this level in chess.

He was someone who could quote Fichte—correctly. Or try to solve the Riemann Hypothesis in his head, while waiting for an opponent's move. Still only 27 and rated No. 4 in the world, he had great potential in chess if it weren't for...

Well, he was odd. Maybe odd was too kind. Suffice it to say that Royce-Smith walked through life along that thin line that separates British eccentricity from clinical psychosis.

"I saw you leave the sheriff's office today," he said, only slightly above a whisper.

"You did?"

"I know why you were there."

"You do?"

"It's about Gabor and the girl."

"It was?"

"You think they were killed. So do I."

That stopped me. I hadn't shared my thoughts about the deaths with anyone except Gibbs. And I didn't tell him about the pills.

"What makes you think that?" I asked.

"All the signs. The clues. And because I can feel them watching us."

"Watching?"

"Watching. All the time. They're watching us now."

"They?"

"Yes, you know. They."

"Help me out here, Eustace. Who are they?"

Royce-Smith looked quizzically at me before continuing. "Surely you understand how close we are?"

"Close to what?"

"You know. Operation Majestic-12."

I just stared at him. I knew from past Sheldrakes how Royce-Smith spoke in riddles. And that you often had to wait for him to get to his point. If he had one.

"The alien bodies," he said. "The flying disc."

I waited. His sigh was his loudest contribution to the conversation.

"Roswell," he whispered.

He looked over his shoulder and down the hall before pulling a dog-eared map out of the inside pocket of his Harris Tweed jacket. Blue ink lines on the map showed that Los Voraces was located less than 100 miles from Roswell.

As in Roswell-the-mecca-of-all-UFO-freaks. Whose number now seemed to include Grandmaster Eustace Royce-Smith.

"They must be responsible for the murders," he said. "We should warn the others."

This is where I got off. All I needed was him panicking the other players with stories of little green men. Little green murderous men.

"No. We can't."

"We can't?"

I shook my head and looked as serious as I could. I used my be-very-scared look.

"We can't because *they* would hear us," I said.

"They would?"

"And that could be fatal."

"It could?"

"Yes, you see, right now they don't know that we know about them."

"You're right."

"That means we can watch them while they watch us."

"Yes."

"You must report to me on what you see."

"Of course."

"And it's vital for the survival of all of us for you to keep this confidential. Can you do that?"

"Absolutely!"

Eustace Royce-Smith walked off, elated at his new responsibility.

Back in the real world, I found the Board One game drawing to a close. It was the kind of draw even Sheldrake would have appreciated. It had begun with:

Bastrikova–Vilković
Sicilian Defense B32

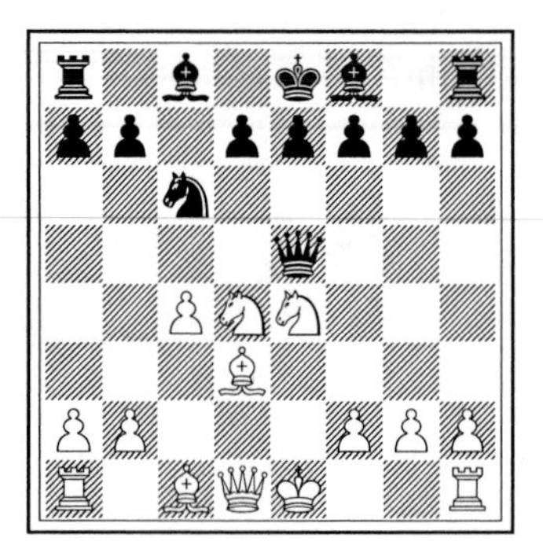

After 8. Bd3

1. e4 c5 2. Nf3 Nc6 3. d4 c×d4 4. N×d4 Qc7 5. c4 Nf6 6. Nc3 N×e4 7. N×e4 Qe5 8. Bd3

A new idea, it seemed. White had never gotten much comp from 8. Nf3 Q×e4+ 9. Be2 Ne5 in the past. But 8. Nb5 Q×e4+ 9. Be2 Qe5 10. f4 Qb8 was a reasonable alternative.

8. ... Q×d4 9. Be3!

There's a saying: In for a penny, in for a pound. Bastrikova had to do something about 9. ... Ne5, so sacrificing a second pawn was an early but justified form of desperation.

9. ... Q×b2 10. 0–0 g6 11. Re1 Bg7 12. Nd6+ Kf8!

Vilković's play was typical of the new breed: "Fritz's kids."

At first it was a putdown—like the way Petrosian used to ridicule young players of the 1970s as the "Children of the *Informant*." He meant the up-and-coming players who thought no one born before 1960 was capable of understanding how the knight moved.

"Fritz's kids" were different. They'd been influenced by computers as much as the earlier generation had been by the latest collection of annotated games in the *Chess Informant*. The difference was that the "kids" had grown up playing machines—in some cases, years before they ever sat down against a human in a clocked game.

As a result, they weren't burdened with the kind of book warnings about king safety and knights-on-the-rim and "don't grab the b-pawn" that had been handed down as scripture since Tarrasch. The "kids" had learned, by playing computers, that calculation trumps all rules. And Vilković appeared confident of his calculation here.

13. Rb1 Q×a2 14. Bc5!

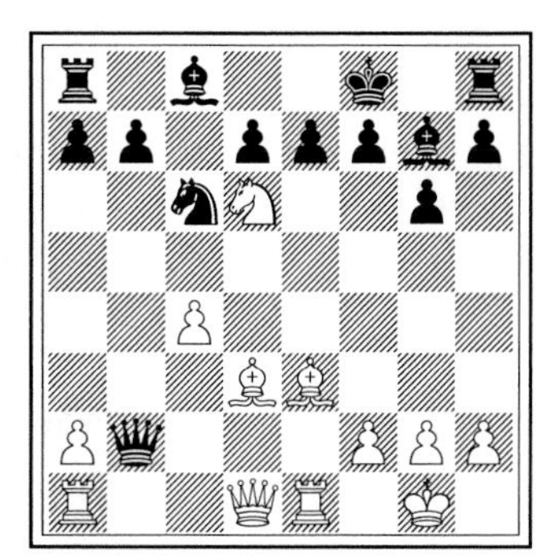

After 12. ... Kf8

But Bastrikova was a pretty fair calculater herself. With this move she set the table for an anthology finish: 15. Qf3 Bf6 16. Q×f6! (or 15. ... f6 16. Qd5).

14. ... Bf6! 15. Qf3

White would be out of bullets after 15. Ne4? Be5.

15. ... Kg7 16. R×e7! N×e7

Not 16. ... B×e7 17. Q×f7+ and mates.

17. Bd4

And now 17. ... Ng8 18. Ne8+! or 17. ... Nf5 18. N×f5+ g×f5 19. Qg3+ would lose quickly.

17. ... B×d4!

"It's not mate," Van Siclen whispered to Krimsditch and Popov, as they watched from two feet away.

"But what is it?" Krimsditch said.

"It's a lottery," Popov said.

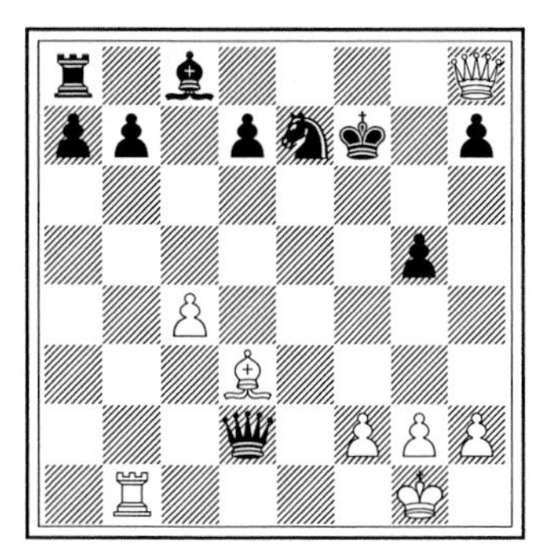

After 22. ... Qd2

18. Q×f7+ Kh6 19. Qf4+ g5! 20. Nf7+ Kg7 21. Q×d4+ K×f7 22. Q×h8 Qd2!

Black offered a draw, which White could probably force if she wanted it (23. Q×h7+ Kf6 24. Qh6+ Ke5 25. Qg7+ Kd6 26. Qf6+ Kc7 27. Qe5+ etc.). After a few minutes Bastrikova accepted.

And it turned out I was right about there being as many as four decisive results this round—but only because Bohigian managed to swindle Karlson in a drawish bishop ending. I posted the updated standings:

SHELDRAKE MEMORIAL

AFTER THREE ROUNDS

Grushevsky, Royce-Smith 2½ points

Bohigian, Klushkov, Qi (with bye) 2

Eichler 1½

Bastrikova, Karlson, Popov, Van Siclen, 1 point

Boriescu, Krimsditch (with bye), Vilković (with bye) ½

As Cel Sims and I closed up the high school for the night, I could tell Karlson was finding it hard to be tied for next-to-last place.

"I should have at least two points."

"This isn't much of a consolation," I said. "But there's a proverb—I think it's Bulgarian—that applies."

"Which is?"

"At the end of the tournament the strong players count their points and the others count their won and drawn positions."

"Yeah, totally."

While the players were at dinner, I made a few phone calls from my hotel room. Among the calls was one to the number in Endoline that Mrs. Nagle had given me.

I remember how strange it seemed the first time I heard there was a town called Endoline. It had a real name once. But that was long forgotten after it became the southern terminus of the old Amarillo & Albuquerque Rail Road. The town soon became known as End-of-the-Line, eventually just Endoline. And, I guess, if there were places in New Mexico called Shakespeare and Weed and Sunspot and Chloride and even Truth or Consequences, then Endoline seemed to fit right in.

Yes, the chemist told me, he could analyze some pills for me. No, it wouldn't take more than a day or two.

"Can't say I've had much business with the people of Los Voraces lately," he said. "Haven't talked with Doc Phelps in a dog's age."

"He must be busy with the whooping cough outbreak," I said.

"Don't know anything about that," he said. "We haven't seen a case of that in the Valley in years."

Yes, he said, the analysis of the pills could be kept between the two of us. No, it wouldn't cost an arm and a leg.

After I hung up, I felt a bit better—and better still after mailing him the pills, making sure no one saw me at the postbox off Main Street. I also felt good about getting the ball rolling with Gibbs. Maybe there was nothing at all wrong here, but I owed it to Gabor. Even to Daphne.

For the next two hours I transcribed about 40 column inches of notes on Round Three for the tournament book, and prepared the day's bulletin. I also started a file about the deaths, for my eyes only. When I looked over at the digital clock radio on my nightstand, it was already 11:15. I left my room and began slipping the bulletins under the doors of the players rooms.

But I didn't detect any sounds at all on the two floors. The Casa's lobby was deserted, and I knew the high school was locked and empty tonight. Moreover, when I ventured out again, Main Street was a ghost town. Just about everyone else in Los Voraces must have been at the church for a town meeting.

But where were the players?

I'd walked about 30 feet from the Casa when I spotted the black-clad figure of Popov slipping in the front door of the Rancho Voraces.

Of course. If there's nothing happening at the tournament site, the players are bound to gather at one of the town's two watering holes, and the Rancho was the closest.

Inside the Rancho I noticed Karlson and Qi at a secluded table nursing organic colas.

"Against d4 she's been playing the Slav and the Nimzo," Karlson said. "Both badly."

"And c4?" Qi said.

"Probably ...Nf6. You'll still get a Nimzo—and squish her like a bug."

They were obviously talking about tomorrow's Qi vs. Bastrikova game. I nodded to them and meandered over to the bar where Eichler was holding council with Krimsditch and Van Siclen. They were using an old-fashioned magnetic pocket set.

"He used to be the one player you couldn't mate. Not any more," Van Siclen said. "Go for it."

"Easy for you to say," Eichler said. "I'm Black."

"Dareh's a tricky old dog," Krimsditch said.

Their subject had to be Bohigian, Eichler's next opponent—although Krimsditch mispronounced his name as "DAH-ree" rather than "Dah-RAY."

But what struck me was that Krimsditch and Van Siclen were talking at all tonight. Since they would be paired tomorrow, this must mean they'd agreed to a draw already.

"You used to play Bohigian in the old days," Eichler said to me. "How do I defend c4 ?"

"You're right, I used to play Bohigian. Now I can't tell you."

"Because?" asked Krimsditch.

"Because now I'm the hall monitor."

"I don't think he's so terrible any more," Van Siclen said.

To be polite I didn't mention that the Dutchman had scored only two points in seven games with Bohigian.

"We just have to find one line he's weak in," said Krimsditch, fiddling with the pieces. "And annihilate him."

"Knock yourself out," I said, and headed across the room.

As I took in the action at the various tables it occurred to me that these little cabals made sense. Without computers or sycophants the players would naturally need to find allies.

I remembered reading about New York 1924. That was back before anyone had seconds. So the invitees broke up into rival groups: Alekhine and Capablanca, later the worst of enemies, somehow became collaborators. They discussed openings each night. In the other camp was Emanuel Lasker. He wasn't speaking to Capa at the time so he fit in well with Yefim Bogolyubov, who hadn't spoken with Alekhine in years. In other words, the enemy of my enemy's friend is my friend.

And times hadn't changed much. At this tournament it seemed only a Klushkov could afford to remain alone. He sat by himself at a corner table, concentrating on the clay tile ceiling.

In a booth across the room I found Grushevsky, Vilković and Bastrikova comparing their grievances against the chess world. They were also talking about Vilković's chances in Round Four.

"Why should I play something you wouldn't?" Vilković said.

"Look, Predrag. This is for your own good," said Bastrikova, playing Earth Mother. "If the world champion gives you advice, you take it."

"What advice?" I asked.

"They want me to play d4 and g3 against the Spaceman."

Grushevsky grunted annoyance. He had the bye the next day, and with nothing to prepare for he was evidently trying to help Vilković torpedo Klushkov.

"It's hard to train someone else the night before a game," I said. "You know, before the last round at Bled '61, when Fischer was trailing Tal, he tried to show Tal's opponent how to play the Najdorf."

"What is wrong with that?" Zhenya asked.

"The opponent was Najdorf."

"Oh."

"You have any stories from *this* century?" Vilković said.

"Tal won the game and the tournament," I said.

"That is simply because Najdorf didn't know how to play the Najdorf," Grushevsky said in his voice-of-authority tone.

"But you think you can teach Predrag a new opening in one night just to beat Klushkov?"

"I am not doing this because of Klushkov," Grushevsky harrumphed. "I am doing this because of my love for chess."

"Odd, how this love so often manifests itself when someone is playing your main rival for first prize," I said.

Grushevsky shot me a poisonous look.

As I got up from their booth I surveyed the scene.

Grushevsky, Vilković and Bastrikova were here. Karlson and Qi were on the side. Eichler, Van Siclen and Krimsditch sat over there. Royce-Smith, Popov and Boriescu were a few booths away discussing … God knows what. Chess, it seems, makes strange co-conspirators.

But if this was confidential preparation, my players were lousy at keeping secrets.

Then it hit me: They wanted to be seen.

Each player, consciously or un-, wanted it known that he or she had help. It was mainly for show, to show they had allies who might be sharing theoretical novelties with them. Whether or not they got any real benefit from their "team," its existence was good propaganda: The threat really is greater than the execution.

But I noticed Klushkov wasn't the only one sitting alone. Bohigian was relaxing by himself at the end of the bar with a snifter of Armenian konyak. The former world champion seemed oddly out of place, overdressed as usual in a dark brown suit.

"You appear to be the only one here who isn't shopping for a new opening," I told him. He allowed himself a grin.

"You have to stick to what you know. As my grandmother used to say: There will be trouble if the cobbler starts making pirogi."

It must sound better in Russian.

"Seems I've heard a lot of sayings today," I said.

"About?"

"Oh, about glitter that isn't gold, snakes that are black and yellow, about pennies and pounds and walls with ears."

Bohigian gave me a "what-are-you-talking-about?" squint, the kind I remembered from the post-mortems of the games we had against one another long, long ago.

"Tell me something," I said. "We're watching grandmasters conspiring against one another. Plotting. Talking about how to crush someone, to annihilate him. Do you think they're capable of doing physical harm to one another?"

He rested his back against the divan, gazing at the ceiling.

"They are capable of at least thinking about it."

"Really?"

"Of course. Players become very passionate after games. Even me."

This was new. Bohigian always seemed like the jovial, good uncle you find in every family. He never seemed to show annoyance—except on those rare occasions when I beat him.

"You wanted to hurt your opponent?"

"At least."

"At least?"

"Yes, there were times I wanted to kill my opponent."

"Do you remember which opponent?"

He looked directly at me and smiled.

"Well, on occasion, you."

Sunday, August 25, 2019

"I THOUGHT I'D CATCH YOU IN," said the voice at the other end of the phone call that jarred me awake.

"Where else would I be at this hour, Sheriff? I'm not the church-going type."

"Might do you some good," Gibbs said. He sounded like someone in much too good a mood for 10:15 A.M.

"Was this call prompted by something other than my spiritual well-being?"

"Well, I've been thinking about what you said yesterday. Interesting stuff. Maybe we could chat a tad more. Say … around noon?"

"I guess that's okay."

"Noon it is."

To say I was curious was putting it mildly. I'd never spent more than five minutes in Gibbs' office until yesterday. Now he wanted to chat, a tad more.

I settled for a soggy burrito and iced coffee as my pre-round nourishment and headed for Gibbs' office on Main Street. I found him alone at the desk. His only companions were a cup of Nescafé and several flies.

"Penny for your thoughts."

"Might only be worth one cent," Gibbs replied. "I just thought it could help if you told me a little about each of your players. Maybe that would help explain the deaths and all."

"You're shopping for a suspect."

"I'd call it preliminary investigating."

"Okay," I said. "If it helps, I can give you a rundown. They're a pretty mixed bag of issues and attitudes."

"I guessed as much," he said, taking out a small, blue spiral notebook.

It made sense to cooperate. It was time to get Gibbs involved.

"First, there's the world champion. Igor Arkadyevich Grushevsky. You've seen him. The barrel-chested Ukrainian with the imposing manner. He can strut sitting down."

"Uh-huh."

"His official bio says he was born in '89, which would make him 30. But I've heard he was really born in '88 and just wanted an edge in junior events when he was a kid. Got away with it, too."

"Do tell."

"There've also been some rumors about his being tied to the mob. He supposedly has friends who are *vory v zakone*."

"Translation?"

"It means 'thieves in law.' That's the term for made men in the *russkaya mafia*."

"You learn something new every day," Gibbs said, underlining the note he had just made. "Even Russian."

"But nothing's ever been proven about Grushevsky."

"What else?"

"Well, there's Dareh Bohigian, the former champion. He's the tallest, and now that Gabor's dead, the oldest of our lot."

"I see."

"Grushevsky beat him for the title seven years ago. Strange match, that one. Anybody but Bohigian, and I'd say it was fixed."

"Fixed?"

"Fixed. Prearranged result. Not exactly unknown in chess. But Dareh's honest. Maybe too honest for this group."

"You like him."

"I'm afraid I do."

"Keep going."

"Next up is Nikolai Klushkov. Tall, blond Russian. Twenty-seven years old—going on four. They call him the Spaceman."

"Because?"

"Because he doesn't seem to be of this planet. Hardly ever speaks—and then usually to himself. At that he's quite a conversationalist."

"Interesting people you have in chess."

"Tell me about it," I said, and continued: "Then there's Johnny Eichler of Germany, the baby of the tournament. He's only 18, and thinks he invented the game. He has some bad habits, too, like adjusting his pieces while his opponent's clock is running. But he's no murderer, as far as I can tell."

"How *do* you tell?"

That was the first time I ever detected sarcasm in Gibbs.

"Doesn't have the killer instinct. Not in his DNA. But maybe in Predrag Vilković's."

"And he is…?"

"He's the height-challenged Serb with the annoying giggle. I know him well. Once at Dortmund I caught him tricking his clock with an electromagnet."

"What?"

"Well, you see, we use timing devices in serious chess. Actually two clocks tied together. Vilković had some gizmo in his wristwatch that allowed him to subtract time if he held it near his clock."

"Sounds like something easy to spot."

"No, he did it really casually, just leaning forward until his hand was close to his clock, and somehow the minute display went *backward.* It wouldn't have worked with the old analog clocks, but it did with the digitals."

"But don't you check the clocks?"

"Of course. Every so often, I add up the elapsed time on both clocks to see if it matches up with the hours and minutes since the round started. Every arbiter does this, to spot malfunctions."

"Go on."

"But Vilković had figured out a way to use his watch device to add about the same number of minutes to his opponent's clock as he took from his own. It always added up, more or less."

"Sounds like a cagey customer."

"Yeah, I suspect there's a lot of anger there. Maybe also in his friend Popov."

"And he is…?"

"He's the Bulgarian with the earring who always dresses in black. I've caught the two of them discussing moves during games. And I forfeited Popov once in a rapid-play tournament for using an EGD."

"Eeegie what?"

"It stands for eyeglass display, a kind of wearable computer. In this case, it fed opening analysis to the lower part of his prescription frames. Sort of like movie subtitles."

"Ingenious people these Europeans," Gibbs said. "By the way, aren't there any Americans in this American tournament?"

"One. Todd Krimsditch. He thinks he's the next Bobby Fischer. But even today, Fischer could probably give him pawn and move—and Bobby will be 77 in March."

"Low self-esteem is not Mr. Krimditch's problem, I take it."

"Not a whit. He also has his little ways of testing the rules. Like with his hair."

"His hair?"

"Yes. Every so often, when it's his opponent's turn to move, Krimsditch examines how much time he has left. He does this by leaning over the board to get a good look and bending his head toward the clock. Like this."

I pulled up my chair to Gibbs' desk and leaned over his ink-stained blotter. Then I lowered my head five or six inches and turned to look to the right.

"Where does the hair come in?"

I leaned back in my chair.

"You haven't seen Krimsditch. He has a huge mane, a WASP's version of an Afro. When he pulls this stunt, he covers at least 50 of the 64 squares. Naturally, he never does this on his own time."

"Who's left?"

"A lot, starting with the women: Kersti Karlson and Zhenya Bastrikova. One's Finnish, the other Russian. Both in their early 30s, which are usually a chessplayer's peak years."

"Really?"

"Really. They're both talented—but totally toxic in each other's company. They make Petrosian and Korchnoi seem like a mutual admiration society."

I could see the question mark spread across the sheriff's face.

"That means Kersti and Zhenya are enemies from way back. They're known for pulling stunts whenever they play one another. Like their J'adoube wars."

"J'adoube?"

"That's something you say when you adjust a piece. After every move, Kersti would turn every knight on the board to face inward. On the next move, Zhenya would readjust them to face outward. Or straight ahead. It didn't matter. As long as it annoyed her opponent. In fact, when they were kids they even tried to take back moves against one another."

"Can they get away with that?"

"You'd be surprised. More than 20 years ago, a world champion took back a move in plain view of his opponent and a room full of spectators. He claimed it couldn't have happened. After all, he said, no one would dare try to do that in front of an audience of witnesses. And in front of a video camera."

Gibbs shook his head. "Getting back to the women. Are they capable of murder?"

"Only of one another—which they haven't done yet despite many opportunities."

"Who's left?"

"The next that comes to mind is Eustace Royce-Smith. A Brit. Very smart. IQ up in the ionosphere. But crazy as a Mad Cow."

"How so?"

"Textbook paranoid. He's convinced Gabor and Daphne were killed by aliens."

Gibbs glanced at the ceiling and grimaced. "Your grandmasters do seem to have some, what do you call them? Idio...?"

"...syncracies. But any city dweller knows that in a random subway car, you're bound to find at least one ambulatory schizophrenic."

Gibbs put down his notebook and looked up.

"One walking crazy," I explained. "And if there's one per subway car, there should be at least that many in a large invitational chess tournament."

"You mean they need medical help?"

"At least."

He seemed to be studying what he'd just written. After a minute I tried to fill the void.

"Speaking of medical, I haven't seen Phelps in days. I know G.P.'s don't do autopsies but he said he'd get back to me with some details on Gabor."

"Doc had to leave this morning. Big professional conference up in Santa Fe. Surprised you missed him. Now as to the others..."

"Yes?"

"I also noticed a thin, uhh, Oriental fellow."

"That's Qi Yuanzhi. Always wears a dark suit, black tie and a pained expression."

"Uh-huh."

"No one had ever heard of him until he was evacuated to Shanghai in '12 after his town was flooded in the final stage of the Yangtze dam project. Once he started playing Western chess he just took off. Went from zero to 2900 in six months.

"2900?"

"That's a rating, a very good one."

Gibbs shrugged.

"No one could tell if it was natural ability or Cordyceps."

"Now that's something I should know about," Gibbs said. "Cordyceps is that drug they talk about on the sports page, right?"

"Actually it's a natural herb. From Tibetan mushrooms, or somesuch. It provides super stamina and endurance. The Chinese used it when they started dominating Olympic running years ago. Everyone suspects their chessplayers use it too but we don't test for that."

"Uh-huh."

"Anyway, Qi is about as good as he's going to get right now. He needs to win this tournament to force Grushevsky to accept his challenge for a title match. So does Klushkov. In fact, Grushevsky needs first place even more."

"But he *is* the champion, isn't he?"

I shook my head. "Yes, but that's not the point. World champions play tournaments only so they can avoid playing championship matches."

I could tell Gibbs was learning a lot more about chess than he really wanted to know.

"Anyway," I continued, "Qi hangs out with Karlson but otherwise doesn't talk much. Neither does Octav Boriescu, our pot-bellied Romanian. But that's probably a language problem."

"He doesn't speak? I mean, English?"

"A little of everything but English. Boriescu's something of a mystery. The grapevine says he dropped out of college one paper short of a degree that would have set him up for life."

"He gave it up for chess?"

It was hard to explain to Gibbs that this was a normal occurrence. I didn't try.

"That's one version. Another is that he got mixed up in some point-selling scandal and had to leave Timisoara fast."

"We all have to make career choices," he said.

I briefly wondered about Gibbs' choices before continuing. "Finally, there's Gert Van Siclen. The laid-back Dutchman with the beard. Former boyfriend of Daphne's, just like Krimsditch. Gert's a real talent but his rating has flat-lined for the last three years."

"Any particular reason?"

"Sure, no self-discipline. Gert's doesn't have a shred of it. He's most at home in extra-large sweaters, tactical positions and anything over 90 proof."

"He drinks."

"Everybody needs a hobby."

"Any other bad habits in your tournament?" Gibbs asked.

"None except occasional nastiness, poor manners and sloppy endgame technique. And none of that's against the law."

Gibbs nodded and closed his notebook. A long pause followed.

"So where does that leave us?" I asked.

"It leaves us with two bodies on cold metallic shelves over at the morgue."

"And no shortage of suspects."

"Perhaps," he said. "But it seems to me that the type of person who would cheat in a big-deal chess tournament is the type of person who might kill."

"Why, Sheriff," I said, trying to act offended. "Everyone knows you can't cheat in chess."

At the high school, I posted the pairings for what shaped up as a fairly mundane day. None of the leaders would face one another. I didn't expect much.

SHELDRAKE MEMORIAL
ROUND FOUR PAIRINGS
Vilković vs. Klushkov
Qi vs. Bastrikova
Boriescu vs. Popov
Royce-Smith vs. Karlson
Bohigian vs. Eichler
Van Siclen vs. Krimsditch
Grushevsky bye

Everyone was at their tables by 1:55, fussing over scoresheets and bulletins. I took the opportunity to remind them of the schedule.

"Just in case some of you have forgotten, there will be a free day on Wednesday for everyone who doesn't have an adjourned game pending. The town has offered to organize a trip to the Los Voraces rock quarry for us."

No one looked up. I continued: "There's a sign-up sheet in my office. Remember, I'm speaking about Wednesday."

Klushkov, sitting almost catatonically at Board One, woke up. "Which one is that?" he asked in a nasal voice.

"The day after Round Six," Bastrikova said from the next table.

Klushkov was still puzzled.

"No, I mean which one is Wednesday?"

There was a long pause until Vilković leaned across the board. "The one after Tuesday," he whispered.

"Ahhhhhh," Klushkov said, nodding. "Thank you."

"Another reminder, people," I said. "I need you to sign both scoresheets when you're done. Not only your own, but your opponent's as well. And please reset your pieces when you're done."

Krimsditch and Van Siclen looked at each other, smiled and shook their heads. Moments later I began the round. The fruit of last night's conspiracy quickly took shape on Board One:

Vilković–Klushkov
Queen's Pawn Game D02

1. d4 d5 2. g3!? Nf6 3. Bg2 c6 4. Nf3 Bf5 5. 0–0 Nbd7 6. Nbd2 e6 7. Nh4

Grushevsky had made a considerable study of Klushkov simply because he'd been his most likely challenger. And Grushevsky had developed a theory about the kinds of positions in which the Spaceman was most vulnerable. Specifically, he thought Klushkov played about 100 points below his rating in simple positions with static features.

That meant, for example, middlegames where he couldn't change the pawn structure much and his opponent held the two bishops.

Looking at the board now, you could tell Grushevsky had prepared Vilković pretty well. White was sure to get one of those low-maintenance positions that arise after, say, 7. ... Bg4 8. h3 Bh5 9. g4 Bg6 10. N×g6 and 11. e4.

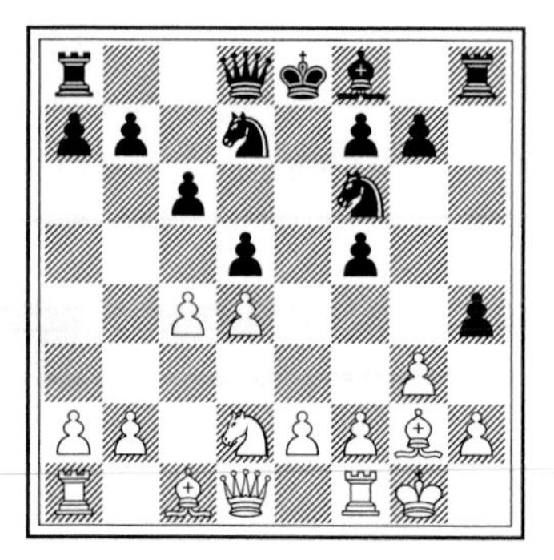

Vilković–Klushkov
After 9. ... h4

7. ... h5!?

But Klushkov had a different middlegame in mind.

8. N×f5 e×f5 9. c4 h4

10. c×d5 c×d5 11. Qb3 Nb6 12. a4!

The old adage says White can't get mated if Black lacks a bishop to trade off for the one at g2. If there's no Black attack on the kingside, Vilković would have a free hand on the queenside and against d5.

12. ... h×g3 13. h×g3 Rb8 14. a5 Nc8 15. Nf3

Black couldn't avoid material losses now (15. ... Nd6 16. Bf4 Be7 17. Ne5 and B×d5).

15. ... Bd6 16. Bg5

Now 16. ... Qe7? 17. Nh4 simply wins the d-pawn.

16. ... Ne7!?! 17. B×f6 g×f6

One thing you could say about him. Klushkov bore no prejudices about pawn structure. But where his counterplay was going to come from was a mystery.

18. e3 Kf8! 19. Nd2

White has his choice. He can pick off the f-pawn with Nh4 followed by Qd3 and, if necessary, Bh3. But the f-pawn wasn't running away. It could always be won in the endgame.

19. ... Kg7 20. Nb1! Rh6 21. Nc3 Qh8 22. Nb5

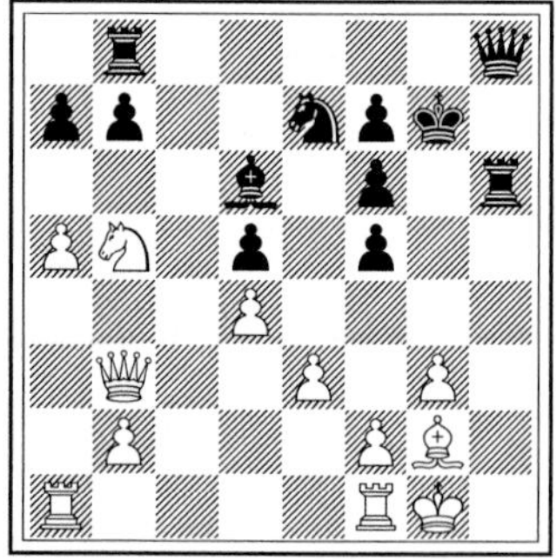

After 22. Nb5

This looked even stronger than 22. N×d5, as the attacked bishop had no retreat.

Grushevsky, who was free today, had been walking around the

stage with a broad smile. At this point he approached me and motioned with his head toward Klushkov's board.

"So many pawns," he said. "So little time."

We were both watching from a distance of a few feet when Klushkov, incomprehensibly, reached for a piece near his king.

"*Chevo*...?" Grushevsky asked himself. "What the...?"

22. ... Qh7!!

I should have remembered Petrosian's Law.

"Opponents always have some kind of weakness in their position—even if it's imperceptible," the ninth world champion used to say. "Against that you have to play."

23. N×d6 Rh1+!

Not 23. ... Rh8 because of 24. f4!, after which the attack is over and White must win.

24. B×h1 Rh8

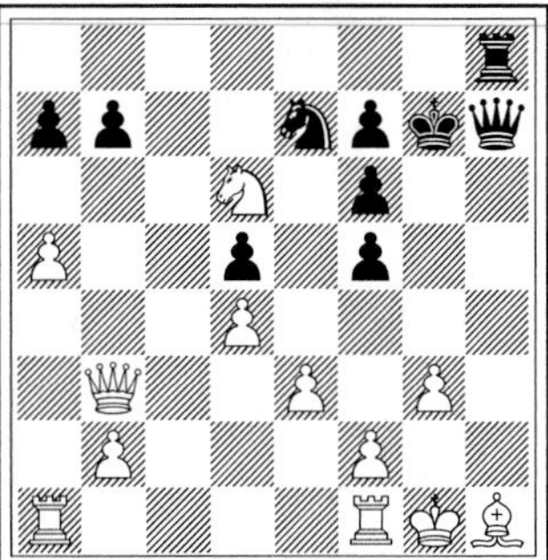

After 24. ... Rh8

Mate is threatened, and 25. Ne8+ Kf8! doesn't change the picture. There was only one saving move.

25. Kg2 Qh3+ 26. Kf3 Qg4+ 27. Kg2 Qh3+ Draw

Even before they'd finished shaking hands, Grushevsky began clutching piece and repositioning them to prove Black must have been lost at some point. I shooed him and the two players off to the post-mortem room. It was only while I was collecting the flags, with my back turned to the auditorium seats, that I noticed an animated discussion going on at the board in the rear of the stage.

Van Siclen had not drawn quickly with Krimsditch. He was still playing at move 22, which he banged down on the board. When Gert looked up and realized he'd caught my eye, he stood up. Without writing down his move, he approached me.

"You realize what's going on, don't you?" he said. "I can explain it to you."

"Let me live in ignorance."

"We agreed last night to draw. By move 15."

"You shouldn't be telling me this," I reminded him. But he was too upset.

"As a result I didn't play my default openings. I never waste preparation."

"Right?"

"But then he starts this ridiculous attack."

Van Siclen had opened 1. c4 e5 2. a3—which Krimsditch answered, a few moves later, with 5. ... g5!?.

"When I asked him about the draw we made last night he said, 'Maybe next time.'"

"I guess you'll know better next time," I said. "But for this event, you might have to draw up a whole new tournament plan."

"But he's cheating!"

"Look, Gert, you can't expect an international arbiter to enforce an illegal agreement that violates both the letter and spirit of FIDE rules."

He left me, muttering in Dutch. Probably something about honor among thieves. I turned my attention to Board Two, where the highest-ever-rated Asian player was taking command.

Qi–Bastrikova
Queen's Gambit Declined D53

1. d4 d5 2. c4 c6 3. Nc3 Nf6 4. Nf3 e6 5. Bg5 h6 6. B×f6 Q×f6 7. e3 Nd7 8. Be2 g6 9. 0–0 Bg7 10. c×d5

I detected Karlson's hand in this move. No GM had played anything but 10. e4 or 10. b4 for years.

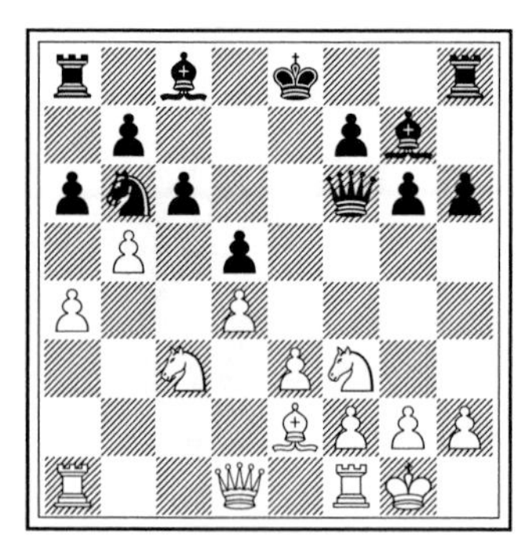

After 13. b5

10. ... e×d5 11. b4 a6 12. a4 Nb6 13. b5

Qi was the opposite of Grushevsky, never betraying his emotions. I was watching his face when Zhenya blundered on the next move. She evidently expected to close the queenside with 13. ... c×b5 14. a×b5 a5.

13. ... c×b5? 14. a5!

Not even a blink from Qi. Bastrikova

thought 25 minutes before convincing herself how awful 14. ... Nd7 15. N×d5 was.

14. ... Qc6! 15. axb6 Q×c3 16. B×b5+ Ke7 17. Qa4! Be6 18. Rac1! Qb2

Of course, not 18. ... a×b5 19. Q×a8 Q×c1 20. Q×b7+ and White wins immediately. But if White had played 18. Rfc1? instead, then 18. ... a×b5 19. Q×a8 Q×c1 would be check.

19. Rc7+ Kf6 20. Bd7! Q×b6 21. R1c1 B×d7

Zhenya could have saved us a lot of time with 21. ... Rhb8? 22. Ne5! and then 22. ... Kg5!? 23. f4+ Kh4 24. g3+ Kh3 25. Qd1! and mates. She had found the only way out of the middlegame without major concessions.

22. Q×d7 Qe6 23. Ne5 Q×d7 24. N×d7+ Ke6 25. Nc5+ Kf6 26. N×b7

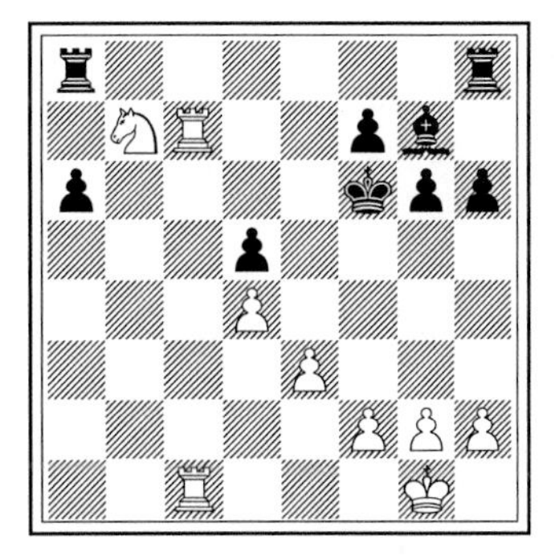

After 26. N×b7

By trading queens, Black earned the dubious right to play at least an additional two hours without appearing ridiculous. But it wouldn't be pretty.

The irony of the day was that the outcome of all the games was more or less decided early on—except for Van Siclen vs. Krimsditch, the one that should have been drawn by now.

Typical of the others was what happened on Board Four. Royce-Smith's chances for first prize suffered a setback when he couldn't budge Karlson's Grünfeld.

Royce-Smith–Karlson
Grünfeld Defense D85

1. d4 Nf6 2. Nf3 g6 3. c4 Bg7 4. Nc3 d5 5. c×d5 N×d5 6. e4 N×c3 7. b×c3 c5 8. Be2 c×d4 9. c×d4 Nc6 10. Be3 Qa5+ 11. Bd2 Qa3 12. d5 Nb4!

Black loses material on 12. ... B×a1? 13. Q×a1. But now she threatens both 13. ... B×a1 and 13. ... Nd3+.

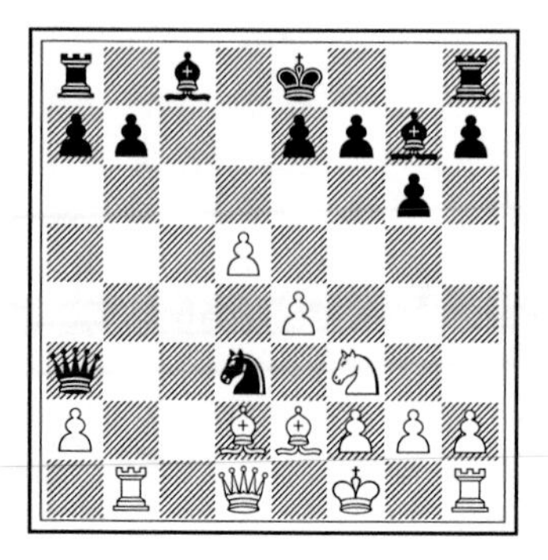

After 14. Kf1

13. Rb1 Nd3+ 14. Kf1!

I wondered if this was a very new trap—White threatens 15. Rb3—or a very old one. On 14. ... Nb2 15. Qb3 the knight is embarrassed, and 14. ... Nc5? 15. Bb4 is just a blunder. Black loses a piece in either case.

14. ... Ne5 15. Nd4! a6!

She doesn't fall for 15. ... 0–0 16. Nb5 Q×a2 17. Ra1.

16. Bb4?

Not best. After 16. Qc2 White threatens to win with 17. Bb4. Then 16. ... Qd6 leaves him with a choice between 17. f4, which isn't bad, and 17. Bb4 Qf6 18. Qc7, which is better.

16. ... Q×a2 17. Ra1

There was nothing but trouble in 17. f4 Ng4! (threat of ...Ne3+) 18. Rb3 Bd7! and ...Ba4.

17. ... Qb2

Now it became clear Royce-Smith had miscalculated. Black was home free.

18. Rb1 Qa2

"Offer draw," Karlson said abruptly as she repeated the queen move.

The Englishman reacted as if he'd been slapped. It was bad manners on Karlson's part, of course. White was the one who should make draw offers in such positions. That's grandmaster etiquette. Besides, he could have forced a repetition if he wanted it.

Royce-Smith tried one more trap.

19. Bc3 Qa3! 20. Bb4 Qa2
Draw

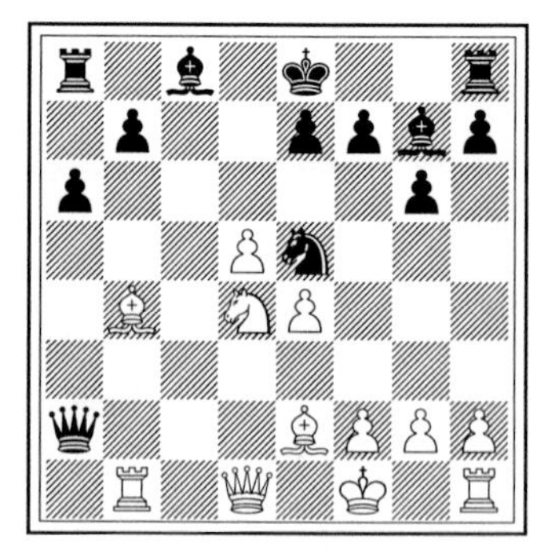

Final position

When I was walking off stage with the scoresheets, I was surprised to find myself again being pursued, this time by Krimsditch.

"What's the deal here?" he asked when he caught up with me inside my office.

"Beg pardon?"

"Why are you letting him get away with it?"

"Getting away with what?"

"With banging the pieces. He's banging down every move he makes. That's against the rules."

"It seems he thinks he's the injured party. You did agree to a draw, didn't you?"

"Duh! Of course. Everyone knew. Even Klushkov could tell. But I didn't realize he was going to play this a3 crap."

"Maybe Gert just didn't like to waste good opening moves on a phony game," I said.

"I couldn't care less what he likes or doesn't like. The point is I can't let him get away with moves like that. I've got a reputation to uphold."

"Then, uphold."

"I will. I have to make sure nobody else gets the idea I'm willing to draw against this crap."

I could see his point. But this was an incident-in-the-making.

"Look, Todd, I can give him a warning about the banging. But you know Gert. It's one thing to break a gentlemen's agreement. It's quite another to delay cocktail hour."

Krimsditch snorted at that, and stormed off.

The room began to empty out by the end of the third hour. One reason was that Bohigian had given Eichler a free ride in the opening.

Bohigian–Eichler
Queen's Indian Defense E14

1. c4 Nf6 2. Nf3 e6 3. d4 b6 4. e3 Bb7 5. Bd3 d5 6. 0–0 Bd6 7. Nc3 0–0 8. b3 Nbd7 9. Bb2 c5 10. Qe2 Ne4 11. c×d5 e×d5 12. Ba6! B×a6 13. Q×a6

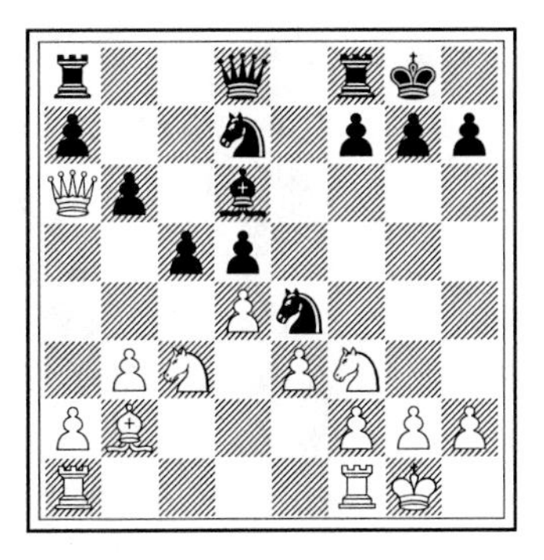

Bohigian–Eichler
After 13. Q×a6

Typical Bohigian, trying to make a mountain out of a few porous queenside squares. His 12th move must have been one of his ideas from 15 years ago that nobody remembered today.

White will stand well if he can squeeze the hanging pawns with Rfd1/Rac1. For example, 13. … Ndf6 is a natural move but then 14. dxc5 Bxc5 has to be a typical plus-over-equals for White, if not more. And 14. ... bxc5 is unpleasant for Black after 15. Rfd1 Qd7 16. Nb5 or 15. Nxe4 Nxe4 16. Qb7.

But Eichler was up to the pop quiz.

13. ... cxd4!

The first point: 14. Nxd4 is met by 14. … Nxc3 15. Bxc3 Bxh2+ 16. Kxh2 Qc7+.

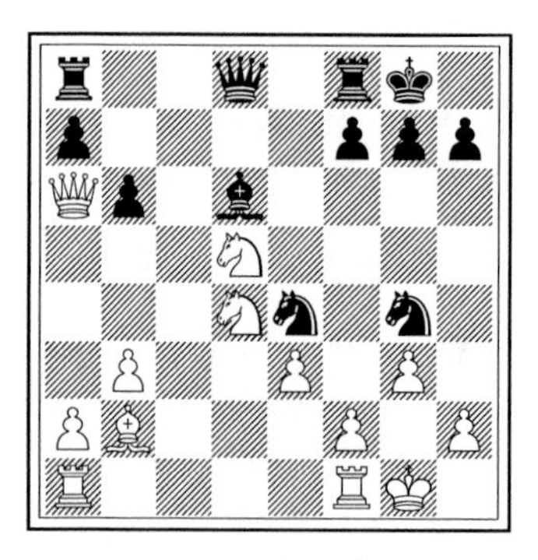

After 16. g3

14. Nxd5

Now 14. … dxe3 15. fxe3 can turn in White's favor after, say, 15. … Ndf6 16. Nxf6+ Nxf6 17. Rad1.

14. ... Ne5! 15. Nxd4

Point two: 15. Nxe5 Bxe5 16. exd4 Bxh2+ 17. Kxh2 Qxd5 is great for Black. Or 15. Bxd4 Nxf3+ 16. gxf3 Qg5+ 17. Kh1 Qh5! and wins.

15. ... Ng4 16. g3

The third trick was 16. h3 Bh2+! 17. Kh1 Nexf2+. And the fourth was coming up.

16. ... Nxh2 17. Kxh2 Nxg3! 18. Kg2 Qg5 19. Nf3 Qg4 20. fxg3 Qxg3+ Draw

As so often happened with Bohigian, there was a lot more game in the notes than on the board. After he put down his pen, he replaced a few pieces and backtracked to the position after Black's 15th move.

This was Eichler's cue that Bohigian wasn't going to give him a free opening lesson. Bohigian just wanted to see what the kid had in mind if he'd played a different 16th move. I knew this wouldn't take long so I let them analyze silently where they were.

Bohigian moved his g-pawn one square and shook his head to

Eichler. Then he replaced the pawn and moved his knight to f4 instead—16. Nf4.

Eichler instantly replied 16. … g5. But when Bohigian reached across the board and moved 17. Qb7! he drew back in surprise.

While his opponent studied the position Bohigian frowned at me. Another missed opportunity?

But in less than a minute Eichler found 17. … Ne×f2!.

Bohigian answered 18. Nde6 and the young German instantly shot back 18. … B×f4!.

This time it was Bohigian's turn to think. After a minute he looked up and nodded: Eichler had passed the test. It should have been a draw after all.

After Eichler left, I helped Bohigian reset the pieces. I could tell he was annoyed. Not by the result as much as by the way he had missed things during the game.

"Those three-move variations," I said. "You can never see all of them during the game."

"I used to make my living seeing all of them," he said. "That's what grandmasters do."

The real shock of the round was Boriescu's comeback on Board Three. Fear of being alone in last place can be a powerful motivation—particularly after you came out of the opening positionally busted, as he did.

Boriescu–Popov
Nimzo-Indian Defense E31

1. d4 Nf6 2. c4 e6 3. Nc3 Bb4 4. Bg5 h6 5. Bh4 c5 6. d5 d6 7. f3 B×c3+ 8. b×c3 e5 9. e3 Nbd7 10. Bd3 Qe7 11. Qe2?

No one liked this move when we got around to the post-mortem. The queen takes away the only good square for White's knight.

11. … g5! 12. Bg3 h5 13. h4 g4 14. Bc2

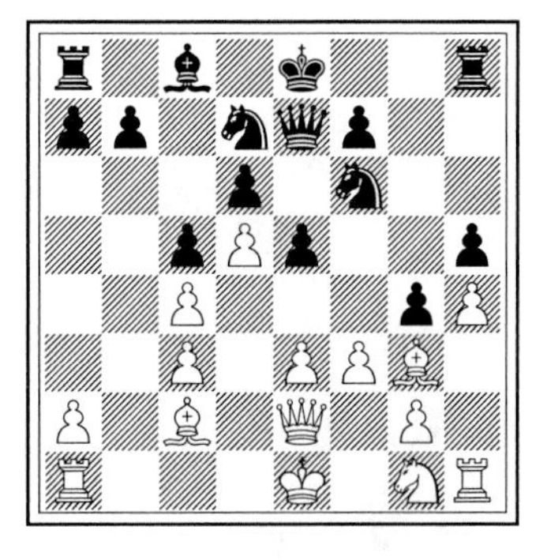

Boriescu–Popov
After 14. Bc2

14. ... Rg8! 15. f4

An ugly move. But taking on f3 was Black's positional threat (15. 0–0–0 g×f3 16. Q×f3 Nb6 or 15. Qf2 g×f3 16. g×f3 e4 and ...Ne5 with advantage) and 15. Bf2?? g3 was out of the question.

15. ... e4

Everything about Black's position looked good except his king. During the P-M, we were getting good positions for Black with ...Kd8–c7—or even ...Kf8–g7.

16. Rb1 Nf8 17. Ba4+ Kd8 18. f5! B×f5?

There was a Popov in every generation of elite GMs: Someone with little real talent and even less imagination, as this hasty grab showed.

Popov had an awesome capacity to study—six, seven, even eight or more hours a day. Like Kamsky, the Polgars and Radjabov he had been home-schooled, so he put in enormous hours of analysis since he was eight. Popov really believed he could out-prepare anyone, even Grushevsky, and one day reach the world championship.

But as Spassky used to say, "Much ambition, little ammunition."

19. Qf2 Bc8 20. Ne2

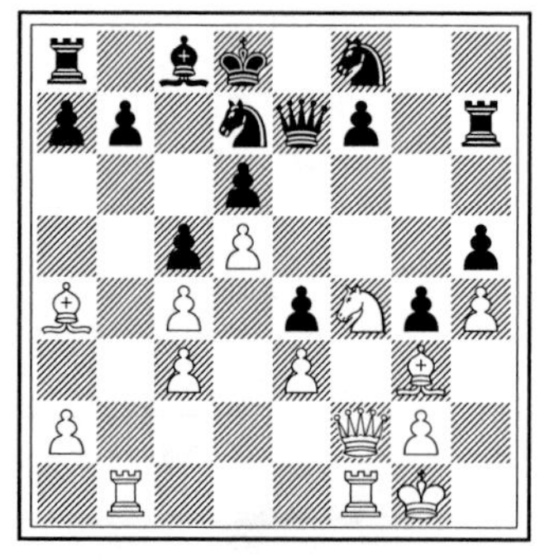

After 22. ... Rh7

It was remarkable how quickly the game turned 180 degrees. White suddenly has great pressure on the f-file and a fine outpost for the knight at f4.

20. ... N6d7 21. 0–0 Rg7

No better was 21. ... f6 22. Nf4 Rh8 because of 23. B×d7 K×d7 24. Rbd1 and 25. Ne6.

22. Nf4 Rh7

The Nimzo-Indian is not a very forgiving defense, and if you find yourself making moves like 22. ... Rh7, punishment is inevitable. All Boriescu had to do now was look for a sack and eventually he'd find one that works.

I suspect he first examined 23. Rfd1, with the ideas of 24. Ne6+ and 24. Bc6!?. But both ideas are handled fairly simply by 23. ... Ne5!.

While I examined the position, I felt a tap on the shoulder. It was Van Siclen, with a new complaint. He spoke in hushed tones but nodded in the direction of his board, near the back wall.

"Now he's humming."

"Krimsditch?"

"Who else?" he said.

"He's humming while he's thinking?"

"Yes, and getting louder. I'm surprised you haven't noticed."

I thought quickly before replying: "You should be pleased."

"What? Why?"

"I thought everyone knew. That's Todd's tipoff. He only hums when he realizes he's busted."

"Really?"

"Really. Maybe you don't appreciate how well you stand. But he does."

That did the trick. Van Siclen quickly returned to his board to see what he'd missed about his position. By that time Boriescu had made a decision on the board in front of me.

23. Ne6+!! fxe6

Also bad was 23. … Nxe6 24. dxe6 Qxe6 25. Bxd7 followed by Rfd1 or 24. … fxe6 25. Rbd1 e5 26. Bc2.

24. dxe6 Qxe6

Black accepts the fact that he has to give up his queen or play out lost lines like 24. … Nxe6 25. Rbd1 or 24. … Qxe6 25. Rbd1 Qxc4 26. Rxd6.

25. Rbd1 Rh6 26. Rxd6 Qxd6 27. Bxd6 Rxd6 28. Qf4 Re6?

A blunder that spared me another adjourned game. White would still have had some technical chores to perform after 28. … Rg6 29. Rd1 Ke7 30. Qxe4+ Re6.

29. Qg5+ Kc7

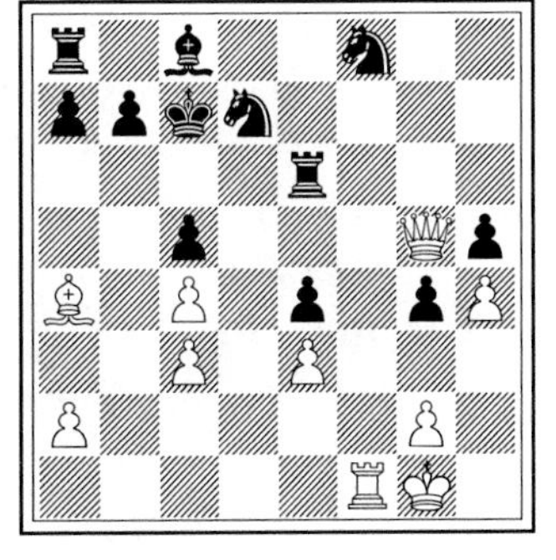

After 29. … Kc7

Black has enough material for the queen but as Botvinnik used to say his pieces don't play.

30. R×f8! Resigns

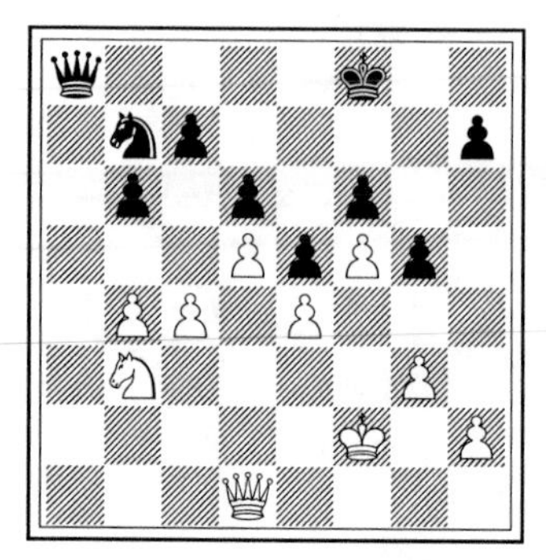

Van Siclen–Krimsditch
White to move

It wouldn't have been much of an endgame anyway after 30. … N×f8 31. Q×c5+ and Q×f8. That only left two games: Qi was still at work on Board Two, but Bastrikova didn't have a chance of salvation from what I could tell. A win would put the Chinese GM in first place, even though he'd already had his "Gabor bye." And on Board Six, Krimsditch was suffering a classic case of fifth-hour fatigue. Both players were in time pressure when the rooks were swapped off along the a-file. They soon reached this position.

Black's attack had evaporated in the blitz as the rooks and bishops were traded off. Van Siclen slapped down **41. Qa1!** just as my watch alarm went off. It was 7 P.M., adjournment hour.

White's position made it clear that Van Siclen could drag this out if he wanted to. And his demeanor made it clear he wanted to. Black couldn't avoid an exchange of queens for long and the only question was whether White could break through on the queenside with his king or on the kingside with his knight. Van Siclen could make Krimsditch squirm all night, literally. The American was known for going through all sorts of gyrations when he had a bad position. Grabbing his head with both hands, nervous arm twitches, you name it.

"This is going to be worth the price of admission tonight," Royce-Smith said to me.

In fact, Van Siclen could adjourn a second time and then analyze the win out to a mathematical certainty before the game would be played off on the free day. No rock quarry for me.

I gave Van Siclen and Qi the envelopes to fill out. Qi performed his duty quickly and left to analyze in his hotel room. Bastrikova, two pawns down on Board Two, probably would have resigned under normal circumstances. But she apparently decided to play it out because she knew she'd have company on the stage tonight.

On the other board, Krimsditch took his time to decide on a sealed move. When he'd made his choice, he tore off the bottom copy of his scoresheet and stuffed it in his pocket. Then he carefully reexamined the original—to avoid ambiguous-move problems—and sealed it. It reminded me of how Tal used to write his sealed move twice—on two separate scoresheets. Because, he explained, "I can't cope with carbon paper."

After Krimsditch and Van Siclen had gone, there were only two of us left on the stage. Bastrikova sat, shaking her head at her position.

While I waited for her to seal, I took Van Siclen's chair at the other board, looking for the breakthrough in what was certain to be a tough knight endgame.

After another 10 minutes, she looked up at me and broke the silence.

"I did not realize you still cared about chess."

"The position's interesting," I said.

"Arbiters are not supposed to be interested."

That struck me as odd. "We're disinterested," I said. "That doesn't mean we're uninterested."

Zhenya understood enough English to get my point.

"Interested enough to help me analyze back at my room?"

She stuffed her scoresheet into the envelope and licked it sealed.

"Nope," I replied. "Not interested."

Royce-Smith was right. The second session was the best show in town.

Often it's just the day's winners who feel comfortable coming back to see the adjournments. But at various points tonight virtually all the players showed up at the high school. It was sort of a death watch for Krimsditch.

Even Grushevsky, who spent the better part of the afternoon berating Vilković for only making a draw against Klushkov, appeared at the end of the session. He was almost cordial to me and Mrs. Nagle.

When Bastrikova's envelope was opened, Qi seemed mildly surprised by her sealed move. He took 20 minutes for his reply. The other game moved along smoothly. But too smoothly for Krimsditch. He had sealed:

41. ... Q×a1

And there quickly followed:

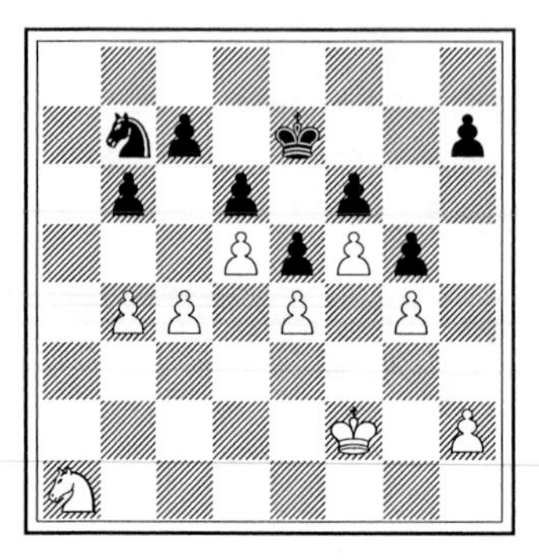

Van Siclen–Krimsditch
After 43. g4

42. N×a1 Ke7? 43. g4!

"Not to be believed!" Royce-Smith whispered to me. "Two hours to analyze, and he blunders on the first move. Doesn't anyone study the endgame in America?"

True enough. Black had to play 42. ... h5 and pray for a blockade on the queenside. Now White could put his knight on h5 and find a way to break into the other wing with his king. Black's knight has to be able to defend f6 with ...Ng8. That leaves him with no useful moves but king "passes."

43. ... Kd7 44. Nc2 Nd8 45. Ne3 Nf7 46. Ke2 Nh6 47. h3 Ng8 48. Kd3 Kc8 49. Kc3 Kb7 50. Kb3

There were no roadblocks to keep the king from b5 now.

50. ... Ne7 51. Ka4 Kc8 52. Nf1 Kd7 53. Kb5 Kc8 54. Ka6 Kb8 55. Ng3

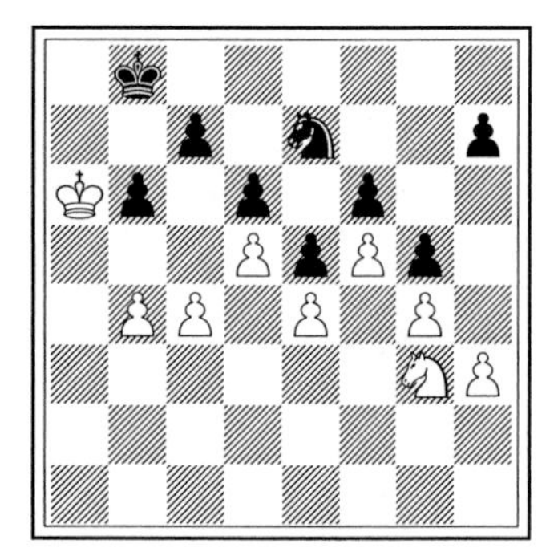

After 55. Ng3

The first mini-zugzwang. Black would be on life support after, say, 55. ... Ng8 56. Nh5 Ka8 57. Ng7 Kb8 58. Ne6 Ne7 59. Nf8 or 58. ... Kc8 59. Ka7 and so on. It wasn't that hard to calculate since Black had zero counterplay.

Next door, Bastrikova was just going through the motions of putting up resistance. She didn't resign until move 58, when it was past 10:30 P.M. Of course, she could have sealed again, since the second time control ended at move 56. But even "Iron Zhenya" had her limits.

A few of the players stuck around, convinced that Krimsditch would soon follow Bastrikova into the loss column. Klushkov also remained, curled up in a chair in the last row of the auditorium.

I posted the standings:

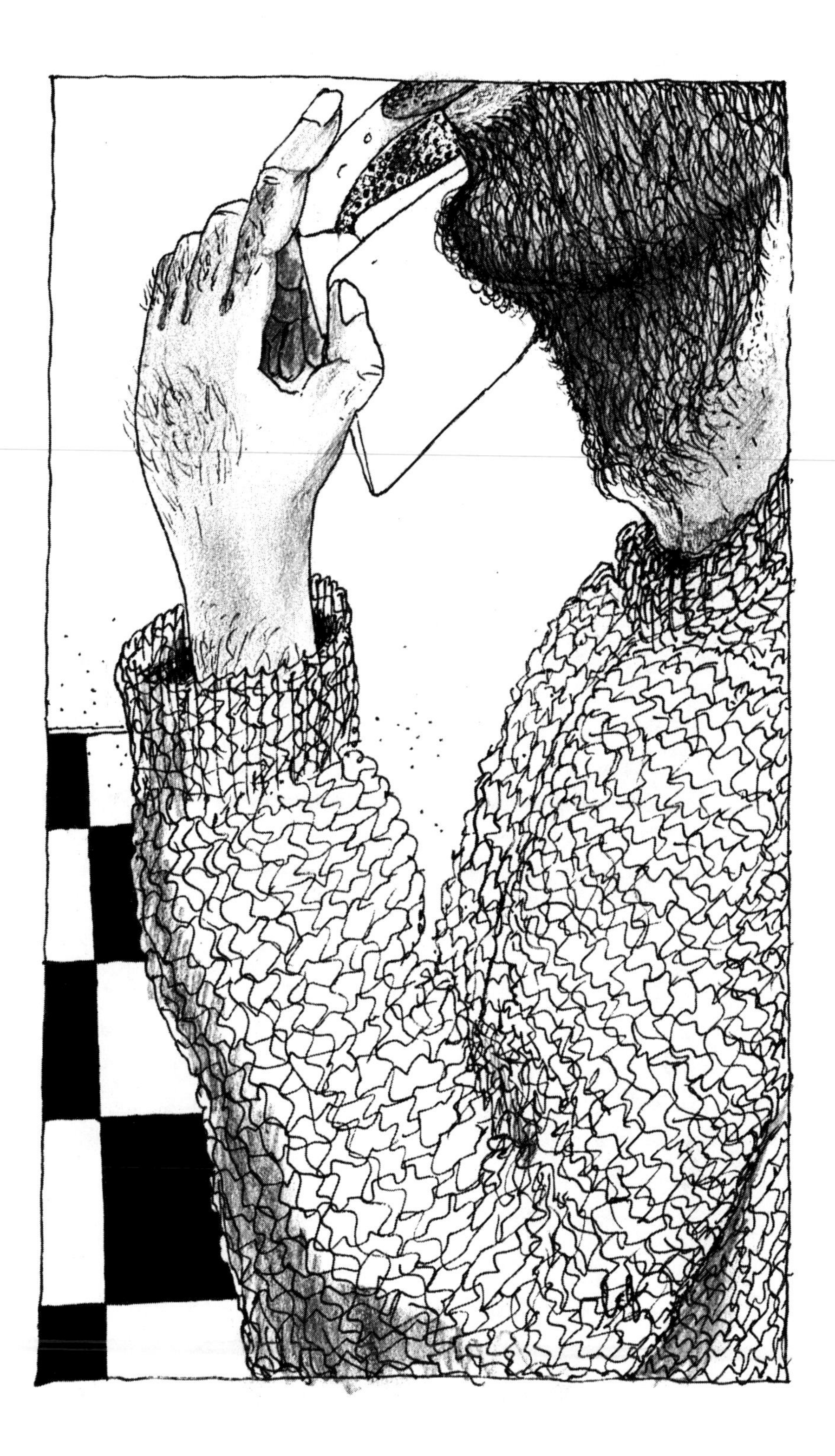

SHELDRAKE MEMORIAL TOURNAMENT

	V	*Q*	*B*	*K*	*P*	*K*	*E*	*K*	*G*	*V*	*B*	*R*	*B*	*G*	*Score*
Vilković	/	0	½	½										—	1–2
Qi	1	/	1										1	—	3–0
Bastrikova	½	0	/									0	½	—	1–3
Klushkov	½			/							½	½	1	—	2½–1½
Popov					/					½	½	0	0	—	1–3
Karlson						/			0	1	0	½		—	1½–2½
Eichler							/	½	½	½	½			—	2–2
Krimsditch							½	/	½					—	1–1
Grushevsky						1	½	1	/					—	2½–½
Van Siclen					½	0	½			/				—	1–2
Bohigian				½	½	1	½				/			—	2½–1½
Royce-Smith			1	½	1	½						/		—	3–1
Boriescu		0	½	0	1								/	—	1½–2½
Gabor	—	—	—	—	—	—	—	—	—	—	—	—	—	—	—

Once Krimsditch had resigned—which couldn't be long off—I'd add his zero to the spot where his line intersected with Van Siclen's column. That would put him alone in last place, with a half point. Van Siclen would move up to sixth, tied with Eichler.

But Krimsditch refused to acknowledge the inevitable. He kept twisting in his chair and leaning over the board. His right knee bobbed up and down under the table as his foot tapped the parquet floor. I always found Krimsditch's nervous energy entertaining to watch. Tonight was no exception.

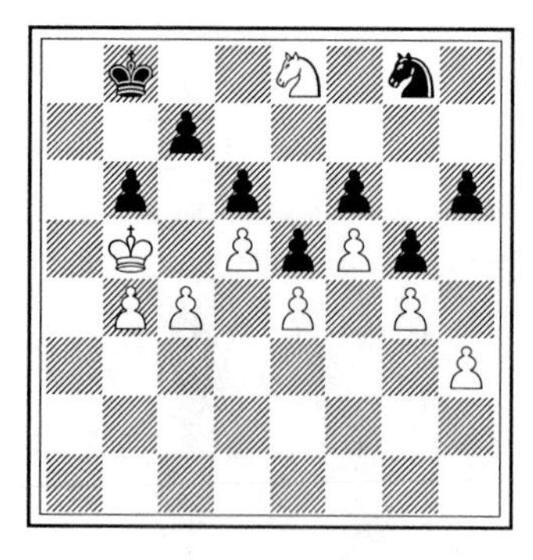

After 59. Kb5

55. ... h6 56. Nh5 Ng8 57. Ng7 Ne7 58. Ne8 Ng8 59. Kb5

Now 59. ... Kb7 60. c5 would decide (60. ... bxc5 61. bxc5 dxc5 62. Kxc5 Kc8 63. d6 cxd6+ 64. Kxd6 Kd8 65. Ng7 Ne7 66. Ke6).

59. ... Kc8

Just before 11 P.M. I went to my office to find another sealed move envelope. Fortunately, there was one on my desk.

I brought it to Krimsditch, and both players got the message that the next move must be sealed. Krimsditch quickly filled out the blanks on the front. Without looking at his opponent, he slid the envelope along the right edge of the table until it was near Van Siclen's left elbow. Then he went back to grimacing at his hopeless position.

It's funny now when I recall the situation. I remember where we were all standing, and how we looked, transfixed, at the board and at Krimsditch's bobbing head. White had a crusher—after 60. N×d6+! he vacuums up the winning pawns with Kc6.

With glacial calm, Van Siclen cupped his left hand around his scoresheet as he recorded his 60th move—a "long" move judging by the motion of his writing hand. Then he put the paper in the envelope, sealed it and handed it to me.

Van Siclen walked away from the board while the rest of us stood behind his chair, calculating the knight sack. I didn't realize what had happened until I heard the thud of Van Siclen's body hitting the stage floor behind me.

Everyone started talking at once. But, of course, no one knew what to say.

A quick inspection showed there was no pulse, nothing in his eyes, no vital signs at all. International Grandmaster Gert Van Siclen was very dead.

It was Bohigian who figured it out.

"The envelope," he sighed. "Poison."

Everyone else looked at him in amazement. Everyone but Krimsditch.

"Serves him right," he sniffed. "Gert cheated."

And I thought to myself: This is becoming a real knockout tournament.

Monday, August 26, 2019

WHAT I FOUND DOWNSTAIRS the next morning could best be described as a grandmaster mutiny. The 12 surviving players had gathered in the Casa lobby. To confront me.

"How could you put the life of the World Champion in danger?" Grushevsky demanded.

The players were waiting, scattered about, as I reached the bottom step of the hotel's main staircase.

"The world only has one champion," Grushevsky said. "One. And you put his life in the hands of a mad killer."

"It's not just Igor," said Bastrikova, standing next to him, at the center of the group. "All of us are at risk."

"Someone who would kill a person as harmless as Gert could kill anyone," said Eichler, to her right.

"You must do something," Popov chimed in.

This wasn't going to be easy.

"Look," I said. "I understand your concern. This is a serious matter. But we need to know more about how Grandmaster Van Siclen died before we take any precipitous action."

"You know more than you're telling," Krimsditch said. "Royce-Smith says you also think Gabor was murdered, and by the same killer."

"And don't forget Daphne," Eichler said.

"Patzers don't count," Vilković mumbled to himself from his seat on the divan.

"What I discussed with Grandmaster Royce-Smith was supposed to be confidential," I said. I glared at the Englishman, who was sitting across the lobby at an oversized coffee table, trying to bury his nose in a Sunday Times double acrostic.

"We devoted some attention to a fanciful theory of his that might explain the deaths of Miss Nardlinger and Grandmaster Gabor," I added. "A theory I'm sure none of you would share."

"Van Siclen's body is no theory," Vilković said.

That was hard to dispute.

"You must do something!" Popov repeated.

"After all, poisoning is illegal," Karlson said.

"Even in New Mexico, it is," Krimsditch said.

I looked from face to face, and saw the kind of incipient panic that drops rooks in time pressure.

"Okay, let's consider our options," I said. "We could, for example, simply cancel the tournament."

"That would be most … unpleasant," Qi said.

"Easy to for you to say," Popov snapped, a none-too-veiled allusion to Qi's perfect score.

"But there are a number of problems with that option," I said. "Starting with the matter of transportation. I arranged for the limousines for your departure to be here on the sixth of next month. Not a day earlier."

It took several seconds before anyone understood what I was saying.

"Surely, there are other ways to get out of Los Voraces," Grushevsky said.

"Yes, there are, several," I said. "It's only ten or so hours to Santa Fe—provided you manage to convince one of the townspeople to drive you."

Even from a distance of seven feet I could see Boriescu's eyes had widened at that.

"Or you could wait for Greyhound. They run on a regular schedule," I said. "The next bus goes to Albuquerque."

"How soon?" Krimsditch and Karlson asked simultaneously.

"Saturday."

Los Voraces was indeed that remote. The situation, as strange as it was, reminded me of old times. Of Lone Pine 1981, to be exact: The night before the first round, Viktor Korchnoi slipped into that tiny California town for the annual GM tournament. This was back in the days when the Soviets were boycotting him because he had defected in '76, and wouldn't play in any event he entered. By the time the Sports Committee *apparatchiks* in Moscow realized they'd been tricked, their two players were already in Lone Pine and there was no way for them to leave Inyo County for a week.

After calling home for instructions, their players reluctantly agreed to play. The result was that Korchnoi ended up scoring a kind of propaganda victory over the U.S.S.R.—at a time when things like that were considered important—by beating one of the Soviets in the seventh round.

Of course, I couldn't admit to Grushevsky that he was more or less a prisoner of Los Voraces. But he was. The others caught on quickly.

"We can't wait until Saturday," Vilković said. "There's no telling how many of us will be left by then."

"*C'est terrible. Tempus fugit*," Boriescu agreed.

At least I think he agreed. Fortunately, I had one ally.

"This isn't helping at all," Bohigian said. "The important thing is to stay calm and let Sheriff Gibbs investigate this matter thoroughly."

Karlson had her own idea: "Or we could catch the murderer ourselves!"

"Right," said Bastrikova, under her breath. "Someone who can't play the Exchange French is going to solve three murders."

"I heard that!" Karlson spat back.

There was one sure way to regain control of this group.

"If it is the wish of the players, we will cancel the tournament," I said. "You will all be invited back next year for another Sheldrake tournament."

"The least you can do," Grushevsky shrugged.

"Of course," I continued, "if this year's Memorial is aborted, it will be as if the tournament had never begun. All your contracts would have to be declared null and void."

"Meaning what?" asked Royce-Smith, suddenly alert.

"Meaning no fees or prize money could be distributed." I let that sink in before continuing. "On the other hand, if we persevered with the tournament, Grandmaster Van Siclen's share would be added to the prize fund. It would … roughly … double it."

Krimsditch was the first to say what I suspected everyone was thinking. "You think you can buy us off to stay here?"

"No, not at all," I lied. "But I think—in fact, I know—that all of you will fulfill your obligations to complete the Memorial. I know you will do this because of your professional integrity and the honorable way in which you will want to resolve our problem and..."

Our problem. That was my point. This was a shared responsibility, not just another trouble for me to make go away.

"...as I'm sure you are all aware, international tournaments have only been suspended in the past due to the outbreak of international hostilities. Even in times of war, there have been tournaments, tournaments that became legends, that continued because of the dedication of the contestants. That's why..."

Vilković was on the verge of interrupting, then realized the mood was softening around him. And he never wanted to be in the minority or, worse, the sole holdout.

"...I know that none of you would want to be associated with the suspension of the Memorial. Quite the opposite, in these trying circumstances I am sure you would want it known that because of your dedication the greatest chess tournament in history continued until its schedule was completed."

Royce-Smith broke the silence that followed. "It would be a shame to waste the four rounds that were played."

"Continuing would ensure that they were rated," Qi said.

"It isn't like this is World War III," Karlson said.

"And if we can't leave town anyway...," Vilković added, leaving the conditional clause hanging in the air.

But Eichler had a question, a good one. "If the tournament goes on, what happens to the schedule?"

I'd anticipated him: "Again, there are various possibilities. We could have a whole new drawing of lots and wipe out all the results so far."

"Clearly, you aren't being serious," Royce-Smith said.

"What's behind door number two?" Krimsditch asked.

"We could stick with the same pairing schedule as before but with two byes," I said.

This brought Klushkov out of his trance. "Bye," he said to himself as he sat in the far corner near the lobby fireplace.

Then, "Bye-bye. Bye-bye!"

Everyone turned to look at him in various degrees of exasperation. But it had no effect.

"Bye-bye!"

Heads shaking, the other players turned away. But this was an opportunity for me. Before anyone could raise another objection, I turned attention back to the pairings, rather than the murders.

"The third possibility is to keep the original draw and, where possible, pair the two players who would have had byes. The only results we would have to cancel would be Van Siclen's."

"And his opponents'," corrected Karlson, who stood to lose the full point she got from the Dutchman in Round Two.

"I'm afraid that is the best solution to our problem," I said.

Again—our problem.

There was another lengthy pause until Qi spoke up. "That might succeed because..."

"...only four rounds have been played," added Krimsditch.

"Everyone would play today," I pointed out.

"If you say so," Karlson said.

"Sounds good," Popov said.

"Works for me," Royce-Smith said.

"*D'accord*," Boriescu said.

"In that case," I said, "I congratulate you all for your generous and forthright decision. See you at the high school at 2."

I watched them file out. The last to go was Bohigian.

"Well, we survived another crisis," I told him. "We might just finish this tournament after all."

He shrugged. "Even that is possible."

What I meant about everyone playing today was this:

SHELDRAKE MEMORIAL
ROUND FIVE PAIRINGS
Popov vs. Vilković
Klushkov vs. Qi
Karlson vs. Boriescu
Eichler vs. Royce-Smith
Krimsditch vs. Bohigian

According to the drawing of lots we made last Wednesday, Grushevsky would have had White against Van Siclen and Bastrikova would have gotten the bye today. Now, with two players free, I simply added a different Board Six pairing:

Grushevsky vs. Bastrikova

What I didn't say earlier, of course, is that this was unique. It would be the only such re-pairing for the rest of the tournament. But for the moment everyone was happy.

Clearly, the Board Two game, between two of the tournament's leaders, was the most important in terms of standings. Grushevsky's game and Bohigian's led the undercard.

On the other hand, one pairing produced something that could hardly be called a game. Less than a minute after the round began, Popov and Vilković submitted their scoresheets. The sheets consisted of just their names, the date, and at the bottom, their signatures and the word "Draw."

"No moves," I observed.

"Very perceptive," Vilković said.

"We believe in absolute honesty," Popov said.

"Anything else would have been deceitful and untrue," Vilković said.

It was hardly original—and wasn't even the first no-move game between these two players. I still didn't like it.

"But you got the date wrong. Both of you. Today is the 26th, not the 25th."

"No, that too is correct," Popov said.

"We agreed to the draw last night," Vilković said.

"That's when we signed the scoresheets." Popov added.

"Exactly as the date says," Vilković said.

On another occasion I would have issued them a warning. Or worse.

The laws of chess give an International Arbiter a menu of six penalties he can invoke in virtually any situation, ranging from subtracting time from an offending player's clock to expelling the wrongdoer from the tournament. But today was not the day to provoke anyone.

"Your devotion to accuracy and integrity will be respected by the entire chess community," I said, and turned around to watch Board Four. That game began:

Eichler–Royce-Smith
Sicilian Defense B29

1. e4 c5 2. Nf3 Nf6 3. e5 Nd5 4. Nc3 e6 5. N×d5 e×d5 6. d4 Nc6

Since 2. … Nf6 came back into fashion six years ago, as an anti-computer weapon, a lot of analytical work had gone into the line. Machines just didn't seem to play well against 4. … N×c3, or against this ancient gambit. Royce-Smith had worked on it and came up with what seemed like a TN, albeit a strange one.

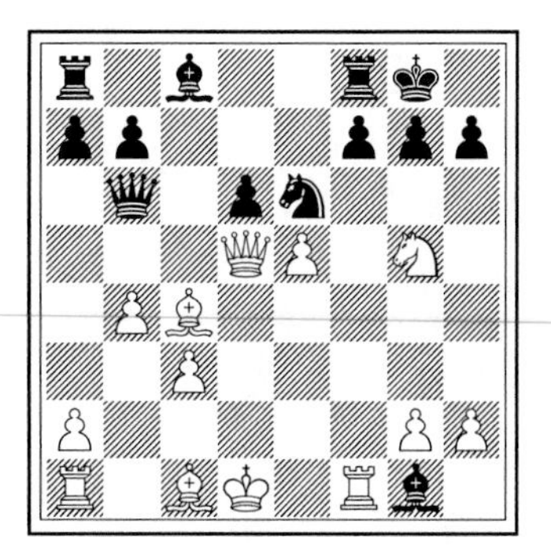

After 15. … Bg1

7. d×c5 B×c5 8. Q×d5 Qb6 9. Bc4 B×f2+ 10. Ke2 0–0 11. Rf1 Bc5 12. Ng5 Nd4+ 13. Kd1 Ne6 14. c3 d6 15. b4 Bg1!?!

The point, incredibly, was to win the h-pawn—16. e×d6 B×h2 (17. d7 B×d7 18. Q×d7? Rad8).

The tactics all seem to work in Black's favor, such as in 16. R×f7? R×f7 17. N×f7 K×f7 18. e×d6 Bd7 19. Qf5+ Ke8 20. B×e6 Q×d6+.

16. Qe4

In the post-mortem, Popov claimed this had all been refuted 60 years ago by 16. Nf3, e.g. 16. … Bf2 17. Qd2 or 16. … Be3 17. e×d6 or 16. … Rd8 17. Kc2.

But Royce-Smith showed him that 16. … d×e5, threatening 17. … Rd8, was a sufficient reply. For example, 17. Q×e5 Qd8+ and the bishop escapes the trap with 18. … Bb6. Or 17. Kc2 Be3.

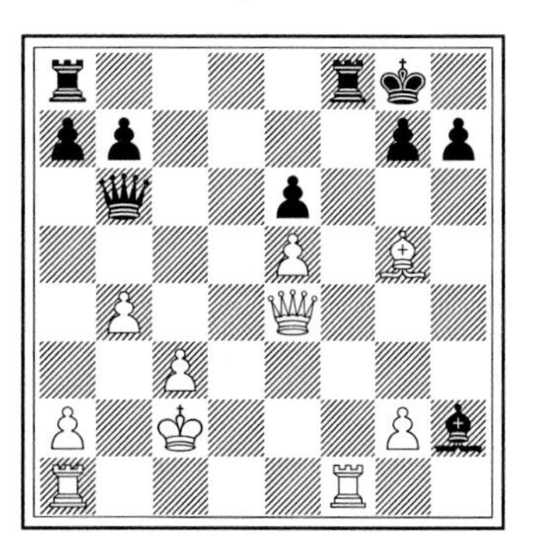

After 20. … B×h2

16. … N×g5 17. B×g5 d5! 18. B×d5 Be6

This forces a trade that exposes White's many weaknesses, e.g. 19. Kc2 B×d5 20. Q×d5 Qg6+ 21. Kb3 Q×g5 22. R×g1 Rfd8 23. Qe4 a5.

19. B×e6 f×e6 20. Kc2 B×h2!

While Eichler was thinking, I realized we had a new spectator. Gibbs, of all people, stood at the end of the stage.

"Sudden interest in chess, Sheriff?"

"Sudden interest in chessplayers. You got a second?"

"Always happy to cooperate with the law. But I can't be away from the boards for long."

"This'll take but minutes."

"Okay. I'll even show you my fine office."

Once inside the office, Gibbs put on his professional face, which was just a bit less smile than usual.

"I think we started tracking the wrong bear yesterday," he said.

"Yesterday?"

"Yesterday in *my* office, when we talked about suspects. Maybe it's time we began considering victims."

"Now that we have three of them," I said.

"Maybe three, maybe just one. I'm not convinced about the first two. But for the sake of argument, let's say three. The question is: Why them?"

"What do you mean?"

"I mean, if someone were to pick three people to send to their eternal reward, he wouldn't do it randomly. Who stands to profit from their deaths? What's the connection?"

At least the sheriff was taking it a lot more seriously than two days ago. I began to think out loud.

"Okay, two of the victims were players. Nothing conclusive there."

Gibbs wrote something in his blue notebook as I continued:

"In a way Krimsditch had the most to gain by Van Siclen's death."

"Because?"

"Because his position was absolutely busted when Gert keeled over yesterday. Krimsditch's impending loss was wiped out, along with all of Van Siclen's previous games."

"Go on."

"Another thing to consider is the financial incentive. I explained to the players on Wednesday that because of Gabor's death there would be a huge increase in prizes."

"How so?"

"Well, the big money in this tournament was supposed to be the appearance fees, not the prizes. Nothing unusual there. These days GMs don't get paid for performance, but rather for attendance."

He raised his eyebrows at that, but I went on:

"Gabor's fee and Van Siclen's were substantial, so when they died, the money went into the prize fund and more than tripled it."

"Which means the likely winner is a suspect," Gibbs said.

"Not just the winner. Every prize would be increased. Everybody stood to gain."

"I see: Fewer players, bigger slices of the pie."

"Precisely—as Vilković would say. But there's a problem with this motive."

"What?"

"It doesn't apply to Daphne. She wasn't a player."

"Then why would someone want her dead?" Gibbs asked.

"That's the question. Oh, she was annoying enough. But..."

"But what?"

"But it's time to do my job."

It was 3:30 P.M., time to make my half-hourly tour of the stage, to check the clocks, acquaint myself with the positions and head off any incidents before they occurred.

This was turning out to be one of the more interesting rounds. Krimsditch's luck wasn't improving. He should have lost yesterday, of course, and today he met Bohigian on one of his ambitious afternoons. I wasn't shedding any tears.

Krimsditch–Bohigian
Bogo-Indian Defense E11

1. d4 Nf6 2. c4 e6 3. Nf3 Bb4+ 4. Bd2 Qe7 5. g3 B×d2+ 6. Nb×d2 d6 7. Bh3

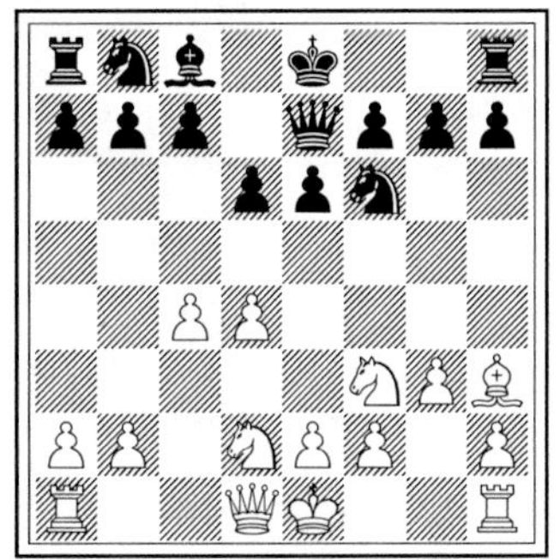

After 7. Bh3

Novelty? Krimsditch wouldn't say, and Bohigian didn't seem to know when I asked later. It was an odd position for a TN to appear—this was only the seventh move and the position was as dry as Tuesday's burrito. But Bohigian went into a long think here.

7. ... Nbd7 8. 0–0 h5!

Here's what he found, the one reason the bishop is misplaced at h3. White can't stop ...h4.

9. e4 Ng4

Among the tricks at Black's disposal is 10. ... e5 and 11. ... Ndf6, threatening ...N×f2.

10. Ne1 e5!

And this makes Bohigian's eighth move work tactically: If White grabs the pawn with 11. B×g4 h×g4 12. Q×g4, Black has a surprisingly strong 12. ... Nf8!.

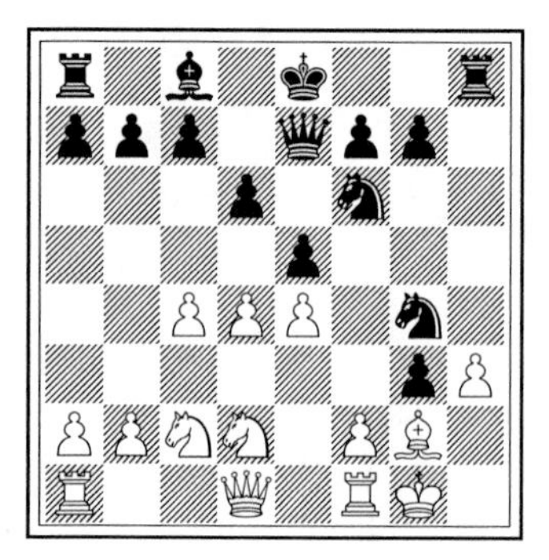

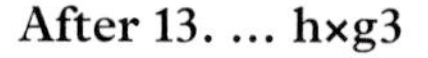

The point is that anything but 13. Q×g7 allows Black to reestablish material equality—but with a positional edge—after 13. ... e×d4.

And 13. Q×g7? turns out to be a blunder that traps the queen after 13. ... Rh7 14. Qg8 Qf6.

11. Nc2 Ndf6

Now 12. Qe2 h4 13. f3 walks into 13. ... h×g3! 14. B×g4 R×h2.

12. Bg2 h4 13. h3 h×g3!

Here White had to try 14. h×g4 and live with what happens after 14. ... g×f2+ 15. R×f2 B×g4 16. Bf3. But after a long study of the position, Krimsditch's memory betrayed him.

Not his memory of theory. No, it was his recollection of his three previous games with Bohigian. He remembered them *too* well. Each time he lost he was crushed by a kingside attack. Despite his public comments about Bohigian being over the hill, he had developed an almost paralyzing fear of being mated by him.

14. f×g3? Nh6 15. d5

Also bad were 15. d×e5 Q×e5 and 15. Ne3 e×d4 16. Nf5 B×f5 17. e×f5 Qe3+.

15. ... Bd7 16. Ne3 g6

Played not just to stop Nf5 but to support ...Nh5!.

17. g4 Nh7!

If Krimsditch had realized he was positionally lost, he surely would have played something like 18. c5!? d×c5 19. d6! and then 19. … Q×d6 20. Ndc4.

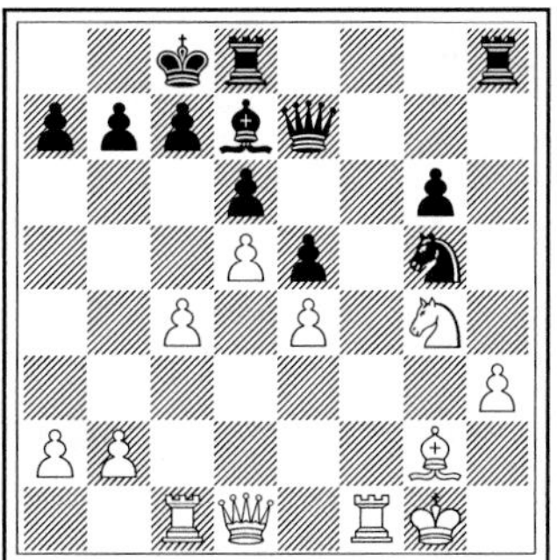
Final position

18. Nf3 0–0–0 19. Rc1 f5!

Now 20. e×f5 g×f5 21. g×f5 N×f5 22. N×f5 B×f5 23. Kh2 Rdg8 followed by …R×g2+ or …Ng5 will not keep the game going on for very long. Krimsditch decided to try to keep the g- and h-files at least half-closed.

20. Nh2 f×g4 21. Ne×g4 N×g4 22. N×g4 Ng5 White resigns

"Already?" Bastrikova asked Bohigian moments after Krimsditch stopped his clock and walked off.

"The frightened crow is afraid of the bush," Bohigian said.

"But if he plays rook to c3?" she asked.

"Then I win with rook to h4, followed by doubling on the file. He can't stop bishop takes g4 and queen to h7. Then rook h1 check must win."

Zhenya nodded in agreement. Impressive as that was, the star move of the day had already been played in the showcase pairing:

Klushkov–Qi
Guioco Piano C53

1. e4 e5 2. Nf3 Nc6 3. Bb5 Bc5 4. c3 Nf6 5. d4 Bb6 6. Bg5 e×d4!?

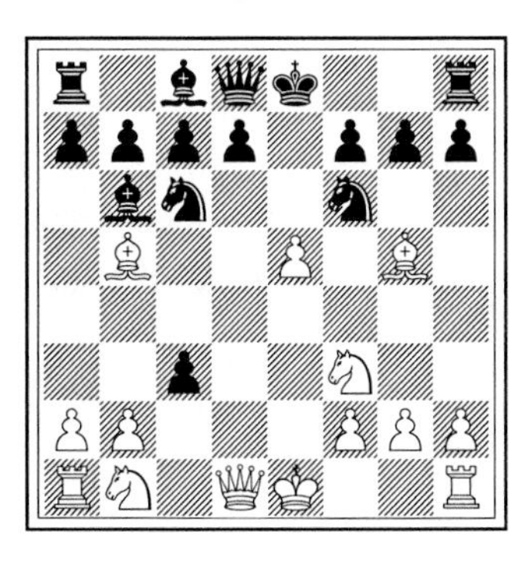
After 7. … d×c3

All I remembered about "book" was that 6. … h6 and the Giuoco-like 6. … Qe7 were played.

7. e5 d×c3!

A daring idea based on:

8. e×f6 c×b2 9. Qe2+ Qe7!

A stunning reply—but quite good. Black surely didn't like the looks of 9. … Kf8 10. f×g7+ K×g7 and then 11. Q×b2+ f6 12. 0–0. Now he must win material.

For the first time in the tournament, Klushkov was in deep trouble. He lay his head down on the scoresheet side of the board and closed his eyes for 15 minutes before continuing:

10. f×e7 b×a1(Q) 11. 0–0 Nd4! 12. N×d4 Q×d4 13. Nd2 c6 14. Nf3 Qc5 15. Bd3 f6 16. Qb2 K×e7

After a brief look at the other boards to make sure the clock times were right—and taking an extra minute to appreciate Karlson's sacrifices and to evaluate Eichler's endgame chances, which were anemic—I went in search of Gibbs.

He was still in my office. I found him bent over the desk, browsing through last year's bulletins, as well as discreetly rifling through the printouts of my notes for the tournament book. I cleared my throat to announce my arrival. He looked up, unembarrassed.

"Sheriff, it occurred to me there are other explanations for Daphne. At least three of them."

"I'm all ears."

"It could be that she was killed because of what she knew or saw. Maybe she found out something about Gabor's death."

"But she wasn't even in town until two days after the event."

Obvious as that was, I hadn't considered it.

"That reminds me," he added. "I'm going to have to check the time when each of your players arrived here. And you said something about two other possibilities."

"Right. The second is that Daphne's death was intended to mislead us."

"How?"

"So it wouldn't look like a pattern. You're the expert here, Sheriff. Wouldn't you agree that criminals are creatures of habit?"

He smiled. "If they weren't we wouldn't catch so many of 'em."

I wondered if he'd ever captured one of them. But what I said was: "Then maybe our murderer is following a pattern. He's targeting the players, all right. But he's also smart enough to break the pattern with Daphne to throw us off."

While he weighed that in his mind, I offered my third idea.

"And it could also be that Daphne was an accident."

"I thought you didn't believe in accidents," the sheriff said.

"No, I mean, it was an accident that she died. I know this is a bit of stretch, but the intended target could have been Eichler."

"Because?"

"Because they were spending time together. We can assume he gave her some things to carry in her handbag. Maybe the killer thought Eichler would reach into it and be the one to come out with a coral snake."

"I think you're right," Gibbs said.

"I am?"

"About that being a stretch."

I had to break away again when Cel Sims stepped into the office.

"Mrs. N neeeeds you," he said.

I had left my assistant in charge but it was time to relieve her.

When I got back to the stage I found Mrs. Nagle watching Board Two, where a series of moves had transformed the position. Klushkov had simply blitzed off his moves. And this unnerved Qi, who matched Klushkov move for move—at considerable expense to his position.

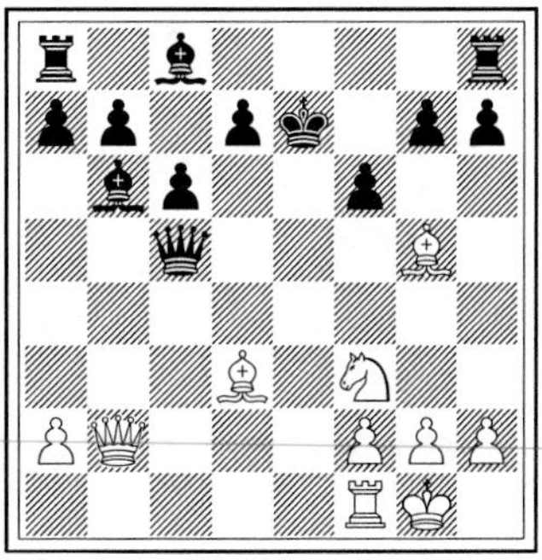

Klushkov–Qi
After 16. ... K×e7

Klushkov–Qi

17. Be3 Qh5? 18. Qa3+ c5 19. Re1 Kd8 20. Rb1 Bc7?

After several years of seeing him up front, I could make an educated guess: Qi would never be world champion. Like Geller and Tarrasch, he was too much the perfectionist.

Qi wanted to play flawless chess—not appreciating how many mistakes the tournament winner makes in the course of a tournament. Here he was being super-cautious, when moves such as 20. ... Kc7 (21. R×b6 K×b6 22. Nd2 d6) needed to be tried.

21. B×c5 Re8 22. Rc1 Re6 23. h3 b6 24. Be3 Bb7 25. Nd4

Now 25. ... Re8 26. Nb5 looked tricky (26. ... Be5 27. N×a7).

25. ... R×e3?! 26. f×e3 Qe8 27. Bf5 g6

Klushkov wrote down his reply then put his pen down horizontally to covered it. After a minute he shook his head, crossed out his move and wrote down another. And played:

28. R×c7! K×c7 29. Nb5+ Kd8 30. Nd6 Qf8

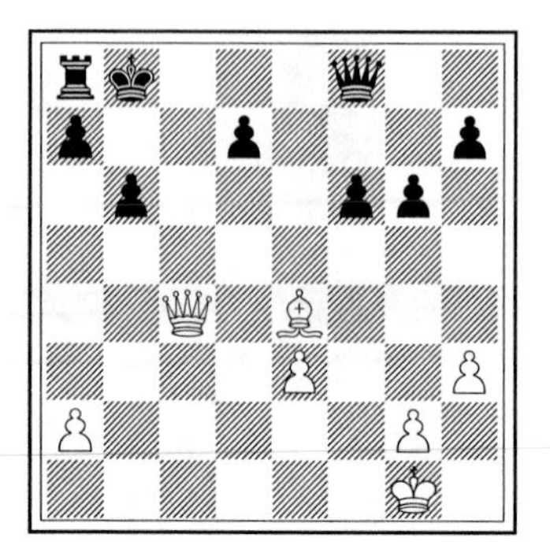

After 34. Qc4

Black would find himself in trouble after, say, 30. ... Qg8 (not 30. ... Qe5?? 31. Nf7+) 31. N×b7+ Kc7? 32. Qd6+!.

31. N×b7+ Kc7

Another pause from Klushkov, who crossed out two moves before making his final decision.

32. Qc3+! K×b7 33. Be4+ Kb8 34. Qc4!

It was absolute alchemy the way Klushkov had recovered—and was now playing for a win (35. Qd5).

34. ... a5 35. B×a8 K×a8 36. Qa6+ Kb8 37. Q×b6+ Kc8 38. Q×a5 Qd6

But the alchemist soon ran out of toadstools and potions, and his position fizzled out to a draw.

39. Qa8+ Kc7 40. Qa7+ Kc8 Draw

This time Klushkov remained at the board after the handshake. Even when Qi was gone he sat huddled over the table, with his long arms wrapped around the right side. I could see from the way he shielded his scoresheet that his pen was working furiously.

"Nikolai, I need the original," I said.

He continued to write.

"With your signature."

Still no response.

"Please, Grandmaster Klushkov, you know the scoresheets are the sole property of the tournament. That's been the standard practice at international events for decades, and I'm afraid I'm going to have to insist that this time is no exception because—

Suddenly Klushkov's head jerked up and his back straightened. His right hand and pen disappeared into one pants pocket, his left hand went into another. He rose from his chair, turned his back and loped off the stage.

I looked at the scoresheet he left. It was spotless.

The headline for the fourth hour was that Eichler was in trouble. You could tell by the way he was thinking at the board, hands pressed against the sides of his face. Or you could tell by the way Royce-Smith paced the back of the stage, with his arms folded across his chest, looking just like Petrosian did when he was more than pleased with his position.

Unfortunately for White, 21. Rh1 allows 21. ... Qf2+ and 22. ... Qf5, among other things.

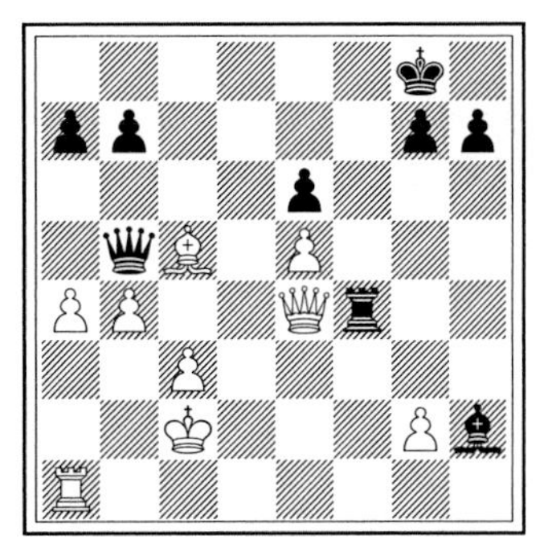

Eichler–Royce-Smith
After 24. a4

Eichler–Royce-Smith

21. Be3 Qb5 22. Rxf8+ Rxf8 23. Bc5 Rf4! 24. a4!?

Eichler found a way to reach the endgame—

24. ... Qxa4+ 25. Rxa4 Rxe4 26. Rxa7 b5 27. Rb7 Bxe5 28. Rxb5 Rc4

—but it was a bad endgame. He had counted on 29. Bd4 Bxd4 30. Kd3. Now when he looked at the position he realized there were no good moves after 30. ... Rxc3+ 31. Kxd4 Rg3.

29. Kd3 Rxc3+ 30. Ke4 Bf6 31. Rb8+ Kf7 32. Bd6 h5 33. b5 Kg6 34. b6 Rb3 35. Bc7

A win, especially with Black, would be a godsend to Royce-Smith, who would move ahead in the race for first. The addition of Van Siclen's fee pushed the top prize to nearly $400,000. That's serious lunch money.

And a loss by Eichler would be his first in 78 games, dating back to early 2017. It would cost him a chance to break Tal's non-losing record of 95 games. Eichler, who hadn't had much experience playing out bad endings against GMs in his brief international career, clearly didn't look happy.

But Grushevsky did. The world champion jumped back into the fight for first with a polished performance.

Grushevsky–Bastrikova
Czech Defense B07

1. e4 d6 2. d4 Nf6 3. Nc3 c6 4. f4 Qa5 5. e5 Ne4 6. Bd3 Nxc3 7. Qd2!?

This was a rare move but no surprise to Bastrikova. In fact, Zhenya and Grushevsky knew each other's secrets too well. They'd been a romantic item for ten years, off and on. They kept breaking up, say at a Wijk aan Zee, and then reconciling a month later at Linares. By now they were like an old married couple. The only thing they argued about was the soundness of the Poisoned Pawn Variation.

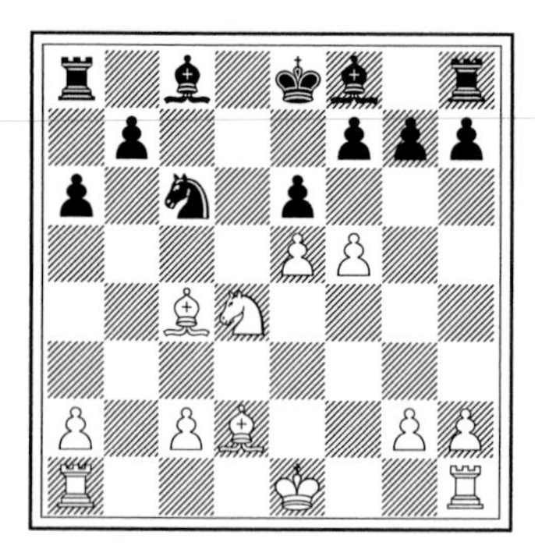

After 14. ... Nc6

7. ... e6 8. b×c3 c5 9. Ne2 d5 10. c4! Q×d2+ 11. B×d2 d×c4 12. B×c4 c×d4

Nobody liked this in the post-mortem. The consensus move was 12. ... Nc6.

13. N×d4 a6 14. f5 Nc6?

Black avoids 14. ... exf5 15. e6 but steps into something much worse.

15. f×e6! N×d4 16. e×f7+ Kd7 17. 0–0–0! Kc6 18. Be3 Nf5?

This had to be wrong. Black must blockade the e-pawn with 18. ... Ne6 19. Bd5+ Kc7.

19. Bd5+ Kc7 20. Bf4

No stopping the pawns now. For example, 20. ... Kb6 21. e6 Bd6? 22. B×d6 N×d6 23. e7 and White is winning.

20. ... Ba3+ 21. Kb1 a5?!

Black hoped to activate her rook along the third rank—but White carried out the idea first on his side of the board. Better was 21. ... Bc5 22. e6+ Kb6.

22. Rd3! Bc5 23. g4

The beginning of the end. White's pawns are an avalanche.

23. ... Ne7 24. e6+ Kb6 25. Rb3+ Bb4 26. c4! Ng6 27. Bd6 Ka7 28. c5!

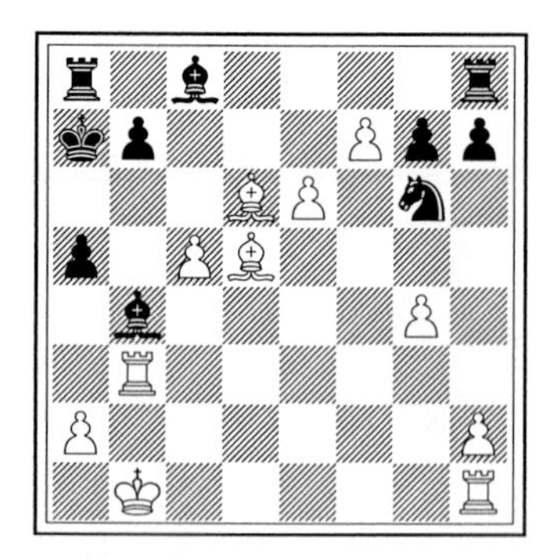

After 28. c5

28. ... Black resigns

While this was going on, Mrs. Nagle handed me a cryptic note: "Call Mr. Schultheiss in E O L," it said with a phone number.

E O L? It took a moment to realize it stood for Endoline.

I made the call behind the closed door of my office. Shultheiss, the chemist, had preliminary results.

"Looked a lot like Drogistal. Even fooled me at first sight—and I know Drogistal," he told me.

"But?"

"But anyone taking it would be making a nasty mistake. This here's Xylot-B."

"Never heard of it."

"You wouldn't, unless you were warned about it. Powerful stuff. Reacts badly with any kind of anti-hypertension drug."

"Reacts how?"

"Messes up your heart rhythm something awful. Eventually triggers a coronary. If you've got even a tiny residue of Drogistal in your system, taking one of these pills would be like swallowing a slow-acting time bomb."

"You're sure?"

"110 percent."

That gave me what I wanted to hear.

"One more thing and I'll get out of your life," I said. "I'd appreciate it if you'd keep this just between the two of us."

"Sure. I've been dealing with people from the Valley for years."

"I'm not certain how to take that," I said.

"It's no insult. It's just that people from your town like to keep their little secrets. A very tight little community."

No disputing that.

"I've noticed they're a bit, shall we say ... insular," I said.

"Insular?" he replied. "You coulda had a full-scale invasion of the town from Pluto—and no one outside of Los Voraces would know about it for years."

I thanked Schultheiss and returned to the auditorium, where the best game of the day was wrapping up. It had begun with a deft treatment of the Winawer.

Karlson–Boriescu
French Defense C19

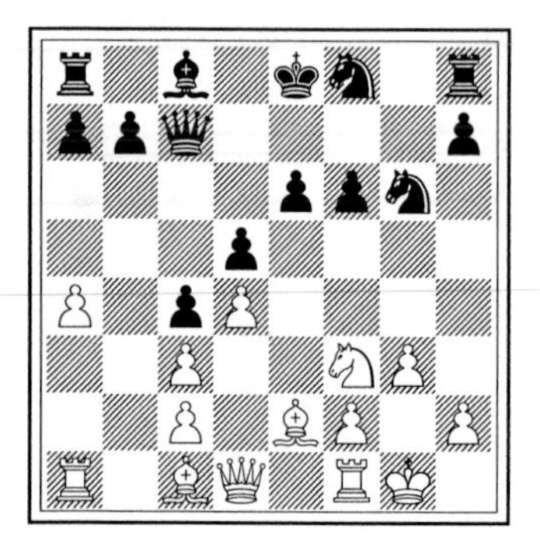

After 13. ... Ndf8

1. e4 e6 2. d4 d5 3. Nc3 Bb4 4. e5 c5 5. a3 B×c3+ 6. b×c3 Qc7 7. a4 Ne7 8. Nf3 Nd7!? 9. Bd3 c4 10. Be2 f6

It was Boriescu who brought this move back into fashion, with his win over Krilinsky at Madrid 2017. Karlson had an improvement.

11. e×f6 g×f6 12. 0–0 Ng6 13. g3 Ndf8

"Something must be wrong if Black has to play this," Bohigian said in the post-mortem.

14. Bh6 Rg8 15. Qd2 Bd7 16. h4! 0–0–0 17. h5 Nh8

"Very wrong," he added.

18. Bf4 Qc6 19. Rfb1 Be8 20. Nh2! Nd7 21. Qe3

White neatly works against the three targets, e6, f6 and b7. For example, 21. ... Bf7 22. Rb5 Rde8 23. Ng4 and White threatens 24. N×f6! N×f6 25. Rc5.

But the irony was that she wins the game by capturing on Black's strong point, c4.

21. ... Nf7 22. Ng4 Nh8 23. Rb5!

Again with the idea of 24. N×f6 N×f6 25. Rc5.

23. ... b6 24. Rb4!

You could tell Boriescue knew what was coming next. But he couldn't figure out a safe way to avoid it. For example, 24. ... Kb7 walks into 25. R×c4! d×c4 26. Bf3.

24. ... B×h5 25. R×c4! d×c4 26. Bf3

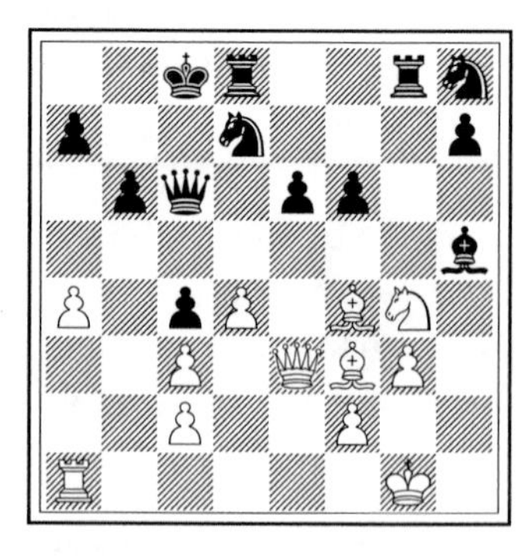

After 26. Bf3

A remarkable trap of the queen. It looks like Black will end up with a lot of wood as compensation but Karlson's combination had several moves to go before it was done. If now 26. ... Qd5 27. Bxd5 exd5 White wins with 28. Qe6! and Qc6+.

26. ... e5 27. Bxc6 exf4 28. Qe6! Rxg4

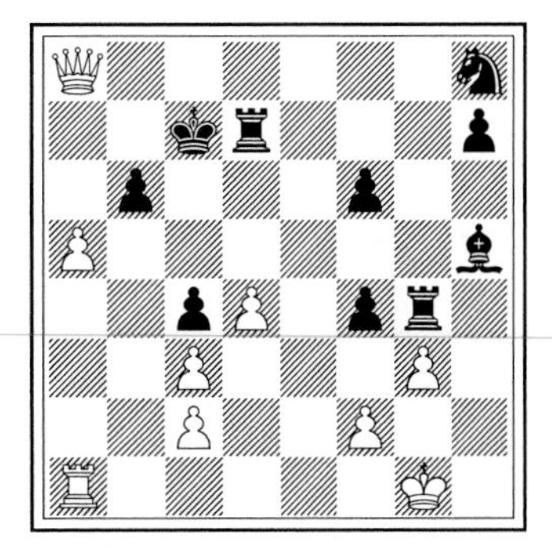

Final position

Or 28. ... Bxg4 29. Bxd7+ Rxd7? 30. Qxg8+ and 29. ... Kc7 30. Qc6+ Kb8 31. Bxg4 Rxg4 (else 32. Bf3) 32. a5! and wins.

29. Bxd7+ Rxd7

And here 29. ... Kc7 30. a5! Rxd7 31. axb6+ would have been a neat finish.

30. Qc6+ Kd8 31. Qa8+ Kc7 32. Qxa7+! Kc6 33. Qa8+ Kc7

34. a5! Black resigns

Either the a-pawn or the entrance of the rook into the attack will decide matters quickly.

There wasn't much to the fifth hour today. Bohigian, Karlson and Boriescu post-mortemed for less than half an hour, and Grushevsky and Bastrikova were long gone by 6:30. Only one game was still alive, Eichler vs. Royce-Smith. It could have a big impact on first prize. Nonetheless there were only three of us on the stage—or in the building for that matter—after Sims left and I gave Mrs. Nagle a "good night."

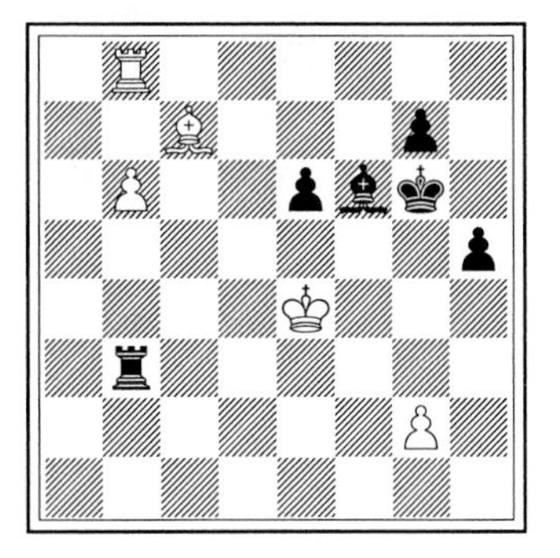

Eichler–Royce-Smith
After 35. Bc7

Black was nursing his extra pawn and ready to bring his king into play

Eichler–Royce-Smith

35. ... Rb4+ 36. Kf3 Kf5 37. Ra8 Rb3+ 38. Ke2 Bd4 39. Rf8+ Ke4 40. Rf4+ Kd5 41. Rh4 g6 42. g4 Rb2+

Eichler was going downhill quickly. Either player could adjourn now but it was as if they both understood they were following a script. White had to continue playing until defeat was obvious. Black had to keep him company.

43. Kd1 Bf6 44. Rh3 h×g4 45. Rg3 Rb4 46. Rd3+ Bd4 and White resigns

Gibbs had left more than an hour before, and I was bit surprised to see him back on the stage at 7:15, while I was alone, posting the standings.

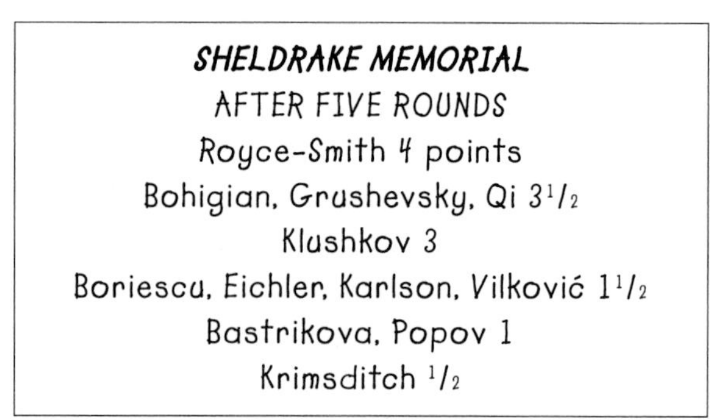
SHELDRAKE MEMORIAL
AFTER FIVE ROUNDS
Royce-Smith 4 points
Bohigian, Grushevsky, Qi 3½
Klushkov 3
Boriescu, Eichler, Karlson, Vilković 1½
Bastrikova, Popov 1
Krimsditch ½

"Any other, uh, explanations come to mind?" he asked.

"One more occurred to me."

"What?"

"Suppose it was Van Siclen that was an accident. The killer couldn't have been sure that he'd end up with the poison last night."

"I'm *still* trying to understand this sealed-move business," Gibbs said with a look of mild disgust. "You mean the guy he was playing might have had to lick the envelope instead of him?"

"Not just him," I replied. "There was a second game last night."

"Uh, huh."

"Qi and Bastrikova. Either of them might have adjourned for a second time after move 56."

"So what?"

"So this: The killer couldn't have been certain that when I brought the envelope from my office I'd be giving it to Van Siclen—and not to one of three other people."

"Unless the killer is a lot smarter than we're giving him credit for."

"Or giving her."

"I stand corrected," he said.

After a long pause I said: "You're right. It could be just about anyone."

"In any case I'll need to pursue this a lot more. Might have more information tomorrow."

"Thanks, Sheriff, I really appreciate that."

"Just doing God's work."

As he left, I took stock. In a way, it had been a good day: I'd prevented a player's revolt. I learned that I had Gibbs' serious involvement in the investigation. And I found out from the phone call that Gabor's pills had been switched—almost certainly by his murderer.

On the other hand...

My talk with the sheriff showed how little we knew about which player—if any—was the killer. Or maybe there was more than one killer? Working together. Or independently.

As Bohigian had said, even that was possible.

Tuesday, August 27, 2019

DURING AN INTERNATIONAL TOURNAMENT, time often passes at the rate of dog years. One week with grandmasters can seem like seven weeks with other people.

That may be why it felt like an eternity since I'd arrived in town. Yet in seven days I hadn't been able to narrow the pool of suspects.

I couldn't even rule out Los Voraces' occasional transients—whose number grew by one today: Boyd Blair. The pride and sorrow of East 93rd Street, Manhattan, arrived in town just after 1 P.M.

"Rejoice! I'm here." Blair called out from across Main Street when he spotted me outside the Casa. "I've come to rescue your tournament!"

"We were doing fine without you, Boyden," I said. He hated when I used his real first name.

"It may be 'fine'—but it's not great," Blair said as he strode toward me.

Blair styled himself "The Impresario of Chess" and tried to live the part. Even in this heat he was wearing his trademark beige seersucker suit and pink lapel carnation.

"I've come at considerable effort, not to say discomfort. You don't know what it's like to sit in front of a 75-gallon hydraulic tank for 13 hours from Tulsa."

Blair, it turned out, had shared the cab of a diesel fuel truck making its monthly delivery to Silas Beadle's service station on the outskirts of town.

"I'd find another vacation planner if I were you," I said.

He ignored that and grabbed my reluctant hand to shake.

"But my suffering is immaterial," he said. "There is work to be done. Grand work."

At 46 he'd lost most of his reddish-blond hair but none of his seventh-grade enthusiasm. I remembered how much I hated him.

"What did you have in mind?"

"I want to build on, to enlarge, amplify and augment what you've done so far," he said. "And I must say I admire what you've accomplished. Even I never booked the 14 strongest players in the world."

"Thank you."

"When I realized the Elo top 14 were missing in action, I did a little investigating and discovered they were all here," he said. "And now I've come to save the day."

"We were doing fine without you, Boyden."

By now Blair, 6 feet tall and 230 pounds, was dripping with sweat. But he was just getting started.

"You don't know the opportunity you're wasting. I have several ideas that will bring this tournament to a much, much larger audience—a minimum of 300 million payable accounts."

"I don't think..."

"Ah, but you must think! *Think* of how this tournament can honor the heritage of chess. We owe it to history to do this, to the memory of Steinitz and Lasker, to Kasparov and Kramnik, to Alekhine and ... that Dutch guy."

As Blair frothed on, we were joined on the sidewalk by Gibbs. He studied Blair's attire, then cocked a squinting eye at me that asked, "Is he for real?"

"We must enhance the tournament's achievement," Blair said. "To make it mythic. Homeric! To make it positively Pantheonic."

He broke out of his reverie when he noticed Gibbs's star badge.

"Ah, you must be the chief law enforcement officer of this town. And, I assume, one of its principal civic leaders. I am Boyd Blair. No doubt you've heard of me."

Gibbs just blinked.

"We need to discuss the necessary changes in your quaint municipality," Blair said.

"Town doesn't like changes," Gibbs said.

"But it needs them. Take the name: 'Los Voraces.' That simply won't do."

Before Gibbs could protest, Blair cut him off with a sharp shake of the head.

"To market this product to the satellite networks and pay-per-click websites we're going to have to rename the town something more electric. More dramatic. More bankable."

"It's been Los Voraces since the conquistadors," Gibbs said.

But Blair had closed his eyes to concentrate. The sheriff and I exchanged shrugs. After a moment Blair opened his eyes wide.

"I've got it. We'll rename the town New Chess. The tournament will be called 'New Chess, New Mex, 2019.' It works. It sings!"

Gibbs shifted his glance back and forth between me and Blair as Blair began to speak quickly.

"I see an underlying theme here. It's ... *The Duel to the Death ... in the Desert.* The gladiators of cerebral combat meet in the wilderness for battle royale. Intellectual Armageddon in the sand dunes! It'll be guaranteed a 45 TV share in North America, and a 50 in Europe, plus 60 million 'Net hits a day. We'll need camera crews and electronic displays. Demo boards with 3-D computer graphics. Player closeups after every move! Monitors with their pulse rates and EEG readouts to document the stress and strain."

He raced on: "Naturally, we'll have to tear up this street to plant the cables. At least 40 tech people, lighting guys, grips, gaffers, everything. I can get them all here by Sunday. Monday at the latest."

Gibbs was looking more uncomfortable by the second. But Blair was just gaining momentum.

"Of course, we'll have to postpone the remaining rounds until then. But that will only serve to build up suspense and enhance the creative tension. We can turn it into a quadruple-round match-tournament. Lasting until November!"

He was having a kind of chess promoter's orgasm.

"We'll have lots of commercial tie-ins. Boards with the tournament insignia. A 'New Chess, New Mex' videogame. Grandmaster action figures! A 900 telephone number so viewers can vote on who they think will take first prize. Autographed T-shirts with a photo of Grushevsky on it. Better yet, Grushevsky and me."

There was no stopping him now.

"Yes, and 'Guess Like a Grandmaster.' That's what I'll call our Internet contest. The mouse potatoes will place bets that they can predict the next move played on each board."

Gibbs had closed his eyes. Blair took no notice.

"We'll post odds: 3-to-1 if you get Bohigian's move right but 5-to-1 for Royce-Smith's. Yeah, and at least 20-to-1 for guessing Klushkov's. Well have cash payouts, plus a grand prize—100 free Elo points—for most correct guesses. It will bring in millions."

Blair's voice resonated as he headed for a big finish.

"And I want to get the President and the Pope to attend the closing ceremony. Maybe also King Charles and what's-his-face from the Kremlin. We'll have marching bands, fireworks, Elvis look-alikes. *Everything!*"

I could tell Gibbs was waiting to make sure Blair was done.

"Well, you got one thing right," he said.

"Which one?"

"The 'Duel to the Death,'" I said.

Blair squinted at the two of us in the bright sunlight.

"What are you ... talking about?"

"Your gladiators are dropping like flies," Gibbs said.

"Dead flies," I added.

"*What?*"

"Welcome to Los Voraces, Mr. Blair," the sheriff said.

It was already 1:40, so I left Gibbs to explain the history of the past week to Blair. By the time I reached the high school I found Bastrikova and Eichler waiting in the lobby with a petition. Nine of the players signed it, asking me to cancel the free day scheduled for tomorrow if there were no adjournments.

"Daphne couldn't get even one signature on her petition," I said.

"We asked nicely," Eichler said.

"I know it took more than that," I said. "It's hard to get nine players to agree that the sun is shining."

Bastrikova looked out the window to check.

"I'll get you an answer to your petition by the end of the day," I added.

They really did want to get out of town quickly. So did I. But the issue would be moot if we ended up with three games headed for move 100.

Of course, you could never tell in advance which games would adjourn once, let alone twice. And there were no obvious candidates on today's schedule:

SHELDRAKE MEMORIAL
ROUND SIX PAIRINGS
Vilković vs. Karlson
Qi vs. Popov
Bastrikova vs. Klushkov
Boriescu vs. Eichler
Royce-Smith vs. Krimsditch
Bohigian vs. Grushevsky

The seventh board would have been Gabor versus Van Siclen. But they would be sharing a different venue today.

Within the first ten minutes, the Board Three game took a strange turn:

Bastrikova–Klushkov
Sicilian Defense B72

1. e4 c5 2. Nf3 d6 3. d4 cxd4 4. Nxd4 Nf6 5. Nc3 g6 6. Be2 Bg7 7. Be3 0–0 8. Nb3 Nc6 9. f4

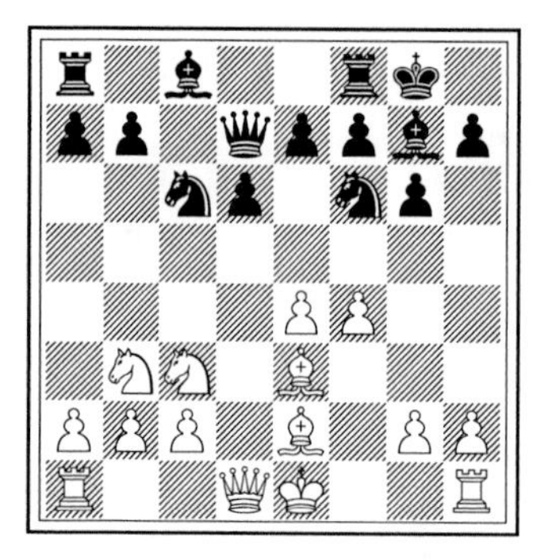

After 9. ... Qd7

I could never figure out if Klushkov's opening moves came from within him or from some bizarre form of divine inspiration. It sometimes seemed as if he was just a vessel through which Caissa was imparting theoretical novelties to the chess world. Whatever the source, Klushkov regularly came up with moves no one else would consider. Such as:

9. ... Qd7!?

At moments like this, I'd learned to look at the position with the eyes of a 1600-player and ask 1600-rated questions: What in God's name did Black's move do?

It stops 10. g4, of course. And it threatens to mess up White's development with ...Ng4. But there had to be something else. Even Klushkov wouldn't play a move like ...Qd7 without a tactical trick, or two, behind it.

Bastrikova, who was the rare left-handed player, reached across the front of her rust-brown blouse to push the h2-pawn one square. She stopped—and looked sharply at her opponent.

Then I saw it, too: On 10. h3 Black has 10. ... Qe6!, attacking the e-pawn. If White protects with 11. Bf3 Black complicates favorably with 11. ... N×e4! 12. B×e4 B×c3+ or 12. N×e4 f5.

After 10 minutes, Bastrikova chose

10. Qd2 Qe6 11. Bf3

and everything seemed in order. White would castle next and begin harassing the Black queen. But:

11. ... Ng4 12. Bg1 B×c3!

Bastrikova hadn't expected this. Hard to believe—but all of a sudden she had the worst of it.

13. Q×c3 f5!

Now 14. h3 Nf6 or 14. B×g4 f×g4 15. Qe3 Qf6! were clearly bad for White.

There comes a point when a player, even a grandmaster, realizes that normal moves have betrayed them, normal chess just doesn't seem to be working that day. That explains:

14. e5!? d×e5 15. Nc5 Qf6 16. N×b7

White was gambling now. It might pay off after 16. ... B×b7 17. Qb3+.

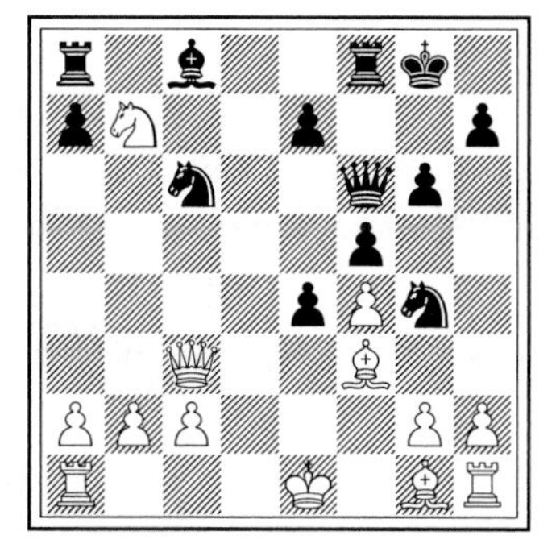

After 16. ... e4

16. ... e4!

Bastrikova went into a 38-minute huddle. But there was no salvation in 17. B×g4 Q×c3+ 18. b×c3 B×b7 or 17. Qc4+ Rf7 18. B×g4 Q×b2!. She never knew what hit her.

While this was going on, I noticed Blair standing behind the Qi–Popov board. He was starting in already.

"I'm sorry, but this area is reserved for the players," I said.

"I am a player," Blair said. "Have you forgotten my 12th place at the World Advanced Championship in 2005?"

"The area is reserved for the players in this tournament."

"Or my bestseller *Think Like a Bohigian*?" he added.

I looked in his eyes and said slowly:

"You ... don't ... belong ... here."

Blair shrugged and took his time leaving the stage. He took a last, long glimpse at Board Four. That's where Eichler had begun his tournament comeback.

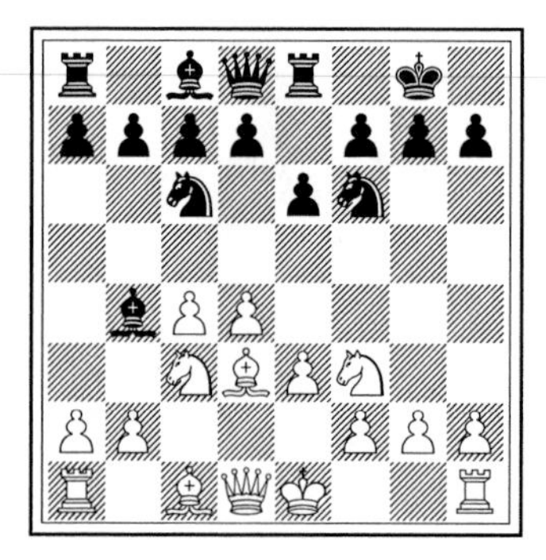

After 6. ... Re8

Boriescu–Eichler
Nimzo-Indian Defense E40

1. d4 Nf6 2. c4 e6 3. Nc3 Bb4 4. e3

Although he eventually won, Boriescu had gotten a dubious middlegame in Round Four with 4. Bg5. This was his Plan B.

4. ... Nc6 5. Nf3 0–0 6. Bd3 Re8!?

They used to play ...Nc6 in this variation with the idea of supporting ...e5, following the traditional Nimzo-Indian recipe of setting up Black's pawns on dark squares. But for some reason all the e-books today had Black playing nothing but ...d5.

Eichler's idea was retro Nimzo. He wants to push the e-pawn while avoiding 6. ... d6 7. a3!, which favors White after the bishop is traded off.

7. 0–0

I'd expected something like 7. e4 e5 8. d5 Nd4—or 7. a3 Bf8! 8. Ne5!? Ne7, after which anything could happen.

7. ... e5 8. Ne4 Bf8! 9. d×e5 Ng4

This last move was played so fast it was almost certainly part of Johnny's preparation. Clearly 9. ... N×e5 10. N×e5 R×e5 11. N×f6+ and 12. Bd2 would have favored White.

10. Nfg5

Or 10. Neg5 g6 and 11. ... Ng×e5 and White has nothing. Eichler took a long time so he must have been thinking on his own from here on.

10. ... Nc×e5! 11. f4

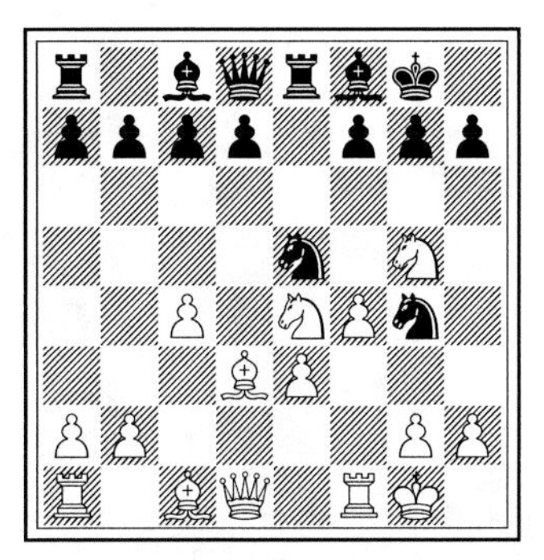

After 11. f4

This seemed to assure White an edge (11. ... N×d3 12. Q×g4 with Qh5 in mind). But Black has two more tricks.

11. ... d5! 12. c×d5

Not 12. f×e5 d×e4 13. N×e4 N×e5 (or 13. B×e4? Q×g5 and 13. N×f7? Q×d3).

12. ... N×d3 13. Q×d3 h6!

Based on 14. Nf3 Bf5 15. Nfd2 Bc5 (since 16. Re1 or 16. Rf3 both allow 16. ... Qh4!), this nice move sentenced Boriescu to a 35-minute think. By the time he made his decision he was left with a little more than an hour for his remaining 27 moves of the time control.

In fact, *Zeitnot* was the theme of the day. After five rounds of trying to adjust to the regimen of 40-moves-in-two-and-a-half-hours—a much slower tempo than they were used to—the grandmasters had fallen into a new rhythm of thinking. They were taking their allotted time today.

And maybe a bit more than that, as Board One showed:

Vilković–Karlson
French Defense C12

1. e4 e6 2. d4 d5 3. Nc3 Nf6 4. Bg5 Bb4 5. e5 h6 6. Bd2 B×c3 7. b×c3 Ne4 8. Qg4 g6 9. Bc1 c5 10. Bd3 N×c3 11. d×c5 Nd7

Up to here Karlson was following her second-round game with Van Siclen. But she tried 11. ... Qa5 in that game and won when White self-destructed.

Vilković, apparently surprised that his opponent varied before he could, spent 25 minutes here. It was time well spent.

12. Nf3 Qc7 13. 0–0!

Another big think by White. Now 13. ... N×e5 14. Qd4! costs Black a piece.

13. ... N×c5 14. Re1 Bd7

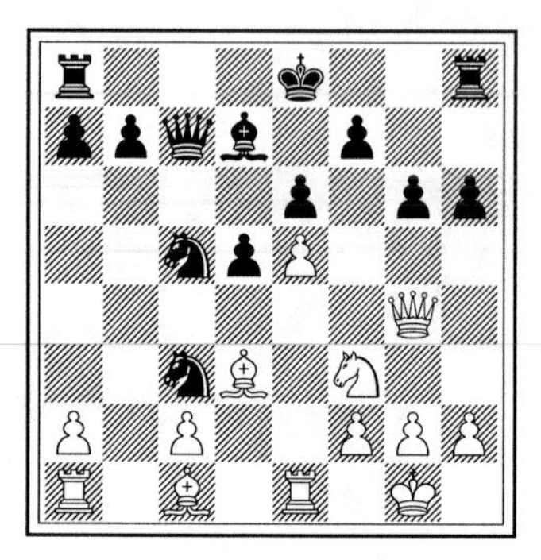

After 14. ... Bd7

Here 15. Qf4 followed by Qf6 would have been thematic and would leave White with at least a small edge. Maybe a plus-over-equals in *Informant*-speak. But as I watched him calculate, it was clear Vilković was becoming increasingly optimistic: He even smiled.

After all, this was his best position so far in the tournament. He was so pleased with it he invested another 33 minutes here and settled on an adventure that looked very promising:

15. B×g6!? Rg8!

White is winning after 15. ... f×g6? 16. Q×g6+ Kf8 17. B×h6+. But after 15. ... Rg8 the defense gets the upper hand following 16. Qd4 Nb5 17. Qb2 R×g6 18. a4 N×a4.

16. B×f7+! K×f7 17. Qh5+ Ke7 18. Q×h6

Both 19. Bg5+ and 19. Qh7+! are threatened, as well as Qf6+ and h2–h4–h5 etc.

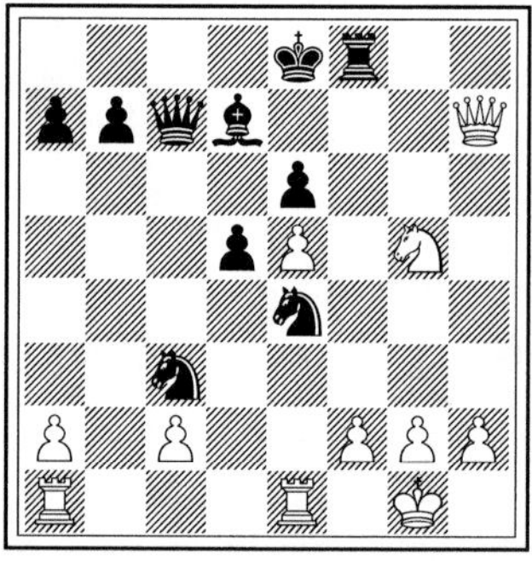

After 21. ... N5e4

18. ... Raf8?

Black decides to throw some material in the enemy's path. But 18. ... Kd8! was the only way to refute the sack.

19. Bg5+ Ke8 20. Qh7! R×g5

Clearly forced. White will have a material edge as well as the attack now.

21. N×g5 N5e4

White exhausted another 17 minutes looking for an alternative to the queen checks and the various ways of trying to promote the h-pawn. In the end he chose:

22. N×e6? Q×e5!!

"Mega-ouch," as Kersti would say. Vilković's jaw dropped when he saw Black was threatening to mate with 23. ... Ne2+!.

For example, 23. N×f8 Ne2+ 24. Kf1 Nd2 mate; 24. Kh1 N×f2 mate and 24. R×e2 Q×a1+.

23. f3 Ne2+! 24. Kf1 B×e6 26. Q×b7 R×f3+! White resigns

The handwriting on the wall read 27. g×h3 Bh3+ 28. K×e2 Q×h2+ and mate next.

Popov, who had taken this all in standing next to me, shook his head.

"It's a lottery," he said.

Also finishing early was the battle of the world champions. But the result was quite different.

Dareh Bohigian was no longer the player he was when he lost the title to Igor Grushevsky. But then neither was Grushevsky. The truth is, there had been considerable—and well-founded—grumbling among the other players about Grushevsky's failure to defend his championship in the past seven years.

It was well-founded grumbling because the Ukrainian seemed to be repeating the strategy that had served Lasker so well at the turn of the 20th century, and was later adopted by Alekhine in the early '30s and by Kasparov in the late '90s:

Grushevsky played only one or two tournaments a year, always including Los Voraces, of course. If he scored at least one clear first place, which he usually did, he would then announce that it was pointless to arrange a one-sided match featuring an invincible world champion. He would spent the next eight or nine months playing exhibitions against computers. Or rock stars. Or legislatures. Or continents.

Whatever the opponent, all his games were for show. They were strictly exhibitions, none with his prestige, or rating, on the line.

Of course, Grushevsky always insisted he was willing to play any legitimate challenger. All they had to do was find a sponsor willing to shell out $12 million in prize money.

Since there were no such sponsors—even Sheldrake wasn't that crazy—Grushevsky hadn't defended his title since winning it from Bohigian. In fact, he hadn't played a rated game since his first place at Los Voraces 2018. As a result, today's pairing would probably be the closest thing to a world championship match game, if only because it involved the former and current champions.

But the 63rd Bohigian–Grushevsky game in the last 12 years turned out to be a letdown. It was their ninth draw in a row.

Bohigian–Grushevsky
Sicilian Defense B52

1. e4

A mild surprise. Against most everyone else, Bohigian played closed openings.

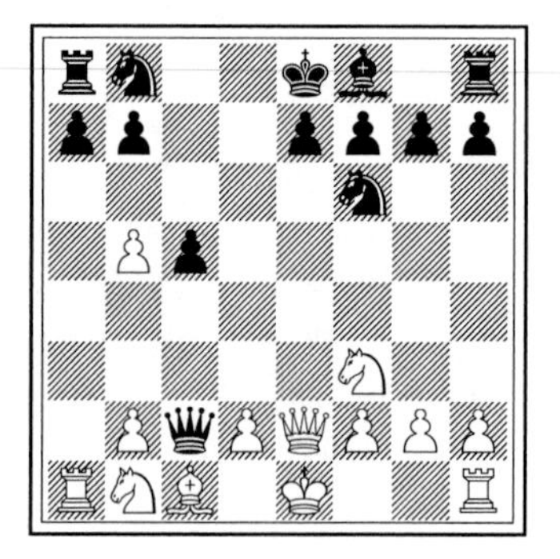

After 9. ... Q×c2

1. ... c5 2. Nf3 d6 3. Bb5+ Bd7 4. a4 Nf6 5. e5 d×e5 6. N×e5 B×b5 7. a×b5 Qd5 8. Nf3 Qe4+ 9. Qe2

As the old saying went, "The game really begins when Tal opens a file, Korchnoi grabs a pawn, Kasparov begins to calculate or Bohigian offers a queen trade."

9. ... Q×c2!

A quick database check later showed that Bohigian had scored 3½–½ against grandmasters after 9. ... Q×e2+. But by grabbing on c2, Grushevsky shifts the burden. Instead of having to prove that Black was equal, the onus was now on White to demonstrate compensation for the pawn.

10. Nc3 e6

Stopping White's next move with 10. ... b6 would give White chances after 11. 0–0 and 12. Ne5.

11. b6 a6 12. Nb5!?

This looked dangerous because of lines like 12. ... a×b5 13. Q×b5+ Ke7 14. R×a8! Q×c1+ 15. Ke2 Q×h1?? 16. Q×c5+ and mates.

12. ... Nd5 13. Nc7+

I suspect the next time this line is played, White will try 13. 0–0 or 13. Ne5. If there is a next time.

You'd be surprised how many promising ideas such as 12. Nb5 get played once and then are completely forgotten. Once a move falls out of practice, everyone thinks it's been refuted, even though they can't find a reason.

13. ... N×c7 14. b×c7 Nd7 15. Ne5

Here 15. ... Bd6 appeared safe enough. But Grushevsky accepted the challenge.

15. ... Nxe5!? 16. Qb5+! axb5 17. Rxa8+ Ke7 18. 0–0!

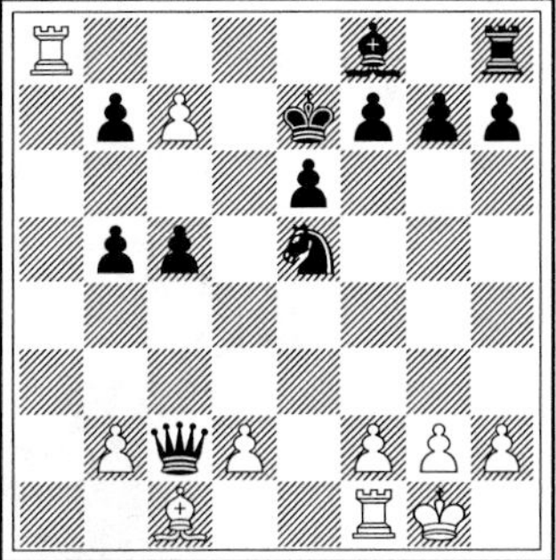

After 18. 0–0

The c-pawn can't be stopped and the onus had shifted again. Black had to find a defense, and his chances would be dicey after 18. ... Kf6 19. c8(Q) Nd3 20. Ra1. But he found:

18. ... Nf3+! Draw

There was no escaping the draw, since 19. gxf3 Qg6+ 20. Kh1 Qh5 leads to a perpetual, and 19. Kh1 Qc4 20. Rg1 Qf4! is worse for White. And 19. Kh1 Qc4 20. Re8+ Kf6! changes nothing.

Grushevsky, as usual, tried to post-mortem at the board, starting from move one. When I reminded him there was quiet room, with comfortable chairs and nice shiny pieces, set up just for that, he got insulted and walked off. Bohigian smiled.

"Another good day," I said. "You've got him and Klushkov behind you now. It's time to start thinking about first prize."

"One doesn't divide the bear skin before the bear is killed."

Right.

"You know," I said. "Out here they have their own saying like that."

"Yes?"

"It goes: 'Some days you eat the bear. And some days the bear eats you.'"

Bohigian gave me an odd look as he stood up.

"Some day I will tell you a story," he said. "The real story of how a bear made me an ex-world champion."

He intercepted my question before I could ask it.

"Some day," he said, and headed for the steps at the right side of the stage.

This was worse than one of his proverbs. As I stood there trying to decipher his words, my eyes focused on something strange: We had spectators, plural. In the first row of the auditorium, Blair had been joined by Beadle, the town's gas station jockey.

Silas was a tall drink of water, 6-4 and no more than 190 pounds,

with a perpetual smile. He was always smiling, as if at some private joke. Silas' interest in chess had never previously been detected, and his buddying up with Blair piqued my curiosity. He had arrived just in time to see some action because this was the hour when Boriescu's game suddenly began to go south.

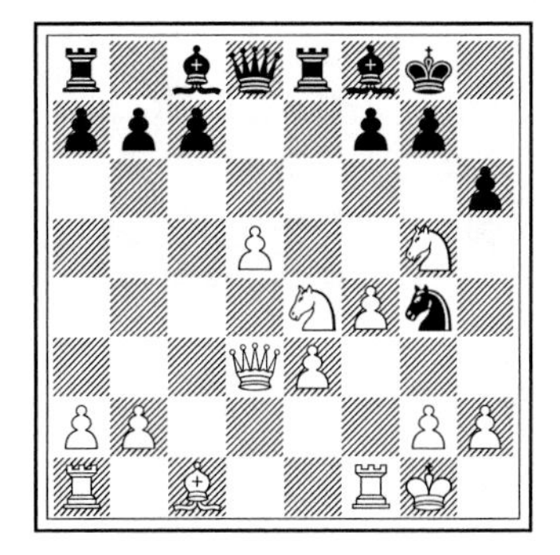

Boriescu–Eichler
After 13. ... h6

Boriescu–Eichler

14. h3 h×g5 15. h×g4 g×f4

Now 16. exf4 Bxg4 17. Ng5 g6 leaves White with a problem meeting 18. ... c6 or 18. ... Be2.

16. R×f4!? Re5! 17. Nc3 Rg5

Black should regain the pawn and keep the two-bishop edge now. This was the first time I felt Eichler really belonged in this tournament.

18. Bd2

This is the type of move you make when you recognize you don't have an edge and you just want to start the middlegame with coordinated (e.g. Raf1) pieces. If Boriescu were more optimistic he'd have made it harder for Black to win the pawn back with 18. Qd4.

18. ... B×g4 19. Raf1 Bh5 20. e4

Boriescu seemed pleased at having solved most of his opening problems. But there were still those weak dark squares.

20. ... Bg6 21. R4f3

Black has made most of the threats so far and here 21. Qh3, intending 22. Rh4, would have been repulsed by 21. ... Rh5 and 22. ... Bd6.

21. ... Rh5 22. g3?

Anticipating ...Bd6 but this was horribly weakening nonetheless. White's house of cards disintegrated quickly.

22. ... Qd7 23. Qe2 Re8

Played with 24. ... Qh3 25. Qg2 Qxg2+ 26. Kxg2 Bxe4 in mind.

24. Qg2 Bb4! White resigns

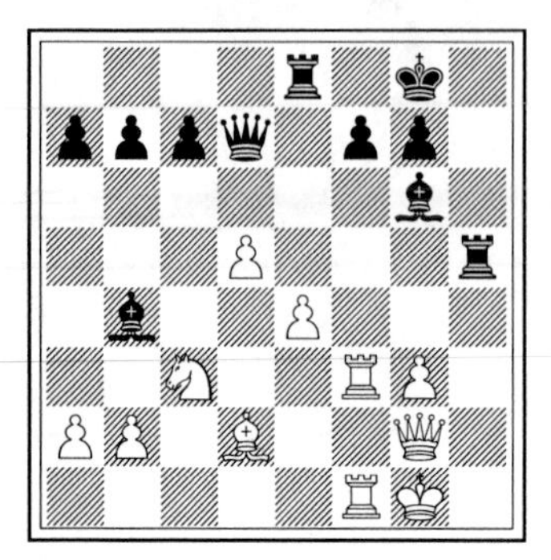

Final position

White loses material after 25. Rf4 Bc5+ or 25. Re1 Bxc3 or 25. Qf2 Qh3.

As I brought their flags and scoresheets to my office, I realized Blair was a half-step behind me. Inside the room he spoke in what for him was almost a whisper.

"This is a matter of some delicacy," he said.

"Delicacy?"

"Yes, you see, I am reconsidering my plans for Los Voraces—"

"That's good because you're not playing any role in this tournament."

"—and I have decided I need to form my local personnel force for future enterprises. Mr. Beadle will be my chauffeur, major domo, secretary and aide-de-camp for the duration of the endeavor."

"And you're telling me because..."

"Because I have encountered a temporary cash-flow exigency."

As I waited for him to get to the point, I glanced about the room.

"My funds have become blocked for financial reasons of a technical nature."

I studied the globe on the next desk. Was Chad really that big? Blair sighed.

"I need money to pay Beadle. Strangely enough, the good people of Los Voraces won't take an I.O.U."

"What happened to your company? What was it called... Cerebral Properties Inc.?"

Another sigh.

"That was last month. I have since acquired a different firm. Intellectual Enterprise and Exposition Corp. A wonderful company, the IEEC, with a magnificent future. But at present we are overwhelmed with unexpected start-up costs."

"Start-up costs."

"Yes."

"Like paying Silas to be your go-fer?"

"Major domo," he said.

"I see."

"And in light of the resources of the Sheldrake Trust and its commitment to excellence in chess I was sure you would be willing to authorize a bridge loan of, say, $200 that will tide us over the next few, exciting days. After all, we must continue the work of Capablanca and Lasker, of Botvinnik and Smyslov, of Spassky and Petrosian..."

I didn't like helping him out. But if finding a few hundred bucks for Silas would keep Silas busy with Blair—and keep Blair away from me—it was money well invested.

He was still thanking me—and invoking the memories of Tal and Fischer and Ponomariov and Anand—when I left to check out the remaining games. It soon became apparent that Board Two was reaching a moment of truth.

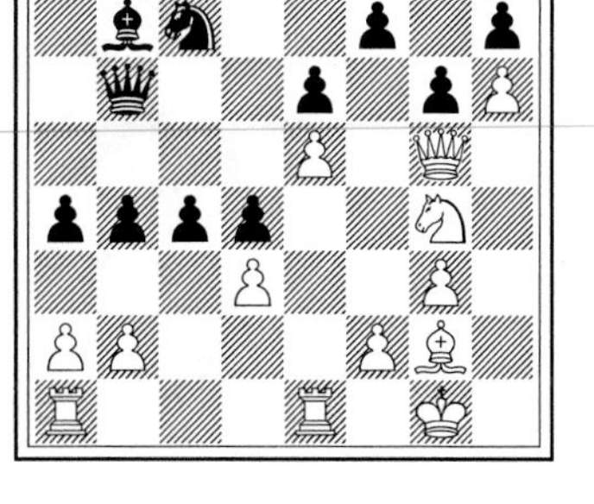

Qi–Popov
Black to move

Qi–Popov

Black saw the idea of Qf6–g7 mate, of course. And he realized 29. ... Nd5 was doomed by 30. d×c4. No better was 29. ... Ne8 because of 30. Nf6+ Kh8 31. N×e8 and Qf6+.

Popov might have tried to keep the game going with the desperate 29. ... f5?! but he preferred:

29. ... B×g2

Qi replied instantly:

30. Qf6! Ne8 31. Qe7!

This is what Popov had missed. The threat is 32. Nf6+, and now it's too late for 31. ... f5 (32. Nf6+ R×f6—otherwise it's mate in one—33. e×f6).

Black no longer had choices to make. He can only respond to specific threats now.

31. ... Nc7 32. Nf6+ Kh8

If Popov had had enough time left he would have resigned as soon as he saw the possibility of 33. Nd7—or when he saw that 33. ... Nd5 would have been met by 34. Q×f8+. But White had an even better move.

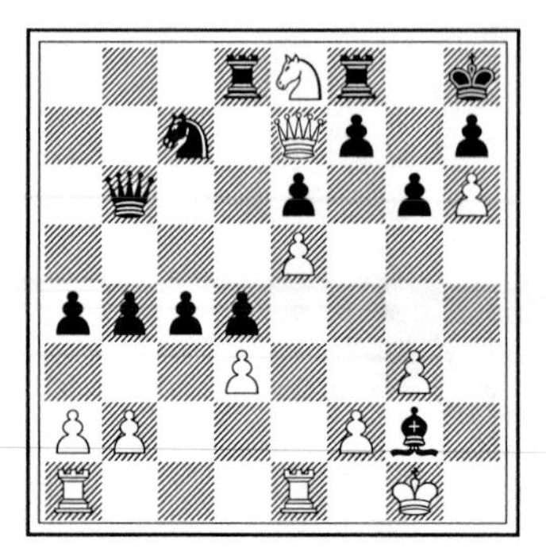

Final position

33. Ne8!! Resigns

Mate can't be avoided. The victory, Qi's fourth, meant that he was in excellent shape in the race for first prize, especially since he had already had one bye. The unfortunate growth in the prize fund meant that Qi's game today may have earned him as much as an extra $50,000. That's more than world champions used to win for entire matches.

Klushkov was also in contention because Bastrikova, down two pawns going on three, had finally resigned on the 37th move. That gave the Spaceman four points and at least a share of third place.

Forgotten in all this was the Board Five game. It had been forgotten because nothing much seemed to happen for the first three and a half hours.

Royce-Smith–Krimsditch
Queen Pawn's Game D02

1. d4 d5 2. Nf3 Nf6 3. g3 g6 4. Bg2 Bg7 5. 0–0 0–0 6. Nbd2 c6 7. b3 Nbd7 8. Bb2 Re8

Black is toying with the idea of 9. … e5 10. dxe5 Ng4. He also tries to tempt White to stop him with 9. Ne5? Nxe5 10. dxe5—which would invite 10. … Ng4 11. Nf3 Qc7 12. Qd4 f6.

9. c4 dxc4 10. bxc4 e5! 11. e3

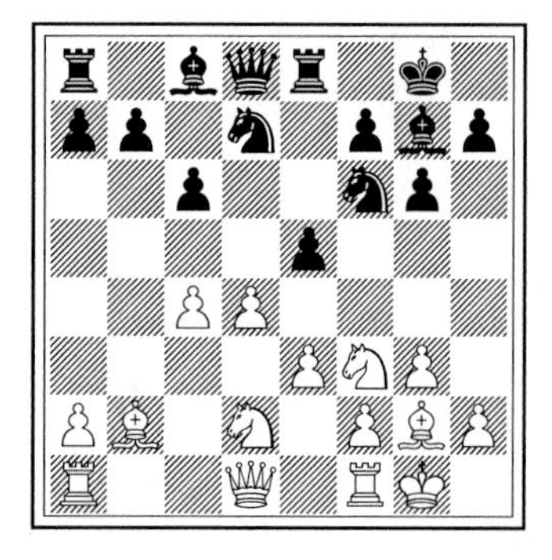

After 11. e3

Krimsditch has liberated his remaining pieces but never quite equalizes now. That's one of the hardest things for young players to learn: In closed openings it usually takes more than one or two good moves to equalize.

11. … exd4 12. exd4 c5?

And it only takes one bad one to get the worst of it.

13. d5 Nb6 14. a4! Bf5 15. Qb3 Qc7 16. Nh4 Bd7

While all the excitement was centered on other boards, such as the innovative opening of Bastrikova vs. Klushkov and the combinations by both players in Bohigian vs. Grushevsky, here it was a case of White's position just getting better move by move.

17. f4! Nc8 18. Be5 Nd6 19. Qb2 Nh5 20. Bf3 f6

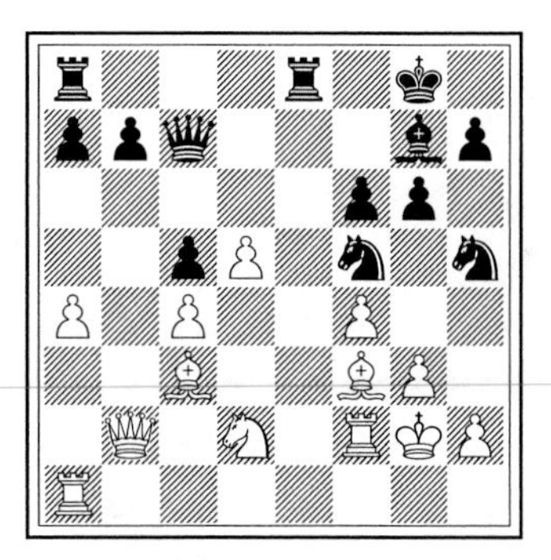

After 24. Rf2

Hardly better is 20. ... B×e5 21. f×e5. Royce-Smith's position was so good, he didn't have to force matters here with 21. B×d6 Q×d6 22. B×h5.

21. Bc3 Bh3 22. Ng2

Threatening 23. g4 or 23. B×h5 g×h5 24. B×f6.

22. ... B×g2 23. K×g2 Nf5 24. Rf2

I have to give Krimsditch credit for ingenuity. Objectively, there might have been a hang-tough defense that could have dragged matters out to adjournment—or later. That was an old grandmaster device, from the days when tournament results appeared regularly in newspapers: If you played out your bad positions to the bitterest end, then when you finally resigned it was too late to make even the final edition. By the next day's paper, your loss was old news.

But that's not what Krimsditch did here. In psychological terms, his choice was inspired.

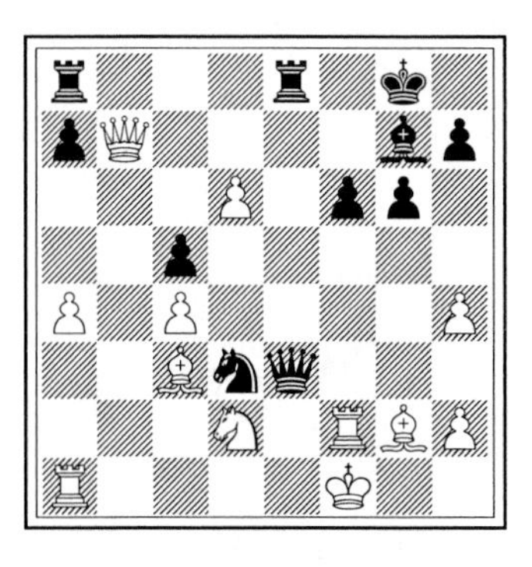

After 29. ... Qe3

24. ... Nh4+!?! 25. g×h4 N×f4+ 26. Kf1 Nd3

Now 27. Qc2 N×f2 28. K×f2 Q×h2+ 29. Kf1 Re3 could have put Black back in the game.

27. d6! Qd7! 28. Q×b7 Qh3+ 29. Bg2 Qe3

For a (brief) moment this looked good: Not only 30. ... Q×f2 mate but also 30. ... Qe1+ was threatened.

I saw 30. Ne4 R×e4 31. Q×a8+ Re8 32. Qd5+ Kh8 33. Rf3 wins for White. But Royce-Smith didn't move.

Then I noticed that Black didn't have to take on e4 but could answer 30. Ne4 with 30. ... N×f2. Royce-Smith still didn't move.

And I spotted a cute trick—on 30. ... N×f2 31. Qd5+ Kh8 32. Re1 Black has 30. ... Ng4!. But White was still thinking.

He thought and thought. Was there something else for White? Or for Black? White's clock ran down to about 20 seconds. Finally he played:

30. Bd5+ Kh8 31. Q×g7+!! K×g7 32. B×f6+

Now it all made sense: 32. ... Kh6 33. Bg5+. The two grandmasters blitzed off the finale:

32. ... Kf8 33. Be7+! Kg7 34. Rf7+ Kh8 35. Bf6+ Kg8 36. Rg7+ Kf8 37. Rg8 mate

That pushed Royce-Smith a bit further ahead of Grushevsky and the other favorites, not counting the byes. It was beginning to look like Los Voraces 2019 would be a two-horse race. And neither horse was the world champion.

SHELDRAKE MEMORIAL TOURNAMENT

	V	*Q*	*B*	*K*	*P*	*K*	*E*	*K*	*G*	*V*	*B*	*R*	*B*	*G*	*Score*
Vilković	/	0	½	½	½	0				—				—	1½–3½
Qi	1	/	1	½	1					—			1	—	4½–½
Bastrikova	½	0	/	0					0	—		0	½	—	1–5
Klushkov	½	½	1	/						—	½	½	1	—	4–2
Popov	½	0			/					—	½	0	0	—	1–4
Karlson	1					/			0	—	0	½	1	—	2½–2½
Eichler							/	½	½	—	½	0	1	—	2½–2½
Krimsditch							½	/	0	—	0	0		—	½–3½
Grushevsky			1			1	½	1	/	—	½			—	4–1
Van Siclen	—	—	—	—	—	—	—	—	—	/	—	—	—	—	—
Bohigian				½	½	1	½	1	½	—	/			—	4–2
Royce-Smith			1	½	1	½	1	1		—		/		—	5–1
Boriescu		0	½	0	1	0	0			—			/	—	1½–4½
Gabor	—	—	—	—	—	—	—	—	—	—	—	—	—	/	—

The good news was that with no adjournments, there was no reason for a free day. I was putting up a notice announcing that Round

Seven would be held tomorrow—and that the trip to the rock quarry was canceled—when I realized Gibbs was paying another visit to the high school.

"How's the chess?" he said, and smiled.

"Could be better."

"Seems like a nice evening for a walk."

"You mean a good time to compare notes."

"Same thing."

I said good night to Mrs. Nagle and left her and Sims to close up shop for the day. Then I joined Gibbs as he began to mosey down the south side of Main Street. The air had a musky sweetness and the temperature was still in the high 70s but bearable.

"Your Mr. Blair is quite a talker," Gibbs began. "Chewed my ear off a good part of the afternoon."

"Don't blame Boyd Blair on the game of chess. They have worse than him in boxing," I said, matching his slow stride. "What else is on your mind?"

"Well, first, I have a bit of news," he said. "The tests came back on the envelope that killed the Dutch fellow."

"I didn't know you sent out for testing."

"Have to. Nobody in town is qualified to do it. Anyway, turns out the glue on the envelope contained a bit of Compound 1080."

I'd never heard of it, and said so.

"Not surprising for someone from out of state," Gibbs said. "It's for killing coyotes. In fact, it's one of the deadliest commercial poisons around."

"That can't be readily available, even in Los Voraces."

"Actually, there was a can of it stolen from the 'Porium last Thursday," Gibbs said. He motioned towards the clapboard storefront, with a faded "Los Voraces Emporium" sign, that we were approaching.

"You've got quite a crime wave going on here," I said.

"Not too shocking in a town where nobody locks their doors at night."

Or where it's still 1955, I thought to myself.

We soon passed the Emporium as well as the town library. We'd gone about 150 feet or so from the high school when I saw Vilković walking towards us in a bit of a daze. I decided it was time for Gibbs to get to know his suspects first hand.

"Good evening, Grandmaster!" I said when Vilković was a few feet ahead of us. He seemed startled.

"Nice night for a stroll," I added.

Vilković blinked. "If you say so," he said.

"But they say it might rain tomorrow."

Another blink. Before I could come up with a way to stretch this into a conversation, Vilković nodded to Gibbs and me and continued on his way. The sheriff was bemused.

"What was that all about?"

"I suspect it was about queen takes e-five."

Gibbs waited for a translation.

"You see, Vilković lost today—badly. And when you lose that bad, you can suffer from a kind of flashback. For the next few hours, your mind keeps coming back to the position where everything fell apart. You can't concentrate on anything else."

"What if you win? Do you start reliving the good parts?"

"No. It's strange, but you rarely do. The high points in chess never quite make up for the low points."

He accepted that with a shake of the head, and we continued along Main.

After about a half block, Bastrikova appeared, headed in our direction and watching us all the way. When she reached us, she shot a doubtful glance at Gibbs and turned to me.

"I think there is something you should know."

"Anything you want to tell me you can certainly share with the sheriff," I said.

She considered that for a moment.

"I do not want to point fingers at anyone."

"No one wants to," I said.

"No. But, ummm, you should … be aware that Karlson arrived here on the afternoon of the 20th."

She was as transparent as Lucite.

"Before Gabor died," I said to Gibbs.

"I just thought you should know," she said.

"Thank you, Ma'am. That's very helpful," Gibbs said.

"You were also going to point out that Kersti was present at both adjournment sessions," I said.

Before Bastrikova could deny it, I added:

"But then again, you were present, too."

She looked sharply at me, then to Gibbs to gauge his reaction. Then she made up an excuse about preparing for Popov tomorrow and hurried back to the hotel. Gibbs and I continued down the street.

"Y'know, I was just about to bring up something like that," he said as we passed the Old Brown Jug Liquor Shoppe.

"Something like what?"

"Opportunity. You see, there are three elements of every murder: Motive, means and opportunity."

It must have been one of the sheriff's rare chances to lecture. That is, with an audience.

"On Monday, we discussed motive in terms of the suspects and victims," he said.

I followed his drift. "And with what you told me about, what was it, Compound 1060?

"1080," he said.

"Okay, 1080. Then now we know more about the means."

"True," but it's not that simple," he said. "Anyone who's ever spent a few hours in town could probably figure out how to get their hands on the stuff."

As the sheriff was talking, a pickup speeded down Main Street. I could make out Beadle was in the front seat—no one else smiled like that—and it looked like Blair was in the jump seat. After they had disappeared in the dust, towards the town limits, I continued the train of thought.

"Every player in the tournament has played here before."

"And anyone that familiar with the town might've even learned where to acquire a coral snake," Gibbs said.

Sunset was giving way to dusk. After a few silent minutes, we reached Paloma's Corral at the east end of Main Street, four blocks from the high school at the other end.

Outside Paloma's, I heard the usual laughter and the sounds from the bar's jukebox, which played ancient Country & Western. We paused there for a moment, while Gibbs seemed to be studying Paloma's neon sign, wrapped up in the strains of "How Come Your Dog Don't Bite Nobody But Me?"

Looking back on it, this would have been a good time to tell him about my phone call to Endoline. He probably already knew—from Phelps, wherever he was—about the true cause of Gabor's death. The information about the pills would help fill in the blanks. But I decided not to interrupt Gibbs while he was still in lecture mode.

"That leaves the third element of murder: Opportunity. Who was in a position to commit all three murders?"

He answered his own question.

"I checked with the Casa, as well as with your limousine service and some other sources. And while I'm not absolutely certain, it appears that every one of your players was in Los Voraces as of 6 P.M. last Tuesday.

"More than two hours before Gabor died," I said.

Gibbs nodded. Then he turned around and looked up Main Street. After a brief pause, we reversed direction and headed back up the street, this time on the north side.

A block and a half later, just short of the Rancho Voraces, Popov spotted us. Even at 10 paces in the dark I could detect a grin I took to be malicious.

"Let me guess: you are sizing all of us up as suspects," he said.

"Guess all you want," Gibbs said.

"My guess is you should consider Eichler."

That came out of nowhere. Gibbs only wrinkled his brow.

"But he was *with* Daphne," I said. "Why would he kill her?"

"I don't know why," Popov said. "But he had the best access to her handbag."

The sheriff smiled to me—as if to say "Opportunity."

"And you do know who his father was, don't you?" Popov continued.

Gibbs looked at me but I had no answers.

Popov did: "Dr. Gustav Eichler."

I drew a blank.

"An internationally renowned authority on herpetology," he said.

"Herpetology?" Gibbs asked.

"Snakes," I said.

I knew Eichler's dad was a big-deal scientist, but I didn't know what brand.

"So what?"

"Simply that a snake was one of the murder weapons, correct?" Popov said. "Also, it makes sense Johnny would have the same interests as his father. And that makes him a prime suspect."

Gibbs nodded but I couldn't tell if he was just being polite.

"After all," Popov said, "If Gabor, Daphne and Gert had died by hanging, you would be interested in someone who came from a family of rope-makers."

The analogy struck me as dumb, and I wondered if we'd be hearing this if Eichler hadn't crushed Popov at last year's Sheldrake. But Gibbs just thanked him for the information. His mission accomplished, Popov ambled back inside the Rancho. We continued our walk.

Along the way we passed Grushevsky, on the south side of Main. I waved. Gibbs noticed how he ignored me.

"World champions tend to outgrow normal human interaction," I explained. "They seem to have a lot more self-importance than the good people of New Mexico."

The sheriff managed a laugh.

"Oh, there are things we're proud of. We're even proud of our state insect."

"You're kidding. State insect?"

"Yup, the Tarantula Hawk Wasp. Ugly critters. They paralyze a tarantula with stings, then drag it down a hole and lay eggs. It's their larvae that finish their victim off."

At that moment we passed Karlson and Qi, who were sharing a pocket set as they studied some position under one of the town's few working lampposts. We went another 50 feet, to the entrance of the Casa, when we were intercepted again, this time by Krimsditch.

"How's the great police dragnet going?" he asked.

"Slow," Gibbs said. "There's a lot to consider."

"Being a chessplayer, you should appreciate that," I said. But Krimsditch was immune to sarcasm. And tonight he was being more than curious.

"I hope you're considering the Chinese factor."

Again Gibbs looked at me—but I didn't know what the hell he meant either.

"Don't you think it strange," Krimsditch said, "how Van Siclen got every big invite in China for the past five years?"

Nowadays invitations to the major Chinese tournaments were among the most-sought-after. But I confessed that Gert's frequent-flyer mileage to Beijing never meant much to me.

"And another thing," Krimsditch said. "How come he was the first *gweylo* recruited for the People's Liberation League? In fact, he's still the only foreigner in it."

"So you're suggesting … what, exactly?" Gibbs asked.

"I'm not suggesting anything. I just think there must be a reason," Krimsditch replied.

This wasn't much more subtle than Bastrikova.

"A reason like blackmail?" I asked. "You think Van Siclen was blackmailing Qi and that's why he was killed?"

Krimsditch looked at me and shrugged.

"Look, you can play deputy sheriff all you want. But so far you haven't come up with a reason for any of the murders. I'm just pointing out an obvious possibility for one of them."

Krimsditch left us in the darkness, alone with the fireflies and the distant strains of "All My Ex's Live in Texas" from Paloma's. I could tell the sheriff was reviewing what we had just heard. A minute or so passed before he spoke.

"Good cop or bad cop?"

I understood what he meant: I could question the players. And I could do it in a friendly manner, using whatever dwindling rapport I still had with them.

Or he could ask the questions, playing the bad cop and using the weight of his office—as well as the veiled threat of jail.

"Let's start with good cop," I said.

"And work our way down," he said.

Wednesday, August 28, 2019

EVERY GM I'D EVER KNOWN had a way of relaxing away from the board. It was like a trade secret. Knowing how to unwind or fight boredom—or just get your mind off chess—was something they needed to survive. At least to survive two and a half weeks in places like Los Voraces.

The secret for Bastrikova and Grushevsky was endless games of dominoes, played off-hours in a booth at the Rancho Voraces. It got their minds off chess but didn't cost them their competitive edge. They still tried to win but losing didn't hurt as much.

Eichler preferred long walks in the Sequoia Gully Campground. Whether he liked to think about his next opponent as he hiked, or review the course of his last game, or just appreciate the cottonwoods and the chollo cactus, he didn't say.

For Bohigian, relaxation meant sleep, as much sleep as he could manage. Sometimes he logged 12 hours a night. Like Kasparov he made it a habit of not shaving until just before the round. And when he was running late, Bohigian would show up to play with a day-old growth of beard.

Popov and Vilković relaxed by arguing with one another about the merits of East European politics, Western European women and soccer anywhere. Boriescu, it was said, took long, hot baths.

And Royce-Smith was into primal scream therapy. When the Englishman lost a particularly painful game he would find his way to the Blue Wolf Picnic Area and bellow out his frustrations, the way

Ivanchuk once howled like a wolf at the park in Linares, after a bad loss.

I knew Karlson's recipe was to unwind in an easy chair in the Casa Yucca Grande, reading a newspaper, preferably the astrology column. That's where I found her this morning.

"Mind if I pick your brain?" I asked.

"Sure, pick away. My moon is in Gemini."

"If you say so."

I had guessed that Karlson would be having an easy day today, because she was paired with Qi, and would be more relaxed and vulnerable to questions.

"How've you been enjoying the tournament this year?"

"Well, I would be enjoying it a lot more if I'd played bishop-takes-d4 against Bohigian," she said. "And if I'd seen queen-to-b4 against Grushevsky. And if—"

"So you've been able to put the other events out of your mind?"

"You mean the deaths."

"I mean the deaths."

"Wasn't that terrible about Gert?" she said. "And Attila? I guess it's been a distraction for everyone. It certainly bothered me, for a day or two. But you know what they say about Sags."

"Sags?"

"Sagittarians. We're always able to focus. We think positive. And we can't lie."

This might be easier than I had thought.

"That's good to know. And Sheriff Gibbs is doing a fine job of investigation," I said. "But there are some questions that have come up."

"Questions? Maybe I can help."

"Maybe you can. We would both greatly appreciate your assistance."

"That's so cool! I don't understand why nobody took me seriously when I suggested we catch the killer ourselves."

I let that hang in the air as diplomatically as I could.

"One question the sheriff had concerned Gabor's hotel room. Did you know which one he was staying in?"

"Sure. The Arroyo Suite, I think they call it. Actually, it's Room 314, right across from me," she said. "But his room was bigger and he had this great view and a throw rug and—"

"I'm sure it did. But, you know, most of the rooms in these old hotels are pretty much the same."

"Yeah."

"Same decor, more or less."

"Yeah."

"Same basic bathroom."

"Yeah."

"Same flimsy security."

"What?"

"Well, you know how you can open most rooms at the Casa with a credit card. You just saw-tooth the edge of the card down the door crevice and slip the lock."

She turned that over in her mind for a few seconds.

"I guess I knew that."

"I guess all the players did," I said. "By the way, the players, do you remember seeing them on the afternoon of the 20th."

"The 20th?"

"A week ago Tuesday. The day before the Players Meeting."

"Oh, yeah. I saw them."

"All of them?"

As she thought a bit, I could tell she was mentally counting to 13.

"Yeah," Karlson said. "Even Grushevsky. I saw him in the lobby. He checked in about an hour after I did. But it seemed like he hid in his room until the first round. Typical of a Taurus."

That helped confirm what Gibbs told me last night about the players' arrival time.

"It's funny, but I've spoken to some of the others," I said. "They seem to recall where you were at certain times this week."

"Like when?"

"Oh, like at the adjournment sessions."

For a player with a rating of 2847, it took a remarkably long time for her to see where I was going. Then it dawned on her.

"You think *I* did it?"

"Someone did."

"*I* killed poor Gert?"

"We have to explore all the possibilities."

"*I* killed Daphne? And Gabor?"

"I'm just asking some of the questions that have been raised."

"But I can't be a murderer. You should know that."

"I should?"

"It's obvious I couldn't kill anyone."

"Obvious? How?"

"Because … because I'm a Sagittarian."

The dirty little secret of round robins, at least at the international level, is that there comes a time when the players in the bottom half of the standings realize where they are. In the bottom half of the standings.

That's when they know their chances of winning a prize compare unfavorably with that of a snowball in … a tumbleweed storm, as they would say in these parts. I knew that time would come at some point and was afraid it would come today. The tailenders—Vilković, Boriescu, Popov, Bastrikova and Krimsditch—had little chance of significantly improving their point totals in the tournament's remaining week. And they knew it.

Some would probably begin to play make-believe games, drawing with one another and thinking ahead to the next tournament on their calendar. Some would try desperately to make up for lost Elo points by taking risks. And some might just crash and burn emotionally. In any case, they wouldn't be playing like the International Grandmasters I greeted eight days ago.

In particular, I wondered how long Vilković would put up resistance. The Serb had the toughest schedule left: He still had to play Grushevsky, Royce-Smith and Bohigian. And he had another stiff challenge to meet today when he faced Eichler, who had been awakened from his slumber with yesterday's win over Boriescu. The day shaped up this way:

SHELDRAKE MEMORIAL

ROUND SEVEN PAIRINGS

Eichler vs. Vilković
Karlson vs. Qi
Popov vs. Bastrikova
Krimsditch vs. Boriescu
Grushevsky vs. Royce-Smith

Bohigian would have had Black against Van Siclen, and Klushkov would have been due for White against Gabor. I had no choice but to give them both byes today, since they had already been paired with one another in Round One.

When I arrived at the high school, I found Blair on the right side of the stage, delivering a sales pitch to Krimsditch, Popov, Royce-Smith and Boriescu.

"That's six percent of the net profits. For each of you, plus stock options in the company. A magnificent opportunity."

"Assuming there are profits," Krimsditch said.

"And assuming there is a company," Popov added.

"Mere details," Blair said with a shrug. "You should worry about the chess and leave the minutiae to a venture catalyst like myself."

"I thought the term was venture capitalist," Popov said.

"That's only if you have the capital," Krimsditch said.

For once, the players seemed to be keeping pace with Blair. Klushkov, who appeared to be meditating at his board several feet away, looked up to listen.

"Handling financial fine points and details," Blair said. "That's why I'm here."

"And while you are here, Mr. Blair," Royce-Smith said. "Let me point out that twelve multiplied by six is 72."

"Eustace was always good at his times table," Popov said.

"I mean, where is the other 28 percent?" Royce-Smith asked.

"Ah, yes," said Blair. "That's what we call an entrepreneurial fee."

"Your fee," Krimsditch said.

Blair spread his arms wide in a grand gesture of acknowledgment.

"For doing what, exactly?"

"And 28 percent of what, exactly?" I said, inviting myself in.

"The proceeds of the tournament I'm organizing," Blair said.

This was worse than I thought.

"There already is a tournament, and I have the players under contract," I said.

"Ah, yes, but I'm talking about the second event," Blair said. "The *grande tournoi*."

Krimsditch explained: "He wants us to stay over for a second tournament, to be played somewhere outside the town."

"So he can take advantage of all of us being here..." Popov said.

"...without having to pay transportation...," Royce-Smith said.

SALOON
DRY GOODS
WELCOM
MUD TURTL
R.I.P.
EST.D 188

"...but call it something else," Krimsditch said.

"I sort of fancy 'Mudturtle Gulch 2019.' That's the appellation of the charming site Mr. Beadle and I were exploring south of town this morning," Blair said.

"It's a ghost town," I said. "There haven't been any residents of Mudturtle Gulch since 1887."

"All the more reason it would make a unique venue," Blair said.

"No residents except wolves," I said.

"That's what they want you to think," Royce-Smith said.

"*Mirable dictu*," Boriescu mumbled.

"Nothing to worry about," Blair said. "Providing security is only part of the services the entrepreneurial fee will cover. Mudturtle Gulch 2019 will go on!"

"That's theft of intellectual property," I said. "While they're here, my players are my players."

"Ahh, but after you're gone, they will be my players."

"Blair, I want my $200 back!"

But the New Yorker, having spotted Beadle's pickup outside, ran off, explaining he had to reconnoiter the drybeds and other possible satellite TV transmission locations around his "tournament site."

This was getting out of hand. Blair was trying to enlist players for some mirage tournament. And he was targeting those in the bottom of the scoretable who would be most tempted. Surely the GMs could see through this.

"Don't you think...?" I asked Krimsditch.

"I can't afford to think," he said. "I'm a professional chessplayer."

Ten minutes later it was 2 P.M., and I began performing my most important official act of the day: Pushing Black's button on chess clocks.

Vilković arrived at his Board One game with stubble and sunken eyes. He looked like he hadn't slept. Unfortunately for him, his game went according to expectations.

Eichler–Vilković
English Opening A36

1. c4 c5 2. Nc3 Nc6 3. g3 g6 4. Bg2 e6 5. d3 Nge7 6. e4

An Eichler favorite, stopping ...d5 at the cost of the d4 hole.

6. ... Nd4 7. Nge2 Nec6 8. N×d4 N×d4 9. 0–0 Bg7 10. Bf4 d6 11. Qd2 0–0 12. Rae1 Rb8?

This made some sense. If Black wanted to play ...a6/...b5 or ...b6/...Bb7, he'd like to safeguard the long diagonal against some e4–e5 trick. He could stop e4–e5 with 12. ... e5. But having taken pains to secure the d4 square Black wasn't about to give up control of d5.

Who would have guessed that 12. ... Rb8 was a blunder—and that White would soon be winning because of his d-pawn?

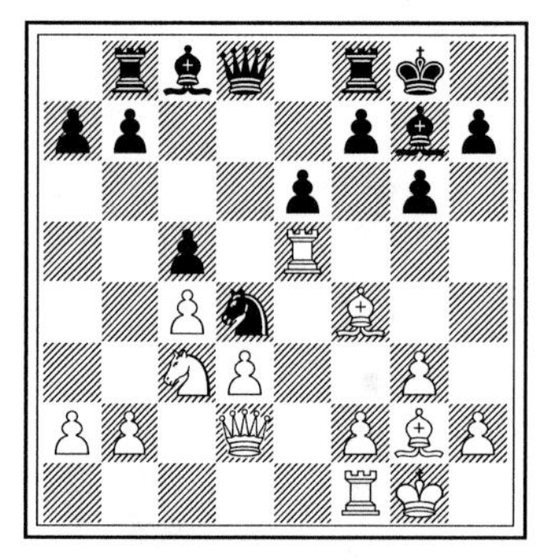

After 14. R×e5

13. e5 d×e5 14. R×e5!

Now 14. ... b6 or 14. ... Qa5 just drop a pawn to 15. R×c5!. Black has to accept the Exchange sack.

14. ... B×e5 15. B×e5 Ra8 16. Ne4 f6

Of course, Black can't allow Nf6+. Worse is 16. ... f5 17. Qh6!.

17. Bd6 Rf7 18. B×c5

One pawn for the exchange isn't enough. But the real compensation lies in White's breaking of the blockade on d4. When we looked at the game later, no one could save Black after 18. ... e5 19. f4.

Of course, that post-mortem consisted mainly of vague comments and shrugs. But I knew from experience that it would be converted into a page and a half of sub-sub-variations once Eichler began to annotate the game with access to the latest Fritz.

18. ... Nc6 19. d4 Kg7

No better was 19. ... b6 20. Ba3 and then 20. ... Q×d4 21. Q×d4 N×d4 22. Nd6.

20. Qc3!

A nice move, lining up the queen against the king and threatening d4–d5–d6. For example, 20. ... b6 is met by 21. d5! exd5 22. cxd5 and now 22. ... bxc5 23. dxc6 Rb8 24. N×c5 or 22. ... Ne5 23. Bd6 Ba6 24. Rd1, with advantage in either case.

20. ... Rd7?

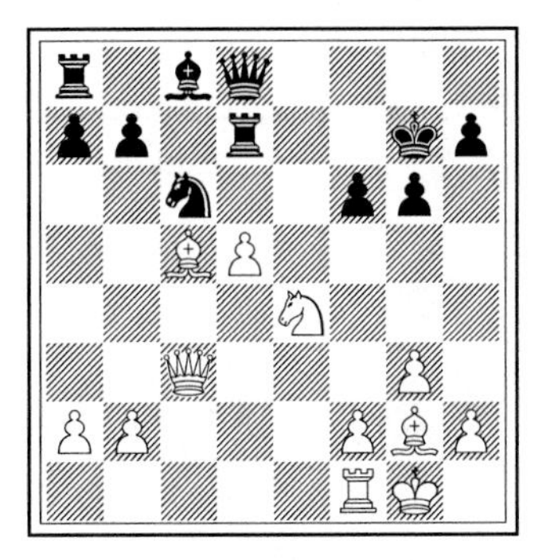

After 22. cxd5

This was supposed to freeze the pawn but just makes its advance worse.

21. d5! exd5 22. cxd5

Now 22. ... Ne5 23. f4 Ng4 24. h3 Nh6 loses to 25. Nxf6!

22. ... Rxd5 23. Nxf6! Resigns

Considering how the tournament was going for him, I couldn't blame Vilković for not playing out 23. ... Qxf6 24. Bf8+!. But I would have liked to see the finish of the king hunt after 23. ... Rxc5 24. Nh5+!.

It would have gone 24. ... Kh6 25. Qg7+! Kxh5 and now either 26. Qxh7+ Kg5 27. Qh4+ Kf5 28. Bh3+ or 26. Bf3+ Kg5 27. h4+ etc. and wins.

But Vilković had already shifted his attention to Mudturtle Gulch, as I feared. On the other hand, my guess about what would happen on Board Two turned out to be wrong. Qi wasn't content with a draw against Karlson. The first hint of that came by move seven.

Karlson–Qi
Sicilian Defense B52

1. e4 c5 2. Nf3 d6 3. Bb5+ Bd7 4. Bxd7+ Nxd7 5. 0–0 Ngf6 6. Re1 e6 7. c3 c4!?

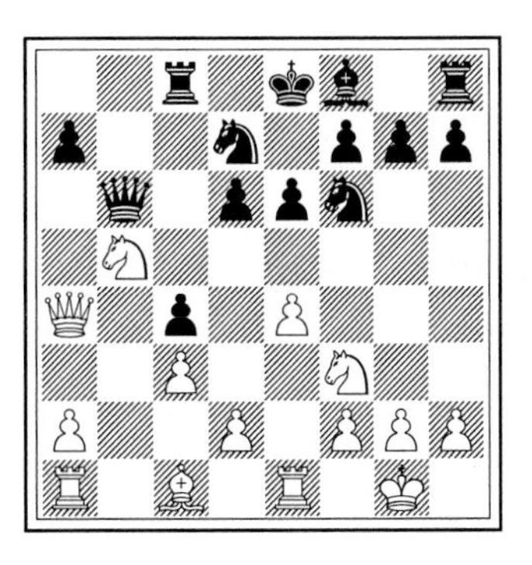

After 12. ... Qb6

Standard play is 7. ... Be7 8. d4 cxd4 9. cxd4 d5 with rough equality. The Shanghai grandmaster plainly wanted to sharpen matters (with ...Nc5, for example).

8. b3 b5 9. bxc4 bxc4 10. Qa4! Qc7 11. Na3 Rc8 12. Nb5 Qb6

13. d4!

Naturally not 13. Nxa7 Ra8. Black now must dance through a warren of complications. For the next few moves he seemed to be on the cusp of tactical disaster—but also close to securing a solid positional advantage.

13. ... cxd3 14. Be3 Qc6!

Not 14. ... Qb7 15. Rab1, threatening Nxd6+.

15. Nfd4 Qc4 16. Qa6! Nxe4! 17. Bf4 Ndf6

Karlson could see that 18. Bxd6 Nxc3! only made matters worse (19. Bxf8 Kxf8 20. Qd6+ Kg8 and 21. ... Nxb5). She sank into thought. You could tell by her pursed lips she was going to be a while, at least 15 minutes, by my guess. Experience had made me good at guessing such things.

I lured Qi into my office by telling him we needed to talk about his win from the previous day, for the benefit of the tournament book. He seemed impervious to praise.

"Nice move, Ne8," I said.

"It was the fastest win."

"Fastest is best."

"Grandmasters often say they prefer the fastest," Qi said. "But then they play the move that gets the most attention."

"They try to have it both ways."

"Actually they sometimes try to have it three ways."

I was trying to make small talk before getting to questions. But the world's third-ranked player seemed even more obscure than usual.

"How is that?" I asked.

"Let me say I have studied the history of your game. And I found the best players always try to pretend chess is something else."

"Such as?"

"Such as art," he said. "First, they claimed chess was more than just a game."

"You mean the Romantics."

"Yes, and then came Steinitz and Tarrasch, who claimed chess was something more advanced than art."

"Science," I said.

"Of course. They were followed by the Russians. But the Russians couldn't promote chess as an art or science."

"Too elitist for good Marxist-Leninists."

Qi seemed pained by that, but continued.

"They composed a new formula: chess equals sport. As a result, chessplayers managed to have it three ways—art, science, sport, depending on what was expedient at the moment."

He didn't seem to mind the possibility that his clock was ticking by now.

"And in the past 60 years this cycle was repeated," he said.

"Repeated?"

"Yes. First, Botvinnik claimed chess was science again because adjournments were the discipline of objective analysis."

"I read something about that…"

"But then the GMs wanted to end adjournments," he said. "They justified that by saying chess was really a test of mental endurance. A sport."

I tried to think of some way to object, but Qi wasn't done.

"And when time limits were speeded up again, they turned around and said, 'This is terrible—it destroys chess-the-art.' And then ten years ago—"

"I get the point."

"All of this to obscure the obvious," he said. "For the top players, chess was never more than a trade."

"But a skilled trade, a craft with a tradition."

"Yes," he said. "Like blacksmithing."

This was already—by far—my longest conversation with Qi. And I couldn't say I enjoyed it.

"I never realized how cynical you were."

"Not cynical. Realistic," he said. "Just as I'm realistic enough to know you didn't summon me here to discuss how I checkmated Zdravko Popov."

"Hold that thought," I said, as I noticed Popov and Bastrikova enter the office to drop off their scoresheets. "I have to earn my paycheck."

Qi took his time heading back to his board while I quickly played through the moves of the mighty Popov vs. Bastrikova struggle. They'd had quite a remarkable game:

Popov–Bastrikova
Queen's Gambit Declined D07

1. d4 d5 2. c4 Nc6 3. Nf3 Bg4 4. c×d5 B×f3 5. g×f3 Q×d5 6. e3 e6 7. Nc3 Qh5 8. f4 Qh4

That seemed odd. Considering their standing in the tournament, I expected 8. … Q×d1+ and a quick draw. But, then again, Popov never plays 1. d4.

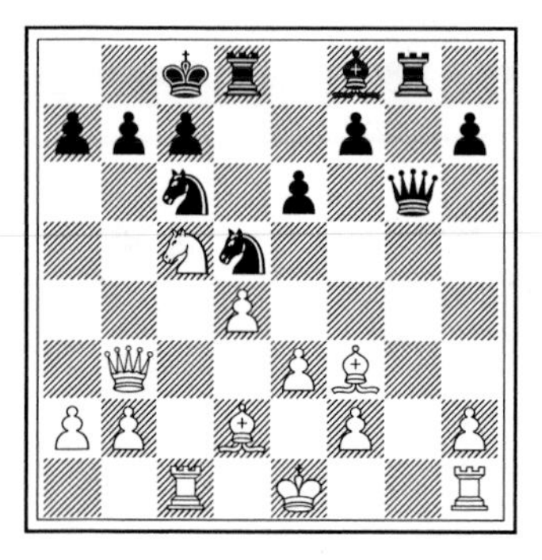

After 16. Qb3

9. Bg2 Nge7 10. Bd2 0–0–0 11. Rc1 g5! 12. f×g5 Q×g5 13. Bf3 Rg8

This all looked suspiciously like theory but I couldn't tell.

14. Ne4 Qg6 15. Nc5 Nd5 16. Qb3

White threatens mate and can meet 16. … Nb6 with 17. N×b7!. Black has a defense of sorts in the form of 16. … b6 17. Qa4 Nb8. But then 18. Nb3 is clearly in White's favor.

My suspicions were confirmed when the scoresheets continued:

16. … Qg1+! 17. R×g1

No choice here. On 17. Ke2 Nf4+! 18. e×f4 N×d4+ 19. Ke3 Nf5+ 20. Ke2 Black disdains the repetition of moves and wins with 20. … R×d2+! 21. K×d2 Q×f2+.

17. … R×g1+ 18. Ke2 Nf4+! 19. e×f4 N×d4+

Both sides were playing "box" moves. That is, forced moves, which would be designated in *Informant* annotations with a small box.

Black would sweep the table of enemy pieces now after 20. Kd3 N×b3+.

20. Ke3 Nf5+ 21. Ke2!

Another "box" (not 21. Ke4?? Rd4+ 22. Ke5 Bg7 mate).

21. … Nd4+ 22. Ke3 Nf5+ 23. Ke2 Nd4+ 24. Ke3 Nf5+ Draw

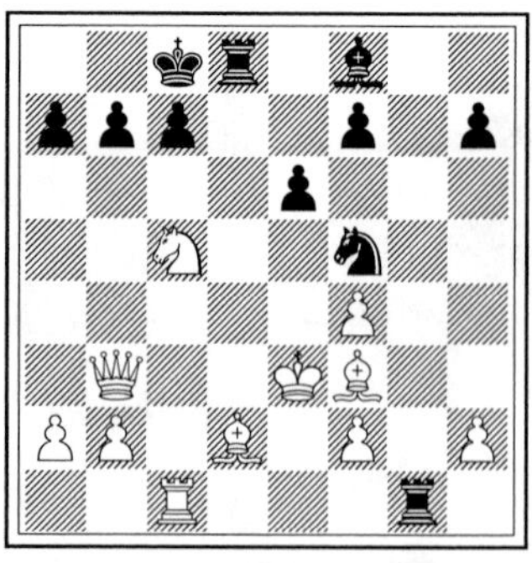

Final position

"How many times has this game been played?" I asked.

"Counting this time? Approximately … six," Bastrikova said.

"Two of the others ended at move 20," Popov said.

"And two others ended after the second repetition," Bastrikova said.

"But we didn't want to cheat the fans," Popov said.

This wasn't much better than the no-move game Popov played with Vilković two days ago. But I was no longer capable of being outraged.

"You're each getting paid a seven-figure fee to play real games here," I said, holding up Popov's scoresheet. "That should come to more than $3,000 a move for each of you for today's game."

They were unrepentant.

"You can't blame us for wanting to draw," Bastrikova said. "Not with where we stand in the scoretable."

"Besides," Popov said, "Isn't it better if the patzers play through games like this and think they're real than if we make 12 book moves and then shake hands?"

I wasn't up to dealing with such logic today, and just filed the scoresheets with a perfunctory, "Thank you for your diligence."

By the time I got back to the playing area, a lot had happened, beginning with the transition to the endgame at Karlson's table.

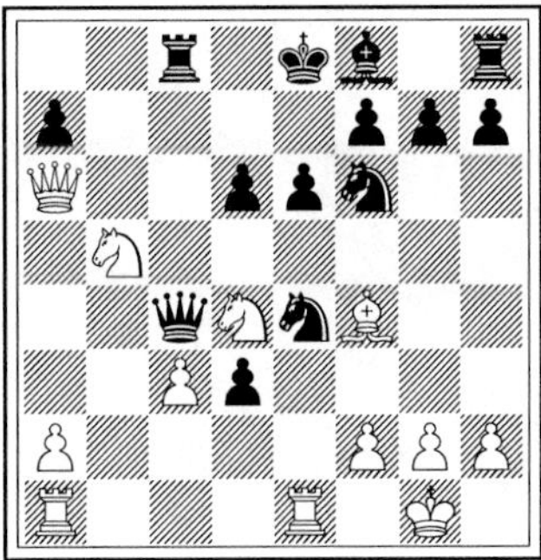

Karlson–Qi
After 17. ... Ndf6

Karlson–Qi

18. f3 d2?!

Not 18. ... N×c3 19. Rac1 Nfd5 20. Bd2 when White is winning.

I made a mental note for the tournament book about this being a possible turning point in the race for first prize. A loss would have doomed Qi's chances. Maybe he shouldn't have spent so much time in my office.

19. R×e4 N×e4 20. f×e4 e5 21. Nf5!

Here 21. ... Qc5+ 22. Be3 Rc6 looked like a defense. For example, 23. Nc7+ Kd7. But the simple 23. Qa4! leaves the queen trapped on c5.

21. ... Qc6 22. Nb×d6+?

With 22. Nf×d6+ B×d6 23. Q×c8+! White keeps an extra piece.

22. ... Kd7!

Again Black avoided a trade of minor pieces (22. ... B×d6 23. N×d6+ Kd7) because of 23. Q×c8+!.

23. Q×c8+ Q×c8 24. N×c8 e×f4!

Another point: The knight is trapped on c8.

25. N×a7 Bc5+ 26. Kf1 B×a7

Bohigian usually treasured his free days, if only to sleep late. But this afternoon he appeared by 5 P.M. to examine games, principally the ones on Boards Two and Five that might cost him prize money.

"What do you think?" I whispered when I found him studying this position.

"Black is playing sloppy but clever," he said. "White is making fewer mistakes but bigger ones."

"And the result?"

He seemed surprised by the question. "Oh, draw, of course."

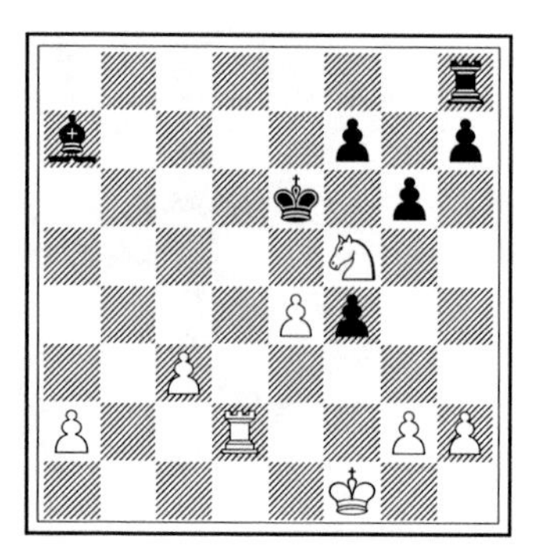

After 28. ... Ke6

27. Rd1 g6 28. R×d2+ Ke6

White has no serious winning chances after 29. Rd6+ Ke5 30. Rd7 g×f5 31. R×a7 f×e4.

29. Nd4+ B×d4! 30. c×d4 Ra8 31. Ke2 Ra3!

Qi arose from the board and headed towards me with the unconcerned air of someone who knew all of the remaining moves of his game. (As it turned out, he did.)

He was eager to continue our conversation in my office.

"This is really about the alleged blackmail, isn't it?"

"Something like that."

"I, too, have heard the rumors," he said.

"And?"

"And there is a very simple reason Van Siclen got those invitations from my federation. He asked for them."

"That simple."

"That simple. Half the players in this tournament expect organizers to approach them, like supplicants bearing invitations to royalty."

"And the others?"

"The other half send their agents to the organizers, like ambassadors trying to arrange state visits for monarchs."

"You're saying Gert was different?"

"He was different. He did the asking himself. That is appreciated in my country."

"Sounds too easy."

"Some things are."

After a bit more back and forth, I found myself with only one remaining question. But Qi anticipated me.

"Besides, I had nothing to do with the death of Gabor. Or of Van Siclen or the girl."

"The sheriff just wants to make sure," I said.

"I don't know the sheriff. But you know very well why I couldn't have killed them."

"And how do I know this?"

Qi raised a single eyebrow in surprise.

"I could never be a murderer," he said. "*I* am a vegetarian."

Back on stage, Karlson was still trying to figure out how to coax a win out of her pawn-up rook ending. Popov, Bastrikova and Vilković didn't wait around to find out if she could. And Krimsditch had taken two hours and 29 minutes to play 23 moves before resigning. His attempt at a comeback had gone:

Krimsditch–Boriescu
King's Indian Defense E62

1. d4 Nf6 2. c4 g6 3. g3 Bg7 4. Bg2

Krimsditch was hardly the literary type, but he knew how to read a tournament bulletin: Boriescu had gotten clobbered in the first round in this line.

4. ... 0–0 5. Nf3 d6 6. Nc3 c6 7. 0–0 Qa5 8. h3 e5

The Romanian lost to Qi six rounds before with 8. ... Qa6 9. b3

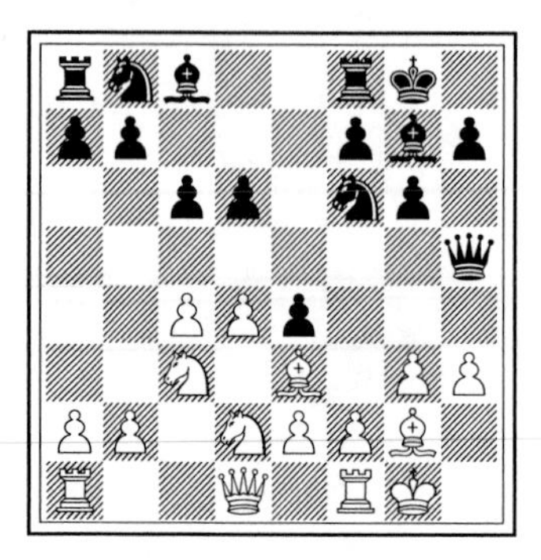

After 10. ... Qh5

b5 10. cxb5 cxb5 11. a4!. Now after 8. ... e5 White gets a nice game with 9. d5. But Krimsditch preferred:

9. Be3 e4 10. Nd2 Qh5?

Black didn't like 10. ... d5 11. Qb3 so he offers an indirect trade of e-pawn for h-pawn. But even I could see it was an awful trade. Surely White realized he could get a solid and substantial edge with 11. Ndxe4 Bxh3 12. Nxf6+ Bxf6 13. Ne4 Be7 14. f3, didn't he?

Krimsditch saw it differently. To redeem his tournament he wanted to make absolutely certain he'd win this game. And to do that he felt he had to prove that 10. ... Qh5 was not just bad, but losing. This meant provoking the piece sacrifice.

But that's a telltale sign of when a GM is in free-fall. He no longer trusts his ability to win a favorable position with simple moves, like 11. Ndxe4!.

11. g4? Bxg4! 12. hxg4 Nxg4 13. Bf4 f5!

This is what White overlooked: ...Bh6 and ...f4 will break the defense of h2, e.g. 14. Bxd6 f4!.

Krimsditch had probably counted only on 13. ... Bxd4 14. N3xe4 and Nf3.

14. e3 Bh6 15. Bxd6

Or 15. Bg3 f4 16. exf4 Bxf4 with a terrific initiative for Black (17. Ncxe4 Bxg3 18. Nf3 Rxf3).

15. ... f4! 16. Re1 Qh2+ 17. Kf1 Nxf2!

By opening the f-file—and avoiding 17. ... Nd7?? 18. Qxg4 or 17. ... f3?? 18. Bxh2, Black forces the win home. Now 18. Nf3 can be met by 18. ... exf3 19. Qxf3 Nd3 or just 18. ... Qg3!.

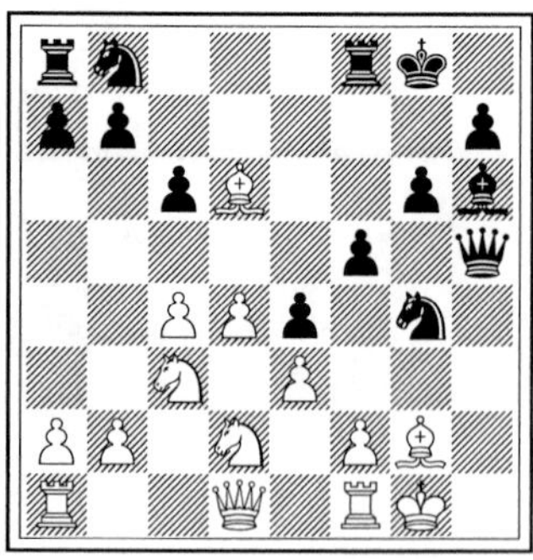

After 15. Bxd6

18. Qc2

Hoping for 18. ... Nd3?? 19. Re2 when White wins.

18. ... Nh3!

The threat is 19. ... Qg1+. And 19. Bxh3 fxe3+ is out of the question.

19. Ne2 Nd7!

By connecting rooks, Black makes 20. ... fxe3+ a killer.

20. Qxe4 fxe3+!

White can keep the game going after 20. ... Ng5 21. Qxf4! Rxf4+ 22. Bxf4.

Then Black would be able to save his queen with 22. ... Rf8 23. Nf3 Qh5 24. Ng3 Qg4 but 25. Kf2 forces him to play an endgame. Now there is no endgame.

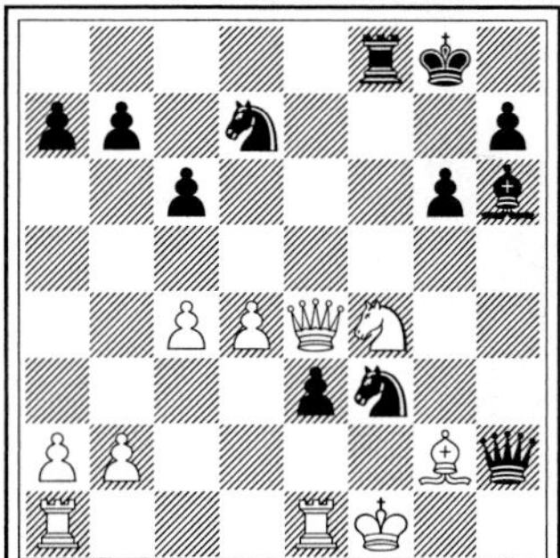

Final position

21. Bxf8 Rxf8+ 22. Nf3 Ng5 23. Nf4

A last-gasp trap: 23. ... Nxe4 24. Nxh2.

23. ... Nxf3! White resigns

When he stopped his clock, Krimsditch had the look of someone ready to abandon 1. d4 for 1. e4—or for Go. The outcome would have been clear after 24. Rxe3 Nd2+ or 24. Qe6+ Kh8 25. Rxe3 Nxd4!.

Finally, there was Board Five, where Grushevsky had arrived with his celebrated thermos.

Each world champion seemed to have his secret elixir. For Fischer it was milk and mineral water. Botvinnik always had some mysterious juice with him at the board. Karpov's purplish yogurt became notorious in the '78 world championship match. For Bohigian it was his gingko-laced, decaf green tea.

No one knew exactly what Grushevsky's formula consisted of. But there was plenty of speculation. A high-protein amino-acid brew? Fruit nectar and honey? All that was known is that Grushevsky resorted to it at crucial points in the game, usually when he was happy about his position. And so it began:

Grushevsky–Royce-Smith
Ruy Lopez C88

1. e4 e5 2. Nf3 Nc6 3. Bb5 a6 4. Ba4 Nf6 5. 0–0 Be7 6. Re1 b5 7. Bb3 Bb7 8. d4

Double-edged, of course. But so is the neo–Marshall (8. c3 d5) these days.

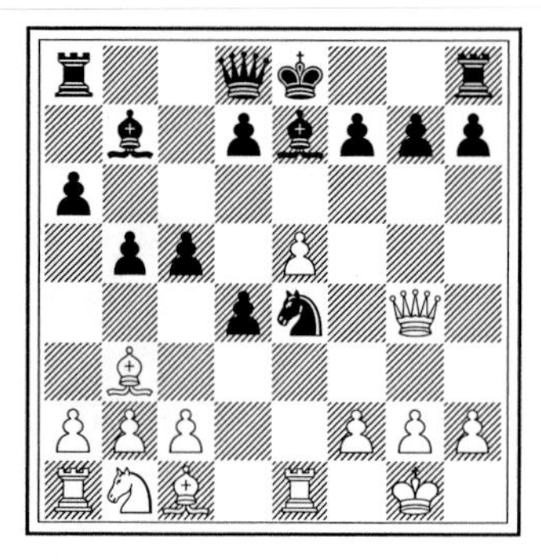

After 11. Qg4 c5

8. ... N×d4 9. N×d4 e×d4 10. e5 Ne4 11. Qg4 c5

When I checked, I found out that "book" was 12. Q×g7 Rf8 13. Q×h7 c4 14. R×e4 c×b3 or 13. ... Ng5 14. B×g5 B×g5 15. e6—with total chaos.

12. c4!

Grushevsky slowly unscrewed the thermos cap and took his first sip. He threatens 13. R×e4 or 13. Q×g7.

12. ... Ng5 13. f4 b×c4 14. B×c4

Now Black can't allow 14. ... Ne6 15. f5 Ng5 16. f6 and White wins.

14. ... h5! 15. Qd1 d5!

At first this just looked like a piece-dropper. Grushevsky again reached for his thermos—then thought better about it and studied the board for several minutes.

Of course, he had to take on d6. It was what happens then after the Black knight check that had him concerned.

16. e×d6 Nh3+! 17. g×h3 Q×d6

Black threatens 18. ... Qg6+ and 18. ... Qc6.

18. Bd3 c4!

Grushevsky always had two fears when he sat down for a game. The first, naturally, was that he might lose. Even he considered that a possibility.

The second fear was that he might lose brilliantly. A loss would damage his standing in a tournament and tarnish his reputation. But there was always another tournament. A brilliant loss, however, would never die. It would live on in the anthologies forever.

Here Grushevsky made sure Black wouldn't get his chance to be brilliant—as he would after 19. Qa4+ Kf8 20. Qxc4 Rc8. Then Black wins with 21. Qa4 Qd5 22. Be4 Qxe4!! 23. Rxe4 Rxc1+ 24. Kf2 Bxe4, for example.

19. Bf5!

White must be able to plug up the h1–a8 diagonal to stop the mating threats. Now he can meet ...Qc6 or ...Qd5 with Be4!.

19. ... Rh6 20. Kf1 Re6!

This ends the Be4 defense (21. Rxe6 fxe6 22. Bg6+ Kd8 23. Nd2 Qxf4+ and wins). But White still had a resource....

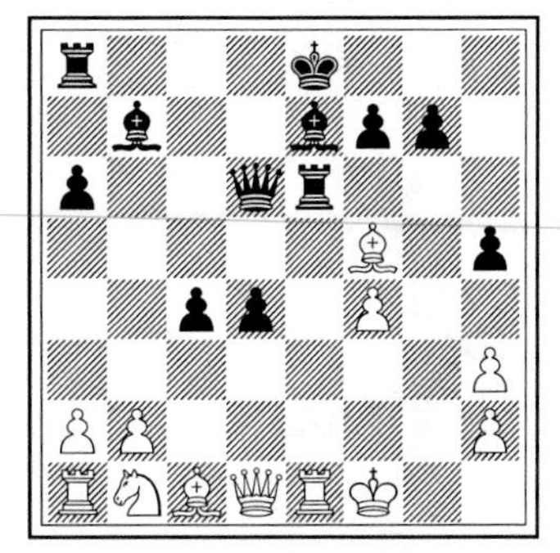

After 20. ... Re6

21. Bxe6 Qc6! 22. Bd7+!

White avoids 22. Bxf7+ Kf8! when Black wins, e.g. 23. Ke2 Qf3+ 24. Kd2 Qd3 mate or 23. Qc2 Qh1+ 24. Ke2 d3+.

Grushevsky signaled his satisfaction by taking a long swig from the thermos. Then he strategically centered it in front of his chest. It stood an inch or so directly behind d1 and e1—and inevitably in Royce-Smith's line of sight. Purely accidental, of course.

22. ... Qxd7 23. Qxh5 Qc6 24. Qg4 Kf8

Although a rook down, it was hard to see a defense for White in view of some devastating mix of ...d3, ...Bc5, ...Re8 and ...Qh1+.

For example, 25. Nd2 Bb4 26. Kf2 d3 27. Rd1 is mated by 27. ... Bc5+ 28. Kg3 Qg2+ 29. Kh4 Be7+ 30. Kh5 Qd5+.

Maybe that wouldn't make it the game of the year. But it would be the only one that players, grandmasters as well as patzers, would be talking about for weeks.

25. Rxe7!

Again the world champion went to the thermos. Clearly he felt he wasn't losing. But was he winning?

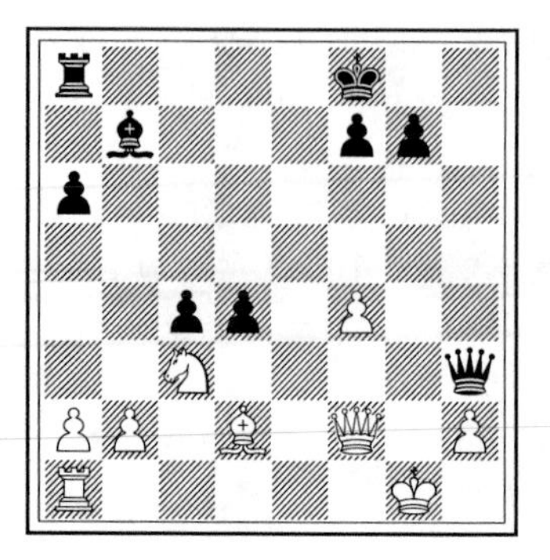

After 30. Kg1

25. ... K×e7 26. Bd2! Kf8

Black had one last tactical idea—27. ... Re8 followed by ...Qh1+.

27. Nc3! Qh1+ 28. Qg1 Qf3+ 29. Qf2 Q×h3+ 30. Kg1

After this, both kings are safe and the material situation is inconclusive.

Grushevsky signaled he was ready to talk peace—by removing the thermos from his side of the table and resting it on the floor.

30. ... d×c3 31. B×c3 Re8

The threat is ...Re6–g6+. Now 32. Qg3 Q×g3+ 33. h×g3 Re2 is loseable. Not lost, but capable of being lost.

32. Re1 R×e1+ 33. B×e1 Qg4+

Royce-Smith got the thermos hint. Unless Grushevsky took leave of his senses (34. Kf1? Be4 35. Qc5+? Kg8 36. Bd2 Qg2+ 37. Ke1 Bd3!) the draw was ready to be recorded on the crosstable.

The Englishman decided to go through a few more half-hearted attempts to win. After all, how often do you get the opportunity to do this to Grushevsky?

34. Qg3 Qe2 35. Qf2 Qe4 36. Qg3 Qd4+ 37. Qf2 Qd5 Draw

A draw with Black was no mean achievement for Royce-Smith. It left him in first place by at least a half point with four games to go. His lead might have been more than half a point but the one remaining game was something of an anticlimax. Karlson was making no progress.

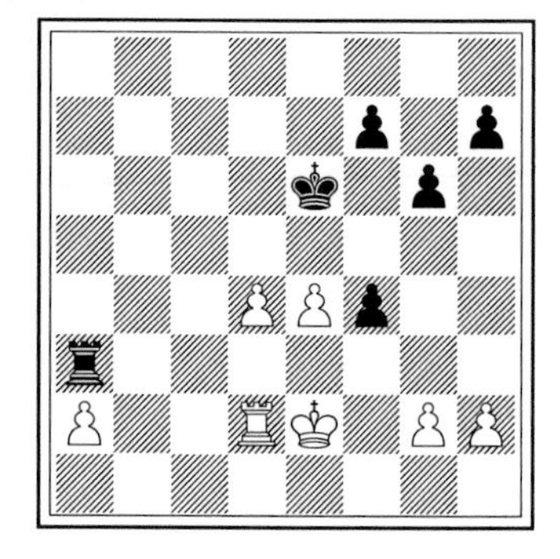

Karlson–Qi
After 31. ... Ra3

Karlson–Qi

It's not just the threat of ...Re3+ that saves Black. White's main problem is that she can't activate her king or rook safely. For example, 32. Rd3 Rxa2+ 33. Kf3 g5 34. Rb3 Rd2.

32. Kd1 Rc3! 33. Rc2 Rd3+ 34. Rd2 Rc3

And here 35. a4 Ra3 is no help to White.

35. Rc2 Rd3+ 36. Rd2 Rc3 Draw

And that was the round, perhaps the best day so far in terms of games, Popov vs. Bastrikova notwithstanding. It was also productive in another way. Besides, Qi and Karlson, I'd also managed to question several of the other players, but without significant success. As I was posting the standings...

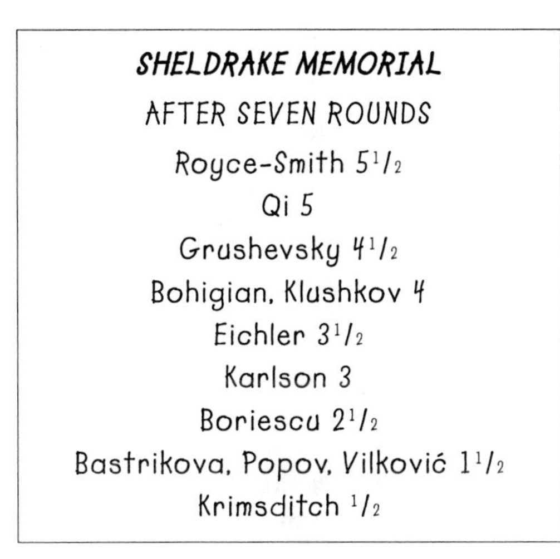
SHELDRAKE MEMORIAL
AFTER SEVEN ROUNDS
Royce-Smith 5½
Qi 5
Grushevsky 4½
Bohigian, Klushkov 4
Eichler 3½
Karlson 3
Boriescu 2½
Bastrikova, Popov, Vilković 1½
Krimsditch ½

...I noticed that Eichler was winding up a chat with Blair. It was time to gather intelligence, about both of them.

"Why don't you simply organize the tournament to get the best quality chess?" Eichler was asking.

"Nah, we focus-grouped and target-polled that idea. It'd never sell."

I waited for Blair to finish—which he did, hurriedly, when he spotted Grushevsky leaving.

"Oh, Igor!" was the last I heard as he disappeared through the auditorium's central door.

"What was that all about?" I asked.

"Conditions, of course" Eichler said.

Conditions being GM-speak for appearance fees, per diems and other tournament perks.

"Good conditions?"

"I really can't tell. Rollie handles conditions."

Rollie Kluytsen was Eichler's Amsterdam-based manager and personal shock absorber. Kluytsen made all of his major decisions, financial and otherwise. There was widespread doubt Eichler could put on his Patek Philippe without him.

"But Boyd is a compelling talker," he said. "He understands my marquee value."

"Your marquee value?"

"Of course, everyone wants to see the next world champion."

"You're pretty sure of that."

"Of course," he said. "In two years, Grushevsky will be over the hill. Qi doesn't have my genius. Neither does Royce-Smith. Boriescu and Popov are butchers, they lack my depth. The women are a joke. And Klushkov is crazy."

"I see what you mean."

"There's nobody else. Very simply, I *am* the future of chess."

The remarkable thing was that he wasn't being arrogant. He really believed this. And since he enjoyed talking about himself I had no trouble nudging the conversation towards Topic A.

"The travel must be taking a toll on you."

"Yes, of course. There is always a next tournament, a next hotel, a next e-ticket, a next set of faces to nod to and names to forget."

"You probably don't get home much."

"True, but my public demands me."

"And you don't get to see your parents often."

"That's the price of celebrity."

Eichler didn't realize where I was going, even when I asked about his father, that is, about which of his interests he shared.

"I enjoy Mahler, of course. And skiing. And any of his favorite dishes with wild mushrooms."

"What about his professional interests?"

"Well, I learned a bit about reptiles. Of course. Who couldn't in that home?" he laughed.

There was no way to set up the next question. I didn't try.

"I see. One more question. In all the traveling you do, all over the world, did you ever hear of something called Compound 1080?"

That drew what seemed like a flicker of recognition in his eyes. But he said:

"I hear about so many things. I can't recall that name."

"Look, Johnny, it's come to Sheriff Gibbs' attention that because of your family background you might have an appreciation..."

That was the best word I could find.

"...an appreciation of the weapon that killed Daphne."

"Yes?"

"And that has certain implications."

"*Yes*. Now I see what you're saying."

"I thought it might be easier for you to talk with me about it than with the sheriff."

"It is. But this is all absurd. Of course, the murderer must be someone else."

"Why is that?"

"You of all people should know. You watch my games every day."

"And your games tell me something?"

"They should tell you I'm certainly not a murderer."

"Because?"

"Because I'm a positional player, of course."

After a depressing margarita-fueled dinner alone, I retired to my room at the Casa with a new appreciation—that was the best word I could find—for law enforcement:

I wasn't cut out to be a cop. Good, bad or otherwise.

I had barely been in the room five minutes before Gibbs knocked. He'd been off my radar screen for hours, apparently at another town meeting he couldn't miss.

"Just wanted to see how the tourists live," he said after I opened the door.

I motioned him to the desk chair, but the sheriff just took a few steps inside and remained standing.

"Am I interrupting something important?" he said.

"Only my preparations for tomorrow. I like to look over the pairings and see what the next crisis will be."

"That part of your job description?"

"No, just a quality I bring to the profession that works."

"On that other matter..."

"Yes."

"Find out anything?"

"Not much," I admitted. "Karlson could have gotten into Gabor's room. Eichler knows snakes."

"Uh-huh."

"And Qi had a pat answer about blackmail. Same story with the others I questioned."

"Not much," he agreed. "Do they have alibis?"

"That's the problem—no one does. And their explanations of their innocence are worse."

"How worse?"

"One says she can't be the killer because right now the sun is conjuncting with Jupiter."

Gibbs frowned.

"Another is not guilty by reason of broccoli."

More frown.

"And the third is innocent because his middlegames are nonviolent—and Petrosians are incapable of homicide."

Gibbs rolled his eyes.

"Ooh-kay," he said slowly, and turned to leave.

"Sheriff, there is something else."

"I hoped there was."

"It has nothing to do with what I found out today," I said. "Just a theory."

"A theory is better than nothin' right now."

"Well, we've limited our list of suspects to people we can see. Is it possible the murderer is someone we can't? You know, Blair got me to thinking about the towns around here…"

"Like Mudturtle Gulch."

"Yeah, like Mudturtle Gulch."

Gibbs smiled as he shook his head.

"Let me guess," he said. "Next thing you're going to tell me is that this fellow Krilinsky did the murders."

"Krilinsky?"

"While hiding out in a trailer, somewhere near town."

"Krilinsky?"

"I didn't know until today that a man named Vyacheslav Krilinsky existed," Gibbs said. "Now I know he was the next best player in the world after this group."

"*Krilinsky*?!"

"And that means he would stand to gain the most if anyone in the tournament went away."

Gibbs' learning curve astonished me. A week ago he didn't know chess wasn't played with dice.

Now he had discovered that Krilinsky—the GM I'd briefly thought of as a replacement for Gabor a week ago—was the 15th-highest-rated player in the world. And that might give Krilinsky a motive for serial murder.

"But I guess from your expression you had a different theory," he said.

It took me a moment to refocus.

"I must confess that idea—Krilinsky—never occurred to me."

"Understandable."

"But something even crazier did."

"I'm listening."

"Well," I said, "Two days ago, I reminded the players how isolated Los Voraces is, how sealed off. And then I spoke to someone who pointed out how, even by New Mexico standards the town sort of keeps to itself."

"So?"

"I mean, something could happen here and the outside world might never hear about it."

"I still don't see—"

"Suppose Sheldrake didn't die."

It was his turn to be surprised. "That's your theory? Sheldrake is the killer?"

"Hear me out," I said. "Suppose he faked his own death last year. Only a few people in town would know. And they're so closed-mouthed, the truth would never get out."

"No way."

"He would have the means—after all, he was a millionaire. And he'd have the opportunity, if he was hiding somewhere over our shoulders. Besides, he had the best motive."

"Mr. Sheldrake sponsored your tournament."

"But suppose he wanted revenge on the players for all the petty incidents of the past. Like three years ago when Van Siclen got loaded at the final dinner in Sheldrake's mansion, and started smashing Sèvres dessert plates in the fireplace."

"No way."

"Or that night when Gabor told him off, and said he was an uncultured imperialist pig. Come to think of it, Sheldrake had a reason to hold a grudge against most of the players. Maybe all of them."

Gibbs waited for me to finish, then studied me for a good twenty seconds.

"You have quite an imagination," he said. "But I can assure you Mr. Sheldrake is no longer among the living. I saw the body."

"But what if—"

"I *saw* the body."

We looked at each other for a moment and then shook our heads. How desperate had we become?

"What do we do now?" I asked.

"Ask more questions."

"I felt uncomfortable asking dumb questions today."

"Ask enough dumb questions," Gibbs said, "and you eventually get some truthful answers."

"That part of *your* job description?"

"No," said the sheriff. "Just a quality I bring to the profession that works."

Thursday, August 29, 2019

Over the years, it always seemed that the most important location at any international tournament I ran—aside from the complimentary food and drink tables in the hospitality suite—was the place where the crosstable was posted. At Los Voraces I always posted two.

One went up in the hotel, along with the day's pairings and results. It inevitably became the earliest gathering spot of the day for the grandmasters. The other crosstable I put up at the playing site, on the back wall, behind the boards and tables. It was close enough to my office and several steps from the players still at work, and it stood directly below the large black-rimmed clock that dominated the auditorium stage.

Why the GMs frequented both spots—visiting the lobby at least once each morning and evening, and checking out the tournament site's crosstable three or four times each game—I could never fathom.

After all, they knew the standings by heart. They also seemed to know how many Elo points they stood to gain or lose at any given moment. They could calculate everyone's Tournament Performance Rating instantly. And, of course, they could recite the key pairings three rounds in advance.

At least when the super–GMs were at the high school, a look at the standings was an excuse for them to stretch their legs. At the Casa, it was just a place to gossip, a 2800-rated chat room. As in:

"Did you hear? New York is canceled."

"Again?"

"Again. But Moscow is back on."

"What about conditions?"

"Good conditions."

"And New Delhi?"

"Unclear."

And so on. But today I found a bit more than gossip at the lobby crosstable.

An animated discussion was going in front of it between Grushevsky, Vilković, Bohigian and Boyd Blair. Or rather between Blair, Grushevsky and Vilković. Bohigian just seemed to be listening for the entertainment value, as he sat in an easy chair enjoying his morning coffee and croissant.

"But you still owe me money for Jakarta," Grushevsky said, jabbing Blair's chest with a stubby forefinger.

"Me, too," said Vilković.

"One hundred twenty-five thousand. That was the agreement," said Grushevsky.

"I also had an agreement!" Vilković said.

Jakarta 2017 had been one of Blair's less successful enterprises: a $2 million "clock-simul" tournament. (Each GM had to play six games—simultaneously, on six boards with clocks—against the opponent he was paired with that day.)

But the tournament collapsed when the players discovered the $2 million existed only in Blair's imagination and they took the next available Garuda Airlines flight home.

"I'm afraid you are confusing me," Blair said.

"This is not difficult to understand," Grushevsky said. "Your check bounced."

"No, I mean you are confusing me with a corporate entity with which I was briefly but am no longer affiliated."

"It was your company," Grushevsky said. "United Thinkers, or ... whatever."

Actually, it was Thinkers United, Ltd. Blair incorporated it in Argentina, established tax-exempt status in Bermuda and set up a mailing address on an island off China. At least, he had all this going until Thinkers couldn't pay its cell phone bills and went bankrupt.

"I was merely a humble employee, carrying out the firm's bidding," Blair said with a dismissive wave of the hand. "An underling, a menial subordinate in the vast corporate hierarchy."

Grushevsky wasn't buying it.

"I lowered my minimum fee—just this once—because you promised there would be three more Jakartas."

"And so there would have been," Blair said. "But unfortunately my Indonesian co-sponsors didn't see matters the same way I did. Something about a nasty fall in tin futures and bad news for the rupiah."

Bohigian shot me an amused glance. He alone among the grandmaster elite resisted playing in Blair's trash-chess shows.

"And you dare to ask me—" Grushevsky said, getting louder.

"To ask me, too!" Vilković said.

"—to ask me to take part in another of your ... money-funny tournaments."

"That's funny-money," I said, joining in.

"I am not amused, either way," Grushevsky said.

But Blair was accustomed to playing defense.

"Don't say 'no' until you've seen what I have in store. Don't pass up the opportunity of a lifetime. Don't close your mind to the future of chess!"

"This is not about the future," Grushevsky said. "This is about the past, specifically my one hundred—"

"Ah, but you must think about the future, about modernization, innovation," Blair said. "Where would the game be if grandmasters long ago had refused to accept the Swiss System? Or if they had rejected the Fischer clock? Or Advanced Chess? Or blindfold team tournaments? Or the World Pawn-and-Move Championship? You must take chess to the next level or it will wither on the vine. It will shrivel and decay. It will die of mental malnutrition. As my old friend Kirsan used to say..."

It was fascinating to watch: His words seemed to have a numbing effect on his audience. Grushevsky went from outrage to contempt, then mere scorn, followed by wariness, then reluctant interest and finally grudging acceptance. Soon Blair was shepherding him in the direction of the lobby's glass door.

"Now, if you will join me and Mr. Beadle in a short jaunt to our next playing site..."

The last I saw of them was Blair, with his arm around Grushevsky, heading to the street. He kept up a steady patter, talking up the scenic wonder of playing an international tournament in a ghost town somewhere in the general vicinity of the Gadsden Purchase. And Vilković was trying to catch up to them.

When I turned to Bohigian I realized we were both shaking our heads.

"How does he do it?" I asked. "With his track record?"

"He sells them the future and that always tastes better than the present," the Armenian said.

"You'd think by now he'd run out of futures."

"He will," Bohigian said. "In the game of life, we all lose on time."

"Is that Tartakower? Or another proverb from your grandmother?"

"No," he said, as he sipped the last of his *espresso doble*. "Me."

Blair or no Blair, this was the day I had been dreading since the drawing of lots on the 21st:

Women's Day. Bastrikova versus Karlson Day. If I could get through the round without a blowup it would be a major achievement.

When I reached the high school, I reviewed the matchups.

SHELDRAKE MEMORIAL

ROUND EIGHT PAIRINGS

Vilković vs. Krimsditch

Qi vs. Eichler

Bastrikova vs. Karlson

Klushkov vs. Popov

Boriescu vs. Grushevsky

The schedule was quickly whittled to four games because Todd Krimsditch was no longer recognizable. Losing yesterday in 23 moves—and with White against Boriescu—was enough to despirit anyone.

Today the nine-time U.S. champion sleepwalked through the opening and even made Vilković look impressive.

Vilković–Krimsditch
English Opening A27

1. c4 e5 2. Nc3 Nc6 3. Nf3 f5 4. d4 e4 5. Nd2

Vilković knew his opponent: If Krimsditch was just playing out the tournament, trying to get to the last round, Vilković didn't need to complicate matters with 5. Bg5, 5. Ng5 or 5. Ne5. Black would find his own way to screw up.

5. ... Nf6 6. e3 g6 7. Be2 Bg7 8. Rb1 Qe7 9. a3 f4?

Black had the typical English task. He needed counterplay since he couldn't stop the advance of the White b-pawn and the usual queenside initiative (9. ... a5 10. Nb5 d6 11. b4). But this move left his center weak and his king vulnerable.

10. Nd5! N×d5 11. c×d5 Nd8 12. 0–0

Now 12. ... d6 13. exf4 0–0 (not 13. ... B×d4?? 14. Qa4+) looked like the best of a bad lot.

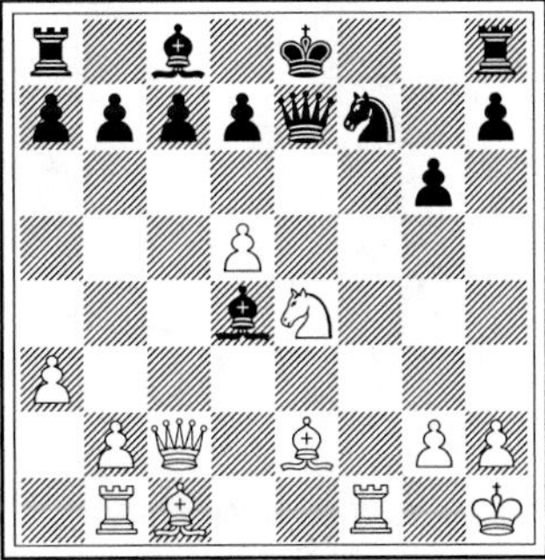

After 16. ... B×d4

12. ... f×e3 13. f×e3 Bh6? 14. Kh1! Nf7

Consistent was 14. ... B×e3. But that was likely to get Black killed after 15. N×e4! Q×e4 (15. ... B×c1? 16. Nf6+) 16. Bd3 and 17. B×e3.

15. Qc2 B×e3 16. N×e4 B×d4

Popov and I were standing behind Krimsditch as he took the pawn. I sensed that the Bulgarian felt the same way I did: White's position is ripe. All the tactical elements were in his favor. But if Black managed to castle, White's moment would be over and Krimsditch would consolidate safely. That meant White needed a big move. The leading candidates were 17. Bc4 and 17. R×f7. But they were, at best, unclear.

Popov looked up at me with shrug of the eyebrows as if to say: White has to have *something*. White did:

17. d6! N×d6

Or 17. ... c×d6 18. R×f7! K×f7 19. Qc4+ and 17. ... Qe5 18. Bc4 N×d6 19. Bf4, winning in either case.

"If I could guarantee getting positions like this, even I'd play the English," Popov whispered to me.

"Everyone would," I said.

18. Bg5! Q×e4 19. Bd3

Prettier was 19. Rbe1—since 19. ... Q×c2 allows 20. Bd3+ and mate in three.

In fact, I was surprised Vilković didn't look for something flashy like that, especially since there was still a six-figure brilliancy prize to be won.

19. ... Qe6

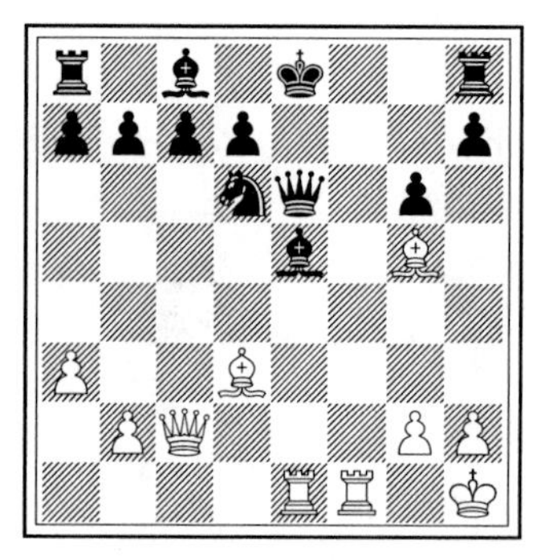

After 20. ... Be5

Black had to keep the queen in the vicinity to defend g6 (19. ... Qd5? 20. B×g6+ and it's time to sign scoresheets).

20. Rbe1 Be5

Hoping to keep the game alive to move 27 or so—which White just might do after 21. Bf6 0–0.

21. R×e5! Q×e5 22. B×g6+! Black resigns

An arbiter is usually happy to clear away one game early in a round, and this, Vilković's first victory of the tournament, was over within two hours. It was also the fifth loss in a row for Krimsditch—and what should have been his sixth had been wiped out by Van Siclen's death. I almost felt pity. But my attention today kept coming back to Board Three.

Needless to say, there was no handshake. The game began:

Bastrikova–Karlson
Sicilian Defense B76

1. e4 c5!

Surprise. Karlson lived and died with the French.

2. Nf3 d6 3. d4 c×d4 4. N×d4 Nf6 5. Nc3 g6

And on the rare occasions when Kersti played the Sicilian, she adopted the Najdorf. It seemed incredible she had prepared an opening as theory-driven as the Dragon for just one game and one opponent.

6. Be3 Bg7 7. f3 0–0 8. Qd2 Nc6 9. 0–0–0 N×d4 10. B×d4 Be6 11. Kb1 Qc7

But, I realized, this was not just any opponent. This was Bastrikova, and to Karlson she was worth a few dozen hours of preparation.

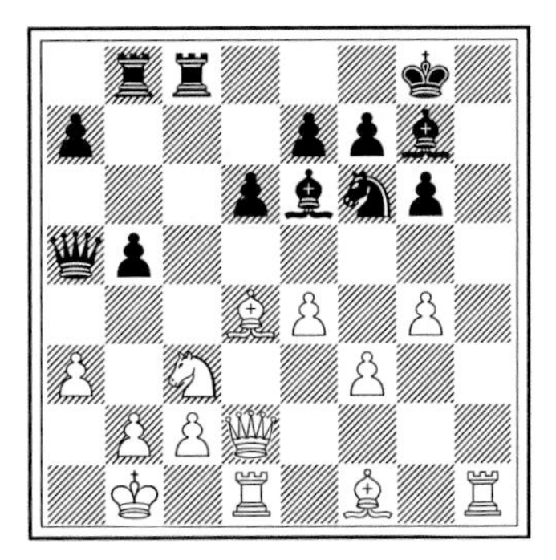

After 16. ... h×g6

12. h4 Rfc8 13. g4 Qa5 14. a3 Rab8 15. h5 b5 16. h×g6!? h×g6

While her opponent was thinking, Karlson got up from her chair and headed towards me. She was an entirely different person on the days when she played Bastrikova, and I could tell she wasn't going to chat about the latest drought report.

"I wish to lodge a formal complaint," she announced.

"I'm shocked, shocked to hear it."

"She is deliberately breaking the rules."

"Which rule?"

"Twelve point two."

Karlson waited while I tried to remember which one of FIDE's Laws of Chess was Article 12.2.

Was it the one about j'adoubing pieces? Or the one prohibiting improper draw offers?

"I give up. What's she doing this time?"

"She's changing her mind too often."

This was a new one. Even for a Bastrikova vs. Karlson.

"First, she wrote down Bishop–e2 as her seventh move," Karlson said. "Then she changed her mind and crossed it out and played f3."

"Right...?"

"Two moves later she wrote Bishop–c4, but then wrote g4 over it—and then crossed *that* off and played something else."

"And...?"

"And just now she wrote h6. But she looked at the position for another 20 minutes—then crossed it out and switched to h-takes-g."

"Kersti, I don't see how she violated anything. Even Kotov changed his mind."

"She's using notes."

So that was it. It all came back to me—FIDE Article 12.2: "During play, the players are forbidden to make use of notes...."

"You think her scoresheet constitutes notes," I said.

"Of course, it does."

"That's a novel interpretation of the rules."

"I *know* the rules," she replied.

I wasn't going to argue the point, not this early in the day.

"Your concern is duly registered."

"She deserves at least a severe warning."

"I would prefer to give her an 'expression of caution.'"

"Whatever," she said, and returned to the board.

Karlson did know the rules. Or at least the ones she could use against Bastrikova.

Over the years I'd seen her harass her nemesis with all sort of petty regulations that were ignored by other GMs:

Like demanding that Bastrikova leave the playing area as soon her game was over ("Players who have finished their games shall be considered spectators."—FIDE 12.3).

Or insisting Bastrikova *couldn't* leave the area during the game ("Players are not allowed to leave the 'playing venue' without permission of the arbiter."—FIDE 12.4).

There was even the time at Amsterdam 2015 when she and Bastrikova sat at adjacent tables, playing other people. But Karlson kept kicking the Russian's chair whenever she got up or sat down.

Karlson insisted it was accidental.

And besides, she said, the only rule that might cover the situation was 12.5—"It is forbidden to distract or annoy the opponent in any manner whatsoever."

But this didn't apply here, Karlson explained. Bastrikova was not *her* opponent that day.

Just as I knew there was likely going to be an incident with the women on Board Three, I had guessed the most interesting game of the day would be played on Board Two.

Qi had only three more Whites left in the tournament and had to get the most out of each of them if he was going to recapture the lead from Royce-Smith. And one of those Whites was today against the resurgent Eichler.

Qi–Eichler
Nimzo-Indian Defense E55

1. d4 Nf6 2. c4 e6 3. Nc3 Bb4 4. e3 c5 5. Nf3 0–0 6. Bd3 d5 7. 0–0 d×c4 8. B×c4 Nbd7 9. a3 c×d4 10. Q×d4

The Chinese GM stays in character. He didn't like hanging pawns (10. e×d4 B×c3).

And he wouldn't dare play a gambit line like 10. a×b4 d×c3 11. b×c3 Qc7 12. Be2!? Q×c3. At least he wouldn't unless he had analyzed it to move 28.

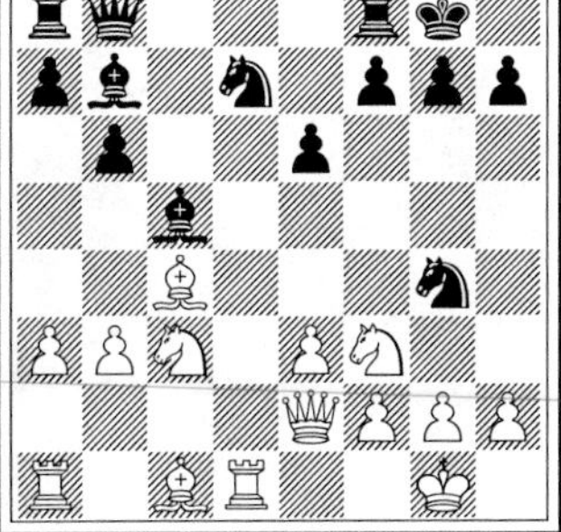
After 14. ... Ng4

10. ... Bc5 11. Qd2! b6 12. Rd1 Bb7 13. b3 Qb8! 14. Qe2 Ng4!

A nasty surprise. Meeting the threat of ...B×f3/...Q×h2+ with 15. g3 Nde5 was hardly appetizing. A series of "box" moves followed:

15. R×d7 B×f3 16. Q×f3 Q×h2+ 17. Kf1 Ne5 18. Qd1 N×d7 19. Q×d7 Rad8

It's hard to criticize a move that wins two pieces for a rook. But Korchnoi once told me it was always better to grab a pawn in positions like this and keep the pressure on than to win more material if it meant easing your opponent's task. For instance 19. ... Qh1+ 20. Ke2 Q×g2 is dangerous because White is crushed after 21. Bb2 Rfd8 22. Qa4 Qg4+ 23. Kf1 B×e3!. Maybe White is alive after 21. Qd3 but he still has to make tough choices to make.

20. Qb7 Qe5!

This was the point: The knight can't move, so Black must emerge from the game's second liquidation with at least one extra pawn.

21. Bb2 Rd2 22. Nd1

No better is 22. Rb1 R×b2 23. R×b2 Q×b2 24. Ra2 although even then Black has a lot of work to do.

22. ... R×b2 23. N×b2 Q×b2 24. Rd1 Q×a3

Even with bishops of opposite color, Black must be winning. On

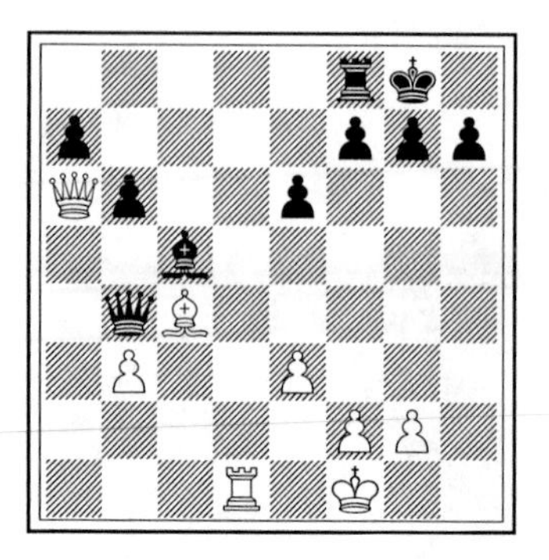

After 25. ... Qb4

25. Rd7 it looks like White is threatening 26. R×f7 and 27. B×e6. But Black can start pushing the a-pawn (25. ... a5 26. R×f7? R×f7 27. B×e6 Qc1+ 28. Ke2 Qc2+ and mates.).

25. Qa6! Qb4

26. Rd7

Or was he winning? Eichler apparently had counted on 26. Q×a7 b5!. Now he seemed to be releasing his hold on the position. White's pieces are very active now, and with bishops of opposite color that means it's very hard to simplify favorably.

26. ... h5 27. g3 Qc3 28. Q×a7 Qf6 29. Ke2

In the post-mortem, Eichler was doing a bit better with ...g5 and ...Kg7. But, for a young player, he won entirely too many post-mortems.

After 29. ... g5 30. Qb7 Kg7 31. Qe4 Re8 32. f4 Re7 Black makes progress but even then it's not clear he has anything after 33. R×e7 Q×e7 34. f×g5 and Qf4.

29. ... h4 30. g×h4 Q×h4 31. Qb7!

It soon became evident that Eichler had run out of ideas. He thought and thought. In fact, he was still thinking when his clock made the characteristic "plonk" at 5 P.M.

For years at Los Voraces I'd used the new adjustable clocks, the ones that could be programmed to make that sound to signify, say, three hours of play. If all the clocks "plonked" at 4 P.M., I knew none was gaining or losing time.

31. ... Qg4+

The g-pawn wasn't going anywhere: 31. ... g5 32. Kf1 g4 33. Be2 g3 34. Qg2.

32. Qf3 Qg5 33. Qe4 Qh5+ 34. Kf1 Re8

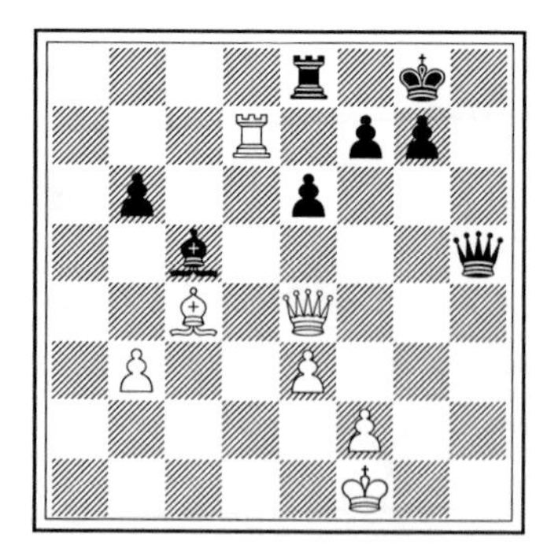

After 34. ... Re8

There was no way to untangle

35. Be2 Qh3+ 36. Kg1 Qh6 37. Bc4 Draw

That gave Qi 5½ points and a possible share of first place. Equally important was that Eichler had missed a golden opportunity to move into contention for a top prize. Maybe his last opportunity.

The two players headed to the post-mortem room. So far, so good. It was 4:20 and already I was done with two of the round's five games. And since Klushkov seemed to be having an easy time with Boriescu, it could be three out of five soon.

But the pace of the women's game had slowed down appreciably after a series of exchanges:

Bastrikova–Karlson

17. Nd5 Q×d2

Black had no choice but to trade both the queens and the remaining pair of knights.

18. R×d2 N×d5 19. B×g7 K×g7

Of course, not 19. … Ne3?? 20. Bd4 and wins.

20. e×d5 Bd7 21. Rdh2

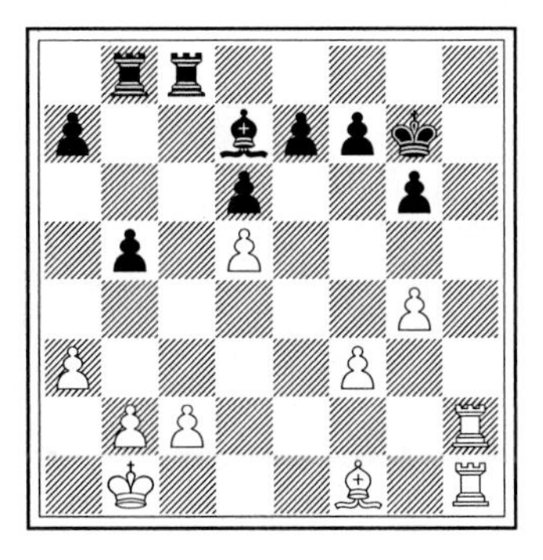

Bastrikova–Karlson
After 21. Rdh2

White had thought 17 minutes on 17. Nd5 and another 12 on 21. Rdh2. Clearly there was no mate. Did Bastrikova think she was going to win a bishop endgame?

After studying the position for a minute or two, it occurred to me she might do just that: Her king would get to b4 very quickly after the rooks were history.

While Karlson began to calculate 21. … Rh8, to stop 22. Rh7+, Bastrikova got up to check the crosstable. That's where I intercepted her.

"Look, Zhenya, I don't want an incident here."

She eyed me warily.

"She sent you."

"Actually, Grandmaster Karlson raises an interesting point about the use of a scoresheet."

I explained Kersti's innovative interpretation of 12.2.

"There are copies of the FIDE rulebook in my office, if you want to check the wording," I said. She was unmoved, to say the least.

"*Ehrunda*! Nonsense."

"I'm not saying I agree with her, but I told her I'd advise you to use caution."

Bastrikova's raised eyebrow spoke volumes.

"Don't provoke her," I added.

"I'm not the instigator. She's the one who starts. You saw what she did at Amsterdam…"

"Please. For once, don't set her off. As a favor to me."

She scowled at that. But she did owe me a favor. And I took it as a good sign that she made a detour to my office to examine a rulebook before returning to the board.

The next few moves were played fairly quickly, with no funny business on White's scoresheet.

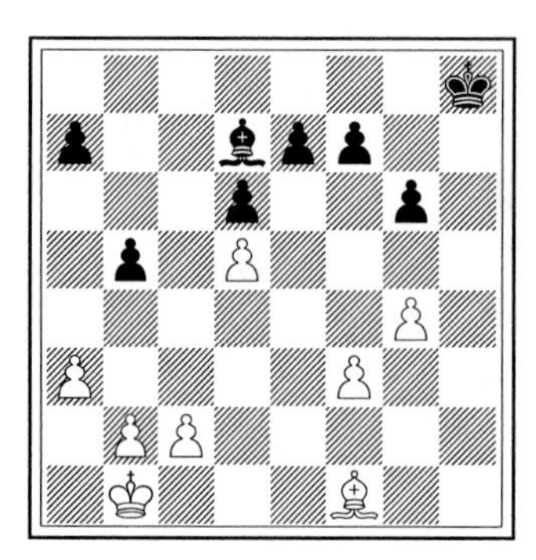

After 23. … K×h8

21. … Rh8 22. R×h8 R×h8 23. R×h8 K×h8

24. Kc1

Bastrikova said later she thought 24. Ka2 e6!? and 24. g5 f6 25. f4 fxg5 26. fxg5 e6 were "too messy." Besides, she thought the king raid to b4 or a5 was winning. What counterplay did Black have?

24. … g5! 25. Kd2 Kg7 26. Kc3 Kf6 27. Kb4

Again Karlson began to study the position at length. I could tell from where I stood that she was concentrating hard—and also doing something strange with her fingers. She seemed to be fumbling with them, in the lap of her skirt below table level. Probably just another nervous habit, like Popov's gum chewing or Krimsditch with his foot-tapping.

While this was going on there was a break in the action on Board Four that gave me an opportunity to play detective again. It happened after:

Klushkov–Popov
English Opening A19

1. c4 Nf6 2. Nc3 e6 3. e4 c5 4. e5 Ng8 5. b4

The Yaroslavl Gambit. Klushkov had a ridiculous winning percentage with it, since introducing it two years ago.

5. ... cxb4 6. Ne4 d5

A lot of those victories came after 6. ... Nc6 7. Nf3 Qc7 8. Bb2, with a dangerous White initiative brewing. Black's move here was designed to simplify the center.

7. exd6 f5

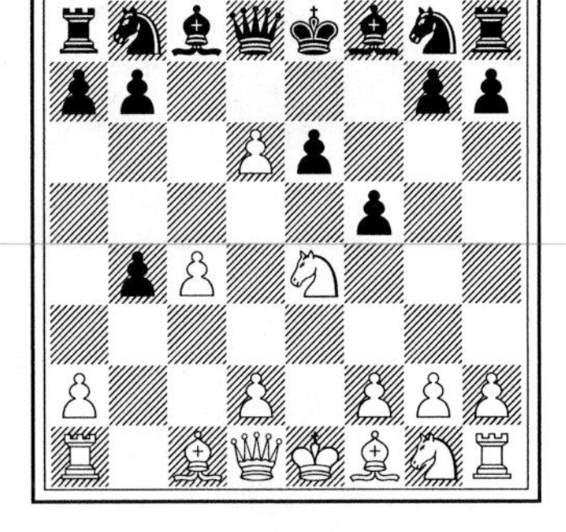

After 7. ... f5

An improvement over Klushkov–Boriescu from the last Sheldrake tournament. That game went 7. ... Bxd6 8. Bb2 f6 9. Qh5+, with an edge for White. He won in 31 moves.

8. Bb2! fxe4 9. Qh5+ Kd7 10. c5

White's compensation was evident. The immediate threat is 11. Bb5+ and 12. Qf7+.

10. ... Qe8 11. Bb5+ Nc6 12. Qh4 Qg6 13. Ne2

The exciting move was 13. ... a6 and then 14. Ba4 b5. White has to take *en passant* and after 15. cxb6 Bxd6 Black seems ready to coordinate his defenses with ...Bb7 and ...Ne7.

But White has 16. Bxc6+ Kxc6 17. Qd8!, with the main point that on 17. ... Qxg2 18. Rc1+ Kb5 19. Nd4+ Ka5 he doesn't have to settle for the queen with 20. Qxd6 Qxh1+ 21. Ke2 Qxc1! but can mate immediately with 20. b7+.

13. ... Nh6

This was designed to prepare a timely ...Nf5, e.g. 14. Ng3 Nf5—but this also indicated Black was groping at straws.

After the natural 13. ... Nf6 14. Ng3 White would have a bind (14. ... Qg4? 15. Bxf6).

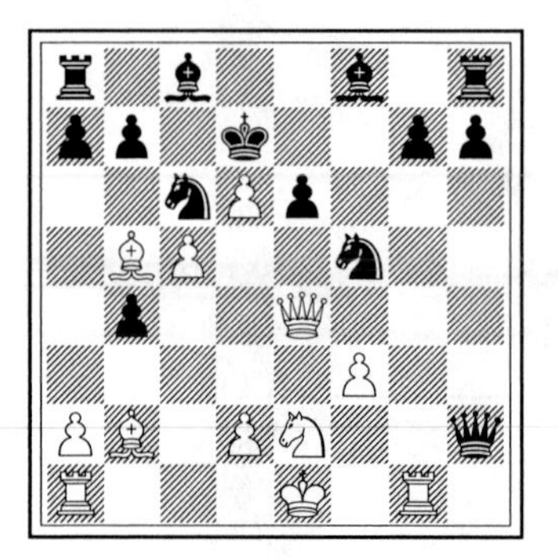

After 16. … Q×h2

14. f3! Q×g2 15. Rg1 Nf5

Or 15. … Q×f3? 16. R×g7+! since 16. … B×g7 allows mate on e7.

16. Q×e4 Q×h2

17. 0–0–0!

Klushkov had exceptionally long fingers, like Fischer. And after castling in his own peculiar way—he always managed to use one hand to pick up both the king and rook and transfer them to new squares in one jerky motion—he left the playing area.

I was close behind as he headed to the P-M room. This was my chance to question him, something I'd been waiting for for three days.

By the time we reached the room, Vilković and Krimsditch were long finished analyzing their game. How much was there to say after 17. d6! anyway?

The only action in the room was at a table to the right of the door where Eichler was making a futile effort to prove to Qi he was lost at some point in their game. Klushkov took a chair at the other end of the room and turned it to the wall where he faced a black-and-white chart of the Periodic Table.

When I sat down next to him he seemed to be asleep.

"Nikolai?" I said.

His eyes opened slightly.

"Nikolai, I know we haven't spoken much in the past. There never seemed much to say."

He looked straight ahead.

"But now there is. I've spoken to some of the others. I need to talk to you now. I think you may have information about the murders."

He appeared to be concentrating hard on the atomic weight of argon.

"I believe you take in a lot that the others don't," I said. "Even with your eyes closed, I'll bet you know everything that is happening around you."

In the background, Eichler was sounding like the first player in history to be frustrated by bishops of opposite color. Surely 25. … Qb2 was winning, he argued. Qi wasn't comforting. Both men were uncharacteristically banging pieces down. I waited a minute before continuing.

"I didn't realize it until I compared notes with some of the players yesterday. But you were present, somewhere in the background, shortly before all three murders."

Klushkov's head slowly turned to meet mine.

"I'm not accusing you. I'm just offering my view. My guess. My guess that you saw someone near Daphne's handbag before she died."

He eyes widened, as if in defense. I was trying to penetrate his shield, and with his grab-bag of neuroses, he lacked a way to shout "Stop."

"My second guess is that you watched someone go into my office before I gave Van Siclen the envelope."

He was focusing intently on me now.

"I'm guessing you even saw someone go into Gabor's room that afternoon before he died."

His head bent forward. Very slightly and very briefly. But it was unmistakably a nod. I paused for several seconds before I went on.

"Are you ready to talk about it?"

His eyes closed. Then his head tilted—again only a fraction of an inch. But this time it went to the left, then the right: No.

"Okay, Nikolai, when you're ready to talk, I'll be ready to listen. But let me just ask one thing more: Did you see the same person all three times?"

He didn't move. On the other side of the room, tempers were cooling. The post-mortem was reaching a negotiated settlement.

"Okay, maybe it wasn't a clear win," Eichler said.

"Yes, perhaps close. But not clear," Qi said.

Finally, Klushkov gave his answer. A sharp, unmistakable jerk of the head left and right.

I was dumbfounded.

All along I'd thought the chances were 99 out of 100 that we were looking for a single murderer. But unless Klushkov was lying—and he didn't seem biologically capable of it—there was at least one accomplice.

One killer must have planted the pills that I found in Gabor's nightstand. But an accomplice might have been the one who removed the rest of Gabor's possessions when I returned to the room that night.

Or was it an accomplice who got the Compound 1080 but the killer who put it on the adjourned move envelope?

I had a million questions but my window of opportunity was about to close.

"Is there anything else you want to tell me now?"

Klushkov slowly stood up. I got up also, not knowing what to expect. Five seconds went by without a word. Then ten.

Finally he spoke, slowly, in his deep nasal voice:

"I ... am ... not..."

"Yes?"

"...a ... spaceman."

And he left the room.

By the time I'd returned to the stage the only other game with a bearing on first prize had bogged down in the opening.

Boriescu–Grushevsky
Catalan Opening E04

1. d4 Nf6 2. c4 e6 3. g3 d5 4. Nf3 d×c4 5. Bg2 c5 6. 0–0 Nc6 7. Qa4

Grandmasters hadn't played the White side of the Catalan this way in decades, until Boriescu started scoring with this line last year.

7. ... Bd7 8. Q×c4 c×d4 9. N×d4 Rc8 10. Nc3 Nb4

The books considered 10. ... N×d4 as the best of several alternatives. But the books didn't include this.

And Boriescu was a player who believed in book moves. You could see how exasperated he was by this: If such a simple move as 10. ... Nb4 hadn't been played before—or at least hadn't been played by grandmasters, the only players that mattered—then there must be something wrong with it. But what was it? He sank deeper into thought looking for an answer. And before he moved again, more than an hour had elapsed.

By that time, the Board Four game was winding up. When Klushkov returned to the playing area, he'd found Popov writing down his move and shaking his head over the position:

17. ... Qh4

Play continued:

Klushkov–Popov

18. Nf4 a6 19. Rde1!

Only when a gambit is young can you get positions from it like this. The threat is Q×e6+ and mates, and 19. … Qh6 is met by 20. Rg6!.

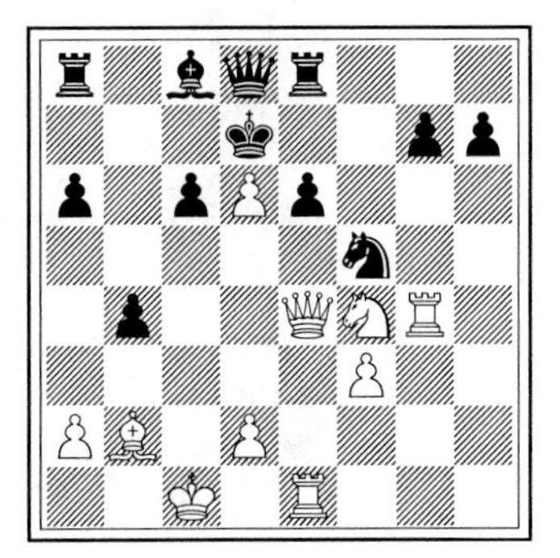

Klushkov–Popov
After 22. … Qd8

19. … B×d6 20. B×c6+ b×c6 21. c×d6 Re8 22. Rg4 Qd8

23. Nd3! Qb6

Or 23. … K×d6 24. Qe5+ Ke7 25. Q×f5 and wins.

24. Ne5+ Kd8 25. R×g7! Black resigns

Another statement game by Klushkov. On 25. … N×g7 he mates with 26. Qh4+, and on 25. … Bb7 he wins with rook checks at d7 and c7. And it was an important win: It gave Klushkov a score of 5–2. He was very much back in contention for first prize.

There was no post-mortem, of course, but there was still a crowd around the board. Vilković was waiting for his pal Popov. Popov was waiting for Klushkov to sign Popov's scoresheet. And I was waiting for Klushkov to finish doing … whatever he was doing to his own scoresheet, as he hunched over the table. After two or three minutes Klushkov pushed the paper away from him and left it in the center of the board. He signed Popov's scoresheet and left without a word.

"Am I the only one who doesn't know what's going on here?" I asked, to no one in particular.

"That's his new thing," Vilković said. "He thinks his scoresheets are too revealing."

"He thinks he's giving away secrets," Popov said.

"By writing down moves?"

"And by crossing them out when he changes his mind," Popov said. "And by the way he scribbles when he's upset or excited."

I looked at the scoresheet. It was a model of penmanship. Even the horizontal line that Russians make through the middle of each "7" was neat.

"But there's nothing scribbled on this," I said. "Nothing."

"That's not his real scoresheet," Popov said. "He slipped the real one in his pocket when you weren't looking."

"That's the copy he made after Zdravko resigned," Vilković said.

"But I just don't get it. A scoresheet isn't a Rorschach test."

"Tell that to the Spaceman," said Vilković. I winced.

Meanwhile, Bastrikova vs. Karlson had taken a sharp turn. The bishops were gone and so was the Black b-pawn that I thought was the key to the ending:

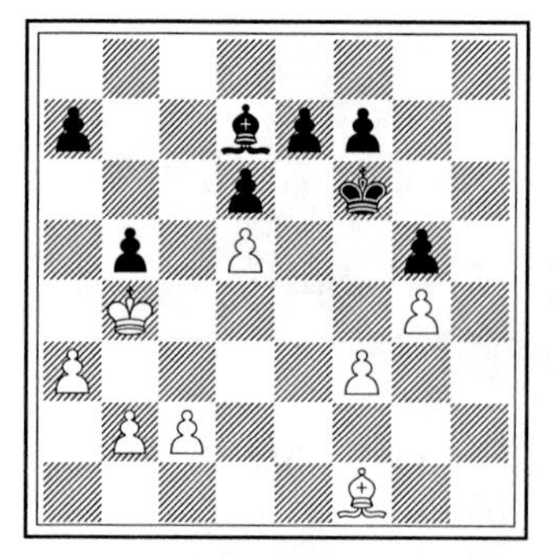

Bastrikova–Karlson
After 27. Kb4

Bastrikova–Karlson

27. ... Ke5!?

A courageous decision, considering how double-edged this could turn out compared with 27. ... a6 28. Ka5 Bc8.

28. B×b5 B×b5 29. K×b5

What was going on here? Black hadn't done anything wrong except follow theory. The 9. 0–0–0 N×d4 Dragon lines had been worked to death in the 1950s—at least the ones with h×g6—and they were rejected in favor of 16. h6. Had Bastrikova found an enormous hole in the analysis? Something no one else had noticed in more than half a century?

It sure looked that way, since 29. ... K×d5 30. c4+ and 31. b4 must be hopeless for Black. It was just a matter of counting the number of squares a pawn must cross to queen. Karlson took only 10 minutes before she smiled to herself and played:

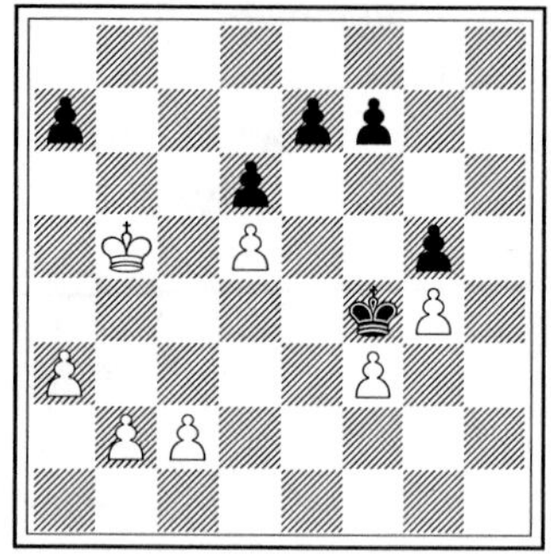

After 29. ... Kf4

29. ... Kf4!

Suddenly it all made sense. It was White's analysis that had a huge flaw:

Black's g-pawn was fast. (30. Kc6 K×f3 31. Kb7 K×g4 32. K×a7 Kf5 and Black queens first—and with check). Now it was Bastrikova's time to think.

There were only two games left at this point, and the other one didn't seem like it would ever reach move 15. That was on Board Five where Boriescu had been wrapped up in the position created by his opponent's TN for what seemed like most of the afternoon. Finally, after an hour and 20 minutes he replied:

Boriescu–Grushevsky

11. Qb3

There followed:

11. ... Qb6 12. Rd1 Bc5!

Kasparov once claimed he had 3,920 innovations stored in his computer, waiting to be played. Grushevsky, naturally, boasted he had at least 4,000.

The question was: How many of the novelties were good and how many were awful? This one looked like it could go either way, and Boriescu understandably took the better part of an hour to reply.

But this one looked genuine.

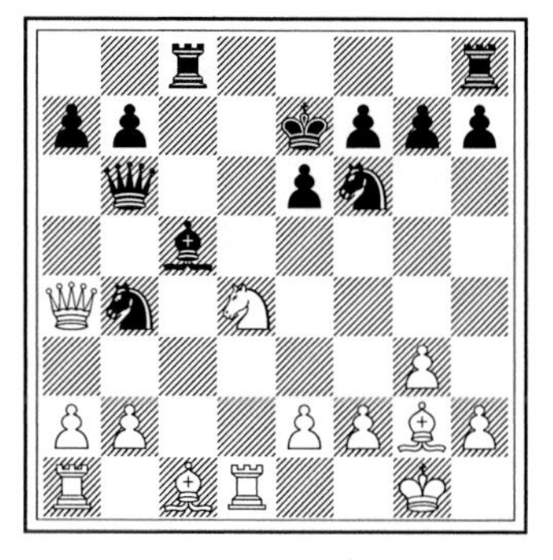

After 14. ... Ke7

13. Na4 B×a4 14. Q×a4+ Ke7

Now 15. e3 Rfd8 16. Bd2 was the way to test Black's TN (16. ... Nd3 17. Ba5).

15. Bd2? Nd3! 16. Bc3

Boriescu indicated later, in his own nonverbal manner, that he didn't think 15. ... Nd3 was playable because of 16. Ba5. But then he saw 16. ... N×b2! and had to find an alternative.

At least now, after 16. Bc3, White can meet 16. ... N×b2 with 17. B×b2 and Rab1. But the flaw with the move he chose is that it wasn't forcing. Black had a free hand and he found:

16. ... N×f2! 17. K×f2 e5 18. e3 Ng4+!

This keeps the White king from escaping to the kingside (19. Kg1 N×e3!).

19. Ke2 e×d4 20. e×d4

I lingered over the position only long enough to decide White was busted—and to judge from Borisecu's expression that he knew it. I returned to my office to squeeze in some time at the computer, grinding out some notes for the damn tournament book.

But within ten minutes Mrs. Nagle rushed in, almost out of breath. Her words reminded me what day it was.

"You've got to get it back from her!"

"Get what back from whom?"

It became clear as soon as I reached Board Three. The position had changed significantly after:

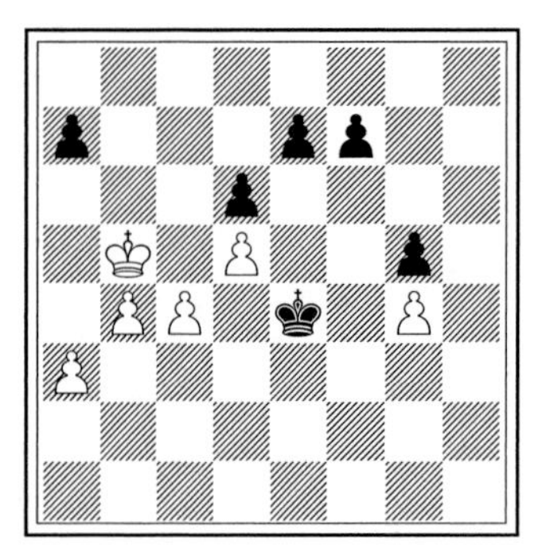

Bastrikova–Karlson
After 31. ... Ke4

Bastrikova–Karlson

30. c4

White could have drawn with 30. Kc6 K×f3 31. Kd7!. But Bastrikova was intent on squeezing a full point out of the position.

30. ... K×f3 31. b4 Ke4!

This was played to meet 32. c5 with 32. ... d×c5 33. b×c5 K×d5 34. c6 Kd6, after which Black pushes the e-pawn and wins.

But when I arrived neither player was at the board. Nor was the clock.

"Where?" was all I asked my assistant.

"The ladies room."

I rushed down the left aisle of the auditorium to the side door and through the hallway, until I found Karlson, arms folded, expression grim, standing outside the restroom.

"What happened?"

"She stole the clock," she said.

"I didn't steal it," said the voice on the other side of the restroom door.

"But you *took* the clock?" I asked the door.

"I had to!" Bastrikova said.

It turned out that minutes earlier, when it was her turn to move, Bastrikova had depressed her clock's button half way—so neither clock ran—and announced she was making a claim.

Karlson instantly pushed her own button, restarting the Russian's time.

Bastrikova immediately pushed hers down again, returning the clock to neutral. And Karlson hit her side again.

The button war continued for four more salvos before Bastrikova grabbed the clock and ran down the stage steps—with Karlson in hot pursuit. Bastrikova soon reached sanctuary in the restroom. And that's how we got to where we were.

"Zhenya, you can't make a valid claim," I said, "unless you are both at the board and I can plainly see the clock."

"I've never heard of that rule."

"I just made it up."

"You can't do that."

"I can, and I did. And if you're not back at the board in three minutes I will add all the time spent on this idiocy to your clock."

And I left the two of them there.

By the time I'd returned to the auditorium, the other game was in the final throes. Grushevsky had replied:

Borisecu–Grushevsky

20. ... Qh6! 21. Re1!

Not 21. dxc5 Qe3+ and Black mates.

21. ... Bd6 22. Bxb7 Rc7 23. Qb5 Rb8 24. Qf5 Nf6 25. Bf3 Kf8

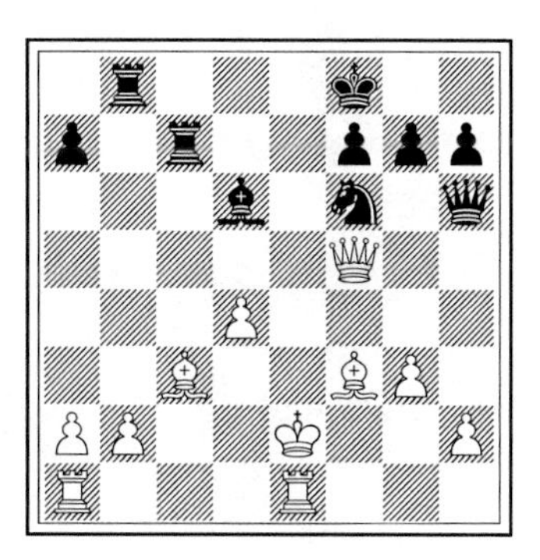

Borisecu–Grushevsky After 25. ... Kf8

White never got to discover check with his king, not that it would have mattered. Maybe he was afraid of 26. ... Rxc3 27. bxc3 Rb2+. But the real danger was losing his h-pawn. Once that happened his position crumbled.

26. Kd3 Qxh2 27. Re2 Qxg3 28. Rf1 Bb4 29. Qe5 Qg6+!

There are only lost endings and bad middlegames after this, e.g. 30. Kd2 Bxc3+ 31. bxc3 Rb2+.

Out of the corner of my eye I saw Karlson, head slightly bent forward, shoulders squared, march into the room. She was soon followed by Bastrikova, still sulking. I made a show of focusing on Board Five until I was sure the women had retaken their seats.

30. Be4 N×e4 31. Q×c7 N×c3+ 32. Kc4 Qa6+! White resigns

I took the signed scoresheets from Boriescu and Grushevsky, and approached Board Three. Both women were waiting.

"All right, let's get this done," I said to Bastrikova.

"What I wanted to say before I was interrupted was—I demand a forfeit," she said, rising to her feet. "My opponent is cheating."

"On what grounds?"

"Twelve point two."

Karlson's eyes were two tiny slits as she stared at Bastrikova on the other side of the table. Zhenya ignored her and looked at me.

"Now *she's* using notes?" I said.

"No," Bastrikova said, and pulled a copy of the rulebook out of her handbag. She read:

"During play, the players are forbidden to make use of notes, sources of information, advice, or to analyze on another chess board."

"So?"

"So, her hands. They are a 'source of information.'"

As I closed my eyes, I realized I had more than the usual Karlson vs. Bastrikova crisis: Zhenya had an arguable case.

That's what Karlson was doing under the table—using her fingers as a personal abacus. She'd been counting out on her fingers how many moves it would take each player to promote to a queen in the various king-and-pawn endgames.

Bastrikova looked at me smugly and waited for my reply. While I turned this over in my mind, Karlson slowly rose from her chair. She was white with rage. I was afraid she was about to overturn the table.

"Stop it, the both of you," I said. "If I have any more problems on this board, I'll declare a double forfeit."

Karlson got the question out before Bastrikova.

"On what grounds?"

"Twelve point one."

Bastrikova fumbled with the rulebook in her hands, but I saved her the time.

"The players shall take no action that will bring the game of chess into disrepute."

"I've never seen this rule enforced," Karlson said.

"Because nobody knows what the hell it means!" said Bastrikova.

"But it's a rule all the same. And being the sole interpreter of such matters in this tournament, I say the behavior of both of you this afternoon would bring disrepute to a tag-team pro wrestling match. Now sit down and finish this game."

And that, incredibly, worked. Bastrikova swallowed her pride and played out the ending.

Bastrikova–Karlson

32. Kc6 f5! 33. gxf5 Kxf5

No better was 33. ... g4 because of 34. f6! exf6 35. c5. Now it seemed certain we were only a move or two away from a draw by agreement and a handshake. Or at least a draw by agreement. With any other opponents, that would have been the case.

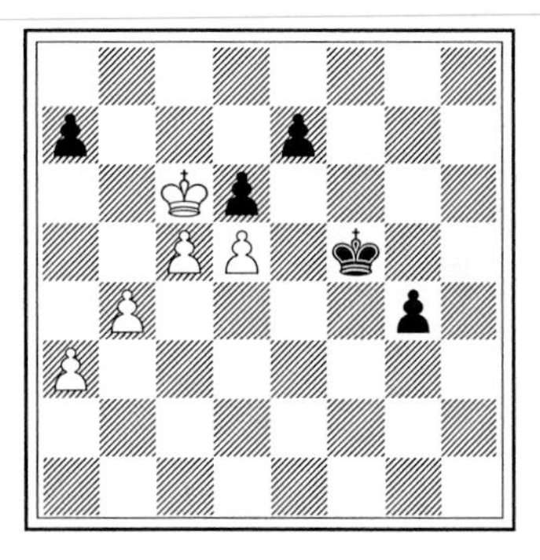

Bastrikova–Karlson
After 34. ... g4

34. c5 g4

35. cxd6??

Grandmasters often play their worst blunders with the greatest confidence. Bastrikova captured the pawn with a look of icy conviction.

35. ... exd6 36. Kxd6 g3

Black queens first now. But White could have drawn with 35. Kb7!.

37. Kc7 g2 38. d6 g1(Q) 39. d7 Qb6+

Of course, Bastrikova could have resigned at any point in the last three moves. But she wouldn't. She just rose from the table without a word, and strode down the center aisle of the auditorium.

Strangely, Karlson also seemed upset. She just sat there as Bastrikova's clock ran and stared daggers at me.

I waited 17 minutes until White's flag fell to update the standings.

SHELDRAKE MEMORIAL

AFTER EIGHT ROUNDS

Grushevsky, Royce-Smith, Qi 5½

Klushkov 5

Bohigian, Eichler, Karlson 4

Boriescu, Vilković 2½

Bastrikova, Popov 1½

Krimsditch ½

Everyone else had gone when Bohigian decided he had played the role of spectator long enough and took his leave of the stage. But as he stopped by where I stood at the crosstable, he seemed concerned.

"They're turning on you," he said. "In a few days they'll all be against you. And then watch out."

Two hours later I was alone in my office, finishing up for the day. I had keyed in some more notes and finished up the Round Eight bulletin when I noticed Gibbs standing just inside the door.

"You won't believe the day I had today, Sheriff. It started around 2:30 when Karlson…"

His look drew me to a halt. Despite his deep tan, Gibbs' face was ashen, almost drained of color.

"What's up?"

"Silas Beadle."

"Yes?"

"…and Mr. Blair."

"And…?"

"Dead."

"No!"

"Yes," he said. "They were probably heading out to the Gulch again. Silas' pickup must have been going 75 when it wrecked on the Cortez."

As he spoke, I recalled the hilly, dusty road south of town that the locals called El Cortez.

"It must've rolled 60 feet down into the ravine."

I visualized Beadle's speeding truck and its plunge. It would have rolled end over end down an embankment until it came to rest. Not much chance anyone could survive such a fall.

"That's horrible."

"Both bodies mangled pretty bad," Gibbs said. "And there's more."

"More?"

"More. There's a trail of brake fluid leading for miles to the scene. It looks pretty certain Silas' pickup was messed with."

His message was clear: After four days the murderer had struck again.

"Sheriff, I don't know what to say."

"I do," he said. "I'm closing down your damn chess tournament."

"You can't do that!"

"Watch me," he said and turned to leave.

"But it's almost over."

"Five dead bodies tell me it's past over," Gibbs said and headed down the hallway.

It took me a moment to recover. Then I raced after him.

"We only have five rounds to go!" I called out.

But it had no effect on Gibbs. The sheriff was already crossing the stage and headed for the auditorium's left aisle and exit. Even at my speed, I would have caught up with him—if I'd continued that way.

But when I spotted the crosstable on the back of the stage, I was stopped cold.

SHELDRAKE MEMORIAL TOURNAMENT

	V	*Q*	*B*	*K*	*P*	*K*	*E*	*K*	*G*	*V*	*B*	*R*	*B*	*G*	*Score*
Vilković	/	0	½	½	½	0	0	1		—				—	2½–4½
Qi	1	/	1	½	1	½	½			—			1	—	5½–1½
Bastrikova	½	0	/	0	½	0			0	—		0	½	—	1½–6½
Klushkov	½	½	1	/	1					—	½	½	1	—	5–2
Popov	½	0	½	0	/					—	½	0	0	—	1½–5½
Karlson	1	½	1			/			0	—	0	½	1	—	4–3
Eichler	1	½					/	½	½	—	½	0	1	—	4–3
Krimsditch	0						½	/	0	—	0	0	0	—	½–5½
Grushevsky			1			1	½	1	/	—	½	½	1	—	5½–1½
Van Siclen	—	—	—	—	—	—	—	—	—	—	—	—	—	—	–
Bohigian				½	½	1	½	1	½	—	/			—	4–2
Royce-Smith			1	½	1	½	1	1	½	—		/		—	5½–1½
Boriescu		0	½	0	1	0	0	1	0	—			/	—	2½–5½
Gabor	—	—	—	—	—	—	—	—	—	—	—	—	—	—	–

Under the crosstable, something had been added to the day's pairings.

The chart read:

SHELDRAKE MEMORIAL

ROUND EIGHT PAIRINGS

Vilković vs. Krimsditch—1-0

Qi vs. Eichler—1/2-1/2

Bastrikova vs. Karlson—0-1

Klushkov vs. Popov—1-0

Boriescu vs. Grushevsky—0-1

But at the bottom was a new entry. A thick pen-stroke had scrawled another line, in red. It said:

Blair vs. Gravity—0-1

Friday, August 30, 2019

GIBBS, IT TURNED OUT, WAS SERIOUS. When Mrs. Nagle's phone call woke me at 10:50 A.M., she asked why there were ribbons of bright yellow plastic striped across the main entrance of Los Voraces High School. Yellow plastic with a message in black lettering that read "Police Line—Do Not Cross." The Scotch tape of the cop business had sealed off my playing site.

Within 20 minutes I'd showered, shaved and thrown on clothes to be presentable enough to make my case in Gibbs' office for why "The Greatest Tournament in Chess History" should be allowed to continue. Beginning with:

"Sheriff, you can't do this."

He looked up expressionless from behind a ten-year-old copy of National Geographic.

"And what is it I can't do?"

"You can't stop the tournament."

"Try me," he said and turned his attention back to a photo essay on fly-fishermen in the Seychelles.

"You can't because the Sheldrake international is a major event. This one is not only the chess tournament of this year but maybe of all time."

"That isn't worth a dead horsefly in this valley."

"I understand that. But this is a lot bigger than the town. It's history."

"So is Silas. Tell that to his widow," Gibbs said.

I tried another tack.

"Look, Sheriff, there's no reason to do this now."

He looked up with a pained expression.

"Of course, there is."

"But you didn't try to shut me down on the 20th when Gabor died. Or two days later with Daphne."

"I didn't know then we were dealing with murder," Gibbs said. "Besides, it's more important now. Silas' death changes things."

"You mean you're taking this more seriously just because one of the townspeople is dead?"

"Well, let's just say that until yesterday it seemed like chess players were killing chess players. But when innocent people start dying, I have to be more concerned."

There was no way I was going to win that argument. Fortunately Gibbs hadn't told any of my grandmasters about Blair and Beadle. The players would be halfway to LAX by now—on foot—if they knew. I decided to gamble.

"Sheriff, if you stop the tournament, you'll ruin our investigation."

The risk was that he would laugh at the reference to "our." Or to "investigation." But instead he narrowed his eyes and said:

"Just how do you figure that?"

"I figure that as long as the players don't know about what happened last night, their guard will be down. They'll act normally."

Well, relatively normally, I thought to myself, thinking of Klushkov staring at the Periodic Table.

"That means I can continue questioning them while they're still cooperative—or at least still talking to me. I'm making progress," I added.

He eyed me doubtfully. I should have told him then what I'd learned from Klushkov. But considering the dubious source, that might not mean much to Gibbs at a time like this. I tried another line of reasoning.

"And also, the killer doesn't realize how much we know. He may make a mistake."

"He hasn't so far," Gibbs said. "He, she or it."

"Maybe, maybe not. But what happened last night might have been a mistake."

"And how might that be?"

"It might be because it breaks the pattern. You agreed with me the other day, when I said that criminals are creatures of habit."

"And?"

"And, all the other deaths happened in front of us, before our eyes. This time it was miles away and in the dark. Maybe it means the killer is scared."

He shook his head.

"Maybe it means he's just getting bolder. After all, last night breaks the pattern in another way," Gibbs said.

"Which way?"

"The way that gives us two new corpses today, not just one."

It was time for one last try, for a compromise.

"Sheriff, give me another day. Just 24 hours. If we haven't solved this by this time tomorrow I'll cooperate in any way.

Gibbs weighed that for a good 30 seconds while he studied the white stucco ceiling.

"Including pulling the plug on the chess?"

"Including that."

He pursed his lips before replying.

"Okay, but if there's one more killing—"

"I know."

"—it will be on your conscience."

One more there would make an even half dozen.

I needed answers. Several of them, and quickly. But all I got in the next few hours was more questions. The most important was: where was Klushkov?

The only person who I suspected had any real clues to the deaths wasn't in his room. Or in the hotel lobby. Or at a table in the Rancho Voraces. Or in any of the other normal places—as well as a few abnormal places—to find grandmasters before and after rounds. None of the players I ran in to had seen him. Our Spaceman was missing in action.

But he had to show up for the game. I decided to try to intercept him before he sat down to play Karlson at 2 P.M. Their game was one of the day's best matchups.

SHELDRAKE MEMORIAL

ROUND NINE PAIRINGS

Grushevsky vs. Vilković

Krimsditch vs. Qi

Eichler vs. Bastrikova

Karlson vs. Klushkov

Bohigian vs. Royce-Smith

If today was going to be the tournament's last round, it was a strangely fitting time to end. Within the first 20 minutes, it had the kind of electric feeling, when you know something remarkable was unfolding.

The first evidence was on Board One, where Grushevsky, of all people, was falling into a trap.

Grushevsky–Vilković
Sicilian Defense B27

1. e4 c5 2. Nf3 g6 3. d4 Bg7 4. Nc3

A younger Grushevsky—one not afraid of having his risky moves refuted in the pages of the *Informant*—would have accepted the challenge and gone into Vilković's pet line, 4. c4 Qa5+ 5. Bd2 Qb6 6. Bc3 Nc6!? and then 7. dxc5 Bxc3+ 8. Nxc3 Qxb2.

4. ... Qa5 5. Be3 Nc6 6. Qd2 Nf6 7. h3?

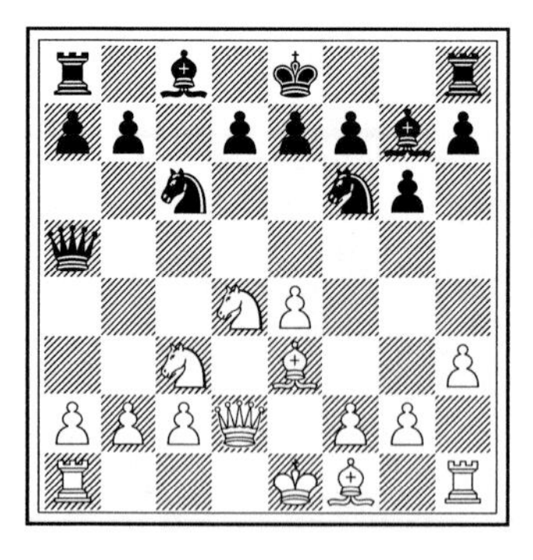

After 8. Nxd4

But this was extraordinary: To meet the ...Ng4 threat, White should try 7. d5!—or just about anything else that stops Black's combination.

7. ... cxd4 8. Nxd4

The world champion had seen 8. ... Nxe4 9. Nxe4 Qxd2+, which wins a pawn for Black.

But he counted on 9. Nxc6, so that 9. ... Nxd2 10. Nxa5 wins White a piece. Or 9. ... Bxc3 10. Nxa5 Bxd2+ 11. Bxd2.

8. ... N×e4!

What he overlooked was:

9. N×c6 Q×c3!!

Now 10. b×c3 N×d2 leaves Black material ahead when the smoke clears.

10. Q×c3 N×c3

"So simple," Popov, standing near me, a few feet from the board, whispered with a smile.

Popov was free today, due to yet another bye, and was clearly enjoying Grushevsky's misery. So was Krimsditch, who had left his board, his clock running in a book position, to see what had drawn our attention. Then Qi finished his examination of the crosstable and came to examine Grushevsky's board. He wore a quizzical frown as if he didn't quite believe what he saw.

Within a minute we were joined by Karlson, Boriescu, Royce-Smith, and Bastrikova. It was as if they had been waiting for this moment all tournament long.

"Now it gets interesting," Royce-Smith said to me.

It took me several seconds to realize what he meant. It wasn't the position that was interesting. Black clearly had an edge, a fairly substantial one. After 11. N×a7 (not 11. b×c3?? B×c3+) Vilković could choose between trying to keep an extra pawn (11. ... Na4 12. Nb5 B×b2) or grabbing the positional trumps (11. ... Nd5 12. Nb5 N×e3).

No, he meant the bigger picture. This could be one of those rare moments when the world championship picture was changing before your eyes:

A loss to a bottom-feeder like Vilković would almost certainly doom Grushevsky's chances for first prize. And if he didn't win the tournament—after playing no serious chess at all in the past year—the pressure on him to defend his title was sure to mount. It would be huge.

My guess is he'd be embarrassed into accepting the challenge from Klushkov he'd been avoiding. Or he could blow off Klushkov and take his chances with Qi. He could always make up some story about how Qi's recent results showed he was stronger than Klushkov. And Qi's financial backing for a match was as solid as the yuan.

"So simple," Popov repeated. "Even the 'strongest player of the galaxy' could miss it."

It took several minutes for the crowd to disperse. But one player who remained at his board throughout was Eichler. As soon as his game began he had stumbled into Bastrikova's preparation:

Eichler–Bastrikova
Czech Defense B07

1. e4 d6 2. d4 Nf6 3. Nc3 c6 4. f4 Qa5 5. Bd2

A minor surprise. Eichler is the first to vary from Bastrikova's loss to Grushevsky four days ago, which went 5. e5 Ne4 6. Bd3 N×c3 7. Qd2.

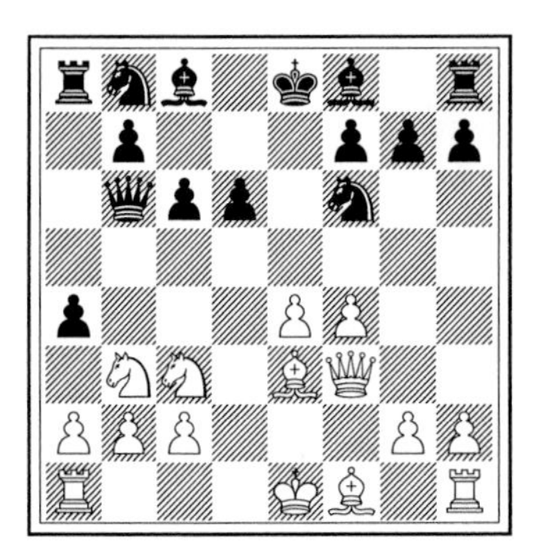

After 10. Be3

5. ... e5 6. Nf3 e×d4 7. N×d4 Qb6 8. Nb3 a5!

This poses surprising problems for White. He wants to castle kingside but can't control the g1–b6 diagonal. And Eichler didn't like the looks of 9. a4 Na6 10. Qf3 Nb4.

9. Qf3 a4 10. Be3

White will stand well after 10. ... Qc7 11. Nd4.

10. ... Qb4!

Allowing—no, forcing White to trap the queen. If, instead, White moves the knight from b3, Black wins with 11. ... Q×b2.

11. a3 a×b3 12. a×b4 R×a1+

This regains the queen, at least, since 13. Nd1?? allows 13. ... b×c2 and wins.

13. Kd2 Bg4 14. Qf2 Rd1+

Bastrikova played this quickly, indicating she was still in her prep. Otherwise, she might have spent some time on 14. ... d5 with the idea of 15. ... B×b4.

For example, 15. c×b3? B×b4 16. Kc2? B×c3! and Black wins. But 15. Bc5 forces 15. ... Rd1+ with something like the game.

15. N×d1 N×e4+

Black has the better of the endgame, even if she can't hold the extra pawn. This was the best position Bastrikova had gotten all tournament long. She milked it for all it was worth. She began to stare at her opponent while his clock ran.

It's funny how this bit of gamesmanship had been tolerated for so many years. People still joked about Benko putting on dark glasses to avoid Tal's piercing glare. Or they spoke admiringly of the way Kasparov and Karpov eyed one another with the cold gaze of python and prey.

Bastrikova had her own twist on this, the classic military strategy of taking the high ground: She always added an extra cushion or two to her chair, so she had a height advantage. Even against the 6 foot 1 Eichler, she was able literally to stare him down.

16. Kc1 N×f2 17. N×f2 Be6 18. c4!

But Eichler had been stared at before. It was Bastrikova who started to swim here. Instead of 18. ... d5! 19. c×d5 B×d5, she began to make mechanical moves, without a plan behind them, as if the extra pawn would win by itself.

18. ... Na6? 19. Bd2 Be7 20. Bd3 f5 21. Bc3

White has just enough piece play (21. ... Kf7 22. g4) to prevent Black from consolidating.

21. ... Rf8 22. Kd2 Kd7 23. Ra1 g6 24. Nd1!

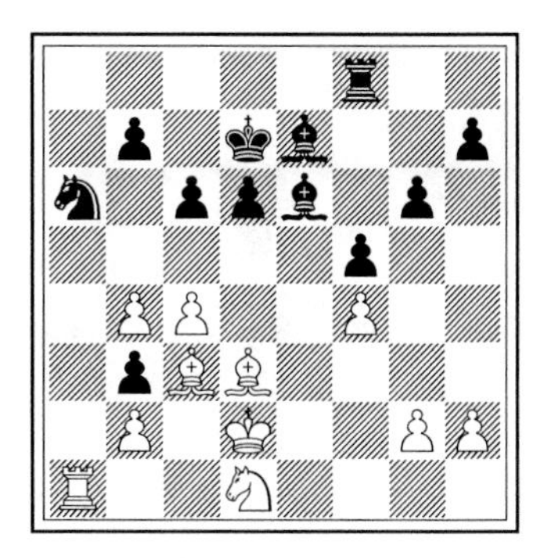

After 24. Nd1

Black winning chances are almost exhausted but she could still try with 24. ... g5, e.g. 25. f×g5 B×g5+ 26. Ke2 Re8.

24. ... Nc7? 25. Ra7 Kc8 26. Ne3 Kb8 27. Ra3 Draw

After a perfunctory shake of hands, Eichler hastily took his leave. When Bastrikova looked up, I offered her a bit of commiseration with a shake of the head, as if to say, "Tough luck." She replied with a scowl.

I couldn't tell if she was angrier with herself—or with me, for yesterday.

The third surprise of the day also came in the first hour of play. Qi appeared to have gotten a free ride in the opening until Krimsditch chose this day to go macho.

Krimsditch–Qi
Queen's Gambit Accepted D27

1. d4 d5 2. c4 d×c4 3. Nf3 Nf6 4. e3 e6 5. B×c4 a6 6. 0–0 c5 7. Nc3

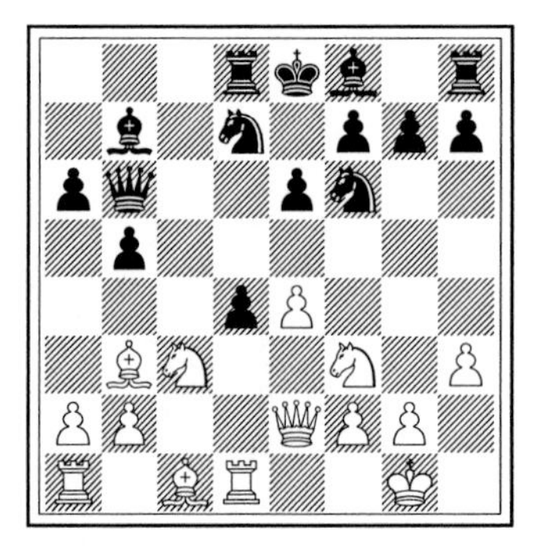

After 12. ... c×d4

It's hard to explain why this natural move had been out of fashion for fifty years. It came back thanks in part to Krimsditch, who won some nice games in the past five years, based on an early d4–d5 sacrifice.

7. ... b5 8. Bb3 Bb7 9. Qe2 Nbd7 10. Rd1 Qb6 11. h3?! Rd8! 12. e4 c×d4

With ...Bc5 coming up after the recapture on d4, Black would stand well. After lengthy study, Krimsditch decided to take the plunge.

13. Nd5!?! e×d5 14. e×d5+ Be7 15. N×d4

The sack was a longshot, and at first I didn't understand it. But as I calculated the prospects of 15. ... B×d5? 16. Nf5! and other lines, I realized the odds were actually in White's favor. The money odds.

Being in last place, Krimsditch had a huge incentive to roll the dice. Solid play back at move 13 might have gotten him a draw and, with more solid moves in the remaining rounds, he could have improved his standing in the tournament—to a tie of 10th place.

But if 13. Nd5 worked, it could earn the brilliancy award, which at half a million bucks, along with his prize money, would guarantee him more than the third-place finisher. It didn't matter if Nd5 was unsound. Krimsditch was like someone who never buys a lottery ticket because of the long odds—but makes an exception when there's a super jackpot.

15. ... Kf8 16. Nf5 Bc5 17. Bf4

While Qi took his time before replying, the game on Board Four finally began—at 2:57 P.M. Three minutes before he would have forfeited for non-appearance, Klushkov floated into the auditorium.

He seemed oblivious to the stares he got from the other players as he found his board, where Karlson had opened 1. e4. The world's No. 2 rated player pushed his c-pawn before sitting down—and my chance to get to him before his game began was lost.

It didn't look like I'd have much of a chance to speak to him during the round, either. Klushkov was in trouble by the 10th move, and appeared glued to his seat as he tried to fend off a vicious Karlson attack.

By 3:30, an hour and a half into the round, it was shaping up as the day when all three leaders would be upset. But by 4 P.M. Grushevsky's chances suddenly improved:

Grushevsky–Vilković

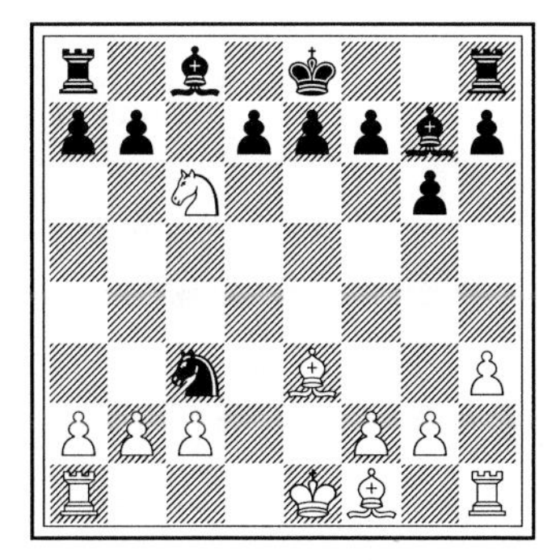

Grushevsky–Vilković
After 10. ... N×c3

11. Bd4 B×d4 12. N×d4 Nd5?!

The first of many small—but cumulative—errors. Black's advantage would remain solid after 12. ... Ne4.

13. 0–0–0 0–0?

There's no feeling in chess like the exhilaration when you see your opponent make a move you know to be bad. Grushevsky had to raise his right hand to cover his smile of relief.

14. Nf5! g×f5 15. R×d5 d6 16. g4!

A nice idea. If Black takes on g4, his h-pawn is doomed (16. ... f×g4 17. h×g4 and 18. Rg5+ followed by Bd3 or Rgh5 with advantage to White).

16. ... Be6 17. Rb5 Bd7 18. Rb4

Of course, not 18. R×b7?? Bc6, forking the rooks. But it was no longer clear that Black was better.

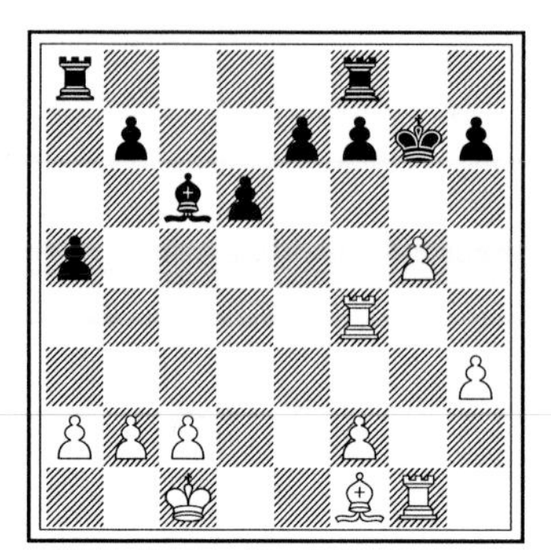

After 22. g5

18. ... a5 19. Rd4 Bc6 20. Rg1 f4?

Vilković later offered the feeble excuse that he was thinking of the best way to draw and chose this move to keep the position closed.

But giving back the pawn—for nothing—was no way to convince Grushevsky to split a point. He had to take on g4.

21. R×f4 Kg7 22. g5!

White solidifies his bind before Black has time to play on the dark squares with ...h6 and ...f6.

Grushevsky wasn't the only player to experience a reversal of fortune this afternoon. Klushkov, when he finally started playing, survived a crisis that began with:

Karlson–Klushkov
Sicilian Defense B70

1. e4 c5 2. Nf3 d6 3. d4 c×d4 4. N×d4 Nf6 5. Nc3 g6 6. Be2 Bg7 7. Nb3 0–0 8. g4!

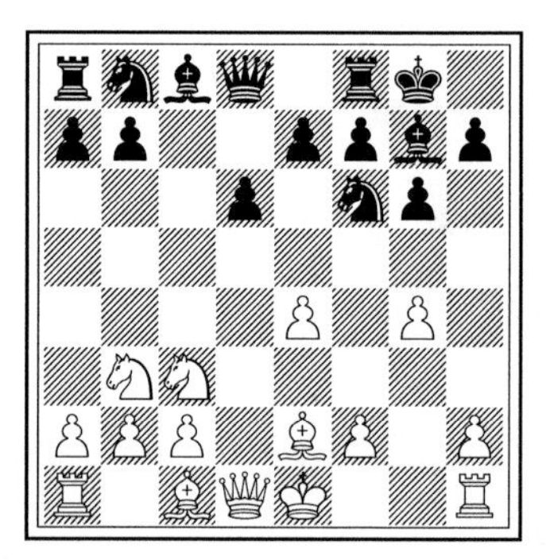

After 8. g4

What happened here is that Karlson had studied the Dragon—for the first time—in her preparation for her game with Bastrikova yesterday. In the course of clicking through games she'd spotted a flaw in the Dragon move order that some players make—some players that included Klushkov.

After the more accurate 7. ... Nc6 and 8. Be3 0–0 Black could have met 9. g4?! with 9. ... d5! 10. e×d5 Nb4 11. Bf3 B×g4! (since 12. B×g4 N×g4 13. Q×g4 N×c2+ and ...N×a1 leaves White with weaknesses all over the board.)

But in Klushkov's move order, White is all ready to play 9. g5 Nd7 10. Be3 with the kind of position even Klushkov wouldn't like to defend.

8. ... Na6 9. g5 Nd7 10. h4! b6 11. h5 Bb7 12. h×g6 h×g6

It was obvious White stood well—but how well? After the methodical 13. f3 or 13. Rh4, White had to have some degree of advantage with Be3/Qd2/0–0–0. But the position also looks like White should have something more forcing.

13. B×a6!? B×a6 14. Qg4 Qc8 15. Qh3 f6

Karlson, realizing she had a rare opportunity to beat the Spaceman, went into furious calculation. You could see she was getting nervous—and she wasn't counting with her fingers today. She cupped her forehead with both hands and bent over in her chair. After 22 minutes of this she played...

16. Qe6+?

But 16. Nd4! Re8 17. Ne6 and 18. N×g7 had to be stronger.

16. ... Rf7 17. Nd5 Kf8!

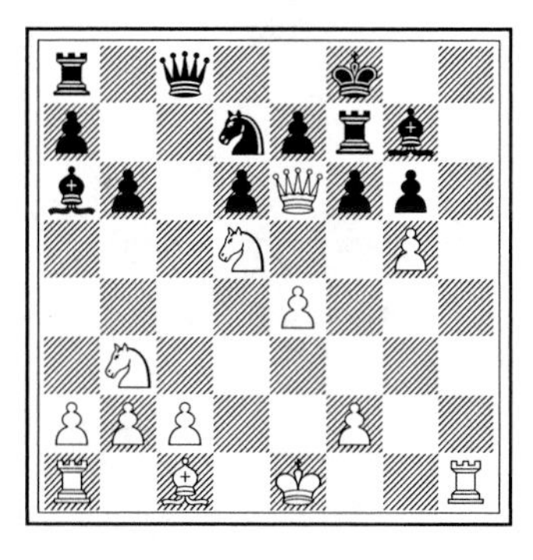

After 17. ... Kf8

Too late, Karlson realized this square was vacant and available. There was a rook on it when she calculated her 16th move.

Here she searched and searched for a sacrifice that might make something out of her powerful piece placement. Great players have a great sense of timing and Karlson knew this was the moment to find a combination.

But it clearly wasn't 18. Nd4 Nc5 19. Qxc8+ Rxc8 20. gxf6 exf6 21. Bf4 Kg8!.

She was searching for something that wasn't there.

18. Nf4 Ne5!

Black avoids 18. ... fxg5 19. Nxg6+ Ke8 20. c3 and then 20. ... Qc4 21. Qxc4 and 22. Bxg5 with advantage to White.

No better is 18. ... Qxc2 19. Nd4 Qc4 20. Nxg6+ Ke8 21. Qxc4 and 22. Nf5.

19. Nd4 fxg5!

Now 20. Nxg6+ Nxg6 21. Qxg6 Bxd4 loses a piece. White decides to trade into the endgame.

20. Q×c8+ B×c8! 21. Nfe6+ B×e6 22. N×e6+ Kg8 23. N×g5 Nf3+ 24. N×f3 R×f3

The dust has settled a bit and it's Black who holds the initiative. But with 25. Ke2 Raf8 26. Be3! White should survive (26. … B×b2 27. Rag1 R3f6 28. Rh6). As long as her pieces are active she shouldn't lose.

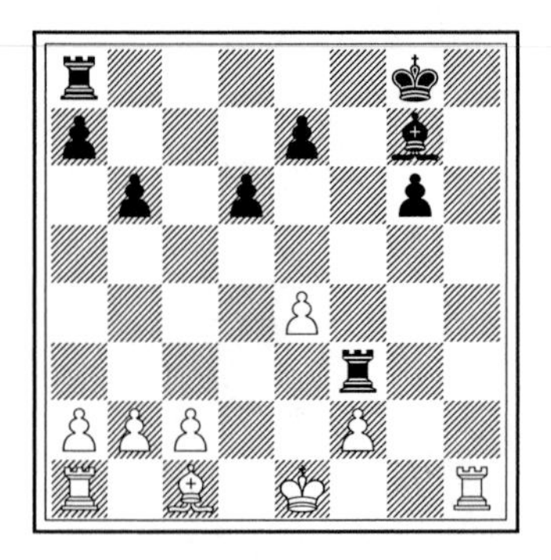

After 24. … R×f3

Karlson wasn't talking, at least to me, after the game, and I'm not certain what went wrong now. Maybe it was a case of an attacker not being able to readjust suddenly to the role of defender. Or perhaps the memory of a bad oversight (17. … Kf8!) just fogged up her thinking and she wasn't able to trust long calculations any more.

In any event, she moved—and lost—quickly.

25. c3? R×c3! 26. Kd2 Rac8! White resigns

After I waited for him to copy his scoresheet, I virtually dragged Klushkov into my office. Today at least we had a conversation. But his side of it was monosyllabic.

"I need to ask you some more questions."

"No."

"It's important, Nikolai."

"No."

"The tournament depends on it."

"No."

"You don't understand," I said. "There may not be any more rounds if I don't get some answers."

"Yes?"

"Yes!"

"No."

After five minutes of this we were interrupted by Mrs. Nagle, who stepped into the office doorway, a few feet from us.

"The new clocks have arrived," she said.

"What clocks?"

"The new ones."

"But I didn't order any new ones."

"Well, somebody did."

"Look, Mrs. Nagle. This is the wrong time for this."

"When is the right time?"

"Later—and besides we don't need clocks. We just got new ones."

"I know that," she said.

"We have enough clocks already."

"But the new ones are here."

"I don't know anything about new clocks!"

"Then where shall I put them?"

I closed my eyes and counted to five—but when I opened them, I realized my error: Klushkov was gone.

I hurried back to the stage, but he was nowhere to be seen. I walked along the auditorium's lefthand aisle and into the lobby, then out the main door and down the school's marble steps. There was no sign of him. Klushkov had probably fled out a back door to the Casa, knowing I couldn't pursue him while my round was still going. And I'd wasted another opportunity.

My round. I reminded myself the tournament was still my responsibility. Regardless of what the players thought about it—or about me—I had an obligation to see it through. By the time I returned to the boards, a quick check revealed substantial changes in the three remaining games.

First, Krimsditch's attack was running on fumes on Board Two.

Krimsditch–Qi

17. ... Re8 18. Qf3 Ne5 19. Qg3 Nh5 20. Qg5

Playing for complications (20. ... Bxf2+ 21. Kf1).

20. ... Qg6! 21. Rac1!

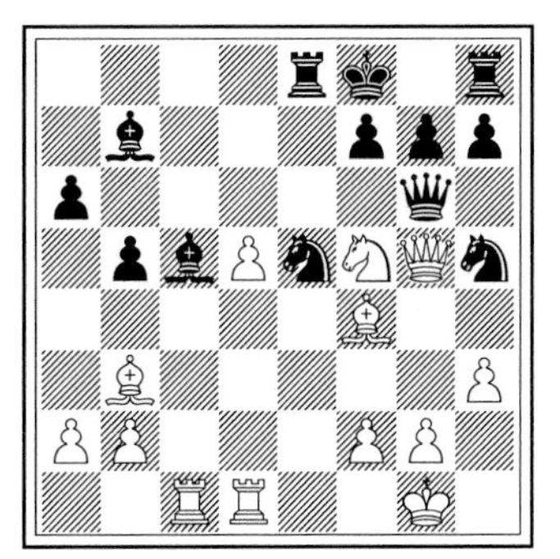

Krimsditch–Qi
After 21. Rac1

Here the Chinese grandmaster took his longest think so far in the tournament. Of course, he could have just played into the 21. ... Qxg5 22. Bxg5 endgame. But the complications remain (22. ... Bb6 23. d6; 22. ... f6 23. Rxc5 fxg5 24. Rc7; 22. ... Nd7 23. d6).

Or he could have found some way of dealing with Rc7 and the prospect of the d-pawn's advance. That was safe but it might not be enough to win.

After about 22 minutes Qi wrote down a move and covered it with his pen. Then he got up from the table—to have a look at Grushevsky's board. This time he didn't register any emotion at what he saw. Before returning to his board he stopped at Bohigian vs. Royce-Smith, at the rear of the stage. He lingered a few minutes more over that position, as if trying to assure himself of the outcome.

When Qi returned to his board he crossed out the move he had written and began to study the board again. It took another 27 minutes before he made his final decision:

21. ... Nf3+!! 22. gxf3 Nxf4

White had no choice now.

23. Qxg6 hxg6 24. Rxc5 gxf5 25. d6

The d-pawn looked dangerous (25. ... Rd8 26. Rc7 or 25. ... Ne6 26. Rxf5 Bc6? 27. d7). However:

25. ... Bxf3! 26. d7 Rxh3!! 27. dxe8(Q)+ Kxe8

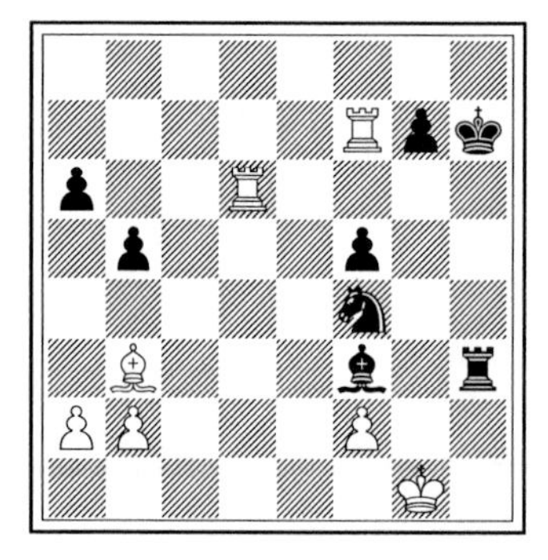

Final position

Mate can't be stopped, and there's no perpetual check by White's rooks because the Black king can dance away to h7.

28. Rc8+ Ke7 29. Rc7+ Kf6 30. Rxf7+ Kg6 31. Rd6+ Kh7

And it turned out that it was Qi who would be staking a claim to the brilliancy prize with this game.

White resigns

This losing streak shaped up as a new record for Krimsditch. He hadn't scored since his first-round draw with Eichler, before Eichler caught fire. The losses meant Krimsditch's Elo would take a nosedive. Probably it would drop him out of the world's top 10. Certainly he wouldn't be invited back here next year.

"Such a pity," Mrs. Nagle told me as we collected the flags and scoresheets. "I always liked Todd."

I shrugged.

"There are always replacements in this business," I said.

She nodded slowly as if deciding whether to agree or not.

The irony of the day was that the biggest change in the standings was the blow suffered by the grandmaster from Manchester:

Bohigian–Royce-Smith
Grünfeld Defense D92

1. Nf3 Nf6 2. c4 g6 3. Nc3 Bg7 4. d4 0–0 5. Bf4 d5 6. Rc1 d×c4 7. e4 Bg4 8. B×c4 Nc6

I'm not a Grünfeld person and my knowledge of the theory ended around here. But there had to be a good reason why 8. ... B×f3 and 8. ... Nfd7 were played instead of this natural move.

9. d5 Nh5 10. Be3 Ne5 11. Be2 N×f3+ 12. g×f3!

There was a reason. Black never recovers from the loss of two tempi now. If Royce-Smith had a TN prepared for today he never got a chance to detonate it.

12. ... Bd7 13. f4 Nf6 14. h4!

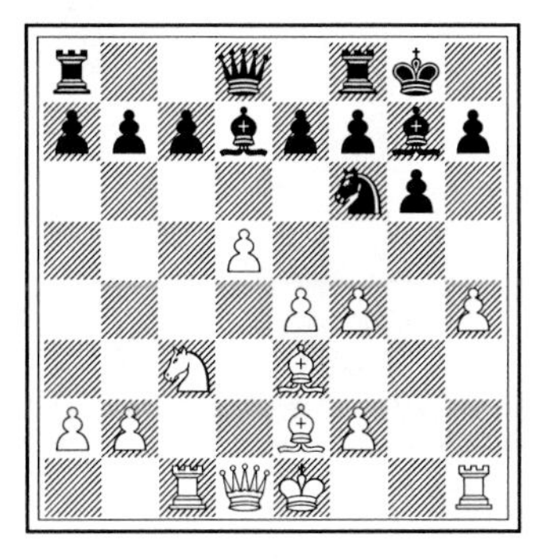

After 14. h4

White has such a solid center, there was no sense of urgency for him to force matters with 14. e5 Ne8. Instead he can open two kingside lines at his leisure.

14. ... c6 15. h5 c×d5 16. h×g6 h×g6 17. f5!

Bohigian nodded to himself just before he pushed this pawn. That was his sign that he was pleased with his play so far—or at least pleased with the consequences of 17. ... g×f5 18. Bh6!.

17. ... d×e4 18. f×g6 Be6!

Black decides on active defense to control the b3–f7 diagonal. He would be losing after 18. ... f×g6 19. Qb3+ Rf7 20. Bc4 e6 21. Q×b7.

19. g×f7+ R×f7 20. Qa4 Rc8 21. Rd1 Qe8

But here Royce-Smith must have had better chances after 21. ... Qc7, e.g. 22. Q×a7 Ng4 or 22. N×e4 N×e4 23. Q×e4 B×a2.

22. Bb5 Qf8 23. N×e4 Ng4 24. Ng5!

Now 24. ... R×f2 25. Qe4! leads to a lost endgame.

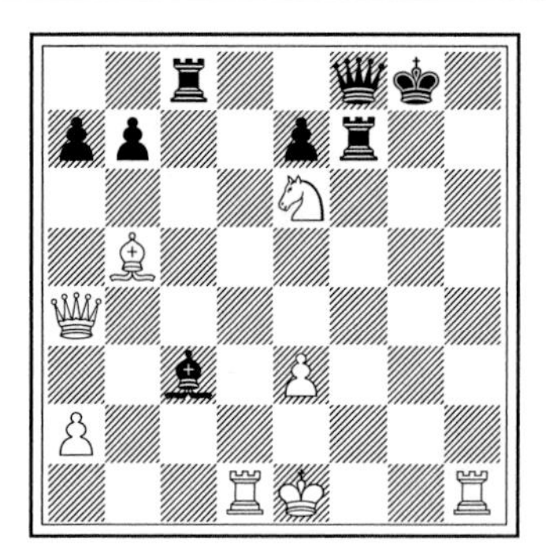

After 26. ... Bc3+

24. ... N×e3 25. f×e3!

How can Black keep the game going now, I wondered? Certainly not with 25. ... Rf6 26. N×e6 R×e6 27. Qb3.

25. ... B×b2!? 26. N×e6! Bc3+

A nice resource: 27. Ke2 can be met by 27. ... Rf2+ 28. Kd3 Qf5+.

27. Rd2! B×d2+ 28. Kd1!

And not 28. K×d2 Rf2+. Now White can capture the queen safely.

28. ... Rc1+ 29. K×d2 Black resigns

Of course, nobody in grandmaster chess ever says "I resign."

Some are clock-stoppers. Some silently extend their right hand in surrender. And a few end the game by starting the post-mortem ("Of course, it would have been a dead draw if I'd played...").

Royce-Smith was so shaken, he just wrote "1–0" on his score-sheet, signed it with a scrawl that would make a general practitioner proud, and slinked away.

I could feel his pain. The loss knocked him out of first place and, at least temporarily, left Qi in command of the crosstable.

But it was only temporary. The last game to end was Grushevsky vs. Vilković. Black was going backwards remarkably fast:

22. ... Rh8 23. Rh4 Rag8 24. f4 Kf8 25. Rh6!

Black doesn't get a chance to play ...h6. If he realized how bad his position was becoming, Vilković would surely have played 25. ... Rg6 26. Bd3 R×h6 27. g×h6 Rg8. But he had plenty of awful moves in him today.

Grushevsky–Vilković

25. ... Bd7 26. Kd2 e6? 27. h4 f5 28. h5 Kg7 29. Rf6!

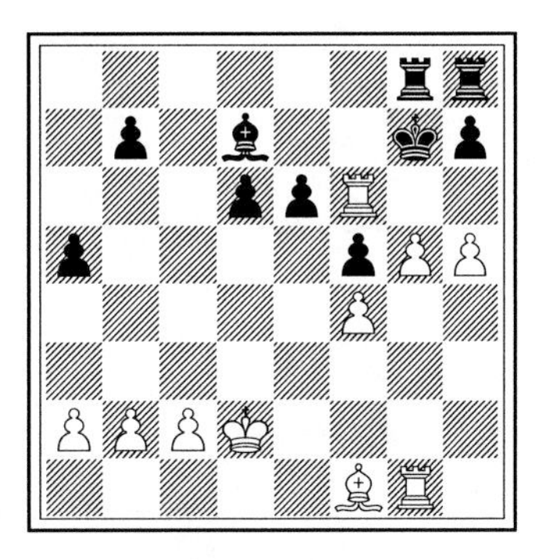

After 29. Rf6

Black's rooks will be trapped following h6+, and then it's just a matter of time before White finds a winning plan.

Say what you will about Grushevsky, his games always seemed to draw attention, even from his peers. Maybe that was true of every world champion, at least while they were still champion. That was true again today. Eichler and Bastrikova had long since finished with their own analysis when I dropped in at the post-mortem room. They were examining the Grushevsky position along with Popov, who had just brought in word of White's 30th move. I took a seat near the board to watch.

"Looks like zugzwang," Eichler said.

"What zugzwang? Show me the zugzwang." Popov said.

"Almost a book position," Bastrikova said.

"What book? Show me the book!" Popov said.

After about 15 minutes—most of it spent with one, two or even three hands hovering over the board—the players came to the traditional consensus.

"Maybe White is winning but it is unclear," Bastrikova said.

"Maybe it's unclear but White is winning," Eichler said.

"Time to eat," Popov agreed.

As they left—not acknowledging my presence—I sat alone.

Suddenly I felt guilty. So far today I'd failed to talk Gibbs out of halting the tournament. I'd missed my chance with Klushkov. And now I was wasting my time watching analysis of how Vilković managed to turn a win into a loss by playing like a C-player.

From behind me I heard: "A trifle jejune, don't you think?"

I turned around and realized the only other person in the room was ... *Boriescu*. He'd been seated at a chair far to my right.

"Their analysis. A bit vapid, prosaic and superficial," he said. "If not epigonic."

"You can speak?" I stuttered. "I mean, in English?"

"But of course," Boriescu replied as he slowly stood up. "I was merely pointing out the naïveté, the outright nescience of my colleagues."

It was as if I were hearing him for the first time. In fact, I was—and I liked him better before.

"They presume to be profound. But it is a well known fact that they engage in rebarbative and vaniloquent excogitation that deserves the opprobrium of the chess world."

"How...?"

"Yet the chess world, or shall I say, the sycophantic elements of such, is continually and constantly confounded, confused and confusticated by their tragically solipsistic superiors in skill."

"Excuse me, uhh ... Grandmaster, but if you could talk—"

"Of course, the immorigerous majority cannot discern the difference between the turgid and the turbid," he said, heading for the hallway.

"—if you could talk all this time—"

"So they are easily misled by the demagogic, perfidious and colubrine," he added and opened the door.

"—if you could talk to us all this time," I said. "Why didn't you?"

"It's quite apodistic," he said. "I had nothing to say."

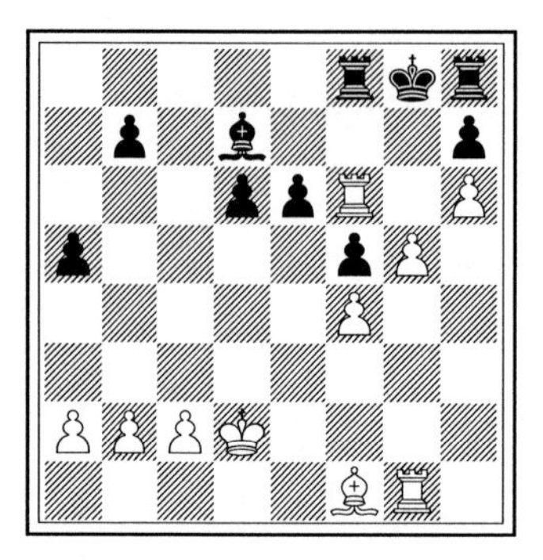

Grushevsky–Vilković
After 30. ... Kg8

Back on the auditorium stage, the final act in the Grushevsky melodrama was playing out:

Grushevsky–Vilković

29. ... Rf8 30. h6+ Kg8

Now Black can't afford to ever take on f6 because exf6+ and Rg7 (+) would be death. Vilković was reduced to passes.

31. Bc4! d5 32. Be2

Mission accomplished: the hole at e5 is ready to be occupied—by something.

32. ... Bc8 33. Bh5 Bd7

As he studied the board, Vilković's shrugged his eyebrows as if to say, "Okay, you have a nice position. But how do you break through?"

The position seems set up for a combination, say with 34. g6 R×f6 35. g7. Then 35. ... R×h6?? loses to 36. Bf7+!. But 35. ... Rf8! is better for Black.

Grushevsky had become world champion by knowing when not to play combinations, Here he finished off by using what amounted to his extra piece.

34. Ke3!

The king. Now 34. ... R×f6 35. g×f6+ Kf8 36. Kd4 followed by Ke5–d6 was winning.

34. ... Bc8 35. Kd4 Bd7

Or here 35. ... Be8 36. Bf3 R×f6 37. g×f6+ Kf7 38. Ke5 and Rg7+.

36. Ke5 Bc8

Now 37. g6 would win eventually. White has a faster way.

37. Kd6 b6 38. Ke7! Black resigns

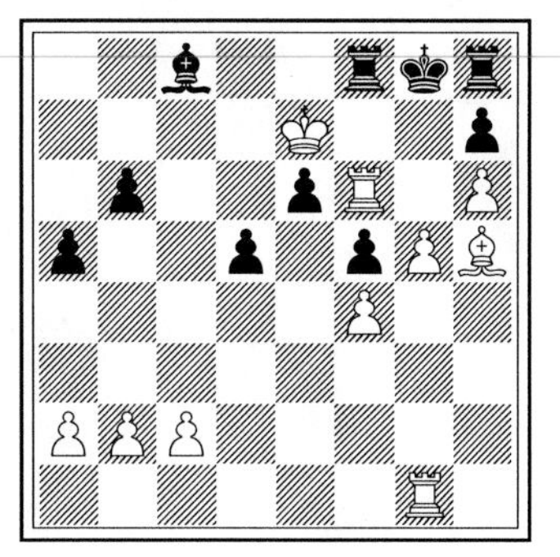

Final position

As a result of the sharp shift in fortunes, the standings looked quite a bit different than I had expected two hours before.

SHELDRAKE MEMORIAL
AFTER NINE ROUNDS
Grushevsky, Qi 6½
Klushkov 6
Royce-Smith 5½
Bohigian 5
Eichler 4½
Karlson 4
Boriescu, Vilković 2½
Bastrikova 2
Popov 1½
Krimsditch ½

There were still four rounds to go according to the schedule. But because of the byes, Grushevsky, Klushkov and Qi each had only three games left.

And after a casual look at the schedule, it was obvious which would be the key remaining game:

Round 10: Qi vs. Grushevsky

While I was considering that and tomorrow's other pairings, I realized Gibbs had been standing a few feet behind me. There was no way to avoid this.

"Sheriff! Good to see you."

"Same here," he said.

"I've made some more progress. It turns out Boriescu can talk."

Gibbs glanced at his wristwatch, then back to me.

"Not only that," I added, "but it seems like he has deep-seated anger toward several other players."

I was trying to read him but his eyes hid behind yellow-tinted glasses.

"Maybe not enough of a motive to cover all the murders, but enough to move him into the top group of suspects."

"Uh-huh."

"Also, there's something Klushkov told me or at least indicated. There may be more than one killer."

I expected … I'm not sure what. But Gibbs just drew his head back a bit and waited for me to continue.

"And it's easy to tell which players are close to which other players. So we can start considering the possibility of a team of murderers, working together."

He eyed me carefully.

"In other words, I'm getting closer, Sheriff. But I'm not there yet. And our deal, our agreement is that I had 24 hours," I reminded him. "That isn't up until 11 tomorrow morning."

He nodded and turned to look away, as if studying something far off in the back of the auditorium. Then he said slowly:

"I'm getting closer, too."

"That's great," I said. "What happened?"

"Not much. I just put two and two together—and found the answer to that question you raised."

"The question about opportunity?" I said, "About who would have been in a position to carry out all of the murders?"

"No. About motive."

Still staring into the distance, he added, "The question about who would stand to gain from them, including last night's."

That threw me. Was there a way that even the deaths of both Blair and Beadle fit into all this?

"You mean there's someone here who benefits from all of the killings?"

"Yes."

"Who?"

He turned to face me.

"*You.*"

"What?"

"You told me yourself you stood to make a lot more money if players died?"

"When did I say that?"

He pulled his small, blue spiral notebook out of a back pocket.

"Monday in my office. You said that the appearance fee for a dead player would go into the prize money. You also disclosed that your salary was tied to the prize fund. You said, and I quote, 'The arbiter always finishes fourth.'"

"But..."

"On Wednesday, and again on Thursday, you made clear your displeasure with Mr. Blair and his efforts to enlist your players in a tournament in which you wouldn't be involved."

"But..."

"His efforts required the assistance of Silas—and that made him another candidate for elimination."

"But..."

"I haven't figured out yet how Miss Nardlinger fits into this. But I'm working on it."

"But..."

"But what?"

"But, Sheriff, this is all just speculation, a wild theory."

"Not just. There is one new fact I was able to uncover today."

He looked again at his notebook.

"Turns out you've been secretly in contact with a Mr. Schultheiss, a chemist over in Endoline. And guess what? The subject of your little conversation was pills. My suspicion is they were the same kind of pills that killed Mr. Gabor."

"Sheriff, I was going to tell you about that the other day, but I got sidetracked. I was pursuing our investigation when I called Schultheiss."

"You didn't mention our investigation when you called him. You didn't mention any investigation. I checked."

"That's because I didn't know who to trust. Now that we're working together..."

"We're not. I have a few more pieces of the puzzle to solve. But when I do I'll be ready to make an arrest."

"Sheriff, you can't be serious!"

"You'll find out how serious I am very soon."

Saturday, August 31, 2019

I'M IN A CAR. NO, IT'S A PICKUP TRUCK. It's dark. The truck is speeding. Signs fly by. We're going at least 50, maybe 60. Maybe more. The windows are open. The air is heavy, dusty. I look at the signs. I can make out letters on one. Hard to read, something about a gulch. Silas is driving. I'm sitting to his right. I can hear someone shouting behind me. It's Gabor. He's shouting at me. I can't make out his words. He's sitting with Daphne. She's also yelling. And holding something. A snake. She's petting a coral snake, and shouting. Suddenly there's a loud crunching sound. The tires screech. I'm jolted to the left, hard. I'm falling. The whole truck is falling. I look at Silas. He's smiling. Now I'm shouting. We're all going to die! Can't Silas see what's happening? Why is he smiling? The truck keeps plunging. Everyone is shouting now. We're going end over end. The truck is spinning. I'm getting dizzy. Dizzy…

When I opened my eyes, I was back in my bed at the Casa. The blinds were drawn and my eyes were bleary. But I could tell there was daylight. It wasn't just morning, the sun must be really bright outside.

As consciousness began to take over I realized I was exhausted. Exhausted, and groggy and damp with sweat. I also realized this wasn't the first time I'd woken up. I remembered trying to focus on the nightstand clock earlier and seeing it was 5:47. And again later when it read 8:22. And now it was … 1:35.

My adrenaline quickly began to kick in. *1:35*? I had just 25 minutes before the round. I rushed to get ready.

By the time I ran the nearly three blocks to Los Voraces High School, the players were up on the auditorium stage. They were milling about, waiting for the round to begin, checking out the crosstable and exchanging gossip. Even Vilković and Royce-Smith, who were due for byes, were there.

None of the GMs paid attention to me as I hurried up the right aisle to the stage. I went to the nearest unoccupied table, Board Three.

"Ladies and gentleman," I began hoarsely.

No one turned.

"Excuse me," I tried again.

Again nothing. I called for order in a more direct way, by banging a rook three times against the tabletop. Several expressions of annoyance looked in my direction.

"I'm sorry to have to do this, but you know I rarely bother you with long announcements," I said.

Vilković made a mock yawn and turned back to the crosstable.

"But today is different," I went on. "You all know how Sheriff Gibbs has been trying to narrow the pool of suspects in his investigation. And I have been helping him."

"Some help," Eichler said. "You suspected me."

"Me, too!" Karlson said.

I hadn't expected this reaction.

"What I am asking each of you to do—and to do it quickly—is to speak to the sheriff and explain exactly where I was and what I was doing at the time of each of the deaths … as well as anything else you might know about the case, of course."

It didn't take them long to realize what I was saying.

"That's good," Grushevsky laughed. "You need an alibi."

"Maybe the sheriff has a point," Popov said.

"Precisely!" Vilković added. "You were present at all the murders."

Klushkov, at least, was silent.

"I always had my suspicions about the arbiter," Royce-Smith said, as if I weren't there.

"Why should we bail him out?" Krimsditch asked, turning his back to me.

"Because it's your duty," I said. "And because without me you don't have a tournament director."

"There *is* an alternative," Qi pointed out, nodding toward Mrs. Nagle. She was dutifully placing blank scoresheets, Round Nine bulletins and clocks on each table. She seemed entirely oblivious to what was going on.

"She'll do," Popov said.

"As long as there's someone to sign the checks," Grushevsky shrugged.

"Or maybe Blair can take his place," Bastrikova said.

They seemed downright eager to replace me—and I couldn't risk telling them why their substitute for me was not available.

"That reminds me. What happened to Blair?" Grushevsky said. "Did you say something to him?"

"Boyd was all full of plans two days ago—plans that didn't include this arbiter," Royce-Smith said.

"And we haven't seen him since," Vilković said.

"It stands to reason you had something to do with his leaving," Popov said.

"Your reasoning is feckless and alogistic," said Boriescu, drawing at least a few curious stares.

I realized I was on my own. My only ally, Bohigian, just closed his eyes.

"Look, I know we've all had a difficult time in the last 12 days," I said. "After all, no one expects to risk their life at a chess tournament. And I admit that I had to consider all of you suspects at one time or another because, well ... because you were."

Karlson and Qi looked at one another and shook their heads sourly. Krimsditch slumped at his board with legs crossed, his attention devoted to a copy of the *Voice of Voraces*. Klushkov seemed to have gone into another trance. I pressed on anyway. I had no choice.

"Now I need your cooperation more than ever. The sheriff is working hard on the case. And I have reason to believe his investigation may be nearing an end. But it's the wrong end. Very wrong. I need your help before he wraps up his investigation. And before he makes a grave mistake and..."

"And...?" Royce-Smith said.

"And your flag has fallen," Bastrikova said, pointing up.

Up to the large clock that stood above our heads on the back wall of the stage. It was 2 P.M. Time to begin the round. Even I had to respect the tyranny of the tournament schedule.

The players knew the drill. They silently headed to their respective tables and prepared their scoresheets. I stood there alone. There was nothing more to say. It took a moment or two before I realized they were all seated, with eyes turned to me. Almost in a daze, I began to walk from board to board, pushing clock buttons.

SHELDRAKE MEMORIAL

ROUND TEN

Qi vs. Grushevsky

Bastrikova vs. Krimsditch

Klushkov vs. Eichler

Popov vs. Karlson

Boriescu vs. Bohigian

Within seconds the only sound in the vast room was the slow hum of ticking clocks. The grandmasters settled into the rhythm of trotting out moves of their preparation and recording them. I just stood at the edge of the stage and watched.

For the first time in eight years of the Sheldrake International Tournament, I was an outsider among them. An intruder who had somehow gotten inside the playing area, where he didn't belong.

"Are you all right?" Mrs. Nagle asked. "You looked a bit peaked."

"I'm fine."

"You don't look fine," she said. "Maybe you should take the afternoon off. I'll cover for you."

"No, really, I just didn't sleep well. I'll be okay."

That's all I needed, Mrs. Nagle playing mother to me.

I knew I had to get my nerves under control. But I needed to do it on my own. And I knew how. I still had a job to perform. I could concentrate on the chess. Whether the players liked it or not, I was still the arbiter, their arbiter. This is where I belonged.

I walked to the center of the stage and planted myself near Board One. I was going to bear witness to the tournament's most important game. This is where I belonged.

Qi–Grushevsky

King's Indian Defense E73

1. d4 Nf6 2. c4 g6 3. Nc3 Bg7 4. e4 d6 5. Be2 0–0 6. Be3 Nbd7 7. g4!?

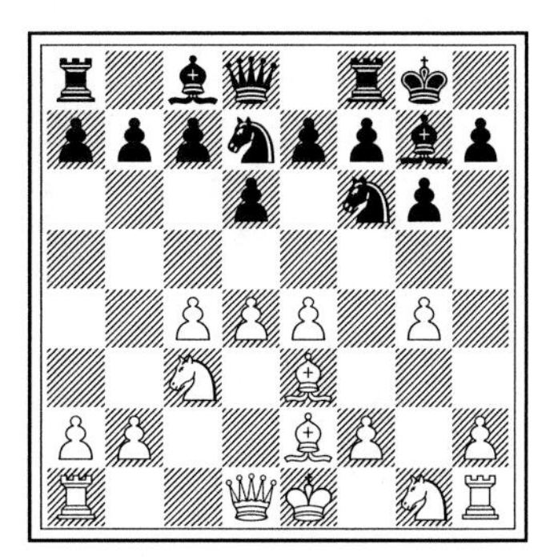

After 7. g4

Thinking back on it, Qi's move should have told me he'd been less than forthcoming when I questioned him. Maybe vegetarians can go for the jugular, after all.

7. ... b6 8. h4! Bb7 9. Bf3 c5 10. d5 a6

I studied the players as much as their board. Grushevsky was sitting to the audience's right side—if we'd had an audience. Qi was on the left, and both players seemed pleased with their position. I stood behind Qi's right shoulder, two feet from the edge of the stage. But something kept drawing my eyes away from the position. Away from the board to ... the clock.

It was new. I hadn't noticed it when Mrs. Nagle was setting up. But she'd replaced the one I usually put on Board One with one of the models she badgered me about yesterday. I'd never even seen this kind of oversized digital before. And I wondered if there was something unusual about it I should know. Yet another thing to complicate my life today.

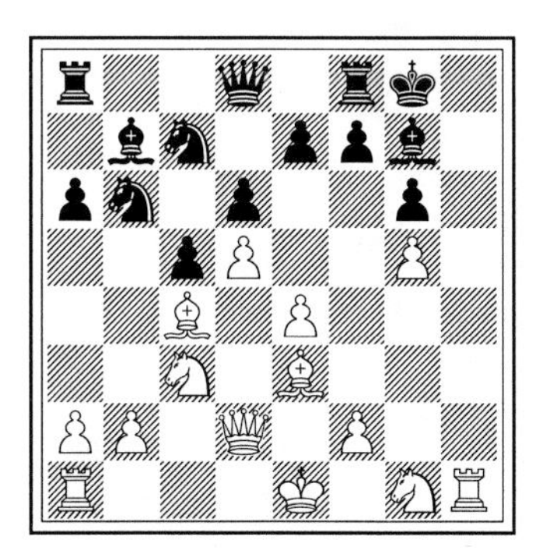

After 16. ... Nb6

11. g5 Ne8 12. h5 b5 13. h×g6 h×g6

Or 13. ... f×g6 14. Bg4 Nc7 15. f4 and Qf3–h3!.

14. Be2 Nc7 15. Qd2 b×c4 16. B×c4 Nb6

17. Bf1!

The fifth move of this piece so far. White already has a winning plan: push the f-pawn, swing the queen to h2 and then meet ...f6 with Bh3.

17. ... e6 18. d×e6 N×e6 19. 0–0–0

My instincts couldn't be that wrong: Grushevsky had to be in trouble. In fact, there was only one other Black position that looked worse than his after the first two hours of play.

And it began this way:

Popov–Karlson
French Defense C15

1. e4 e6 2. d4 d5 3. Nc3 Bb4 4. Bd3

Just about everything had been tried in recent years against the Winawer Variation. Popov had played a leading role in the revival of the line that went 4. ... dxe4 5. Bxe4 c5 6. Ne2.

4. ... c5 5. exd5 Qxd5

Black can chicken out with 5. ... exd5 6. dxc5 Nc6 but I could tell she was going for broke. It made sense: A win here would move Karlson into a share of fifth place. That may not sound like much. But thanks to the deaths and the changes to the prize fund, a win could mean another $200,000 for her.

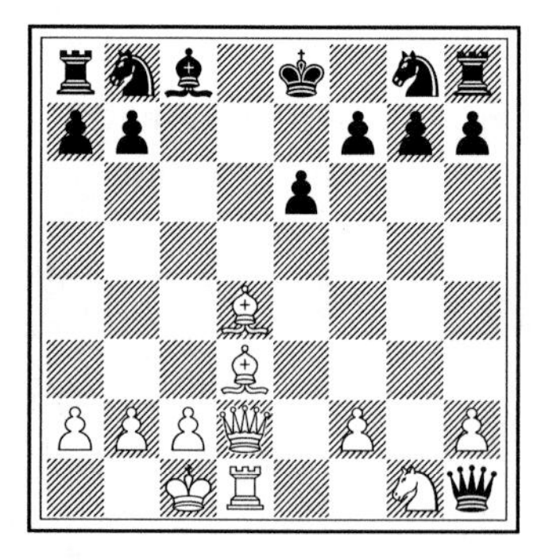

After 10. 0–0–0

6. Bd2! Bxc3! 7. Bxc3 cxd4 8. Bxd4 Qxg2

Of course, not 8. ... Qxd4?? 9. Bb5+. After the text, White will be a rook down. But we're still in a book position.

9. Qd2 Qxh1 10. 0–0–0

10. ... Nf6

This was a bid to improve on 10. ... f6 11. f3 Nc6 12. Bc5, which had been winning for White lately.

11. f3 Nbd7

Concentrate on the chess, that's what I told myself. I realized Black didn't just want to connect knights—on 12. Bxf6 she had to play 12. ... gxf6! 13. Qf2 Rg8! to save her queen. Karlson's main idea, aside from just furthering development, was ...e5.

12. Qf2

And that was why White should have prepared the queen-trap with 12. Qe2. The text might have been busted by 12. … e5! and then 13. Bc3 e4!.

12. … Ng4

This saves the queen (13. Qg3 Qxh2 14. Qxg4 Qh6+ and …e5) but at a cost. Better might have been to accept the consequences of Ne2/…Qxd1+ and try to get her king some cover.

13. fxg4 Qd5 14. Kb1 0–0

While studying the position I felt a tap on the arm. Not on the shoulder—Mrs. Nagle couldn't reach that high. It was more like on the elbow.

"Cel is going to need some help," she said.

"What?"

"I said Cel is going to need help. Downstairs. In the sub-basement."

"Mrs. Nagle I can't be bothered with that now."

"Not now," she said. "Later. He needs to bring up the demo board. It's down there somewhere."

It took me a moment to realize she was talking about the hi-tech, $14,000 whistles-and-bells demonstration board. I'd bought it for the first Sheldrake tournament and never used it.

"Cel needs help finding it and carrying it up. You know, for the spectators."

I turned my back on the stage and scanned the auditorium. None of the 226 seats was occupied.

"Mrs. Nagle, we have no spectators."

"We should be prepared for them, just in case. After all, today is the big game."

"Mrs. Nagle…"

"Not now. Later. Just in case," she said and headed for the hospitality suite. I refocused on chess.

15. Qh4 f5?

Up a pawn and the exchange, Black's defense must have been easier after, say, 15. … h6 and 16. … e5.

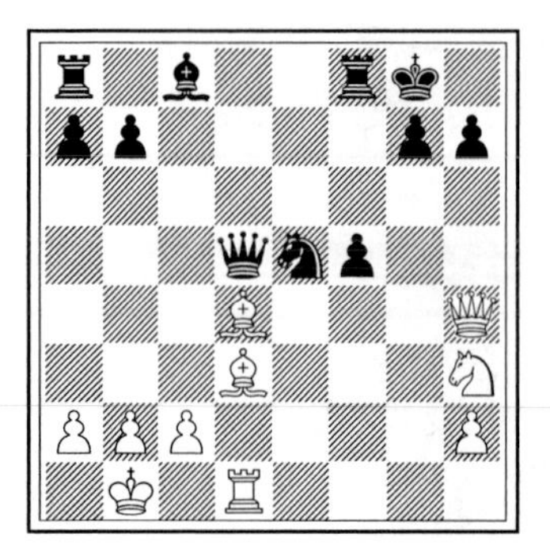

After 17. ... Ne5

16. g×f5 e×f5 17. Nh3

Now it was obvious Black was in trouble: She loses quickly after 17. ... h6 18. Rg1 Rf7 19. B×g7 (and Bc4).

Or after 17. ... Qf7 18. Rg1 Nf6 (18. ... g6 19. Ng5) 19. Ng5 followed by Bc4+ or B×f6.

17. ... Ne5?

Immediately fatal. Karlson had to try 17. ... Qc6 and then 18. Rg1 Nf6 (because Black is alive after 19. Bc4+ Q×c4! 20. R×g7+ K×g7 21. B×f6+ R×f6 22. Q×c4 Be6).

Black never had another choice of moves:

18. B×e5 Q×e5 19. Ng5 h6 20. Bc4+ Kh8 21. Nf7+ R×f7 22. Qd8+!

The endgame could have become problematic after 22. B×f7 Be6 23. Rd8+ Kh7! 24. R×a8 B×f7.

22. ... Kh7 23. B×f7 h5

Here Popov looked up and whispered something to his opponent as he played...

24. Qg5

Karlson resigned on the spot and got up to turn her attention to the Grushevsky game.

As I collected the scoresheets, Popov grinned.

"I said 'Mate in three.' I always wanted to do that."

Aside from Qi vs. Grushevsky, the only other game that might influence the top prize was on Board Three. Klushkov, a half point behind the leaders, was scheduled for one more game with White after today. That meant he had to win against Eichler this afternoon if he had any hopes of finishing first.

But since suffering his only loss of the tournament back in Round Five, Eichler had scored 3–1. And it might easily have been 3½–½ if the German had better technique. He was a completely different player now.

Klushkov–Eichler
Slav Defense D16

1. d4 d5 2. c4 c6 3. Nf3 Nf6 4. Nc3 d×c4 5. a4 Nd5

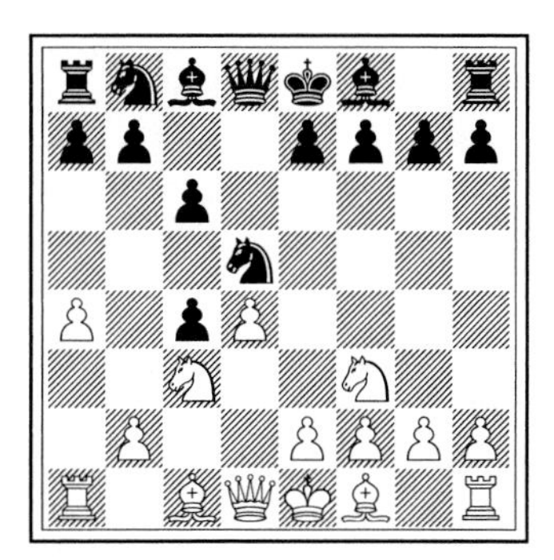
After 5. ... Nd5

This was Capablanca's long-forgotten idea, preparing ...N×c3 and ...b5, as well as ...Bf5 and ...Nb4. It had finally come into vogue, thanks to "Fritz's kids." It was the perfect defense for players who love to hold onto pawns.

6. a5 Bf5 7. Nd2

Played to prepare e2–e4 (but not 7. e4? N×c3 8. b×c3 B×e4).

7. ... Nb4 8. e4 Be6

Black's opening looks questionable after 9. N×c4—until you see 9. ... Q×d4! (and 10. Q×d4 Nc2+).

9. Nf3 Bg4 10. Be3 B×f3 11. g×f3 e5!?

Safer was 11. ... e6, but after 12. B×c4 White has the usual positional advantage that nearly put the Slav Defense out of business 90 years ago.

12. B×c4!

This was clearly a better test of Black's last move than 12. d×e5 Q×d1+ .

Then 13. K×d1 Nd3 14. B×d3 e×d3 15. Kd2 Nd7 is fine for Black, and so is 13. R×d1 Nc2+.

12. ... e×d4 13. Qb3

Once again there was a fork trick, 13. B×d4? Q×d4! 14. Q×d4 Nc2+.

13. ... Qf6!

Naturally, not a piece capture, because of B×f7+ and Rd1+ (or 0–0–0+). For example, 13. ... d×e3? 14. B×f7+ Kd7 15. 0–0–0+ Bd6 16. Q×b4 and wins.

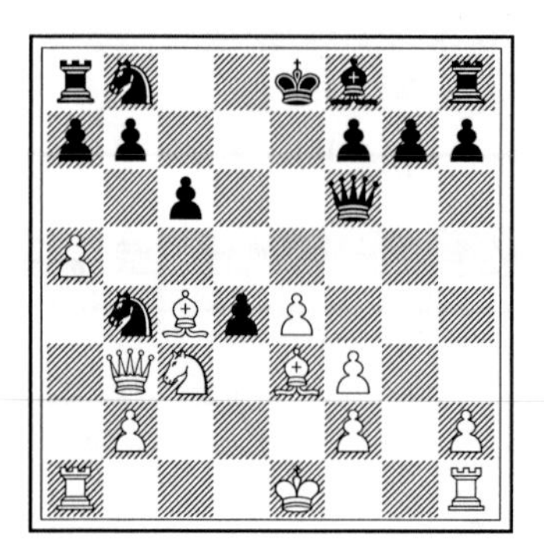
After 13. ... Qf6

Johnny was moving remarkably quickly and was soon nearly an hour ahead on time. He was normally a fast player, but not this fast. Could this still be part of his opening preparation?

14. B×d4! Q×d4

It must be. Eichler didn't pause to consider another move. That was a tipoff because 14. ... Q×f3 was a perfectly reasonable alternative. White has compensation after 15. Rg1 Nd7 16. Rd1 0–0–0 17. B×a7 but Black can quickly win back the initiative (17. ... f5).

Klushkov didn't look comfortable. How could he when he was going to be a piece down and still trying to wade through his opponent's home analysis?

15. B×f7+ Kd8 16. 0–0

This is a gamble but Klushkov couldn't play conservatively, even if he was inclined. For example, 16. Rd1 is met by 16. ... Nd3+.

Even though the knight is lost behind enemy lines, Black ends up with the advantage after 17. R×d3 Q×d3 18. Q×b7 Bd6 19. Q×a8 Bf4. Or after 17. Ke2 Q×f2+ 18. K×d3 Nd7.

16. ... Kc7 17. Rac1 Qe5

Another quickly played move. Eichler got up from the board to check out Grushevsky and Qi. A win today would move Eichler into a tie for fourth, with reasonable chances of moving up in the standings. And the chances of a win today would be pretty good after 18. Nd5+? N×d5 19. e×d5 Bd6!.

18. f4! Q×a5

Not 18. ... Q×f4?? 19. Nb5+ and White wins.

19. Rfd1 N8a6 20. Qe6 Rc8 21. Ra1!

White's move is surprising but useful: Black can't allow Qe5+. But on c5 the queen takes away the bishop's best square (compared with 21. Qd7+ Kb8 22. Be6 Bc5!).

And most important—by driving the queen from control of d8,

White can force a draw. If only someone would offer a draw so I could get another chance to question Klushkov....

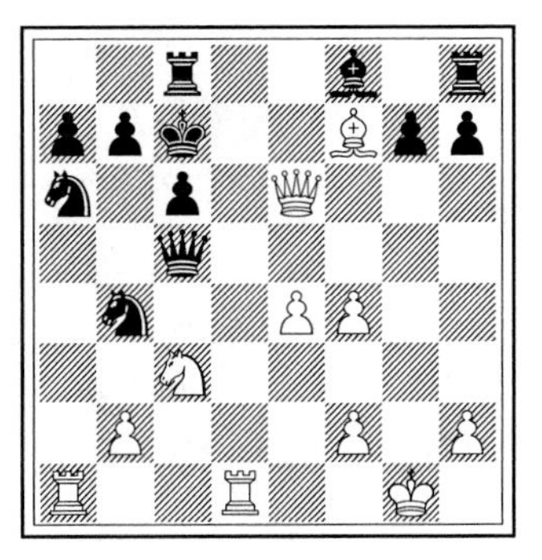

After 21. ... Qc5

21. ... Qc5

22. Qd7+!?!

But he doesn't want it.

With 22. Q×c8+! Klushkov could have taken the perpetual check (22. ... K×c8 23. Be6+ Kc7 24. Rd7+ Kb8 25. Rd8+ Kc7 26. Rd7+, since ...Kb6?? always allows Na4+).

Eichler stared at the position. In his preparation he must have counted on 22. Q×c8+. Now he was on his own.

22. ... Kb8 23. Be6 Be7 24. Na4! Qc2

It was more exact to kick the White king to f1, e.g. 24. ... Qh5 25. Q×e7 Qg6+ 26. Kf1 Q×e4.

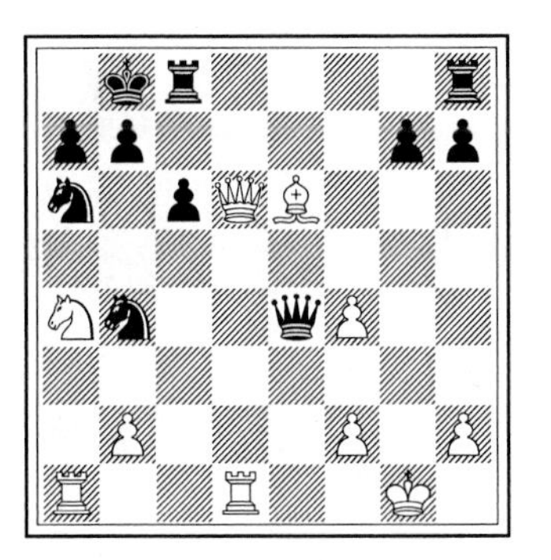

After 30. Qd6+

25. Q×e7 Q×e4 26. Qd6+ Rc7 27. Qd8+!

Now I understood. White still had the draw in hand because 27. ... R×d8?? allowed mate. Black had to allow the position to be repeated.

27. ... Rc8 28. Qd6+ Rc7 29. Qd8+ Rc8 30. Qd6+

Eichler studied the position with the look of someone who was in no rush to make up his mind.

After all, he could take the hour and 23 minutes left on his clock to make a decision—and then claim a draw with 30. ... Rc7 because that would be a third-time repetition.

Or he could play something crazy and go for the win, by giving back the Exchange. For example, 30. ... Ka8!? 31. B×c8 R×c8 and then 32. Qe5 Qg6+ 33. Kf1 Nd3 34. Qg5 Qe4 with some chances.

But they were mainly chances to lose.

While his clock ran on, I walked a few steps to Board Two, where Krimsditch was fighting to avoid last place. In grandmaster jargon, a player has "castled" if he's lost two in a row (0–0). Bastrikova had already castled queenside—scoring zeroes in rounds four, five and six. But there was no way to describe the record of Krimdsditch, her opponent this afternoon. Since the third round it was 0–0–0–0–0–0.

Today, however, it was Bastrikova who looked like the one in the throes of a bad streak:

Bastrikova–Krimsditch
Sicilian Defense B80

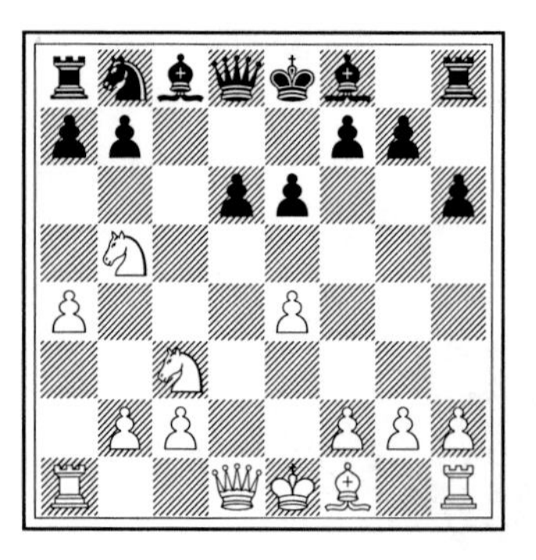

After 9. a4

1. e4 c5 2. Nf3 d6 3. d4 c×d4 4. N×d4 Nf6 5. Nc3 e6 6. Bg5 h6 7. B×f6!?

A new idea, taking quick aim at d6.

7. ... Q×f6 8. Ndb5 Qd8 9. a4

White has Qd2 and Rad1 in mind. When Black hits the knight with ...a6 White resumes the attack on d6 with Na3–c4.

9. ... Be7 10. Be2 0–0 11. 0–0 a6 12. Na3 Qc7 13. Qd2 Nd7! 14. Rad1 b6 15. Nc4 Rd8 16. f4

But now the d-pawn was safe: 16. N×d6 is met by 16. ... Ne5—and only a computer would like White's chances after 17. N×c8 R×d2 18. N×e7+ Q×e7 19. R×d2 Qb4 20. Rb1.

16. ... Nf6 17. Ne3 Bb7 18. Bf3 Rac8 19. Kh1

White shifts gears. He plans 20. g4 and 21. Qg2, which defends e4 and prepares to push the g-pawn. But Black acts first.

19. ... d5! 20. e×d5 Bb4 21. Qd3 B×c3 22. d6!

Otherwise Black retakes on d5 with a textbook advantage.

22. ... Qd7 23. B×b7

As Krimditch reached to recapture, I felt a huge, warm hand, almost a paw, on my shoulder. I turned around.

"Mrs. N says I need your help," Sims said.

"She says that."

"She says I do. Help with the *chairrrs*."

"What chairs?"

Sims looked blankly at me.

"She says I need help finding them," he said. "They're in the basement. You have to go downstairs with me."

"Are you sure this isn't about a demonstration board."

He pondered that for a moment.

"Oh, *riiiight*. The board."

"Look, Cel, I'm busy right now. Why don't you go downstairs and start without me?"

He gave me a nod that seemed to involve every muscle in the top half of his body. By the time he'd left the stage. Krimsditch had moved.

23. ... Q×b7 24. b×c3 Ne4!

This is the safest. White would have cheapo chances after 24. ... Rc6 25. Nc4 Nd5 26. f5.

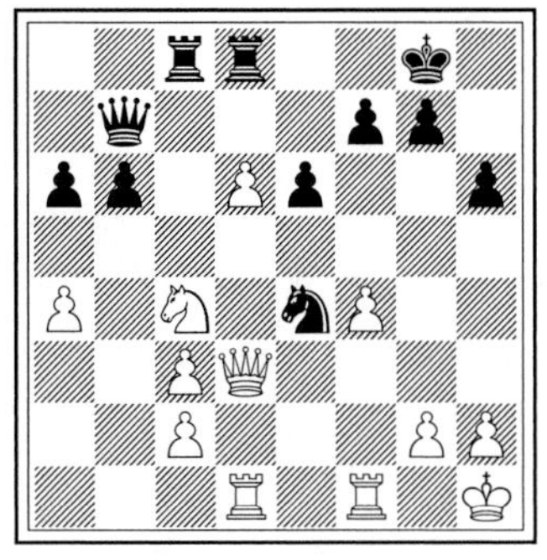

After 25. Nc4

25. Nc4

But there were few chances of any kind now. It looked like Krimsditch would finally win a game.

I took a quick survey of the stage. Qi was still at work against Grushevsky on Board One. Bastrikova was just hanging on at Two. Popov and Karlson were off post-morteming the game they'd had on Four. Boriescu was in trouble against Bohigian on Five.

That left Board Three—where Eichler was still thinking over his 30th move. At this level of GM play, psychology plays a much greater role than amateurs can imagine. And it was obvious that there was some sort of heavy mind game going on there.

Every few minutes Eichler would stop staring at his position—or at Klushkov, and get up from his table. He would walk a few steps to examine Board One. Grushevsky was losing, that much seemed clear to him. But then he'd look back at Klushkov. What was going on in Klushkov's mind? Was Klushkov daring him to avoid the repetition? Or did Klushkov suddenly want a draw after all?

Eichler had never experienced this kind of situation before and you could see him try to turn over the possibilities in his mind as he sat at his board.

A draw by Klushkov, coupled by a Qi win, would be a bonanza for Qi. He would have a one-point lead with two games to go. That would virtually ensure him first prize—and likely force Grushevsky into accepting his challenge to a world championship match.

Then Eichler shot another glance at Klushkov. If Eichler could see what was happening, surely his opponent could too. And maybe that was the point. Maybe Klushkov's repetition of moves acknowledged the obvious: That his shot at the title was gone. That he would never become world champion. That he was destined to be remembered as a near-champion, like Pillsbury, Keres and Shirov. And that he just wanted the tournament to be over so he could go home.

Was that the real message of 30. Qd6+?

Klushkov gave no clue. He closed his eyes and slumped in his chair. And Eichler got up one more time to check out Board One.

While this was going on, Bohigian was reminding everyone how well he once played:

Boriescu–Bohigian
Catalan Opening E04

1. d4 Nf6 2. c4 e6 3. g3 d5 4. Nf3 d×c4 5. Bg2 c5 6. 0–0 Nc6 7. Qa4 Be7 8. Nc3

A Boriescu favorite. White never seems to get much from the old 8. Ne5 Nd5 9. N×c6 Qd7 any more.

8. ... Nd7 9. Ne5!? N×d4 10. e3

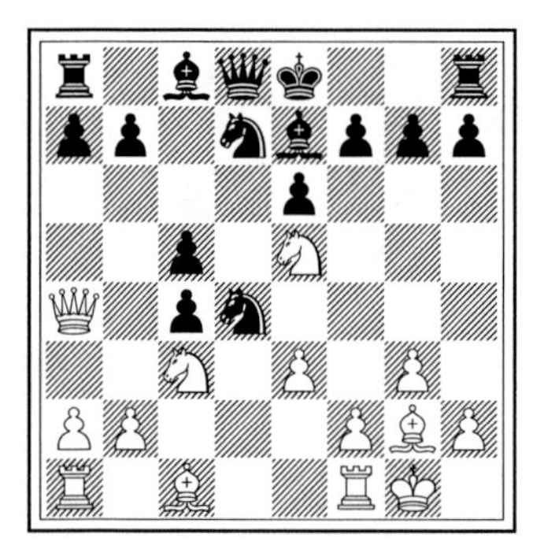

After 10. e3

The Romanian had won several games that continued 10. ... Nf5 11. Rd1. But Bohigian had an improvement on published analysis. In fact, it was an improvement on Boriescu's own notes.

10. ... 0–0! 11. e×d4 c×d4

Now 12. N×d7 B×d7 13. Q×c4 turns out poorly (13. ... d×c3 14. Q×c3 Bb5 and 15. ... Rc8). Boriescu replied quickly.

12. B×b7

So did Bohigian.

12. ... B×b7!

In his notes in *Informant #131*, Boriescu had considered only 12. ... N×e5 13. B×a8 Bd7 14. Q×a7, leading to an unclear endgame. It was hardly the first time that the *Informant* had published bad analysis, and not the first time someone had confronted a grandmaster with his sloppy note over the board. Boreiscu's ears reddened nonetheless. He took 20 minutes to recover his composure.

13. N×d7 d×c3 14. N×f8 Qd5! 15. f3 c×b2 16. B×b2 Bc5+

Now 17. Kh1 allows Black to end the game with the pretty 17. ... Q×f3+!.

17. Kg2 Qd2+ 18. Kh3

The king looks stupid here but 18. Kh1 would have lost to a different queen sack, 18. ... Q×b2 19. Rab1 Q×b1!.

18. ... Q×b2 19. Nd7 Be7 20. Rab1 Qe2 21. Ne5 c3

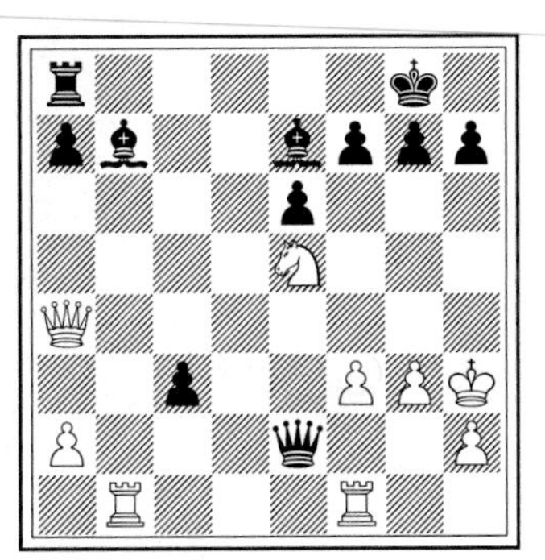

After 21. ... c3

Since 22. Qb5 loses outright to 22. ... Q×b5 and 23. ... Ba6, White is stuck in a very unpleasant middlegame.

As I studied the position, my wristwatch alarm went off.

It was 5:30 P.M. Time to make my half-hourly check on the clocks, to see that the times added up to the three and a half hours that had expired since the round began. In the key game, Grushevsky was making his counterattack. Play had continued:

Qi–Grushevsky
After 19. 0–0–0

Qi–Grushevsky

19. ... Nd4 20. f3 d5

This was the high water mark of Black's counterplay. It didn't last long:

21. b4!

White points out the Achilles' heel. The c-pawn cannot be reinforced, and Black's position crumples if the knight retreats (21. ... Rc8 22. b×c5 Ne6 23. Qh2 and 24. e×d5).

Worse is 21. ... c×b4 22. B×d4 b×c3 23. Qh2 Q×g5+ 24. Kc2 and wins, e.g. 24. ... Qh5 25. Qg2.

21. ... Qc8 22. b×c5 Ne6 23. e×d5 N×c5 24. Bd4

The shape of things to come was 24. ... N×d5 25. Qh2 f6 26. Qh7+ Kf7 followed by 27. Bh3 or 27. Rh6, and White wins.

24. ... f6 25. g×f6 R×f6!

This was the only way to keep the game going past move 30. After 25. ... B×f6 White finishes off with 26. Qh6 Kf7 27. Qh7+ and Re1+.

26. Bh3! Qf8 27. Nge2

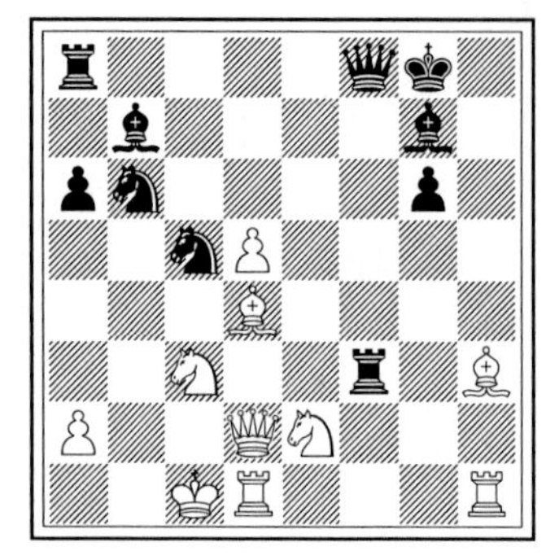

After 27. ... R×f3

Simplest. Black can't withstand a slow buildup of force, such as after Rdg1.

27. ... R×f3

28. B×c5! Q×c5 29. Be6+ Kf8 30. Rdf1 R×f1+ 31. R×f1+ Ke8

Suddenly I felt a sharp tug on my right arm. This time it was Mrs. Nagle, all 117 pounds of her, trying to pull me away from the board.

"You have to leave—now," she said.

She seemed alarmed. Or maybe just anxious. But certainly determined. Whatever it was, in eight years I'd never seen her in such a state.

"This had better be good," I said. "Or very bad."

She nodded at the latter and headed off to the right side of the stage, her left hand clutching my right. I walked with her down the aisle, guessing she wanted to talk out of earshot, beyond the auditorium door. I looked back once, over my shoulder, but all I saw on stage were heads bent over boards.

Once inside the school lobby Mrs. Nagle kept going with me in tow.

"Mrs. Nagle," I said but got no response.

I let her tug me as far as the front door.

"Mrs. Nagle, I'm not going another step."

"You must. He's coming."

"Who's he?"

"Sheriff Gibbs"

"Why is he coming?"

Now she seemed perplexed, like a teacher dealing with a slow third-grader.

"To arrest you, of course."

I was stunned. I looked at her with my mouth open, no sound coming out. I offered little resistance in the minute or so it took her to lead me by the hand out the front door and down the school steps.

I was momentarily blinded by the sunlight, still fairly bright, as we headed down Main Street. Mrs. Nagle's strides were short but within a short time we'd already passed the Los Voraces Emporium.

"Where are we going?" was the first thing that came to mind. She said nothing.

I just followed her, thoughts racing. We passed the library and the Old Brown Jug Liquor Store when I tried again:

"I can't just run away, Mrs. Nagle. I'm the arbiter. There are still four games going."

But she held her tongue. We walked on. I tried to sort out in my mind what I'd heard and what I knew to be true. But the synapses didn't seem to connect.

Ten, twenty, thirty feet further east along Main Street, I made my stand, outside the Casa Yucca Grande.

"Mrs. Nagle, I'm not going any further until you answer some questions."

"All right."

"Why is Gibbs going to arrest me? And how do you know he wants to?"

She paused a bit too long before replying.

"I was in your office when the call came in. From Doc Phelps. He was in the sheriff's office when they heard the new tests came back."

"The tests?"

"The test results showing your fingerprints were on the bottle."

"The bottle?"

"The bottle."

"What bottle?"

"The bottle in Mr. Gabor's bathroom cabinet." she said. "You know, the poison bottle."

"That bottle," I said.

"The first murder weapon," she said.

Suddenly, my head was spinning again.

Gibbs actually had evidence that pinned one of the murders on me? It couldn't be.

Mrs. Nagle continued to yank at my arm, towing me 20 feet further down the street—before it hit me…

My fingerprints couldn't be on the bottle from Gabor's cabinet. I never touched it. I saw it in Gabor's room early on the 21st. But it had disappeared when I went back that night.

Besides, it wasn't the murder weapon.

The pills that killed Gabor were the ones I took from his nightstand and sent to Endoline. None of this made any sense.

I stopped abruptly, pulling Mrs. Nagle up short, just before we'd reached Paloma's Corral.

I squinted a bit as I looked her in the eyes.

"How did you know there was a bottle?"

"You must have told me," she said. "Yes, last Saturday."

"No. All I told you is that I had some medicine I needed to have analyzed."

"You must have told the doctor."

"No. I haven't even seen Phelps since the morning after Gabor died."

"Well, then you must have told the sheriff."

That's when I realized she was making it up as she went along.

"Wrong again," I said. "In fact, Gibbs told me last night I was the chief suspect because I *hadn't* told him that I'd talked with the chemist."

"I don't understand what you're saying," Mrs. Nagle replied, and again began to grab at my arm. But this time I just let her pull on my sleeve. Something was very wrong here.

"Where is Gibbs?" I asked slowly.

"I told you. He's on his way to arrest you."

"But you said he was in his office with Phelps."

What looked like a bit of fear crept into the corner of her eyes.

"His office is on Main Street," I added. "We just walked straight down Main Street. If Gibbs was on his way to make an arrest, there's no way he could have missed me."

She just wagged her head.

"There are some things you just can't explain," she said. And looked at her watch.

In reaction, I glanced at my watch, too. It was 5:57.

I suddenly realized she wasn't just upset. She was terrified. Terrified about something that was about to occur.

"Mrs. Nagle, what is going to happen at 6 P.M.?"

She opened her mouth to say something then abruptly closed it, and just looked at me.

Then we both turned and looked, almost involuntarily, to the west. At the high school, four blocks away.

I don't know exactly what I thought. But the next thing I knew, I was running. Running to the school, back up Main Street.

I'd gotten as far as the Casa when suddenly Brendan Menendez appeared on the sidewalk.

"Where's the fire?" he said with a forced smile—and then tried to block my path.

I sidestepped him by running into the middle of the street, and began to run faster.

As I ran, I noticed something: From out of storefronts and offices, the townspeople of Los Voraces began to appear. They looked surprised that someone ... some crazy person ... was running up the middle of their red clay main street.

In less than two minutes I'd reached the marble steps of the high school. Standing at the top—in my way—was an unlikely figure.

Silas Beadle.

Without a word, he tried to body-block me as I tried to dart to his left.

Mustering all my strength, I reversed direction and threw my weight at him. I caught him off balance and managed to slam him to the school wall. He crumpled to the ground.

"You're pretty spry for a dead man, Silas," I said and headed for the main door.

I continued to run, into the school lobby. By the time I reached the auditorium, I was winded and wheezing. From the back of the center aisle I could see that four games were still going on.

I wanted to shout. Something. Anything.

But years of respect for silence in chess tournaments—that and a lack of breath—stopped me.

Instead I stood and took in the scene 20 yards in front of me:

Above the stage, the huge clock read 5:59 and seconds. Directly below it was Board Three—where Eichler was *still* thinking about his 30th move.

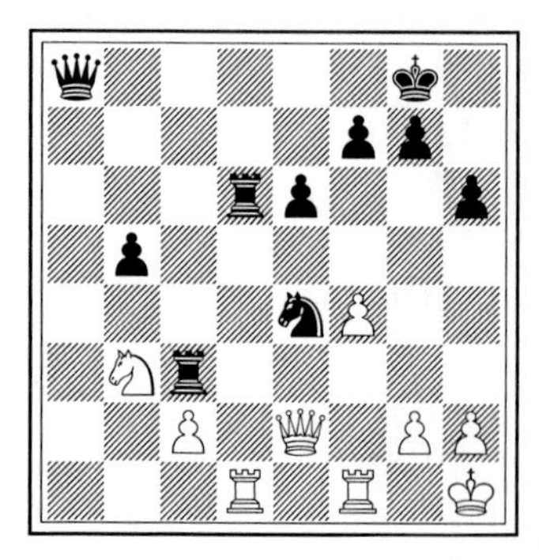

Bastrikova–Krimsditch
After 30. Qe2

I couldn't see Bastrikova's board at the next table but, it turned out, her position had collapsed utterly:

Bastrikova–Krimsditch

25. ... b5 26. a×b5 a×b5 27. Na5 Qa8 28. Nb3 R×d6 29. Qf3 R×c3 30. Qe2

Even from this distance I could see Krimsditch grin as he screwed a piece into the board, with three theatrical turns of the wrist. (I later found out it was the killer, 30. ... Rh3!.)

A few feet to the rear, on Board Five, Boriescu had just resigned to Bohigian, who was walking off the stage.

And right in front of the center stage, Popov, Karlson, Royce-Smith and Vilković stood around Board One—as Qi was about to deliver the coup de grace.

In the time I'd been drawn away by Mrs. Nagle, play had continued:

Qi–Grushevsky

32. Qc2! Kd8 33. Rf7 Bh6+ 34. Kd1 Nc4 35. Rd7+

Grushevsky played 35. ... **Kc8** and punched his clock. The new clock.

Suddenly I realized what was happening.

"NO!" I shouted from where I stood.

Qi looked up at me.

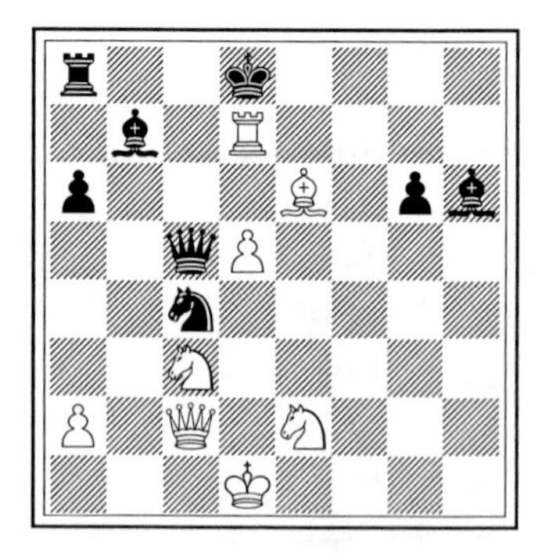

Qi–Grushevsky
After 35. Rd7+

Then he shook his head. He turned back to the board.

And played **36. Q×g6.** And pressed his clock button. And that's all I remembered.

That and a flash of intense white light from the clock as eight ounces of plastic explosives blew the auditorium stage of Los Voraces High School to smithereens.

"He's coming around now, Doc," I heard someone say.

When I opened my eyes I was back in my bed at the Casa.

Hours had passed. How many I couldn't tell. But I knew from the window that it was night outside.

"What....?" I managed to say.

"You've had a nasty concussion," said Dr. Josiah Phelps, standing over me to my left. "But nothing serious. You should be fine by tomorrow. Monday at the latest."

Phelps wasn't alone. There were at least four others in the room.

Slowly, images and shapes began to form, and things began to come back to me, things that happened hours before:

Mrs. Nagle leading me away from the school. My run up Main Street. The struggle with Beadle. The blinding light.

"I guess it's time we told you what's been happening," said Gibbs, standing to my right.

"From the beginning," said Nurse Barnes, behind him.

"Riiiiight," agreed Sims, near the window.

"The beginning?"

Mrs. Nagle, next to Phelps, explained:

"I guess it all began on the 20th when you and the chessplayers were just arriving. That's when you told us this wasn't going to be the last tournament as we'd been led to believe."

"We didn't like that *one* bit," said Gibbs, back to a smile.

"We chose Mr. Gabor because we felt, well ... he had already seen so much of life," Mrs. Nagle said.

"He was the oldest," Beadle, next to Sims, said.

"Also the most unpleasant. Always putting down the town," Phelps said.

"And there was that incident when he flooded his bathtub two years ago," Menendez said. "We thought his dying might frighten all the players out of town," Gibbs said.

"Didn't wooooork," said Sims.

I found myself turning from face to face, as each speaker added a new detail.

"But we made a mistake with the pills," Mrs. Nagle added. "Brendan switched the heart medicines when Mr. Gabor went to dinner that night. Silas was supposed to remove all the pills the next day."

"We didn't realize you'd taken the ones from the nightstand by then," Gibbs said.

"Then we knew we had to clean everything out of the room," Menendez said.

"I'd gone into hiding by then," said Phelps. "Because we didn't agree on what more I could tell you about his death."

I was too bewildered to speak. There was a long pause before Gibbs continued:

"What happened to Miss Nardlinger was different."

"We really didn't know her at all until she broke into the swimming pool," Barnes said. "But then she started threatening to sue the town."

"So Cel slipped the coral snake into her purse while all your players had their eyes glued to some damn-serious chess position," Gibbs said.

Sims nodded shyly. I couldn't tell from the way he turned his head away if he was proud or ashamed. Mrs. Nagle was next to speak.

"We thought that would do the trick. There'd be a panic and that would be the end of it."

"But when you came to see me last Saturday," Gibbs said, "It sounded like you were the only one who was the least bit concerned."

"We also knew you were asking about the state troopers," Phelps said. "So the sheriff had to show he was interested in finding the killer."

"I was a little worried when you said he could be anyone, even a townsperson," Gibbs added. "But then you provided a motive for yourself—'the arbiter always finishes fourth.'"

"So, dear, we knew the sheriff could always deal with you," Mrs. Nagle said. "That is, if you became too much trouble."

My eyes widened at that.

"Later that day, you asked me about finding a chemist...," she said.

"...And I listened in on your phone call to Endoline...," Menendez said.

"...So we knew you had the rest of the pills," Gibbs added.

"But swiping them would have been too suspicious," Phelps said. "Besides, we didn't know where you'd hidden them."

There was a long pause.

"When we realized the tournament wasn't going to stop, we had no choice but continue," Mrs. Nagle said.

This seemed like some sort of incredible, bad dream.

"It was Nancy who thought up the business with the envelope," Phelps said. She blushed.

"Cel supplied the Compound 1080," Gibbs said.

"And Mona coated the envelope edge with it," Beadle said.

"This time, we thought we'd succeeded," Menendez said. "The way the players got jumpy, an' all."

"But then on Monday morning, you managed to convince them to stay—by promising them more money," Gibbs said, shaking his head. "And it got worse when Mr. Blair arrived on Tuesday and started talking about running another chess tournament."

"And ripping up Main Street," Beadle said.

"And changing the name of the town," said Phelps.

"You see why we couldn't allow that, dear," said Mrs. Nagle. "So we voted on Mr. Blair."

"Your players were accusing one another of murder by then," Menendez said.

Gibbs chuckled.

"You even thought the killer might be Mr. Sheldrake," he said.

"But when I saw you talking to Mr. Klushkov on Friday, we knew you were getting too close," Mrs. Nagle said. "So the sheriff figured it was time to scare you."

"Nearly worked too," Gibbs said.

I'd been silent throughout the series of revelations. But something Mrs. Nagle said was too cryptic to allow to pass.

"You said you voted on Blair?"

"Yes, dear, the whole town did."

"You voted to *kill* him?"

"Oh, my yes," said Phelps. "For each victim. Every adult resident of Los Voraces cast a ballot."

"In our town meetings, you know," said Menendez.

"It's prairie democracy!" Mrs. Nagle added.

Even in my condition I could recall: There had been a town meet-

LOS V RACES TOWN MEE
lcf

ing the evening I arrived in Los Voraces, just before Gabor died. There was another town meeting three days later, before the adjournment session when Daphne was killed. And another last Saturday, the day before Van Siclen got the poison. And yet another two days ago, before Gibbs told me Blair had been done in by the booby-trapped brakes. The most recent town meeting was yesterday.

They had been voting each time on whether to commit murder.

"You killed the 14 best chess players in the world!" I said.

"Actually, only 13," said Phelps.

"Mr. Bohigian was off the stage when the clock blew," Mrs. Nagle said.

"He's only suffered memory loss," added Phelps. "From a concussion, like yours. Can't remember a thing."

"*But I do*," I said. "Why didn't you kill me, too?"

"Oh, but you'd never tell what happened."

"Why not!?"

"Because nobody would believe you."

There was silence for nearly a minute as they waited for me to object.

But I knew they were probably right.

Whatever I said about the events of the past 12 days would be contradicted by the testimony of the 183 citizens of Los Voraces, New Mexico.

Phelps explained the final stage of their plan:

"After you and Mr. Bohigian have left the Valley, we'll notify the state police that there was a tragedy."

"A terrible tragedy," Menendez said, shaking his head. "All the other chessplayers died in a gas explosion at the high school."

Gibbs spoke next: "I have a lot of friends in Albuquerque. They'll send investigators, of course. But it will be strictly procedural. All they'll find is the rubble at the school. We'll show them the ashes of the bodies we had to cremate. Nothing else to look at. Terrible tragedy. Case closed."

There was another awkward pause, broken only when Mrs. Nagle said:

"And it wasn't so bad, was it, dear? As you said yesterday, 'There's always replacements in this business'"

I was beyond shock. But I still managed to ask:

"But why? Why did you do it?"

No one said a word as I looked from face to face.

Finally, Doc Phelps shook his head and said:

"The sheriff tried to tell you."

"More than once," Menendez said.

"Town doesn't like the chessplayers," Mrs. Nagle said.

"Never did," Gibbs said. "Never will."

A day later, Bohigian was able to travel, and we left in my car.

I drove down Main Street one last time and headed towards the Interstate, reversing the path I'd made 12 days earlier. And as I drove, it occurred to me.

Every time I'd come to Los Voraces, I learned something about grandmasters—more, in fact, than about Los Voraces.

This time was different.

Index of Openings

Descriptive

ECO